Flora's Wish

Center Point
Large Print

Also by Kathleen Y'Barbo and available from Center Point Large Print:

Beloved Castaway
Beloved Counterfeit

This Large Print Book carries the Seal of Approval of N.A.V.H.

Kathleen Y'Barbo

CENTER POINT LARGE PRINT
THORNDIKE, MAINE

ISBN: 978-1-62899-257-1

Library of Congress Cataloging-in-Publication Data

Y'Barbo, Kathleen.
Flora's wish / Kathleen Y'Barbo. — Center Point Large Print edition.
pages ; cm
Summary: "An engaging story of how God can move circumstances to bring love, joy, and lasting fulfillment to the most hopeless heart"— Provided by publisher.
ISBN 978-1-62899-257-1 (library binding : alk. paper)
1. Large type books. I. Title.
PS3625.B37F57 2014
813'.6—dc23
2014025785

To My Bonus Kids
Clint and Katie Turner
Emily and Josh Miller
Alex and Liz Turner
Austin Turner
Bailey Turner
Kyle Turner
Logan Turner
I love you like my own . . .

Over all these virtues put on love,
which binds them
all together in perfect unity.
COLOSSIANS 3:14

"I was in the middle before I knew that I had begun."

~Jane Austen,
Pride and Prejudice

"To believe every man to be honest till he is found out to be a thief, is a motto most self-respecting men cling to; but we detectives on the contrary would not gain salt to our bread, much less the bread itself, if we adopted such a belief. We have to believe every man a rogue till, after turning all sorts of evidence inside out, we can only discover he is an honest man. And even then I am much afraid we are not quite sure of him."

~Andrew Forrester,
The Female Detective (May 1864)

❀ ONE ❀

May 1887
The Crescent Hotel
Eureka Springs, Arkansas

The last thing Flora Brimm needed was to lose another fiancé. While there was no evidence to prove Will Tucker had met the same unfortunate fate as the other four—an early and untimely demise—there was also no prospective groom in residence at the Crescent Hotel this evening.

Flora stepped off the elevator and walked toward the ballroom to make her entrance late and alone. She paused to take in the grand sweep of glittering chandeliers and the wide expanse of floor-to-ceiling windows reflecting the electric light back into the room. Oversized potted palms climbing almost high enough to touch the ceiling hid the four corners of the grand room.

Though the ballroom was crowded with guests, Flora glanced around in hopes of finding the man she hoped to wed. The search was futile, of course, as tonight's celebration of the Crescent's first anniversary was a masked ball. Those who dared ignore the requirement were given a generic mask, white for the ladies and black for the gentlemen. And yet she hoped that somehow she might recognize him.

Or, perhaps, he would recognize her.

Flora waved off a liveried man with a tray of white masks. At her grandmother's insistence, a disguise of pale blue silk dotted with seed pearls had been created to match her gown. She tied the mask in place and then touched Grandmama's diamond choker with its half dollar–sized aquamarine set into a butterfly shape. The heirloom weighed heavily against her throat, but it was lovely and she would endure it for the evening. Tiny earrings with perfectly set pearls dangling among sparkles of diamonds, aquamarines, and sapphires completed the ensemble and caused her to smile. The earrings had been Mama's favorite.

On any other occasion, Flora would have happily joined the dancers on the floor and been the belle of the ball until the orchestra played its last tune. Tonight, however, her worry over wedding plans possibly gone awry caused her to wish she could spend the evening anywhere but smiling for strangers or, worse, for those who knew her well enough to offer condolences on her most recent loss.

Perhaps Mr. Tucker was trying to find her at this very moment. Perhaps he'd left a note with the desk clerk in the hour since she last checked. Yes, of course. She'd meant to stop and ask again

10

about messages. Yes, she would do that now.

Just then the elevator doors opened, and a crowd of unmasked familiar faces from Natchez spilled out. The conversation she knew she would have to have should any of her father's friends recognize her made her scurry inside. As she crossed the threshold, the orchestra struck up a waltz. Flora noted the time as she toyed with the silver watch she'd received as an engagement gift from Mr. Tucker. Even arriving as late as she had, the evening threatened to stretch on interminably.

From across the room, she met her grandmother's approving gaze. While Millicent Meriwether Brimm might feign dislike of such large events, Flora knew quite well that Grandmama was in her element. The gathering of important dignitaries around her proved that while she was no young beauty, she could still hold her own socially. The lift of one iron-gray brow told Flora she'd be hearing a lecture on tardiness tomorrow.

Turning from Grandmama, her attention was once again drawn to the windows. Thus far her favorite spot among all the lovely offerings at the Crescent Hotel had been the rooftop belvedere. The view of the countryside had been like nothing she'd seen since her trip up the steps of the Sacré-Coeur at Montmartre to take in the view of Paris below.

And though Eureka Springs was nothing like the City of Light that had so captivated her on her grand tour before Mama took ill, there was something about the hills and valleys that settled a deep peace in her heart. Or perhaps it was the great height from which she viewed them.

Indeed, that was likely the case. Had she been born a boy, Flora could easily imagine herself climbing the Alps or ascending some faraway mountaintop to plant a flag of discovery. The thought of it caused the beginnings of a smile, as did the recollection of how many times she'd been called down from the roof of their Natchez home to receive a scolding on the impropriety of a female attempting such a climb. Of her promise to Violet to continue the dizzying fun the sisters once had together.

The smile fled when she realized that being born a boy would also have alleviated the problem of finding a groom who could stay alive until an heir was born.

"Flora!" someone shouted over the music. "Is that you, Flora Brimm?"

Spying the mother of her second fiancé heading her way, Flora cast about for a means of escape. The last thing she needed was a reminder of the loss they shared.

Worse, she would likely be drawn into a discussion about the other "unfortunate incidents"—code words, of course, for the fact that even after Simon Honeycutt's death, Flora continued to lose fiancés at a higher rate than the local chickens shed feathers.

Well, not tonight. Not when her nerves were already stretched so tight. And not when Will could possibly overhear the conversation or Mrs. Honeycutt could tell him exactly what she thought of Flora.

Flora lifted her fan to her face and slid it open. Pretending to wave away the heat of the room, she used the distraction to seek a place to hide until she could make her exit.

A trio of well-placed palm trees set into a corner of the room just might provide a spot where she could find sanctuary, especially given the fact there was a window behind them. Ignoring Grandmama's pointed stare, Flora dodged out of the way to hide behind an overlarge politician and his argumentative companions. A pair of matrons strolling toward the refreshments provided a second means of preventing Grandmama and that awful Natchez gossip from spying her.

With freedom almost within reach, Flora darted behind a waiter and very nearly upset his tray. After offering a hurried apology, she managed to reach the safety of the trees.

The shadows were deep behind the palms, and the air held the earthy combination of fresh soil and patchouli. The window had not been thrown open as she'd hoped, but there was plenty of room to relax and wait for the time when she might make her exit the same way she arrived.

Peering around the foliage, she watched her almost-mother-in-law pause to look around. A moment later, the matron headed toward Grandmama.

Flora ducked back into the shadowy depths and tucked the fan back into place, and then she heaved the best version of a sigh she could manage, given the restriction of her corset. "What a waste of an evening," she said as she slumped against the wall and closed her eyes.

"Agreed," a deep voice responded. "Though I find the situation much improved over just a moment ago."

Flora snapped open her eyes to see someone standing nearby. He wore the hotel-issued black mask, but there was no disguising the impertinent look in the dark-haired man's gray-green eyes. He looked away just long enough to stash a peculiar-looking copper object in his jacket pocket.

The urge to tell him exactly how she felt about his cheeky behavior warred with the practicality of remaining silent. Neither appealed, so Flora decided to say a curt, "If you'll excuse me," and then make an escape.

"The window would be a better choice. That is, if you're looking to avoid that woman." The stranger peered through the foliage and then returned his attention to Flora. "Unless I miss my guess, that's Mrs. Milburn Honeycutt of the

Natchez Honeycutts. But apparently you knew that."

She did. Just how he knew it gave Flora pause to wonder, but only for a moment. She straightened her spine and edged back into the shadows. "What makes you think I want to avoid anyone?"

His brow wrinkled. "You're hiding behind a collection of potted palm trees. And though I would never claim to understand what goes on in a woman's mind, I do have some experience in knowing when a person wants to hide." The man's gaze swept the length of her. "And you want to hide."

Flora ignored him. Or rather she gave her best impression of it, for there truly was no ignoring a man with his presence, especially in such close quarters.

"The question is why," he continued in a smooth-as-silk voice.

"Maybe I'm disappointed because I wanted to play chess, and all these people seem to want to do is dance."

"An attempt at humor," he said slowly. "Which is just another way of creating a diversion. Further proof that you have something to hide. But what?"

"It's no business of yours, sir, I assure you," she said as she looked beyond him to the window.

"When you arrived at my hiding place, it became my business."

"Oh, really?" Flora returned her attention to the

stranger. "That begs the question of why an invited guest might need a hiding place. And for that matter, I'd like to know what you tried to put away in your jacket pocket."

A muscle in his jaw twitched. Nothing in his expression or his stance gave Flora cause to believe he might respond.

She decided to make light of his stern demeanor. "No, of course you would refuse to answer. So I'm left to guess." She paused to brush a palm frond out of her way as she inched closer to the window. "I'd say you're either waiting for a certain favored female or you're some sort of spy. Which is it?"

Something in what she'd said must have struck a nerve, for he looked away. "That is much too heavy for you to lift," was his odd response. "The window," he added. "You appear to be trying to decide whether to open it."

"Not the answer to my question . . . Oh, never mind. I truly do not care why you're hiding behind the potted palms. Now, if you'll excuse me." She pressed past him to open the window, but though she was no weakling, it remained sealed tight.

On the other side of the palms, the waltz ended. While the guests clapped, Flora gave the window one more tug. Nothing.

Letting out a long breath, she turned around to face the man who stood between her and the way back into the ballroom. "You look strong enough,

16

sir. Might I trouble you to see if you can do better?"

A smile rose slowly, and then came a nod. "I suppose I could do that. It helps if you unlock it first." He reached to easily accomplish the task, and then he turned to regard her again. "You do understand we're several floors up. Suggesting this exit was my attempt at humor."

"Thank you." She gave him her best smile. "And yes, I'm well aware of the height, though I much prefer the view from the belvedere on the roof above us. Have you seen it?"

"No, I've not had the pleasure."

"You should really find the time to go up and take a look. It's breathtaking." Flora leaned out the window and heard his gasp behind her. "Unless you're afraid of heights." She cast a quick glance over her shoulder and found him once again watching her intently.

"Madam, in my line of work I've found little that gives me concern." He gave her another sweeping glance. "You, however, just may be the exception."

"And what line of work is that?" She arched a brow to emphasize the question. When he remained silent, she shrugged and then returned her attention to the glorious scene on the other side of the window.

The stars glittered as bright as the chandeliers behind her, and the moon washed the grounds below in a pale silver light. Beneath the window Flora spied a wide ledge that could easily accommodate two people walking side by side. The ledge wound around the side of the building to meet up with a balcony and a second set of doors that would allow her to return to the ballroom on the opposite side from where she'd spotted Mrs. Honeycutt. From there it was a quick jaunt to the elevators.

She took a deep breath of pine-scented air and let it out slowly as she braced herself on the window frame. With care, she pivoted to place both feet on the ledge. Slowly she eased into a standing position. As she pressed against the building, a brisk wind lifted the edge of her skirt and then swirled up to tease at the back of her neck.

Suddenly the fourth floor seemed much higher than it had moments ago. A rail might have helped, as it had in Paris, but alas there was none.

For a moment Flora clutched the window frame. Then, with her eyes fixed on the path before her, she took a step.

The crazy woman was actually going to do it!

This was certainly not how Lucas McMinn had expected the evening to go. And now, thanks to the woman whose eyes matched the jewel at her throat, he would have to abandon his surveillance in the Pinkerton investigation that brought him to the Crescent Hotel in favor of saving a disguised debutante from herself.

He tossed his irritation aside and followed the vision in blue out onto the ledge, making sure the miniature listening device he'd only just sent off the patent for was safely tucked in his pocket.

The woman had taken two more steps before the paralyzing fear he'd expected of her kicked in. "Wait right there. I'm coming after you."

"No, truly, I'm fine," she said without turning around. "I practically grew up following my sister around places . . . well, nearly like this."

"What are you, some kind of circus performer?" He stepped out onto the ledge just as she moved out of his reach.

"Hardly," she said with a soft chuckle. "Though my sister and I certainly dreamed of such a thing as children."

Before following the subject, Lucas paused to assess the situation. Out here the air was fresher and the breeze unexpectedly stiff. Staying close to the wall would not only be prudent, but it also would keep him from any unexpected wind gusts. Apparently she held no such scruples, for she had inched close to the edge and now stood with her back to the danger and her attention focused on the goings-on inside.

Light poured out of the windows, flanking the ballroom to slide across the woman's high cheekbones and mass of coppery curls before spilling over the edge of the ledge and onto the lawn four floors below. Were he not in such a ridiculous predicament, Lucas might have stopped to admire her beauty.

Instead, he was forced to keep his mind on how he might bring her back indoors without causing harm to either of them. He had a fine filament rope in his hidden pocket and the spikes he'd worn last time he had to climb, but neither was likely to save both of them.

At least not at the same time.

Of course, he still had the one weapon that had seen him through many a tough spot. He'd been a man of prayer ever since he was dunked in the creek by the circuit-riding parson some ten years back. Tonight, however, Lucas petitioned the Lord as he never had before.

Wings would help, Lord, but until I've perfected a pair that works well enough, I'd settle for a good bit of patience and a nice patch of solid ground. At that moment, he stumbled on a crack in the ledge and had to grab for the wall.

"If it's all the same to You, Lord, I would prefer to reach that ground under my own steam," he muttered as he fought to catch his balance along with his breath. "And using the elevator."

"What's that?" The woman glanced his way. "Why are you following me?"

"I've nothing better to do." He gestured to the far side of the building, now some thirty yards away. "How about we both head that way?"

But her attention had already gone back to the ballroom. Her fingers toyed with the bauble at her throat, and she appeared to be concentrating on something other than her own safety.

Lucas cautiously moved a few steps closer. "Is something going on in there?"

He spied Mrs. Honeycutt speaking with an older woman. Their conversation, while animated, did not appear to be worthy of deep interest, and yet his companion seemed unable to look away.

"Someone you know?" he asked gently. "Other than Mrs. Honeycutt?"

She nodded.

Apparently the daredevil was a woman of few words, for she offered nothing in the way of explanation. "All right," he said. "We really ought to get back inside."

Nothing.

Again Lucas fought the choice words biting at his tongue. The irony of two adults in ridiculous masks standing on a ledge four floors up hit him. What Pinkerton agent worth his badge would get into a predicament like this on what was supposed to be a simple reconnaissance mission?

He glanced up to gauge the distance and then reached into the special pocket in his jacket. Moving the hearing device aside, his fingers retrieved an ebony pipe.

"Please don't smoke that near me."

His attention was jerked back in her direction as he unscrewed the bowl from the pipe. Again he found her watching the pair of women instead of him.

"As you wish," he said as the specially made bullet containing filament line dropped into his palm.

He returned the pipe to its place and pulled his climbing spikes out of a tobacco pouch he retrieved from another pocket. Then he took his revolver from his chest holster and removed the bullets from the chamber, replacing them with the one holding the filament line. Then the gun went back into its hiding place beneath his jacket within easy reach for the moment he might need it.

Lucas carefully knelt to fit the spikes into place along the soles of his boots. Rising, he said a quick prayer and then closed the distance between them.

She jolted at his sudden move and said with surprise, "Do you mind, sir? I'm rather busy here."

"Busy doing what?" He could only surmise that she was still staring at the partygoers. "If you're so interested in what's going on inside, why don't you let me escort you there? Then we can both get back to what we came to do."

"That depends," she said as she adjusted her mask. "If you were doing something illegal behind those palms, I'd rather not be associated with your return to the ballroom."

"I assure you there's nothing to fear."

Her gaze moved down from his eyes until it rested on his feet. "There is if you insist on wearing those while we dance."

❀ TWO ❀

Lucas couldn't help but grin. "So we're dancing, are we?"

"We are. In the absence of an opportunity to play chess, that is." She continued to stare at his feet. "Are those spikes? What were you planning to do, climb the wall?"

"Never mind." He made short work of removing them and returning them to the tobacco pouch. "There. Back to normal."

The wind swirled around them, but the woman seemed oblivious. "Are you some sort of inventor?"

Another gust of wind buffeted him. "Could we talk about this inside?"

She turned her back on him and walked away as if she were taking a stroll down a garden path. If she and her sister weren't circus performers, the reason was not for lack of talent. Or looks. Though her clothing spoke of wealth, it didn't take much to imagine her dressed for participation in high-flying antics at Mr. Barnum's circus.

That thought almost undid him, as did the breeze that skittered past. Lucas leaned against the stone wall to catch his breath.

"Do you need my assistance?" the object of his thoughts tossed over her shoulder.

"No, just . . ." He shook his head. "It's not important."

Erasing the image of a red-haired aerialist from his mind, Lucas followed close behind, one hand resting on the hotel's facade for balance. Finally they reached the broad expanse of balcony on the far end of the building.

"Avert your eyes, please."

When he complied, she climbed over the railing and onto the balcony. He discovered this when she told him he could follow her. Lucas caught up to her just as she reached the entrance to the ballroom.

To his surprise, Blue Eyes linked arms with him. "Now, if you would do me the honor of waltzing me across the dance floor, sir."

He looked down at her and shook his head. "Don't you mean *around* the dance floor?"

"Oh, no. Across the dance floor, and promise me you won't stop until we reach the elevators."

Understanding dawned. "So I'm your cover?"

"Spoken like a lawman," she said as she led him inside. "Or a criminal. I'm still not certain which."

"Does it matter?"

"Not tonight."

Her smile was easy to reciprocate, and before Lucas knew what was happening, the woman had him parading her across the room in time to the music. She was light on her feet, which made the experience uncomfortably pleasant.

Such was his concentration on trying not to enjoy himself that he almost missed the fact they had danced themselves past the Crescent Hotel employees stationed at the doors and almost to the elevator. Lucas gave her one last twirl, and then she reached to press the down button.

The music still swirled around them, and Lucas found himself reluctant to let her go. "It would be a pity to waste the music while we're waiting for the doors to open."

"Why not? You're a wonderful dancer."

"Thank you." Finally a good reason for all those dancing lessons his proper New Orleans grandmother had made him take.

They fell into step beneath the grand chandelier that dominated the passageway. When the elevator chimed, Lucas swung her around one last time and then drew her close. "I believe that's your ride home."

"Yes," she said slowly as she peered up at him. "It is."

Was that reluctance Lucas heard in her voice?

"We could always dance another round. Or

perhaps you would like to go back into the ball-room and hide behind the potted palms again. Whomever you were looking for is likely wondering where you've gone."

She seemed thoughtful. "No. I've decided the man I'm looking for isn't in the ballroom." A pause. "I should know my own fiancé even with a mask on, don't you think?"

Now that was an odd question. "I guess so."

She shrugged. "What about you? I don't suppose you found the person you were searching for either."

"Why would you think that?"

She shook her head. "You're with me, and I'm certainly not whom you were hunting."

Lucas ignored the loaded statement. "I suppose not. And despite the fact I've struck out tonight, I'm pretty good at finding folks. Maybe you could tell me whom you're looking for. I might have seen him."

The doors began to shut, and she reached over to cause them to open again. "I doubt you would know him," she said as she stepped inside the elevator car. "He's with the railroad."

"Try me."

"His name is Mr. Will Tucker."

The elevator doors closed, and only then did Lucas realize he didn't even know the woman's name.

But he would. Soon.

• • •

The next day, Flora gave up any pretense of practicing the watercolor lesson she'd learned that morning and chewed on the end of the brush as she tried to convince herself that Will Tucker was still alive. A check of her watch showed that Mr. Tucker was exactly seventeen hours shy of being two weeks late for his promised arrival. And he was a half day late for their debut at last night's dance.

With neither a telegram nor a note to offer any reason for his tardiness, the evidence did not favor a positive outcome. And with Grandmama likely to pack up at any moment, the situation had become dire indeed.

The last thing Flora needed was to return to Natchez without a solution to the problem Grandfather Brimm handed them all with his will. Perhaps she could find the fellow who had entertained her on the ledge and then danced her across the ballroom. He'd seemed like the sort who might know how to hunt for someone.

At least, he'd given her that impression last night.

How she would find the fellow was a mystery in itself, but though he was masked, she did have clues in his impressive height, his dark hair, and the unique shade of his gray-green eyes.

A movement caught her attention, and Flora turned toward it. The man who had openly watched her from across the dining room this morning and then regarded her impassively from the south portico at midday now stood in the shadow of the very gazebo she'd been trying to capture on canvas.

And while she'd endured no small measure of stares, the way this man watched her was different. His look was predatory.

With a mere lift of her hand, the lady's maid attending her would remove herself from her spot beneath the portico and come immediately. A gesture less subtle would alert the woman to fetch hotel security.

Knowing this, Flora decided to make a game of it. If this man was a reporter or some hired gun Father had sent, she'd have great sport in calling his bluff.

Moving slightly so she could better observe him from beneath the feathered edge of her hat, Flora sized him up as if he were just another object to paint. Broad at the shoulders and narrow at the waist, he wore the garments of a man of leisure with the catlike grace of someone ready to spring. The silver chain of his pocket watch glistened in the afternoon sun as he leaned deeper into the dappled shadows of the gazebo.

She dabbed her paintbrush into the jar of water on the table beside her and then smeared a dab of brown paint atop the green of the Crescent's south-facing gardens. If she squinted, Flora could almost convince herself the blob resembled a bowler hat. Continuing her attempt, she rinsed the brush. When she looked up again, the man was gone.

Good. Perhaps he'd lost interest. That certainly ruled out the possibility of a hired gun.

Unfortunately, she'd also lost interest in her painting. Not that she'd held any real hope of picking up the skill Mama had mastered. In fact, she was completely useless at the task.

Flora dabbed the fine hairs of the paintbrush in water until the mud-colored paint was gone and then set the brush aside. With a nod to the maid, she tossed all attempts at continuing aside along with the brush.

"Would you mind terribly having a porter come and take this away?" To her credit, the maid kept her expression neutral, though Flora couldn't help but notice that her gaze lingered a bit on the brown blob at the edge of the poorly painted garden. "I would like my writing materials, please." She gestured toward the gazebo. "That spot over there looks like a nice place."

As the maid hurried away, Flora tried not to think of anything but the lovely flowers and the view of the Ozarks that tumbled down the hill at the edge of the gardens. The Lord's provision had stood her in good stead until now, and He was certainly not in the business of ignoring the pleas of His children.

The north wind, heavily scented with pine and portending a spring shower, teased at the tendrils of hair that refused to remain coiled beneath her hat. Flora paused to admire the hotel, a delightful wedding cake–like structure with balconies stacked five stories high. Were she not pressed to recall her reason for attending Grandmama's taking of the waters this year, Flora might have found enjoyment in the leisurely pace of the quaint but more than comfortable resort.

Though the gazebo was of a much simpler design than the more opulent Crescent Hotel's main building, Flora preferred the secluded spot as a place to be alone with her thoughts. Or, in this case, with her letters.

Likely Father would want news of Grandmama's imminent return. He always tended to plan his trips around his mother's presence at Brimmfield. For when Grandmama was in, Father was most always out. Then there was the letter she must write to her grandmother. The one that would explain why she had taken the drastic step of marrying Will Tucker.

She would hold off writing this one until Mr. Tucker actually arrived at the hotel. And surely that would be soon. And though Flora had already written to her this morning, her sister would certainly appreciate yet another letter in the post-box detailing what she would consider Flora's great adventures. A momentary pang of regret stung as she thought of the injuries that kept Violet Brimm mostly bedridden.

"Be fearless for me," her sister had said once. "Bring the world back to me. But most of all, be fearless. Climb to new heights."

And so Flora had, but never without thinking of Violet. She also couldn't help thinking of Cousin Winny and his taunts . . .

Her thoughts were disrupted when she heard footsteps behind her. It was too soon for the maid to have returned. Flora glanced over her shoulder to see the man in the brown bowler approaching. "There's my dancing partner. Ever find someone to play chess with?" When she ignored him, he continued, "You're going to pretend you don't recognize me? Well, I believe I know you. Fatal Flora, I presume?"

Cold dread stopped any chance of response.

To acknowledge the awful name that had apparently followed her from Natchez would be to admit her irritation as well as her identity. Flora Brimm intended to do neither. Instead, her polite smile faltered only slightly as their gazes met and her heart skittered to a quick stop.

Unmistakable gray-green eyes regarded her with what she guessed was cool contempt. Was it in recollection of their last meeting?

A dark brow rose, as did one corner of his mouth. Now amusement seemed to color his handsome features.

"You *are* Flora Brimm of the Natchez Brimms, are you not?"

"Of course she is. Who, may I ask, is inquiring?" The matriarch of the Brimm clan swept across the garden path as if she owned the place. Two maids and a uniformed employee of the hotel followed at a respectable distance behind. The trio stopped at her grandmother's gesture to halt, and the nearest maid offered the elegant lady her ear trumpet.

After regally glancing over the interloper, Grandmama turned her attention to Flora as she pressed the hearing device to her ear. "Do explain what you're doing out in the afternoon sun, dear." Her gaze lifted heavenward for only a second. "And with rain showers coming. Next thing you know, you'll be waltzing under the raindrops like some common—"

"Truly, Grandmama, you're exaggerating." Flora paused, unable to resist another comment. "And what's wrong with dancing under the rain-drops?"

"It's not done. At least not by a Brimm, of course." Grandmama looked as if she had given the ultimate answer to all responses. Of course, in her circle, it was the ultimate response.

Some things just weren't done. At least not by Brimms.

Flora made a note to dance in the rain at her earliest opportunity. Not to show Grandmama, but to take one item off the list of things that just weren't done by Brimms.

"As for you, young man." Grandmama focused again on the stranger. "We offer no alms to the poor, but if you'll leave your name with Isabella . . ." She motioned for the nearest maid to move forward. "I'll be happy to have a box meal sent down."

If the man found Millicent Brimm the least bit off-putting, he did not show it. Rather, he tipped his hat and walked away without so much as a word of explanation or an expression of thanks. He did, however, give Flora a look that promised they would meet again.

The prospect did not entirely disappoint.

"Grandmama," Flora chided softly as she turned her back on the stranger. "He could very well be one of the guests here. He's certainly dressed well enough."

"Darling, breeding tells, and that was no gentleman." Her grandmother lifted an iron-gray brow. "You don't know this man, do you?"

"No, of course not."

Her grandmother linked arms with Flora. "And yet he knew your name." She paused just long enough to make her point. "Curious."

Of course he knew her name. She was the legendary Fatal Flora, the bride who had lost four fiancés to their untimely graves. All of Natchez knew that, so why not total strangers as well? He also knew she had an ability to navigate heights, decent skill on the ballroom floor, and an interest in finding Will Tucker.

Flora swallowed down a response and allowed her grandmother to lead her up the path toward the hotel. The girl she'd sent for her writing materials met them at the door to the lobby.

"I'm so sorry, Miss Flora. There was a problem with the elevator, so I was forced to take the stairs, and then—"

"Put those away," Grandmama said to the poor, out-of-breath maid. "She has no need of them now. We'll be taking tea here on the veranda." She turned to the fellow in hotel livery and said, "Do hurry. The rest of you may leave."

As the servants scurried away, Flora glanced back over her shoulder at the expanse of green and the Leatherwood Valley beyond. The man in the bowler hat was nowhere in sight.

It did not escape her notice, though, that somewhere out there was a strange man who knew her as Fatal Flora. A man who could ruin everything with Mr. Tucker.

That is, if Mr. Tucker ever saw fit to arrive for his wedding.

Lucas had been summarily dismissed by a woman three times his age—and offered alms for the poor as well. Not his best afternoon.

He took his wounded pride off into the shadows

on the far side of the property and watched as the ladies and their entourage made their way up the steps to the veranda. The spark in Flora Brimm's eyes had dimmed immediately upon the arrival of the woman his research indicated was Millicent Augusta Meriwether Brimm of the Natchez Brimms and the Atlanta Meriwethers.

The idea that Mrs. Brimm might be in on the scheme Tucker had going was impossible. It was rumored she had caused more than one fellow to be placed in political office in Mississippi, not counting her own husband, who had been elevated from a law career to a state senator before the war. No one with that sort of power did business with criminals.

Not personally, anyway.

Lucas knew this not only from his years as a Pinkerton agent, but also from his own experience as the grandson of a man who was used to getting his own way. He leaned back against a tree trunk and reached for his handkerchief. The day was warm for May and getting warmer.

Watching Miss Brimm didn't help. Something about the woman made him hot under the collar. Especially when he recollected how she felt in his arms as they danced, and the way the moonlight washed over her features on the ledge.

He reached for his watch to confirm the time, and then he nodded to the security man he'd hired to keep tabs on Miss Brimm. At present the fellow wore the livery of the Crescent Hotel. Just yesterday he'd been wearing a Eureka Springs deputy's uniform and badge.

Lucas decided his next move was to head toward town and his meeting with the local sheriff. After the pleasantries were exchanged, he got down to the business at hand.

"I appreciate the loan of your best man, sir, but after today I'll not be needing him."

"Is that so?" The sheriff, a man of sufficient size and trigger speed to incite fear in those who came across his wrath, shook his head. "I like to cooperate with the Pinks when they ask. Seems a bit odd they sent you all the way down here without letting me know first, though."

Lucas paused only a moment. "You have a con man here, Sheriff, and if I'm right, he's using a woman with money to get him close to the wealthy guests at the Crescent. No offense, but we can't be certain who else he's using."

"Including me," the lawman said with a chuckle.

A warm breeze blew in from the lone window, bringing with it the scent of the local livery stable. Not an altogether pleasant aroma, especially in the tight confines of the office.

"Are you satisfied I'm not playing nice with the crooks?" the sheriff asked with a small smile.

"I am."

Lucas's assurance had come in the form of a coded telegram from Kyle Russell, the one man inside the agency he could trust. But with the assurance had come a warning to wrap up the matter quickly and quietly and hightail it out of Eureka Springs before anyone got wind of the fact he was there. No explanation as to why.

The older man shifted positions and gestured for Lucas to take the chair across from him. "What can I do for you, Agent McMinn?"

Lucas decided to get straight to the point. "I need you to arrest a Mr. Will Tucker."

"On what grounds?"

"I thought I would leave that to you," Lucas said carefully. "As long as he's locked up before sundown, I really don't care."

A full minute went by with nothing but some serious staring to show for it. Finally, the sheriff leaned back in his chair. "I'm not in the habit of arresting a man without cause, McMinn, even when it's the Pinkertons doing the asking." He paused. "Or is it just you doin' the asking?"

Lucas didn't flinch. "I don't recall asking."

More silence stretched between them as the fellow appeared to consider his options. "I'll see what I can do. But without any grounds I won't be able to hold him much longer than it would take for you to come get him."

"That's all I need, sir. Just long enough to come get him. I'll take it from there."

"As long as I know I'm not turning him over to some kind of vigilante, I'll see that you get him."

Lucas's eyes narrowed. "I'm not sure what you're saying, Sheriff. Are you worried I'm going to harm a prisoner?"

"Stranger things have happened." He shrugged. "Just stating my feelings on the matter."

"Duly noted." Lucas rose and the older man did the same. A handshake later, Lucas pointed his boots back up the hill to the hotel. An official case file might not be open on Will Tucker yet, but there would be just as soon as Flora Brimm cooperated.

And if she didn't cooperate, the next arrest warrant he swore out would be for her. Lucas paused to think on that and then turned around. It wouldn't hurt to get the paperwork started on that warrant, just in case. And unlike with Tucker, he would have Flora Brimm on receipt of stolen property, if nothing else.

His grin broadened. That was a charge that would stick, for he could personally testify to her guilt as an eyewitness, and it wouldn't take much to confiscate the property in her possession, either.

❊ THREE ❊

"Sit, Flora." Grandmama gestured to the chair nearest where she'd settled. "And do not dawdle." With a nod, Flora joined her grandmother, though her thoughts continued to be divided between the strange man and the plan she hoped would include Grandmama.

They were in a quiet alcove with a lovely view of the Crescent Hotel's grounds. Though other chairs were scattered down both sides of the long veranda, only a gray tabby dared come anywhere near Millicent Brimm without permission. And even the cat kept a respectable distance as she stretched lazily in the shade and peered through half-open eyes at the waiter who brought the tea tray.

"Lovely, isn't it?" Grandmama mused as she added sugar to her tea. "It reminds me a bit of home."

"Mmm," Flora said though she could see little to compare with Brimmfield and its indigo fields that rolled down toward the Mississippi River.

"Violet should be here."

Flora gave her grandmother a sideways look. "We've been over this. She refuses."

Grandmama reached to pat Flora's hand. "She

refuses thus far. One must give prayer time to work. You know this, dear."

"Yes, but I also know my sister. If we can't get her to move back into the main house, how will we get her back out in the world?" She looked away. "It's just been too long."

"A pity Brimmfield is in jeopardy of leaving the family." Grandmama's words were a surprising change of topic as well as a none-too-subtle jab.

"Is it Brimmfield you would miss or the fact that it would go to Cousin Winny?" Flora met her grandmother's level stare even as her thoughts raced. "After all, he is family."

The teacup rattled against the saucer as Grandmama set it down with a force that was echoed in her expression. "Winthrop Brimm is merely a blood relative, Flora. First cousin and family are distinctly different."

"And yet family all the same," she dared.

Grandmama's expression sharpened. "Like his father before him, Winthrop has been known to associate with persons of unsavory character. Unlike his father, he has not yet married one of them."

Sipping her tea, Flora let the comment pass without response. Bigger arguments were yet to be fought. Or perhaps Grandmama would fall into league with her without difficulty.

It was a good plan.

"Yes, I would miss Brimmfield. And for the

record, no child of Clothilde is family of mine," Grandmama continued as she leaned back in her chair and regarded Flora with an I-dare-you-to-argue look.

Whether it was Clothilde Brimm's questionably dusky hair and skin or her disdain for the restrictions of polite Southern society, Grandmama piled reason upon reason to dislike her daughter-in-law. For those same reasons, Flora had loved her aunt dearly.

But she loved her grandmother more, and thus she let the comment pass unanswered rather than allow Grandmama to continue to harp on a feud that should have been long ago resolved. Talking about her plan to marry would have to wait until Millicent Brimm was in a better mood, as would reminding her that feuding with a dead woman rarely left a person feeling they had won anything of value.

"Tell me about tonight's dinner plans. Will we be dining with the Culbersons again?"

"You cannot change the subject so easily, Flora Belle Brimm."

"I can and I have," she said gently but firmly. "Though if you would prefer not to discuss the Culbersons, perhaps you might regale me with another of your lovely stories of your travels. You know I wish to follow in your footsteps."

And soon was best left unspoken.

Grandmama's lips remained closed tight, her

irritation etched into the lines of her forehead. Flora watched her grip the arms of her chair and then slowly lean forward as if to stand. Instantly, one of the hotel porters hurried to assist her.

"Leave me be," she said as she shook off his assistance. When the young man had gone back to his post, Grandmama turned toward Flora. "Something else is on your mind."

"There is, actually." She worried with the words she longed to say and the trim on her sleeve in equal measure.

"Then you'd best just get it over with and tell me. You never were much on keeping secrets. At least not from me."

Flora smiled. "You were always willing to listen."

"I still am."

"All right." She let out a long breath and seized her courage. "I have a plan that will save Brimmfield."

One iron-gray eyebrow rose. "Go on."

"It's a bit far-fetched, but I've decided to marry." There. She said it.

"Of course you'll marry," Grandmama said with a polite chuckle. "I'm sure some brave fellow will manage to make it all the way to the altar. We'll just have to give the Lord a bit more time to find him." She leaned forward again to press her palms against her knees. "And to strengthen his health."

Though her grandmother was far too proper to

reference the reasons, time was certainly not something they had in abundance. Grandfather Brimm's will stated that Flora was heir to Brimmfield—but only if she produced an heir before Winny turned thirty. Her cousin had recently celebrated his twenty-eighth birthday. Given the fickle nature of timing the birth of a child, not much time remained for Flora to find a husband who could survive to the altar and give her the child she needed.

"Actually, I have a candidate," Flora said with what she hoped would be the appropriate amount of enthusiasm. "He's well qualified and willing to accept the terms as I've outlined them."

"A candidate? With terms?" Grandmama leaned back and shook her head. "Flora, you sound as if you're talking about a potential employee."

"In a manner of speaking, I suppose I am." Before Grandmama could protest, Flora hurried to continue. "You see, the fellow in question is most trustworthy. His character is above reproach, and he's indicated he will sign a contract outlining his duties as my husband."

This time her grandmother's chuckle was accompanied by a sideways look. "Darling, I believe most men are well acquainted with the expectation of their duties as a husband without the likes of you outlining it in a contract."

"Do be serious," Flora snapped. "I'm not talking about *that* sort of marriage."

"In order to beget the required heir within the allotted time, I'm afraid you must have *that* sort of marriage, my dear. I know of no other way."

"He is of high esteem. He will see that an heir is . . ." She felt herself blush to her roots. "Is begat," she finally managed. "The care and raising of that child, however, will be exclusively my domain."

Grandmama appeared to take that assertion with unusual calmness. Perhaps she didn't believe the statement. Or, more likely, she was busy formulating a plan to counter it.

Finally, she let out a long breath. "I'd be hard-pressed to believe you could find a man of such high esteem who would be willing to be bound to such an agreement. I would certainly have no respect for him."

"Well, the Frisco Railroad finds him worthy of respect. He's made quite a name for himself as one of their special railroad detectives."

"Is that so?" Her grandmother appeared to consider the news with more than a little interest. "And this railroad man is willing to take on a loveless marriage for what I assume is a tidy sum? That isn't the sort of fellow I would call above reproach."

This was not going as Flora had hoped. "You don't understand, Grandmama. He's seeing to the needs of his family as well."

"Likely a wife and a half dozen children

tucked somewhere back on the railroad line in Springfield or St. Louis, unless I miss my guess." She let out a long breath. "Truly, Flora, you must rethink this plan. I'll not approve this sort of misbehavior."

"Forgive me, but I'm not asking for your approval. Rather, I am informing you of—"

"Flora, please." Grandmama's expression sobered as she held up a hand to cease the discussion. "Dear, I believe we've been followed." She gestured to the row of chairs on the far end of the veranda. "That man on the end. I've seen him before."

Flora followed the direction of her grand-mother's gaze and found Will Tucker smiling in her direction. With a grin that even from this distance could charm a woman's heart, there was no mistaking the railroad detective.

Worse, the man looked as if he hadn't a care in the world as he tipped his hat.

"You've seen him before?" Flora managed. "Are you sure?"

"Yes, I'm certain of it. Perhaps on the train from St. Louis? Or was it at that dreadful reception for the governor last week?" She nodded. "Yes, that's where it was. He was skulking about as if he didn't want to be seen. I couldn't help notice he'd taken an interest in you, though."

The taut string of nerves holding her in place threatened to snap as Flora watched Mr. Tucker rise to stroll inside. As the doors closed, she gripped the arms of the rocker, her thoughts reeling.

"Are you certain?" That came out sounding as though someone else had said it.

"Dear, I am old and I may have need of my hearing trumpet on occasion, but I'm neither dotty nor blind. Nor do you need to ask the same question more than once. Yes, I am absolutely certain." Grandmama's eyes narrowed. "Only a careless fool would assume I don't take notice when any fellow has set his sites on my unmarried and quite wealthy granddaughter. And that is the man I saw."

"Last week?"

"Now who needs this ear trumpet? Yes, that is the man."

Irritation and relief rose in equal measure as Flora returned her attention to Grandmama. "Would you excuse me?"

"Flora Brimm, I'll do no such thing. You and I were in the middle of an important conversation that we need to take upstairs and continue in private."

"And we shall. Just not right now."

"Whatever did they teach you at that Yankee boarding school?"

"To behave in a manner befitting my station in life and to do nothing to disturb the peace of that station," Flora said sweetly as she quoted from

Dillingham Ladies Preparatory's oath. "And to see to the needs of my family before my own. Which is exactly what I plan to do."

Flora straightened her back and took her leave. Later she would pay the price with a lecture or perhaps a ticket back to Natchez. By then, however, neither Father nor Grandmama would have any say in what she did.

That honor would go to her husband, at least in theory. And in reality, she would leave the name of Fatal Flora Brimm behind.

As to her grandmother seeing Will Tucker last week? That was preposterous. Had he been in Eureka Springs, there was no reason for Mr. Tucker to hide himself from the woman he planned to marry.

No, Grandmama must certainly be mistaken.

The Crescent Hotel's double doors once again opened, and a pair of liveried doormen stepped back to allow Flora entry into the main rotunda. Up ahead she spied Mr. Tucker sidestepping the fireplace of Eureka marble that anchored the center of the room. Such was the throng in the corridor leading to the staircase and elevators beyond that she easily caught up to the scoundrel.

He was tall and fair, with eyes of stormy gray and impossibly long lashes that a woman might envy. His hair stood in stark contrast to his dark hat and suit, and it had been cropped shorter than she remembered upon their last meeting. Still, he bore that dreamy Mr. Darcy quality that women who liked that sort of man might adore.

Had she planned on marrying for love, Will Tucker would not likely have made the topmost tier of her wish list, but with four former fiancés in their graves and a rumor that she might somehow be a party to their demises, Flora had long since given up on any sort of demands she might place on a husband.

For that matter, she'd almost given up on a husband due to the lack of possible candidates until her fortuitous meeting with Mr. Tucker on the steamboat between New Orleans and Natchez. She'd just left an interminable visit where she'd been forced to listen to Winny speak at length on what he would do with the profits gained from the sale of Brimmfield. Rather than hide away on a packet ship to a remote location, she'd climbed aboard the *Lady of the River* with a headache and a prayer.

Mr. Tucker and his talent for conversation had been the answer to both. That and his interesting ability to quote literature and to remember almost anything he read with perfect clarity and recall.

Then there was the fact that almost immediately after petitioning the Lord for the perfect husband, he appeared.

"A moment of your time, sir," Flora said as she linked arms with her intended and led him away from the staircase toward the office and front exit.

If he was surprised by her forward behavior, Mr. Tucker did not let on. Rather, he dipped his head in greeting. "Well, hello there, Flora."

She slid him a sideways look. " 'Hello there' is not what I'd hoped to hear from you, Mr. Tucker. But this is not the place to discuss it."

"I have been meditating on the very great pleasure which a pair of fine eyes in the face of a pretty woman can bestow," he said, quoting Mr. Darcy from the novel *Pride and Prejudice* as he had upon their first meeting. The cad.

"It's a bit late for that sort of behavior, Mr. Tucker. You'll need to stop quoting others and begin by telling me the cause of your delay." She nodded toward the front exit of the hotel. "Perhaps a walk is in order. Will you join me?"

He offered a smile. "After you, Miss Brimm."

When they had made their way around the side of the building away from the prying eyes of other guests, Flora released her grip on his arm. A sweep of his person from the tip of his well-shod toes to the top of his head, covered in a most fashionable hat, told her Mr. Tucker's trip to Eureka Springs had not been uncomfortable. Nor had it been recent, for there wasn't a single spot of soot or a wrinkle in his clothing to indicate he'd just traveled by rail.

Several responses came in response to the grin that lifted the corner of his mouth. "You're late," was the one she chose.

He dared to chuckle. "I'm right on time, darlin'." He glanced around and then swung his attention back to Flora. "You'll understand if I don't elaborate. Official business and all."

But she didn't understand. Nor did it matter what sort of business kept him from arriving two weeks ago as promised. Or, worse, kept him on the periphery of her life without any indication he'd been there, if that had indeed been the case.

She looked past him toward Magnetic Springs and the mountains beyond, a lovely scene to soothe her rumpled thoughts. But gazing at the vista would do nothing to remedy the fact that her carefully laid plans were quickly falling by the wayside. Flora crossed her arms over her chest and willed her temper to cool.

"Mr. Tucker," she said firmly. "You are not 'right on time.' You are, in a word, late. Two weeks late, and without so much as a note of decent explanation or apology." He moved toward her, but Flora easily sidestepped him. "No you don't, sir. I'll have that explanation and the apology. You've caused me no end of trouble."

"Have I?" His look of contrition almost worked. Almost, but not quite. The gleam in his eye gave him away. His expression told Flora that Mr. Tucker was actually enjoying her irritation. "And I thought I was the solution to all your troubles."

That did it.

Flora Brimm was no wide-eyed girl intent on

marriage to the first fellow who offered it. Rather, she was a grown woman who had mourned more than one man making the same offer as Tucker.

Straightening her shoulders, she let out a long breath and fixed him with a stare. "You and I had an arrangement. Please understand that this arrangement is in grave danger of being declared at an end. And lest you misunderstand, it is you and not I who is in breach of its terms."

Instantly his arrogance disappeared. Apparently, he'd counted the cost of his cheeky behavior and deemed the loss too great to chance. "Let's walk."

Before she could protest, he linked arms with her and led her past the gazebo and around the side of the building before pausing once more near the empty croquet field. Here the scent of freshly cut grass drifted toward her on a light breeze.

"Surely you're not thinking of changing your mind, Flora? I'm here now." He paused to inch toward her, and he placed his hand on her arm. This time she allowed the familiarity. "I know once your feathers get unruffled, you'll—"

"You are truly insufferable." She yanked her arm away and began to retrace their steps. "To think you were the solution was pure madness," she said over her shoulder.

He fell into step beside her. A moment later Mr. Tucker snagged her wrist to cease her progress.

"You could have sent a note. Something." She sounded like a petulant fool. A woman scorned.

Flora bit her lip and looked away. In truth, she felt a little like both.

"Hey, now," he said with no small measure of irritation in his tone. He looked away briefly, and when he once again met her stare, his expression was neutral.

"Please, Flora. Can't we discuss this elsewhere?" He led her away from the path to the more private shadows of a bench some yards away from the main building. He sat down and gestured for her to join him. "I *am* the solution. And far as I'm concerned, our arrangement's still good. Why would I have bought this if I didn't intend to go through with our marriage?" He reached into his pocket and pulled out a gold wedding band encrusted with rubies and diamonds. "Do you like it?"

In order to maintain control over the conversation, she elected not to allow any indication that she was impressed with his offering. She did, however, concede to joining him on the bench. "It's lovely. However, it proves nothing, especially when you're *two weeks* late to the wedding with not a word to me in the meantime."

His face told her nothing of what he must be thinking. When he did not respond, she looked away. "I found you easily enough, Mr. Tucker. I'm sure I can find a replacement for you."

"What with those Fatal Flora rumors and all? Four down at last count is what they say. But I suppose it's possible you wouldn't have a reputation this far from home."

She gasped. How could he know this? Of course. He was a detective. She should have taken that into consideration. The only thing to do for it now was to feign indifference. And perhaps add a bit of bravado to her flagging attitude.

"Excuse me, sir," she said as she stood, "but are you insinuating something?" With the question, her backbone straightened and her ire rose. "For I would much prefer you just say it now while you have the chance."

Mr. Tucker's penitent look was instant if not completely believable. "Look, Flora. I was going to save this for later, but maybe this will repair your frayed nerves a bit."

"My nerves are fine," she snapped. "It is your calendar that needs repair."

He produced a folded piece of paper from his coat pocket and offered it to her as if he hadn't heard her comment. "Our marriage license," he said with a wink. "I even spoke with the parson before I checked in. He can marry us tomorrow morning." He glanced over his shoulder and then back at her. "See, I *have* been busy."

"But—"

"Honey, I'm not going anywhere, but apparently the reverend is. It's the soonest he would agree to marry us. Go ahead and look at the license if you don't believe me."

Flora inspected the document and decided it looked every bit as legitimate as the marital property agreement upstairs in her suitcase. Convincing an attorney to draw up the contract under a vow of silence had taken work, but she would not be sharing any more of the Brimm fortune with this stranger than the agreed upon amount.

A brisk north breeze lifted the edge of the document and almost pulled it from her hand as Flora met Will Tucker's eyes. She had one more thing to clarify with him. "My grandmother swears she saw you at a party we attended last week."

She watched carefully for any response. Instead, his face went blank. "Mr. Tucker? Did you hear me?"

Slowly a grin lifted the corners of his lips. "I did but I figured you had to be teasing."

Flora schooled her own features. "So you weren't there?"

"Honestly, how can you think I would watch you covertly and not make myself known?" He shrugged. "Your grandmother is mistaken."

"Yes, I suppose she must be," Flora said slowly as she allowed his words to take hold. She quickly folded the license and returned it to him. "I shall need a meeting time for tomorrow morning."

He cocked his hat back and seemed to think a moment. "Nine o'clock. I'm to deliver you to the parsonage."

The way he stated things, Flora felt as if she were some sort of package to be deposited on the porch. Truly, for an educated man, Mr. Tucker hid his accolades well.

"Very well, then. I shall meet you in the hotel lobby at half past eight."

He reached to draw her fingers to his lips. The odd thought occurred that this intimate act should not feel so off-putting, not when the man would be her husband by this time tomorrow.

The man who would father the favored heir.

"Flora, dear, if I didn't know better, I would think you were dismissing me. And only hours before our wedding."

Something in his demeanor, in the flippant way he addressed what was a topic of great concern, jabbed at her. She glanced around to be certain they were alone and then paused to offer a look she hoped would measure up to Grandmama's do-not-mistake-my-meaning expression.

"You do not know me better, Mr. Tucker, nor am I much acquainted with you. Any attempts to suggest otherwise, and that marriage license is worthless."

Lucas leaned further into the shadows beneath the back stairs and adjusted his specially constructed and soon-to-be-patented bowler hat, being careful not to allow the acoustic tube that enhanced his ability to listen in on Flora Brimm's conversation to show. She thought she was marrying Tucker in the morning.

He would see about that.

"So, yes, I *am* dismissing you, Mr. Tucker," she said clearly as her groom-to-be clutched the document he'd shown her. "There are preparations to be made." At the man's dense look, she continued. "Do you wish to draw attention to the fact you and I are here together?"

"They'll know soon enough, won't they?"

Miss Brimm shook her head. "Perhaps you've forgotten what I've told you regarding my grandmother. She would neither approve of nor allow any sort of dalliance with someone I barely know. She said as much just now, so I've work to do to get around the issue."

Tucker's chuckle and the familiar way he touched Miss Brimm's sleeve made Lucas clench his fists. "What can one old lady do?"

The Natchez belle easily slipped from the criminal's grasp. "That 'old lady' spotted you before I did," she said sharply.

"I told you it wasn't me she saw last week—"

"I meant today," she insisted with a shake of her head. "And trust me. Should Grandmama get wind of our plans beyond the general statement I made regarding our contract, she would call in any number of favors to guarantee we would never get away with anything less a long engagement followed by what would surely become an overblown circus of a wedding. Is that what you want?"

"She won't hear it from me." Tucker spoke just quickly enough to let Lucas know the man was more than a little worried. "You have my word."

Tucker said something else, but a trio of squealing children skipped past Lucas's hiding place, followed by their loudly complaining mother. A moment later, the trolley pulled into the drive and clanged without ceasing for a full half minute. By the time the extraneous noise ceased, the pair appeared ready to part ways.

Miss Brimm glanced around, but her gaze swept past Lucas's hiding spot without pausing. "Let's do this my way. I shall order up transport for us for eight thirty tomorrow morning. Please alleviate my fears and go to your room until then, sir. Order your meals sent up. I'll gladly pay for them once we've finalized our bargain. Just stay out of sight."

He paused to give her a look that was hidden by the shade from his hat. "I'll agree to it, but only because you asked so nicely, my dear. Consider it a wedding gift. Though I still don't see why you're so afraid of that old . . ." Tucker shook his head. "Forget I said anything. I'll meet you in the lobby tomorrow morning after a night's rest and an evening of behaving myself and staying out of your grandmother's way. How's that?"

She gave him a sideways look. "By staying in your room?"

He held up his hand. "I promise."

"Then I think that's a good plan."

He winked. "As do I. Can't be tired if I'm heading off on my honeymoon tomorrow."

The trolley bell rang again, hiding her response. What could not be hidden, however, was the expression on her lovely face. Though Will Tucker was looking forward to a honeymoon, his bride was not.

Or perhaps she affected such an angry stance for some other reason. With his listening tube temporarily unusable and no other way to gauge her emotions, Lucas was left to wonder. It didn't take a Pinkerton man, even one who specialized in advanced science and modern crime-fighting gadgetry, to tell Miss Brimm was not counting the minutes until the after-wedding celebration.

When she led Tucker toward the hotel's front entrance, Lucas lost any ability to either see or hear them. He removed the bowler, made the adjustments that hid the listening device, and then returned the hat to his head to follow his prey. Keeping to the edges of the path where the foliage was dense, he easily trailed the pair until they separated at the front entrance.

Their parting left him momentarily baffled. Had Miss Brimm been his intended, Lucas knew for certain he would have offered at least an embrace. With lips that lovely and begging to be kissed, he would gladly have accommodated her.

Unfortunately, dwelling on a kiss that would never happen caused him to miss the direction in which Tucker headed. Flora Brimm, however, was impossible to miss as she swept past and hailed a doorman. Rather than access his listening tube to overhear her request, Lucas kept still until the doorman sprinted toward the entrance. Then, with Miss Brimm's attention elsewhere, Lucas followed the employee inside.

"A moment of your time," he said as he opened his coat just enough to allow the fellow to see his badge, but not enough to allow a viewing by any of the other hotel guests.

Especially not Miss Brimm, who had slipped inside and was now hiding—or, rather, attempting to hide—in a dark corner near the elevator.

Lucas nodded toward the manager's office, hidden behind an etched glass enclosure. Releasing his coat lapel, he pressed a finger to his lips in a bid for discretion. "I'll need to know what that young lady requested of you, and I'll also need to speak with the manager."

"She wishes to go into town. The post office, I believe."

An odd request, considering that she could easily post a letter here at the hotel. "The manager, then. I need to speak to him right now."

"Yes, of course, sir," the man said as he hurried to his task. A moment later, the manager returned to usher Lucas into his private domain.

"Before you go," he said to the fellow, "that same woman is skulking in the shadows near the elevator. Would you let me know the minute she leaves her hiding spot?"

A discreet glance and his eyes widened. "But that's Miss Brimm, sir."

"Yes, it is. Do not let her know you're observing her."

"Of course not, sir."

"To what do we owe a visit from the Pinks?" the manager asked as he closed his door and gestured toward a chair in front of his desk.

"A matter of discretion," Lucas said. "I'm afraid I have to inform you that two guests in this hotel are engaged in illegal activities. One has an arrest warrant pending. The other warrant should be active as of this afternoon at the latest." He would confirm that with the sheriff as soon as he could manage it. "I am not at liberty to disclose these names as it might cause the parties to flee should attention be directed to them. However, I'm certain you would wish them to be dispatched quietly from your establishment."

The manager's brows gathered. "Indeed I do. We don't condone anything of the sort at the Crescent. Consider the entire resources of our hotel at your command."

Miss Brimm was seeking a personal visit downtown. Lucas grinned as he patted the handcuffs in his pocket. Indeed, she would have one. Unfortunately for her, the woman who was in collusion with Will Tucker would be heading for a jail cell and not the post office.

"Actually," he said with a grin. "All I need right now is a buggy, the omnibus transport arrival schedule, and a little assistance from one of your men."

·❈ FOUR ❈·

Flora kept to her hiding place near the hotel entrance until the green-eyed man with the bowler hat disappeared around the corner. The last thing she needed was to have another conversation with him. He knew far too much, and worse, he continually seemed to appear from nowhere.

Perhaps she should post her letter to Father tomorrow after her appointment with the pastor. *Their* appointment, she corrected, though she tried to ignore the stab the reminder gave her conscience.

She patted her reticule, in part to reassure herself that the quickly penned missive, a brief note scribbled on hotel stationery moments ago, was still there. Somehow, telling Father about her intentions to marry before the ceremony made the pact seem all the more official and the subterfuge less disrespectful. That her father would be livid when he read the news of the already completed nuptials was a given. Flora's concession to respect and propriety would be in the timing of his receipt of this news.

Knowing Grandmama had her ways of finding things out, Flora did not consider posting the letter here at the hotel. Better to go into town and deliver it to someone less likely to be swayed by the matriarch of the Brimm clan.

Leaning against the carved post, she watched the pendulum swing on the oversized clock on the wall behind the reception desk and thought back on what she'd seen. The man had seemed insistent that he speak to the manager. Then he'd gone behind the glass enclosure only to reappear a few minutes later with at least two hotel employees in tow.

Whatever the reason, the expression she had spied on the hotel manager's face before the door closed was unmistakable. He was not happy. Likely someone, possibly one of the escorts Grandmama insisted upon, had informed him of the man's penchant for bothering innocent young women.

Indeed, the fellow certainly seemed in a hurry to leave. Perhaps he was being escorted off the property. Until she knew for certain, though, she realized he could pop up again at any time. Not a welcome thought.

She thought for a moment of seeking solace in

Mr. Tucker's suite—the number of which he'd offered though she had not requested it—until she could be certain the stranger would not return to follow her. Unfortunately, Mr. Tucker would likely misunderstand her motives for contacting him again so soon after dismissing him.

Another look in both directions revealed no familiar faces, so Flora stepped from the shadows. She waited a moment for someone to notice, but no one appeared interested in her actions.

She let out a breath and smiled. That she'd eluded security and her grandmother emboldened her. With her head held high, she maneuvered herself around a cluster of chairs, most occupied by older gents with newspapers and too much time on their hands, to march over to the reception desk. When the fellow merely stared at her rather than jumping to assist her, Flora rang the bell.

"Yes, Miss Brimm," the rather skittish doorman said. "Your carriage is being brought around now."

"Thank you," she said as she glanced over toward the double doors and then back at the hotel employee. "I can't imagine what's taking so long."

The poor man colored bright red as he cleared his throat, his eyes skimming the top of her head rather than meeting her gaze. "I . . . well . . . that is, we have a new fellow who will be driving you and . . . ah, here he is." Relief appeared to wash over him as he nodded toward the entrance where yet another man stood. "You have a nice trip into town now," he said as he reached for a handkerchief to mop his brow and then ducked back behind the glass enclosure.

"What an odd man," Flora said under her breath as she moved cautiously toward the doors.

Mindful that Grandmama, one of her minions, or, worse, the green-eyed man, could still pounce at any moment, she quickly slipped outside and then glanced around for the buggy. Other than the Frisco Railroad's omnibus, which rolled to a stop a few yards away, there appeared to be no private vehicles waiting.

Sending a sideways look to the doorman, Flora shook her head. "Where is my carriage?"

"Other side of the depot transport, ma'am. I will be happy to escort you," he said as he offered his arm.

"Thank you." Flora stepped off the curb as a crowd of train passengers emerged from the omnibus. At once several dozen men, women, and children flooded the area. Thankfully, the doorman pressed his hand atop hers and skillfully steered her around the chaos.

And into the waiting arms of the green-eyed man with the bowler hat.

"Good day, darlin'," he said with a grin that might have been appealing had he not been addressing her in such an uncouth manner. "I thought you and I would take a buggy ride.

Maybe find a chessboard and play a game or two. Or we could just have a nice friendly talk."

Before she could react, the doorman released his grip on her arm. "I'm sorry, Miss Brimm," he hastened to mutter before slipping into the crowd. "The boss said I was to cooperate with this fellow here."

A few feet away, a mother scolded a crying child while the omnibus driver hauled luggage onto the curb. Flora made a dart in their direction, but the stranger grabbed her arm and hauled her back against him.

"Unlike last night, I am now quite mindful of your identity, Miss Brimm. I believe I tried to tell you as much earlier," he said, his voice low, his breath warm against her ear. "Unless I miss my guess, your friend Mrs. Honeycutt is over there playing a cordial round of croquet with a general's wife and a few other society types. I also know your banged-up reputation can't stand another dent in it, so why don't you make this easy on both of us and not draw her attention over here?"

"I have no idea what you're talking about, sir, but I demand that you unhand me." Her heart raced as she worked to clearly and distinctly enunciate the words her grandmother had taught her. "The Brimm family will refuse any ransom, so I'm quite worthless to kidnap."

The statement was a total fabrication, of course, for surely Father would pay any price to see her returned . . . and to keep Cousin Winthrop from his inheritance.

Or so she hoped.

"There will be no ransom requested. It's not that kind of buggy ride. As to that woman, Mrs. Honeycutt? You know exactly what I'm talking about," he said with deadly calm as he released her. "Poor Simon. I wonder how his mama will ever get over losing her only son just days before his wedding. Maybe you and I ought to go see how she's doing."

Flora saw a woman who could possibly be her almost-mother-in-law in conversation with two other women on the far end of the hotel gardens while yet another lady appeared to be playing her turn at croquet. From this distance it was impossible to know for sure.

"Of course, you'll have to explain to her why you have me with you. You don't think she'll tell anyone you're in trouble with the law, do you?"

"The law? You have no proof of that."

The man chuckled, sending a shiver down her spine. "Do I need it? My guess is Mrs. Honeycutt will take a look at the badge I carry in my pocket and be inclined to believe me." He paused. "And repeat it. I'm sure the manager and his desk clerk will back her up."

"That woman over there could be anyone," Flora said as she sent up a fervent prayer she was correct.

"Oh?" He handed her an ordinary-looking pair of wire-rimmed spectacles. "Take a look using these."

"Honestly, I fail to understand why—"

"Just take a peek and then you'll understand."

She fitted the spectacles in place, blinking several times to adjust her vision. To her surprise, Mrs. Honeycutt's image came into view. Flora could clearly see not only the older woman but also her companions, one of whom she thought she recognized as a friend of Grandmama's from the garden club. Another was definitely the wife of the general who had hosted them for dinner just last week.

All of this she saw in great detail. And from a distance too far away to be visible.

"How do these spectacles do that? They look perfectly normal," she said as she handed back the spectacles, her knees threatening to buckle. "Obviously they're some sort of special lens. It's so far, and yet I could clearly see."

"It doesn't matter how they work. What matters is whether you and I are going to have a nice walk over there to visit with your Natchez friend or not."

He had her. "What do you want?"

"Turn around slowly, and while you're at it you might want to think about smiling. That lady looks a little worried, and I don't think it's because her child won't settle down. You wouldn't want her to think I'm upsetting you."

Flora spied a woman watching from her place near the back of the omnibus as she bounced a squalling baby against her shoulder. A nod or, failing that, a scream, and she would likely go for help.

A glance around, and Flora decided there were plenty more who could come to her assistance: men piling suitcases on the curb, women preening in tiny purse mirrors in an attempt to smooth their road-ruined coiffures, and even a pair of curious youths who were currently poking at the flank of the lead horse in the team.

If she managed it just right, she could escape without Mrs. Honeycutt being any the wiser. For surely the Natchez matron did not possess a pair of oddly powerful spectacles.

"Flora Brimm," the man said, "you need to turn around slowly and keep your hands where I can see them."

"Don't be ridiculous," she said as she made eye contact with the mother.

"I've been called a whole lot of things in the commission of my duties as a Pinkerton agent, but ridiculous isn't one of them."

"So now you're not just the law, you're a Pinkerton? If that's true, why didn't you admit to it last night?"

"Last night I had no reason to believe I needed to."

The lawman put a hand on her shoulder and

slowly turned her around to face him. "Get in the buggy. We're going to take a ride."

"Not until I see a badge."

He regarded her with some measure of amusement. "You'll see a badge when I decide you're not going to take off and run." One dark brow rose. "Remember, Fatal Flora, you're the one with the most to lose here."

Drawing herself up to her full height, Flora looked him in the eyes. "I demand you either release me or offer proof of your affiliation with the Pinkerton Detective Agency, Mr. . . ."

"McMinn," he said as he peered down at her from under the brim of his hat. "Lucas McMinn. Under other conditions I'd say I was pleased to make your acquaintance. The best I can do right now is to tell you one last time to climb up into the carriage before I put you up there myself. Or I can put handcuffs on you and march you inside. The manager and a few of his employees have all confirmed my identity, and I'm sure they'll be glad to tell you that." He paused. "So will the sheriff for that matter. So do I pick you up and situate you in the buggy? Might cause a scene."

"You wouldn't dare," she said, even though the expression on the rogue's face told her he would.

"Just like a fine lady like you wouldn't climb out a window to act as lookout for your boy-friend? Oh, excuse me. Your fiancé. And you did. Last night. With me tailing you."

"Truly, sir, I have no idea what you're talking—"

"Will Tucker is what I'm talking about." He almost spat the words, such was his obvious distaste for the topic. "And don't bother denying you know the man. You told me yourself last night you were looking for him. You called him by name."

Flora gasped. "Looking for him and finding him are two different things!"

This time his grin was swift, though the sobering expression that followed was swifter. "Don't take me for one of those Natchez boys you can fool by batting your pretty blue sky eyes and acting cute, Miss Brimm."

"What did you just say?" *Blue sky eyes?* She hadn't heard that term in many years. The phrase conjured up an Irish kitchen and an old friend of her Aunt Clothilde.

Or had she heard him wrong? The memory slipped back into place and was gone.

"Please, Miss Brimm. Interrupting will not have the desired effect. I know you found the man. I watched you two getting reacquainted not thirty minutes ago. And I heard every word you said about your wedding tomorrow." He paused as if to allow her to absorb the information. "Now, how about we finish this conversation elsewhere?"

"I still demand a badge and some answers," she managed as she gripped the edge of the buggy to remain upright.

70

A glance behind her showed Flora that all the occupants of the omnibus had disappeared inside the hotel. Only Mrs. Honeycutt and her companions remained in sight, but thankfully they had not moved any closer.

"This isn't a Sunday social, Miss Brimm. You'll have plenty of time to get your answers just as soon as I get mine. Only thing is, I don't plan to stand around and let your fiancé size me up for a coffin, which he just might be doing from any one of those windows up there." He let out a long breath. "Look, here's my identification."

The man discreetly opened his coat to show her what appeared to be an authentic Pinkerton badge. "Now up you go. We can finish talking once we get clear of this hotel."

She complied, but only to buy a few moments of time. As soon as he left her to step around and take the reins, Flora planned to jump out and run. What she didn't plan on was for the man to slap a pair of handcuffs on her before he slid into the driver's spot.

"I'll scream."

"Go ahead. The sheriff won't care if I bring you in quietly or shouting from the rooftops, but my guess is you have an opinion on whether people are watching."

She did, and so she refrained from any response, especially as Mrs. Honeycutt had left the other women behind in the garden and was now strolling toward the hotel's front entrance.

"Just go," Flora said as she held her back straight and tried not to give any indication that she was trussed up like a turkey at Thanksgiving. "But do not think I will be locked in a jail cell. My father will certainly have something to say about—"

The horse lurched forward, almost knocking her backward. "Easy there, girl," Mr. McMinn said, though Flora couldn't tell whether he was addressing her or the spirited steed.

She braced herself as the carriage made a sharp turn onto the road leading toward the city below. While the Crescent Hotel perched high above Eureka Springs with a view on all sides, there was not much to interrupt the vista except for trees. Thus, in what seemed like seconds they left the bustling hotel behind in favor of the bracing mountain air and the thick shade of the surrounding forest.

Though the city lay just down the road, they might have been miles from civilization, a thought that was foremost in Flora's mind when her companion turned onto a tiny trail and stopped.

Silence reigned, interrupted only by the furious staccato of her heartbeat. The cold metal of the handcuffs bit into her wrists, but she refused to let him know.

"Look," he finally said. "I'm not enjoying this."

Oddly, his tone gave an impression of truth.

Flora shifted her attention to the canopy of green and the deep blue sky beyond while she collected her thoughts. A crackle overhead drew her attention to a fat squirrel perching on a pine limb, his attention divided between her and whatever he held in his cheeks.

"First, I want to be sure you understand the purpose of this carriage ride." He paused and seemed to be studying the toes of his boots. Abruptly he returned his attention to her. "I've shown you my badge that proves I'm a Pinkerton agent, but I want to be sure you're convinced of it."

"Why does it matter?"

He shifted positions and the carriage creaked. Though he was not an overlarge man, he was of sufficient size to cause her to look up to meet his eyes. "It just might, and that's all I will say right now."

Flora studied him a moment, carefully weighing what little she knew of the dark-haired fellow. From his penchant for hiding to the deference shown him by the hotel staff, she had deduced there was something out of the ordinary about him. That he was a lawman had been one of her assumptions last night. To have it confirmed with the evidence of a badge gave Flora no reason to doubt his claim.

"Mr. McMinn, is it?" When he nodded, she continued. "Yes, Mr. McMinn, I do believe you. And I assume we've stopped here because you're amenable to an arrangement other than jail, though I cannot imagine what charges anyone would have against me."

"The charges are easy enough to explain." He reached for her arm with, Flora hoped, the key to the handcuffs. Instead, he ran an index finger over her watch.

For a moment his stern expression went soft. Then, in an instant, the lawman's hard stare returned. "Flora Brimm, you are charged with accepting stolen property, aiding and abetting a known criminal, and a few other things I might choose to add once I get you situated in the jail-house."

❊ FIVE ❊

"Of all the nerve! Stolen property? I have no need of stealing anything, Mr. McMinn. The idea of it is preposterous." Flora shook her head. "And how dare you accuse me of colluding with a person of that ilk? I am a woman of careful associations."

His chuckle belied his formidable presence. "Careful associations? Is that what you're calling your engagement to Will Tucker? A careful association?"

It was. Though she was loath to admit it to the

man now, Flora had used those exact words in her letter to Father.

Again he touched her watch. "Tell me where you got this."

"It was a gift."

"From?"

Once again, Flora met his gaze. Under other circumstances she might have allowed herself to note the way the dappled sunlight played across the angles of his face. The way his lashes, raven dark and thick as a woman's, brushed high cheekbones when he closed his eyes.

Now, however, she willed herself to form a more dispassionate opinion. Considering the man held the key to the handcuffs circling her wrists, the effort was not difficult to manage.

"From my fiancé." She let out a long breath. "Mr. Tucker."

A nod. And then another shift of positions as if he were seeking to assure himself they were truly alone.

"Look, I want Tucker, not you. He is the true criminal. At least, that is my current assessment. It could change." Before Flora could protest, Mr. McMinn held up his hands to stop her. "Did you ever wonder why the letter *M* was engraved on the back?"

Indeed she had, but Mr. Tucker had explained it quite well. "That's the initial of his mother's given name. The watch was hers." Flora gave him a sideways look. "How did you know about the engraving?"

He said nothing for a moment, allowing her to draw her own conclusion. "Because I have an affidavit on file proving the watch's ownership." Another pause. "And asserting that your fiancé stole it."

She looked up sharply but said nothing. The handcuffs weighed heavily against the skin of her wrists. If only she'd thought to bring her gloves along when she left the suite this morning.

"Miss Brimm? Don't you have an opinion on what I've told you?"

"Of course I do. I don't give one whit for what your affidavit says. The assertion is preposterous." She said it as much to convince herself as to make her companion see reason. "I know Mr. Tucker, and he wouldn't . . ." Again she shook her head. "He just doesn't appear the sort."

"And appearances are everything with your set, aren't they? Which is why you're willing to marry him." His eyes swept the length of her and then returned to meet her gaze. "You know very little about him. Just enough to become his wife but not enough to say for certain that he got that watch from his dead mama. Am I right?"

"Please understand you've said nothing to change my mind about my . . . that is, about Mr. Tucker. However, you are correct in your assertion that because it was a gift, I have no bill or receipt for the watch. And until its true owner can be determined, I would like you to remove it from my wrist and place it in the sheriff's custody."

He certainly hadn't expected that. This much she could tell from the way he covered what had to be surprise with a nod. "At least you've been honest about one thing." He made quick work of releasing the clasp on the watch to slide it off her wrist. "I'll be sure and note that in the report." After dropping it into his pocket, he swiveled to face her. "Now there's just one more thing you and I have to decide."

She tamped down on the urge to respond with sarcasm. Instead, she opted for charm school manners, the better to sooth the irritated beast. At least that was her hope.

"And what might that be, Mr. McMinn?"

"Will you help me catch this criminal, or should I deliver you over to the Eureka Springs sheriff and continue my investigation unassisted? I should warn you that I will be successful in either case."

"Successful in catching him or successful in finding him guilty?" Again she offered a demure look. "For the two are not mutually exclusive. And for the record, though you've convinced me of your identity as a Pinkerton agent, you have not yet convinced me of my fiancé's identity as a criminal. Are we quite clear on this?"

"Fair enough, Miss Brimm. How about this? You point me in Tucker's direction, and I'll see that he gets a fair trial."

"And if I choose not to? Just so I know the full array of options available."

"If you choose not to, I'll turn you over to the sheriff and bring Tucker in without you."

"Not much of a choice, I suppose." She gave the matter a moment's thought. "All right, Mr. McMinn. But understand I will only help you find Mr. Tucker because I believe his innocence will be easily proven." She ignored his expression of disagreement to gesture toward her reticule. "Might I post this letter before we return to the hotel?"

Mr. McMinn pulled his watch from his pocket to consult the time. "I don't suppose it will hurt to let you do that."

"Thank you." She lifted her hands. "Now, about these handcuffs?"

He shook his head. "They're staying right where I put them. I won't have you running off before I'm ready to turn you loose."

"Don't you think people will wonder why I am riding around with a stranger wearing these?" She tried not to smile at the man's obvious irritation. "I would think a man who is conducting an investigation might not want to attract too much attention. Of course," she added sweetly, "I'm just a novice, so perhaps I'm wrong . . ."

"All right," he said sharply. "No need for sarcasm. I see your point." He paused only a moment before shedding his suit jacket and draping it across her lap. "There," he said with a grin. "All fixed. Just be careful not to make any sudden moves. You never know what I have in my pockets."

Thinking of the odd spectacles and the things she had noticed last night, she had to wonder.

Still, her reputation would remain safely guarded and her letter would be posted. As he set the buggy in motion again, Flora resigned herself to a partial victory.

As they neared the bustling downtown area of Eureka Springs, she gave brief consideration to an escape. However, the thought of a possible arrest warrant frightened her almost as much as her grandmother's reaction should Flora arrive back at their suite wearing a Pinkerton agent's handcuffs.

In stark contrast to the lush forests of the surrounding countryside, the streets of Eureka Springs were narrow and winding. Ramshackle buildings edged in amongst hotels and bathhouses, all hugging the muddy thoroughfares with only the most rugged of walkways to separate them. Here and there gaps in the wood, limestone, or brick structures gave way to rock formations that, in places, trickled with the same spring water that bathers paid dearly to soak away their ailments.

The sidewalks, such as they were, teemed with people who appeared not to care whether they edged one another out of the limited space and into the muddy street. Occasionally Flora spied an oversized feathered hat or a flash of finely made skirts that might indicate someone of her social set. Thus, she kept her head low and her handcuffs well hidden beneath Mr. McMinn's coat.

When the buggy paused near the intersection of Spring and Short Streets, it only took a moment for attention to be drawn their way. "Truly, Mr. McMinn," Flora said. "Might you dispense with these handcuffs and allow me to post the letter myself? People who know me could be within sight, and I—"

"You're staying put, Miss Brimm. Unless you've changed your mind. I'm sure the sheriff would be happy to let you roam a jail cell without those handcuffs."

Ignoring him rather than offering a response seemed prudent. Still, she couldn't help wishing she had some means of removing the ridiculous restraints. With obvious reluctance she extracted the letter from her reticule and gave it to him.

"You, boy!" The lawman gestured toward a youth who might have been a newspaper hawker or perhaps in the business of shining shoes. He showed the ragamuffin three coins and nodded toward the post office across the street. "What do you say? Will you see that the postmaster sends this out?"

The young man adjusted his cap and offered a gap-toothed grin. "It's a deal, mister!"

Mr. McMinn handed over the letter and the coins and watched until the messenger disappeared inside the building. As the buggy moved away from the post office, Flora looked back to be certain the boy had indeed done as he'd been charged.

"Worried about something?" Mr. McMinn asked as he guided the horse back up the narrow street.

"Just making sure the letter gets posted."

He gave her a quick sideways look. "You wouldn't want your father to miss the news of your wedding, would you?"

She gasped. "How did you know what the letter said?" She paused to reflect on a better choice of words, and then she began again. "About that. While I appreciate your need to follow through on your commitment to whatever case you're working on, I would very much like you to allow my marriage to go forward as scheduled. So if at all possible, could you conclude your business with Mr. Tucker today?"

Mr. McMinn laughed even as he urged the horse around a throng of buggies and wagons. "Miss Brimm, you are possibly the most self-centered woman I have ever had the bad sense to join forces with."

To correct his assumption and let the man know her concern was for home and family rather than herself would be counterproductive at this point. And likely he wouldn't believe her anyway, especially if he had indeed secured a warrant for her arrest.

So Flora remained silent, her back straight and her expression such that anyone who might recognize her would think she was merely out for an afternoon drive with a handsome acquaintance. Unfortunately, her acquaintance had the irritating habit of tipping his hat and making conversation with every person who slowed down their drive.

By the time the carriage had traveled the length of downtown, Flora was ready to scream. When three pigs, two children, and a goat ran out in front of them, she did. Loudly and without apology.

Thankfully, he was able to maneuver around the obstacles without calamity, though she had to wonder how he managed it. She might have asked except that she spied the unmistakable form of the railroad executive who had hosted her and Grandmama for dinner just two nights ago. And with him was his wife, who had quizzed Flora at length about her unmarried state.

Flora immediately slid to the floor, where she hid as best she could under Mr. McMinn's jacket. While the sounds and smells of Eureka Springs were only slightly muffled, she hoped she might be hidden well enough to keep the gossips from talking.

"You're awfully skittish," he commented as the buggy began the climb up toward the Crescent Hotel.

"With good reason," Flora snapped.

"Oh, I see." He chuckled. "I guess you're not keen on being seen with the likes of me."

"Actually, I'm unsure as to which of two issues of concern would most damage my reputation."

One dark brow lifted. "Oh, do tell me what those are, darlin'," he said with an exaggerated drawl. "I care so much for all of your issues of concern."

"Thank you," she said, as sweetly and sarcastically as she could manage despite her predicament. "Since you asked, I'll be happy to tell you. Not only would it be disastrous to be seen riding through the middle of Eureka Springs with handcuffs—that's awful enough—but worse?" She shrugged as she feigned abject horror. "What if someone actually thought I was enjoying a ride with you?" A shudder completed the statement, though she wasn't keen on glancing over to see how he had taken her jab.

"At least I remained in my seat. I wonder if anyone spied the drunken woman who couldn't remain upright long enough for the law to discreetly return her to her hotel?"

"Of all the nerve!" Flora fixed Mr. McMinn with a withering look. Unfortunately, he ignored her. Finally, she tired of staring and turned her attention to twisting around so as to be in a position to climb back onto the seat.

She took in a deep breath of pine-scented air and let it out slowly. With her hands bound by the cuffs, her corset far too tight for exertion, and her pride dented, Flora found the process difficult at best. Each time she managed to get her elbow up on the seat, the buggy would hit some sort of rut and she would bounce back down on the floor. After a point, she suspected the lawman was not completely innocent in this, though his expression belied the fact.

She peered up at him. "Mr. McMinn, I demand you either help me or release the handcuffs so that I might help myself."

"You demand?" He paused to allow his eyes to sweep over her before returning his attention to the road ahead. "From where I sit, you don't appear to be in a position to demand anything, Miss Brimm."

"And yet eventually you will have to explain to someone why you returned to the Crescent Hotel with Flora Brimm trussed up and cowering on the floor of your buggy. For if I am such a wanted woman, you would have seen me jailed. Instead, you're forcibly returning me to the hotel in handcuffs. Inquiring minds might ask what nefarious purpose you have in mind." A pause for effect. "And me, a defenseless woman?"

"Defenseless?" His tone combined with an inelegant snort told her his opinion of the thought. "Miss Brimm, were I to testify in court as to many of your other attributes, lunacy among them, I would have much to say on the matter. But defenseless? A woman who treats a walk on a fourth-floor ledge like a stroll in the park? Hardly."

"Fine." She maneuvered around to alleviate a cramp jabbing at her shoulder and fixed her eyes on the canopy of bright green leaves overhead. *Lord, You are in control, not this overbearing fool. While I know I'm supposed to love all Your children, I just cannot imagine You meant him too.*

"What are you doing?"

"I'm praying."

He flicked the reins and the horse picked up its pace. "While you're at it, say a prayer for me."

"Don't worry. I've already mentioned you." Flora slid him a look. "Twice."

"I see." He nodded toward the road. "We're almost back to the hotel. I'm going to strike a deal with you. I'll take off those handcuffs if you'll promise not to run."

"Brimms do not run," she said as the wheels bounced over another rut and she braced herself against the seat. "Except for office."

"Right." He pulled back on the reins until the buggy came to a stop. Slowly he swiveled to look down at her. "And Pinkertons don't run either. They shoot."

"Then neither of us has anything to worry about, do we? Now get these handcuffs off." At his cross expression, she said, "Please?"

He hauled her up onto the seat as if she weighed nothing and waited while she settled into place. When she held her hands out in his direction, he drew the key from his pocket. "Hold still now," he said as he grasped her wrists.

Flora did, but the horse did not as a hawk swooped nearby and caused the mare to jolt. The lawman fumbled with the key and then lost it on the floor. Retrieving the key while holding tightly to the reins took some time, but Mr. McMinn finally emerged victorious. This time, he quickly stabbed the key into place and released the lock on the cuff encircling her right hand.

As the cold metal fell away, Flora flexed her wrist and offered up the other. "What?" she asked when he shook his head.

"No, I think I'll wait on removing that one," he said as he dropped the key into his vest pocket.

"Wait?" She shook her arm and felt the cuff's weight against her skin. The other half of the contraption dangled free, its cold metal sliding against her palm until she grasped it with her fingers. "Stop joking and remove this at once. I've done what you asked."

"No, not completely." He settled back in his

seat and set the horse in motion again. "I'll remove the other handcuff when you hold up your end of the bargain. Until I get Tucker, you get to wear the cuff."

"Of all the nerve! I am completely trustworthy, and I resent the fact that you assume otherwise."

"Trustworthy?" His irritating chuckle made her want to pinch him. "If you recall, Miss Brimm, I first made your acquaintance behind a collection of potted plants. I was there on official business, but you? I believe we can agree you were *not* looking for a chessboard." He held up his hand to prevent a response. "Then there was our little stroll on the fourth-floor ledge. And I can't say as I would call a woman who waltzes across the dance floor and into an elevator with a stranger—"

"I did *not* dance with you into the elevator, sir," she said, her patience nearly at its end.

"Fair enough. But I have the key to those cuffs, and you're the one who still needs to finish your part in this investigation. Find Tucker and I'll take off the other one."

Apparently this was Mr. McMinn's final word on the subject, for he turned his attention to the road ahead and did not spare Flora another glance. A few minutes later, the carriage rolled up the final hill, and the cedars and pines parted to allow the Crescent Hotel to come into view.

Flora pulled her sleeve down over the cuff on

her wrist and then reached for her reticule. The drawstring bag, if situated just right, would allow the other handcuff to slide down inside where only the chain connecting the two pieces would be visible. At best, she would draw no attention. At worst, she might appear as if she wore some sort of odd chained purse on her arm. Either was preferable to walking through the lobby of the Crescent Hotel with the restraint in full view.

"Welcome back, Miss Brimm, Mr. McMinn." This from the same doorman who had led her to her doom less than a half hour ago. Though his expression did not show any emotion, he averted his gaze when she turned toward him.

"Why, thank you," she said as sweetly as she could manage, and then she allowed the fellow to help her down from the carriage.

Mr. McMinn waited until the doorman came around to take the reins and then walked over to join Flora at the curb. "All right, my dear," he said as he offered her his arm. "Shall we?"

Flora shook her head. "If it's all the same to you, I'd rather not offer the other guests any indication of familiarity between the two of us, sir. We have a business deal pending and nothing else."

His dark gaze swept the length of her in a manner that might have caused a lesser woman's knees to buckle. "I see," he said slowly. "So basically it's the same as your engagement. Just a business deal."

Flora gasped. How could he know this? But before she could respond with any sort of well-formed protest, the Pinkerton agent had pressed his palm against her back and was guiding her through the open front doors of the hotel.

"Shall I give you Mr. Tucker's room number?" she asked as they passed the front desk.

"You're going with me anyway, Miss Brimm. Lead on." He ushered her to the elevator, and then he shadowed her every step until they reached the second floor. "Which room is his?"

She told him and then asked, "Should I knock or do you prefer I leave you here to do that yourself?"

"Oh, no," Mr. McMinn said. "I have no assurance the man I'm looking for is behind that door. You're coming with me. And yes, I believe I'll have you knock. I'll stand out of the way. You get him to open the door and I'll do the rest."

She held out her hand. "What about the hand-cuffs?"

"I'll take them off once I have Tucker."

Flora shook her head. "But what if I run?" she asked in her most sarcastic tone.

"And not for office?" was his quick response. "You won't. Not when I have the only key. I have a feeling that no matter what happens after you knock on that door, you won't go far until I reclaim my cuffs. Let's get this over with."

Flora took a few steps toward the room Mr. Tucker had indicated was his and then stopped to turn and face her captor. "You do realize I am only helping you because I believe Mr. Tucker is innocent."

"Of course. I have no doubt you believe that. You also want those cuffs off. Now, can we please get back to business?"

"Yes, but I want you to understand why I'm doing this—"

"I understand just fine." He nodded to her wrist. "It doesn't hurt that you know you'll be trotted back down the hill to be handed over to the sheriff if you don't cooperate."

He had her there. Still, she managed to give the man a look she hoped would show him how wrong he was.

"Come on," he urged. "I don't like standing out here. We're starting to look obvious."

She nodded and straightened her back, clutching the reticule so the chain wouldn't clink. When she reached the proper door, Flora lifted her free hand to knock twice.

And then twice again.

Nothing.

She looked over at the man who had flattened himself against the wall, his right hand now resting on the barrel of a pistol tucked into a holster under his jacket.

"Knock again. It wouldn't hurt to call him by

name, either. Criminals can be a skittish bunch."

She rolled her eyes and then complied, calling Mr. Tucker's name as she implored him to open the door. Again there was no response. Flora looked to Mr. McMinn for their next move.

He reached over to wrap his fingers around the doorknob and then slowly turned it. As the door cracked open, Flora peered inside. He nodded as if urging her to enter.

She shook her head. "A lady," she whispered, "does not enter the room of—"

Mr. McMinn pressed his palm to her back and gave her a gentle push, sending Flora through the open door. When she turned around to glare at him, she instead watched him press past her.

"He's gone."

❦ SIX ❦

"Gone?" Flora's gaze swept the room as her heart and her hopes fell. Indeed, the place appeared as if no one had been in residence for some time. "But that's not possible," she said with difficulty. "He told me this was his room number. I'm certain of it."

Mr. McMinn made quick work of searching every inch of the room and then turned to face her. "Maybe you remembered wrong. Or he told you wrong. In either case, there's no sign of him here."

"No, I . . ." She shook her head. How could she remember wrong when the room he'd claimed was his sat one floor beneath her own? "I just couldn't be . . ."

"Wrong?"

Flora nodded, though she knew that the error to which he referred was not the same as the one she was considering. While she might have misheard or incorrectly recalled the room number, she was most concerned that she had once again chosen the wrong groom.

An image of Will Tucker lying on a mortician's slab rose, and she quickly blinked it away. No, he couldn't have succumbed to the Fatal Flora curse already. She'd just seen him not more than an hour ago.

Flora walked to the window to get a breath of air. A flash of pink caught her attention, and she opened the window to get a better view. Easily within reach should she lean out just a bit was an object that appeared to be strangely similar to the bookmark she kept in the thirteenth chapter of First Corinthians in her traveling Bible.

"No you don't," McMinn said as he came up behind her to wrap an arm around her waist. "No escapes out the window, Miss Brimm. I don't have the patience for it today."

"Unhand me. I was merely reaching for this." She jabbed him with her elbow just enough to cause him to release her. "Here," she said when her fingers caught the fabric.

It was her bookmark. But how did it get on the ledge?

Mr. McMinn holstered his gun and gave the ribbon a cursory glance before once again pressing past her. "Come on."

Flora ran her hand over the embroidered edge before tucking it into her reticule alongside the still-attached handcuff. "Mr. McMinn," she called to his retreating back. "Can't we renegotiate this?"

"This?" he asked over his shoulder.

"This." She nodded toward the handcuff still on her wrist. "Truly, what is the purpose—"

"The purpose is to find your friend Mr. Tucker. I don't see as how we'll do that here, so come with me while I'm still of a mood to only make you wear the one cuff."

"Where are we going?" she asked as she hurried to keep up.

"Downstairs. And while we're heading that way, you need to think long and hard whether your fiancé ever used any aliases, because I guarantee there won't be a Will Tucker registered as a guest here."

"Are you sure about that?" she asked as they stepped off the elevator into the lobby. "I still think you're wrong about him."

She had also begun to believe she was wrong about his premature demise. Surely this was all an unfortunate case of miscommunication that could easily be remedied.

Flora stepped up to the desk and rang the bell. A moment later, the desk clerk appeared around the glass. "I am inquiring as to the room number of a certain gentleman. Mr. Will Tucker, please."

"Will Tucker," the clerk echoed. "Sure, I remember him."

"So he did check in under his actual name. How about that?" Flora turned to give her captor a triumphant look. He ignored her.

"Are you sure?" Mr. McMinn asked. "Tucker's a common name. This fellow's about my height. Slender build. Blond hair. Blue eyes."

"They're green," Flora corrected.

The Pinkerton agent ignored her as he waited on the desk clerk's response.

"Isn't hard to remember someone when they just checked out," the clerk said. "But the lady's right. His eyes were green." He offered Flora a smile. "I guess ladies usually notice these things, but I tend to—"

"He checked out?" Mr. McMinn glared at Flora. "You knew he was going to run for it. That's why you wanted to go to the post office." He turned to stare down the clerk as he produced his badge. "How long ago and where was he headed?"

All the color drained out of the man's face. Flora knew the feeling, for she felt the same. Still, she clung to the hope that there was an innocent explanation to Mr. Tucker's sudden disappearance. Likely a break in the case that had kept him occupied up to today.

Yes, that was it. The idea of her intended racing off to solve some sort of trouble with the Frisco Railroad bolstered her confidence and caused her knees to still their shaking.

"How long?" Mr. McMinn repeated, his voice low and insistent.

"Probably twenty minutes ago," the clerk stammered. "And I'm sorry, but as to his destination, he didn't say. Seemed in a hurry, though."

McMinn let out a long breath and leaned toward the clerk. "I need a place where Miss Brimm can wait for me. Someplace private and secure."

"I'm sure I can find—"

"That won't be necessary. I will wait for you in my suite, Mr. McMinn. And I insist you return quickly." She gestured to the hidden handcuff. "For obvious reasons."

"You will do nothing of the sort. For obvious reasons."

The clerk adjusted his cap. If he had any inkling of the issue between them, the man gave no indication. "What if I put Miss Brimm in the accountant's office? He's out for the day."

"Has he locked up all the money? I don't trust her farther than I can toss her." His wink was more irritating than the ridiculous statement.

Flora swept past the two men, her head held

high. "I'll have the manager's office. He appears to be out as well."

"Yes, Miss Brimm, he is," the clerk said. "At least for an hour or two. But I don't know . . ."

Flora ran her finger over the spines of the books on the shelf behind the manager's desk. Choosing a slim volume of Longfellow's poems, she slowly turned to face the men standing in the doorway as she settled behind the desk as elegantly as she could manage. The lawman might hold the advantage legally, but she was a Brimm of the Natchez Brimms, and as such she would remain unflustered, even in the face of possible incarcera-tion.

Not that she completely believed he would turn her over to the sheriff. And even if he did, the stolen property charge was absurd. Still, she offered him a sweet smile that belied her thoughts.

"I don't think I'll be intruding on the manager's hospitality long. Will I, Mr. McMinn?"

"You'll be here until such a time as I or the sheriff comes for you." He patted his vest pocket and then turned his attention to the clerk. "What is your name?"

"Henry, sir."

"Well, Henry, should she attempt escape, feel free to shoot her."

At Flora's gasp, the poor clerk's eyes widened. "Sir, I don't think I could possibly—"

"It was a joke, man."

Mr. McMinn shook his head as he walked toward Flora. Placing his hands on either side of the desk chair, he rolled her out of the way and opened the desk drawer to produce a sheet of hotel stationery. Grabbing the pen from the silver desk set, he wrote a name on the paper and then folded it in half and carried it back to the clerk.

"Do you know this fellow?"

Henry unfolded the page and then nodded. "Yes, sir, I do."

"He should be here at the hotel somewhere. Go find him and bring him here. Hurry."

"But who will see to things at the desk in my—" At the lawman's glare, he hurried away, leaving Flora alone with the perturbed Pinkerton agent.

"I understand why you're thinking I had something to do with Mr. Tucker's departure," she said when the weight of the lawman's stare became too heavy to ignore. She traced the edge of the Longfellow book with her index finger and thought of the mystery of the pink bookmark in her reticule. "But I assure you I am as surprised as you that he has supposedly left the hotel."

A dark brow rose. "Supposedly?"

"Under the circumstances, I have to wonder if there is more to the story than the clerk's offhand recollection."

"It didn't sound like an offhand recollection to me." He shifted positions to cross his hands over his chest. Someone rang the bell out at the front desk, but he ignored it. "What do you think is going on?"

She simply shrugged as she silently sorted through the possible reasons, all related to whatever investigative work caused his tardy arrival. Perhaps that also led to an early departure. To admit she knew any of this, however, might breach a confidence and possibly threaten an ongoing case.

Again the bell rang. This time Mr. McMinn turned around, showing Flora his back. The thought occurred that she might possibly slip past him and escape. But to where?

She let out a long breath and opened the book of poems. Better to read about the forest primeval than to invoke the man's ire any further.

The clerk returned alone and muttered something about the man in question that Flora only partly heard. Perhaps he was late, or was it that he would be due in soon? In either case, the men spoke to each other in low tones, occasionally stealing glimpses of Flora she pretended to ignore.

As the door closed behind them, she set aside all pretense of attention to Longfellow and his Acadians. Suddenly evading Grandmama and her minions did not seem like so grand an idea. If only one of the Brimm spies clothed in servant's garb had been watching closer.

Perhaps Father's offer of a bodyguard should have been accepted, his insistence on being careful of her personal safety heeded. Flora sighed. Nothing could be done to change things now.

She moved quietly toward the exit, skirting the edge of the desk and the bookshelf to touch the doorknob. To her surprise, the door flew open and she stood nose-to-nose with the desk clerk.

"You gave me such a fright!" Flora said as she took a step backward and slammed into a chair.

"You didn't help my ticker much either, Miss Brimm. Mr. McMinn says I'm to watch you until his man shows up." Henry shrugged. "Me, I don't see what he's worried about, you being a woman and all. And I do have plenty to do already without adding guard duty to the mix."

Flora offered her sweetest smile. "You're a busy man. I can certainly see that."

"Well, I am at that." He adjusted his cap and stood a notch taller. A second later someone on the other side of the glass partition rang the bell. "I need to see to a guest. You won't run off and get me in trouble, will you?"

"No, of course not," she said, though she wished it were possible. "I'll be fine. You just do whatever it is you need to do."

He gave her a nod and hurried over to attend to what appeared to be pressing business with someone on the other side of the glass. As Henry inclined his head toward the customer, Flora moved to the doorway to look around.

The enclosure was nothing more than a narrow hall with a wall that was half wood and half window on one side. The glass had been frosted so as to hide the lobby from the offices, or perhaps the opposite was true. In either case, she could easily walk around without being seen by the hotel guests. On her right stood the clerk and what she could only presume from this vantage point was an overlarge hotel safe. To the left she spied the door that provided the only means of escape.

"Need something, Miss Brimm?" Henry called as he stepped into view.

"No, thank you. Don't worry about me. Just go on about your work."

He looked at her for another moment and then turned back to the counter where a stack of papers now drew his attention. Flora waited only long enough to see that he had become fully engaged with his task before she moved slowly toward the door.

Before she could touch the handle, the door flew open. "Oh, so sorry, miss," a red-haired fellow said. "I didn't expect to find anyone on the other side there." He nodded to Henry as he pressed past her, and, for a second, Flora considered reaching out to stop the door from closing. However, when she saw one of her grandmother's maids standing only a few feet away, she panicked.

Explaining to Grandmama why she wore a

handcuff would be trouble enough. Finding a way to remove it, more trouble still. Especially given the issue of an arrest warrant.

Flora sighed. Better to stay and wait rather than seek an easy exit. For she was innocent of everything but planning a wedding without informing her family. For that she would plead guilty.

Now to pray her fiancé arrived at the church on time.

"Seamus, tell the lady what you told me." Henry paused. "Seamus is the wire operator."

"Oh. I see."

"Well, there was this fellow. A nice man but in a hurry, he was." Seamus the wire operator reached for the stack of papers and was sorting through them. "Yes, here it is. He told me to throw this away if he wasn't standing right there when I finished sending it. I was going to, but I figured I'd wait to see if maybe he came back for it."

Flora shook her head. "I'm sorry, but what does this have to do with me?"

Henry took the paper from Seamus and walked over to hand it to Flora. "It's a receipt for a telegram. Name sound familiar?"

She glanced down at the recipient. "Jack Wilson. No, I don't know this man."

The clerk shook his head. "Not him. I meant the sender."

Flora returned her attention to the paper. On the

bottom of the page was the unmistakable name of Will Tucker. The telegram's text was cryptic at best: *Full steam ahead.*

Had she intercepted some sort of important statement pertinent to a railroad investigation? Or was this some other coded message? Either way, only Mr. Tucker knew the answer.

Her heart racing, she looked past Henry to Seamus. "Can you tell me the location where this was received?"

"Natchez Under-the-Hill. The man is the telegraph officer, I believe."

She clutched the paper. "I wonder if I might keep this."

"Keep it?" He looked perplexed. "I don't know, ma'am. I'm supposed to be saving it for Mr. Tucker."

"Actually, I believe you said he instructed you to throw it away should he fail to return for it. So I'm sure he would be most happy if I delivered it to him personally first thing tomorrow morning." Flora paused. "He and I have a previously arranged appointment."

At least she intended to be there. And if Will Tucker was not, at least now she knew how to get a message to him. Either way, it was an excellent plan.

Full steam ahead to Natchez, indeed.

Should the missing Mr. Tucker prove impossible to locate in Eureka Springs, Mr. Jack Wilson of Natchez Under-the-Hill had best be prepared to explain just exactly what his connection to her fiancé was and how she could locate him.

"Can't see as how it would hurt," Seamus said. "Though if Mr. Tucker comes back to ask me where his receipt is, I will have to tell him I gave it to you."

"Yes, would you?" she said. "I welcome another visit with him, and I promise I'll keep the receipt right here in my reticule." She gestured to the purse at her wrist and quickly covered it with the receipt lest either of the men notice the handcuff she was hiding.

"I'd be pleased to," he said as he offered his goodbyes to the desk clerk and slipped out the door.

Flora felt Henry watching her. "Miss Brimm," he said slowly, "I ought to tell that Pinkerton man about what Seamus gave you. After all, he is looking for the fellow, and he is the law."

With her best boarding school manners, she regarded the man who just might give her whole plan away. "Of course, I can see how that would appear to be the best way to handle the situation, but I wonder if I might appeal to your discretion in the matter."

"I don't think I know what you mean."

A burst of laughter on the other side of the glass temporarily ended the possibility of discreet conversation. She pressed her finger to her lips and then motioned toward the manager's office.

"I ask your discretion," she said when he stepped inside the office, "because the matter of Mr. Tucker and myself is a bit problematic." Flora paused to decide how much more to say. "You see, Mr. McMinn—"

"That's the Pinkerton?"

"Yes," she said. "As I was saying, Mr. McMinn has learned of my engagement to Mr. Tucker and is quite unhappy about it." All true, though Flora hoped she would not be questioned any further on the details of the statement. "Mr. McMinn has certain erroneous beliefs regarding my fiancé's activities, but at the moment I cannot correct them." She leaned forward conspiratorially. "I can only say it is a matter of utmost importance to the Frisco Railroad."

"The Frisco? I worked for them for ten years before I settled down here in the Springs and married my wife. You mean Tucker's a railroad man too?"

She ducked her head and then peered up at him. "I fear I cannot answer that officially due to the nature of his business. I'm sure you understand."

"Of course. I'm guessing he's one of those railroad detectives. We get them here sometimes. You know, a little rest and relaxation before heading back on the rails to keep folks safe."

"Or to elope."

"Elope? Well, of all the . . ." He shook his head. "Why didn't you say so?"

"Actually, due to his special duties for the railroad, Mr. Tucker and I felt it important to—"

"Never mind," he hurried to say. "Forget I asked. I wouldn't want you to betray any confidences. Just tell me how I can help you and your intended."

Flora smiled. "Are you certain?"

Henry adjusted his cap and put on his broadest smile. "Anything for a fellow railroad man."

"Well, in that case . . ."

❧ SEVEN ❧

Flora turned the key, took another look down the hall to be sure she hadn't been followed, and then slipped inside her suite to find the parlor blessedly empty of Grandmama and her entourage. The door on the other side of the room was shut tight, a good sign that her grandmother was away or indisposed.

Either option was fine as long as Flora kept her solitude a little longer. She knew eventually Lucas McMinn would come knocking at her door. The weight on her wrist bore the truth of that. And when he arrived, he had best bring the key that would rid her of the ridiculous restraints. Once he stomped and sputtered a bit, which as a man—and a lawman at that—he was entitled to do.

She smiled at the thought of besting him. Surely he would not expect to find her released from the prison of the manager's office. And yet she hadn't run. Rather, she'd happily allowed the clerk to escort her to the elevator and promised to stay put in her rooms until Mr. McMinn returned.

Easing the strings of her reticule over the remaining handcuff and off her arm, Flora held the empty cuff and tried to figure out how best to hide it until the Pinkerton agent arrived. Shoving the thick metal ring up her sleeve proved difficult, but under the circumstances it appeared to be her only choice.

She held her arm down at her side to be sure the evidence did not show. The final result left much to be desired, including the fact she now bore a large and suspicious lump beneath her left wrist.

At least she'd done a passable job of disguising her current situation—or so she hoped. Flora went to the mirror in her dressing room to look and decided that only Grandmama, who never missed a single errant detail, would notice.

Now, to hide the remainder of the evidence. She reached into her reticule to retrieve the receipt and then walked over to stoke the embers in the sitting room fireplace. A moment later, Flora dropped the paper into the flames and watched until it burned completely to ashes.

Next she found the pink ribbon and then went looking for her Bible. It had been moved from her bedside table to the chair beneath the open window. The window above the rooms Will Tucker had taken for himself.

Her fiancé had been here. In her room.

How dare he?

Outrage mixed with curiosity coursed through her as she picked up the Bible. Flora sat down and thumbed through the pages, intending to put the ribbon back in place. In the spot where the bookmark had been, she found a folded slip of paper.

Pulling it from its hiding place, she unfolded it to see the letterhead of the Frisco Railroad emblazoned across the top. Beneath it were bold letters: *Until tomorrow. W.T.*

Tomorrow. Flora smiled as the tension between her shoulder blades relaxed. He had left a message before making his escape. Wherever Mr. Tucker had gone, he intended to return for their marriage vows. That he'd gone to such lengths to let her know was a comfort, but Flora couldn't help wondering why he had chosen this course of action.

Somehow his shadowed life as a railroad detective no longer seemed glamorous or exciting. Instead, the man's penchant for disappearing without warning was becoming a little troublesome.

But more than that, Flora heard a whisper of worry that until now she'd managed to silence. Was this man God's best for her? Was he God's choice?

"Beg pardon, ma'am," a soft feminine voice said.

Flora fumbled with the Bible, dropping it on the rug at the maid's feet. "Goodness, how did you get in here so quietly?"

"I'm terrible sorry, Miss Brimm." She picked up the Bible from the carpet and handed it to Flora. "Your grandmother sent me up to ask if you would like to take tea with her at the home of the general's wife. She's down in the carriage and in a bit of a hurry. She said you shouldn't tarry if you would like to come along."

"Please tell my grandmother I must decline due to a previous commitment." Flora held the Bible against her chest, her heart still beating at a mad pace. "And that I send my best wishes to the general's wife."

"Yes, ma'am." The maid curtseyed but remained in place.

Flora looked up to see her staring, her expression oddly confused. "Is there anything else?"

"No, Miss Brimm," she said as she hurried off. "I'll see that your grandmother is given the message."

Only when the girl was gone did Flora realize that the handcuff she'd so carefully hidden had come loose from her sleeve and was dangling free. She hurried to the door, but the maid was gone.

"Oh, well," she said under her breath. "Either Grandmama will come upstairs to set the situation to rights or I'll be left alone until Mr. McMinn returns."

Neither option appealed.

And yet she'd given her word to the clerk that she would remain in her suite until released by the lawman from her prison. She slid the folded page from her Bible and set the book aside.

"Until tomorrow," she said softly.

Once again, thinking of her wedding as an appointment set poorly with Flora. Knowledge that she might have traveled a few steps ahead of the Lord on her path toward marriage gave her too much to consider.

She wandered into the sitting room. She would burn this piece of paper too, but knowing Mr. Tucker had somehow managed to place it in her Bible . . .

Flora shook her head. How had he managed all of that? How could he have known she would find the pink bookmark on his ledge? That she would go to the Bible and find the note?

Her finger traced the edge of the marble fireplace as she tried without success to fit the pieces together. Finally, she crumpled the note and threw it into the fire.

Orange flames reflected against the cold silver

of the handcuff as she watched the small piece of paper turn to ash. If Grandmama had been told about the handcuff, she'd likely arrive soon. If the maid chose to be discreet, Flora knew she would have a bit more time to await the Pinkerton agent.

And if Will Tucker was the Lord's choice for her, He would see that she and the railroad detective successfully repeated their vows. "Close this door if I'm not to walk through it," she whispered even as she silently prayed that nothing would stop tomorrow morning's wedding.

Lucas stalked across the lobby toward the elevator, his temper rising with each step. He should have known the woman would talk her way out of the manager's office. If he didn't find her in her room, others beside Miss Brimm would pay the price.

Starting with the deputy he'd hired to shadow her. It hadn't helped much that the man had fallen ill. Lucas wouldn't have had to leave the Natchez belle under such unprofessional care as the hotel desk clerk otherwise.

Then there was Tucker. With no sign of him at the depot and a pair of deputies watching the roads in and out of town, there was little else Lucas could do to find the man today. At this point, his best option was to shadow Miss Brimm until tomorrow morning's supposed wedding. If Tucker showed, he'd be jailed on the spot. If he didn't, the next move would be to shadow Fatal Flora until she led the law to him.

For as little as he knew about women, he could see that this one was protecting Tucker. Whether the affection was mutual would soon be apparent.

Lucas stepped off the elevator and headed for the Brimm suite. Propriety demanded he bring along someone else as a chaperone, but at this point Lucas cared less for reputation than for getting the job of finding Will Tucker done. This was an investigation and not a social call. Investigations meant all bets were off when it came to reputations.

And it was just as possible that Tucker had doubled back and was hiding in the Brimm rooms as it was that he'd hightailed it out of Eureka Springs.

Lucas stopped in front of the door and drew in a long breath, letting it out slowly in hopes of diverting some of the aggravation that was eating at him. Failing that, he placed one hand on his revolver, pounded twice, and then called, "Flora Brimm, open the door this minute."

That did the trick, for in far less than a minute the woman he'd once thought of as Blue Eyes opened the door. "Must you make a scene, Mr. McMinn? Hurry and get in here before anyone sees you," she said as she stepped back to allow him to enter.

He glanced around at the marble fireplace where

a fire burned bright. To the right was a corridor that led to a bedchamber. From this vantage point Lucas spied a canopy bed with curtains matching the ones on the parlor windows. Behind those curtains he could just make out a pile of neatly stacked pillows. A carpet embroidered with roses crossed the distance from the bed to where he stood, marching past to end at another door down the hallway to the left.

Tucker could be behind that door. Or he could be watching from the other chamber. A second cursory glance around the parlor revealed no place for him to hide other than possibly behind the drapes. Palming the revolver, he walked over to snatch them back.

Satisfied the criminal wasn't hiding in the window hangings, he moved carefully toward the open bedchamber door. The room was decidedly feminine, as were the belongings strewn across the bed and lined up in colorful jars and containers across the dressing table.

A plumed hat sat atop a tall dresser. Beneath the windows, which had been thrown open to allow the fresh breeze to ruffle the curtains, was a chair that held a Bible. Numerous slips of paper, as well as a pink ribbon, looked to serve as bookmarks.

Something about the ribbon seemed familiar, so he picked up the Bible and found the spot where it lay. As he ran his hand down the length of the pink fabric, he recalled Miss Brimm capturing one just like this off of Will Tucker's window ledge.

In his line of work there were no coincidences. And Tucker's room being one floor below was certainly not by chance.

"Just how close are you and Mr. Tucker?" He replaced the bookmark and set the Bible back in place and then peered out at the ledge. While there was no physical evidence of a connection between the two rooms, Miss Brimm had already exhibited her ability to ignore heights to stroll on a ledge. Perhaps she had taught that same skill to the scoundrel.

Or learned it from him.

"This is my private bedchamber, Mr. McMinn," she said, her voice high and strung tight. "Not only is it quite improper that you're in here, but your presence is also an invasion of privacy."

He affected an amused look, though the thought of Flora Brimm and Will Tucker in collusion made him feel anything but entertained. "You're not going to answer my question? That in itself is an answer, Miss Brimm."

"Not at all. I am merely demanding that we hold this conversation elsewhere."

Lucas ignored her to search behind the curtains and under the bed. Nothing but an errant shoe was hidden there. Straightening, he nearly collided with his hostess.

"Truly, sir, what are you doing?"

He nodded toward the bed. "Finding a lost shoe, apparently," he said as he went past her to move quietly back down the hall and across the parlor toward the second bedchamber.

Holding his revolver at the ready, Lucas turned the knob. The door slid open on noiseless hinges to reveal a limited view of a room similar to the other.

Unlike the other chamber, however, the curtains had been pulled tight to shut out the sun. The result was a room set in shadows, but a space that did not hide Will Tucker, he determined after throwing open the curtains and conducting another thorough search.

Stepping back into the hall, he shut the door and returned to the parlor.

"All right," Miss Brimm said. "If you're satisfied that we're alone, let's get this over with."

He swung his attention to her as she walked toward him, her wrist extended. Oh, but she was pretty. A man less inclined to recall her association with the outlaw Will Tucker might have allowed that beauty to sway him.

Not Lucas.

He shrugged off any thought of the woman's exterior and considered instead the request she was making. "Not just yet," he said as he stepped past her to walk toward the windows. "You have a mighty fine view of things from up here, Miss Brimm."

He turned to face her and found her staring, hands on her hips and the lone handcuff glittering beneath the wagon-sized crystal chandelier that marked the center of the parlor ceiling. She looked madder than a wet hen, not that he could blame her.

Still, he reminded himself, this was Tucker's woman. And whether it was in name only or some kind of setup concocted by the two of them, she was still tied to the man Lucas had vowed to hunt down.

"He's not here, but I have a reason to believe Tucker hasn't left town yet." He waited for her reaction and saw that her expression didn't change. Either she'd known it or she had suspicioned it. "You don't look surprised."

She shook her head as she crossed her arms over her waist. "I could have told you he wasn't here, so no, I'm not surprised."

Lucas found the nearest seat and made himself comfortable. After giving her just enough time to start fussing again, he looked up at her, schooling his features so that she could not guess his thoughts.

"All right, Miss Brimm," he said in his best country boy drawl. "I'm going to ignore your obviously deceptive response. Instead, I am just going to ask once more. Where is he?"

Her face went red and her fists clenched. Lucas was completely sure if she'd been holding something, she would have already thrown it at him. Instead, her eyes narrowed and her breath heaved.

"Honestly, I wish I knew, but I don't."

Though he didn't want to believe her, Lucas's gut instinct told him she was telling the truth. "Any idea why he might have hightailed it out of here?"

"Anything I say would just be a guess."

"Then guess."

Flora looked beyond him a moment as if she might be chewing on an idea. "All right," she said as she swung her gaze to meet his again. "In his line of work, he is often called away on short notice. I assume that is what has happened here."

"Assume," he repeated. "But you don't know this for sure?"

She shook her head. "No, but if you really did hear any of our earlier conversation, you would know he promised to go to his room and stay there until tomorrow morning."

"And that wasn't some kind of code for—"

"Mr. McMinn, really! Do I look like some sort of spy? It wasn't code for anything."

He'd met his fair share of spies, and though he'd never tell her this, she would have made a fine one. No man in his right mind would believe that a woman with her looks and class would ever be anything more than she professed.

"Fair enough. And what line of work is he in?"

"It's not for me to say," she replied demurely.

"Even if it meant you were impeding an ongoing investigation?"

She sighed. "He works for the railroad."

A plausible response. From what he had gathered, Tucker tended to pick his women from stops easily accessible by railroad or steamboat. "What does he do for the railroad?"

"I would prefer he be the one to tell you."

Lucas watched as the expression on the woman's face softened. If she knew anything incriminating about Will Tucker, she gave little indication of it.

He shifted positions just enough to allow a good view of both the door and a reflection of the windows in the mirror over the fireplace. Either were possible points of entry—or exit. "Then why don't you tell me how Tucker managed to escape?"

"I am going to pretend you haven't just insinuated that I am somehow complicit in Mr. Tucker's absence." She let out a breath. "Rather, I will assume that in your ignorance of me you have made a misstep. Would you care to rephrase your question?"

"No, I don't think I do. And for the record, I don't mind you knowing I believe you have information about Tucker you are withholding."

"I am withholding nothing of any value to your investigation, Mr. McMinn."

"I would prefer to make that determination, Miss Brimm."

The crimson on her cheeks made her eyes all the bluer. He tried not to think of how she felt in his arms as he danced with her across the ballroom.

She shook her head and then moved across the room to settle herself in the chair nearest him. From where he sat, he could almost touch her. He could also see what appeared to be fear in her eyes. "Then we will just have to agree to disagree. Now about these handcuffs. Do you mind?"

Lucas leaned forward and caught a scent of something sweet. Lilacs?

Slowly his gaze met hers. Before he could respond, she pointed at him. "Don't say it. Yes, I know you mind. Yes, I know you haven't found Mr. Tucker. However, I am willing to give you access to him tomorrow if you will just allow me two things."

Finally the truth. "And they are?"

"First, of course, is for you to remove these ridiculous handcuffs."

"And the other?"

"I wish to be married."

"Well, I should hope so." A distinctly elderly and female voice from the vicinity of the parlor door spoke the words sharply.

Lucas stood so quickly his chair fell backward. When he got himself untangled from the furniture, he found Millicent Meriwether Brimm peering up at him with what appeared to be a combination of amusement and curiosity.

"Grandmama? I . . . I thought you were with the general's wife."

"I changed my mind. I felt the beginnings of a sick headache and decided halfway there to return home and send my apologies instead." Without taking her eyes off of Lucas, the matriarch of the Brimm clan reached behind her to close the door. "Flora, dear," she said, turning now to her granddaughter. "Where are your manners? Your young man and I have not been introduced."

"Really, Grandmama. This is not who you think—"

"I'm Lucas McMinn, Mrs. Brimm." Sometimes a man finds opportunity, and other times opportunity finds him. Lucas grinned as he made his way across the parlor to the opportunity of a lifetime. "Pleased to meet you, ma'am."

She accepted his hand, though her gloved fingers barely grazed his palm long enough to call it any sort of a shake at all. Lucas had met a few folks with royal titles. If this old gal didn't have any, it wasn't because she couldn't pull off the look.

"My pleasure indeed," she said in a smooth-as-magnolias tone. "And it appears my grand-daughter has already told you of me."

"No, actually I have not."

Lucas could see some of Flora's pretty features in the older woman, though time had softened the blue in her eyes to the color of faded denim. Just

119

enough of the original hue remained threaded through the lady's fashionable hairstyle to attest to where Flora came by her copper curls.

Apparently she had also inherited her grandmother's temper, for Millicent Brimm was giving her granddaughter a wait-until-I-get-you-alone look. Had he not been watching closely, Lucas might have missed it, because by the time Mrs. Brimm returned her attention to him, she'd pasted a smile back in place.

"So, Lucas McMinn. I understand there is to be a wedding."

❈ EIGHT ❈

"Yes, ma'am," he said, smiling. "I understand wedding plans are afoot. What I wonder is whether you're in on them."

"In on them?" the older woman asked. "I fail to understand how I could be 'in on' anything to which I have neither been invited nor properly informed." She shot Flora a look. "And a brief declaration is not my idea of being properly informed."

Flora rose to stand between her grandmother and the Pinkerton agent. Unfortunately, she failed to remember that she'd brought the handcuff out of hiding in hopes that he would remove it. Now

Grandmama stared at the silver cuff, her face decidedly pale and her eyes wide.

"My dear, please do enlighten me. Why are you wearing . . ." She shook her head and lifted a gloved hand to point toward her granddaughter's wrist. "That thing," she finally managed.

"That," Flora said as if it were a Tiffany bracelet, "belongs to Mr. McMinn. It's a rather funny story how it all happened."

"Do tell," Grandmama said as she moved past them to take her favorite spot on the settee nearest the window.

Flora followed, her heart racing. "Actually, I need a moment with Mr. McMinn in private, and then we will be happy to explain."

Somehow, though Grandmama was seated and they were both standing, the family matriarch managed to look down her nose at them. "I shall await your return. And in the interim, Flora, would you please send one of the maids back in? I feel the need for tea and perhaps an herbal compress. They are probably skulking about in the hall trying to listen in on our conversation anyway."

"Yes, of course," she said as she motioned for Mr. McMinn to follow her.

True to her grandmother's assumptions, both maids were waiting nearby. After Flora informed them of Grandmama's orders, she waited until they disappeared into the elevator before returning her attention—and her wrath—on Lucas McMinn.

"Honestly. I thought I had seen the worst of your . . . your . . ." Description escaped her, so she settled for clenching her fists and sending a quick prayer for calm upward.

"My charm?" he offered.

"Under no circumstances would that question ever be answered in the affirmative," she snapped. "But never so much as today. Do you have any idea the trouble you've just caused?"

"Trouble?" He shook his head. "Me?"

Flora stalked off in the opposite direction of the elevators, and with each step tried to think of what to say. Of how to squeeze out of the tight space she'd wiggled into. Then it came to her.

"All right, Mr. McMinn," she said as she turned and closed the distance between them. "You and I are about to strike a bargain." She reached out to press her index finger into his shoulder. "And when that bargain is struck, you will remove the handcuff from my wrist and you will follow me back into the suite and nod when I indicate you should do so. Other than that, you will remain silent. Is that clear?"

Mr. McMinn's laughter echoed down the hallway. "Nicely put, and I do admire a woman with spunk." He paused as if to attempt to cease his chuckling. "However, I cannot think of a single reason to agree to this plan of yours."

"I can."

One dark brow rose. "I'm listening."

"You somehow learned of my plans for tomorrow morning—"

"Your wedding plans. And yes, that's true." The lawman lifted a dark brow. "Don't ask how."

She waved away his response. "I no longer care how you've learned about our marriage. What I do care about is getting out of this mess. And that means soothing things over with my grandmother."

"How?"

"She knows the generalities of my wedding arrangements but not the details. With my grandmother, it's wise not to underestimate her ability to wreak havoc over anyone's best laid plans. If she knew where and when I am to be married, I have no doubt that at the least she would show up to watch. At worse . . ." She paused to shudder. "In either case, you and I must be careful."

"You and I?" He shook his head. "Since when are we a team?"

"Since you clamped this *thing* on my wrist and refused to remove it! And since you intruded into my plans with your badge and gun and intention to arrest my fiancé."

After a brief pause to tamp down her irritation again, Flora continued. "Each of us has something we're looking to achieve. I'm simply saying that without cooperation, neither of us will get what we want."

He leaned against the wall and crossed his arms over his chest. "Go on."

"You want to find Will Tucker." Flora paused. "Did you find any leads on where he might have gone?"

"No," he said with obvious reluctance.

"Then it's possible he may have checked out of the room he registered under his own name and into one under an assumed name. Or he might have had more than one room all along."

"It's possible," he admitted.

"If I do not arrive at the appointed place on time, we will never know if he is still in Eureka Springs or not." She held up the hand from which the cuff dangled. "And if I am wearing this when I step off the elevator tomorrow morning, my fiancé may be a little suspicious, don't you think?"

She could tell Mr. McMinn hated to admit that she'd made her case. Still, she couldn't resist one last jab. "Though if you truly believe I am complicit in Mr. Tucker's alleged crimes, I demand you place this other cuff back on my wrist and take me down to the Eureka Springs jail immediately."

That got his attention. His brows rose, though he said nothing.

"Either you and I form a team to prove Will Tucker's innocence—"

"Or guilt," he interjected.

She glared at him. "Either we form a team to

find Mr. Tucker or you turn me over to the authorities to be judged fairly. I am certainly not finding any fairness in your judgment of me at the moment, sir."

Apparently her comment hit its mark, for he appeared to be considering her statement with some care. Finally, he nodded. "Agreed. I'll take off the cuff, but you are still legally in my personal custody, do you understand?"

"Whatever does that mean?"

"It means you acknowledge you have been informed of the fact you're wanted in connection with an open investigation into the criminal activities of Will Tucker. However, because you are agreeing to help me with this case of your own free will—"

Flora's chuckle of derision earned her a frown from him. She returned it with her best smile.

"As I was saying, because you have agreed to help me with this case, you are considered to be remanded into my custody until such time as I return you to the sheriff in Eureka Springs for justice to be served in your portion of this case." He paused to allow his gaze to sweep the length of her. "Of course, if your help is valuable enough and it is proven that you had no knowledge of Mr. Tucker's criminal activities—"

"Or the lack thereof."

The lawman shook his head. "Or the lack thereof," he grudgingly added. "Then you will be released from my personal custody and the warrant for your arrest will be dismissed."

Flora grinned. "Because I'm confident of my fiancé and his innocence, I gladly accept your terms for personal companionship, Mr. McMinn."

"Custody," he snapped. "Personal custody."

"Yes, whatever." She once again thrust her arm in his direction. "Now, the handcuff, please?"

He reached into his pocket and retrieved the key. His eyes met hers briefly before he cradled her hand in his. His palm was warm, his fingers wrapping around her wrist as he made quick work of releasing her.

When the cuff slid away, Flora smiled. "Thank you," she said as she once again met his eyes. "I know you will understand that as a lawman, there are things that cannot be public knowledge. Just know that when all the facts come out, I am confident Will Tucker will be found innocent."

His expression softened unexpectedly. "I know you believe that, Miss Brimm."

"But you're not willing to accept it as a possibility?"

He ducked his head. "No, I'm not."

"Care to tell me why you're so certain of this?"

Mr. McMinn squared his shoulders as he tucked the handcuffs back into place in his pocket. "Like you said, there are things that can't be public knowledge. I would put how I know this man is guilty in that category."

Flora bit back the remainder of her response as the elevator door slid open. One of the maids stepped out bearing a tea tray. The other hurried to catch up, the herbal compress wrapped in a steaming towel cradled in her arms. While their faces showed interest, they looked away as they slipped into the suite.

After the door had closed behind them, Flora said, "About my grandmother—"

"Let me handle her. Old ladies love me."

Flora laughed. "Well, there's your first mistake. My grandmother has yet to realize she's an old lady. She still thinks she wields all the power in the Brimm family. And if you ask my father, she's right."

He adjusted his lapels and had the audacity to wink. "All the better. Now, are you coming? Or do you plan to wait out here in the hall while I turn on the McMinn charm?"

"I wouldn't think of missing the McMinn charm, sir. I don't believe I've seen any of it yet." She reached for the doorknob only to have the door fly open. Both maids went scurrying. "As I said," Flora continued, "after you."

Lucas crossed the room. "Now, where were we?" he said with his most charming tone.

When the matriarch of the Brimm clan gave him a look as though she smelled something unpleasant, he backed off to settle in a chair a safe distance away. *All the better to assess the situation,* he told himself.

"You're the fellow in need of a box lunch." Her gaze traveled the length of him. "Though on closer inspection you look nicely fed to me. And somewhat familiar, actually."

"No, ma'am. I'm afraid that was just a misunderstanding. You see, I'm a—"

"So," Millicent Brimm interrupted before taking a sip of tea from a flower-covered teacup. "You are the candidate with terms."

Lucas frowned. "Candidate with terms?"

Flora waved away the question, though her expression told Lucas she knew exactly what her grandmother was talking about. "He's in law enforcement, Grandmama. I'm merely helping him with a case."

"Not your candidate?"

"No," was Flora's brief response.

Mrs. Brimm returned the cup to the tray and rested her hand in her lap. For a moment, the old woman appeared to be engaged in a staring match with her granddaughter. Then she gave up and shrugged. "Suit yourself, but I know there's more to this than either of you are admitting."

"That's true, ma'am. I believe I'm safe in telling you more about the case we're working on. You see, your granddaughter is helping me catch a thief."

"Is she now?" Mrs. Brimm gave him a look that

would have terrified a lesser man. "And why is it that a man of your stature and obvious physical prowess would have need of someone such as my granddaughter to complete his duties?"

"I . . ." He thought a moment. "You see . . ." No, he couldn't let her know too much or he would be giving information out that was best not shared.

"Exactly. You do not." She turned her attention on her granddaughter, giving Lucas a chance to once again draw an unhurried breath. "Were you two conspiring to fool an old lady? Did you not recall that I myself caught you and this man in conversation out on the grounds when you were pretending to paint?"

"Believe what you wish, Grandmama," Flora said, her tone even despite the crimson climbing into her cheeks.

"I shall. Now as for you." She returned her attention to Lucas. "What did you say your name was?"

He leaned forward and rested his elbows on his knees. The last time he'd been questioned under such terms, he'd been on the witness stand in a particularly nasty political corruption trial. That defense attorney had nothing on Millicent Brimm.

"McMinn, ma'am. Lucas McMinn."

"Pinkerton agent Lucas McMinn," Flora added.

"Pinkerton agent Lucas McMinn," Mrs. Brimm echoed. "How nice. We'll have a lawman in the family. We've had our share of lawyers but never a lawman."

"Grandmama, I believe you need to use your hearing device. You seem to be missing the point. We are not—"

"I am missing nothing, Flora Brimm. I see what's going on here, even if you two don't think I do. Now, is there or is there not going to be a wedding?"

Flora opened her mouth. Whether it was to answer her grandmother or just in surprise, Lucas couldn't say. Apparently, neither could Miss Brimm.

"Yes, ma'am," he supplied. "A wedding is scheduled for tomorrow morning." As soon as the words were out, he wondered how she'd gotten the information out of him.

"What time?"

Rather than respond, he turned to Miss Brimm, who was regarding him with an I-can't-believe-you-said-that glare. Of course, he ignored her. Or at least he hoped he gave her a reasonable impression of being ignored.

"Nine," Flora said under her breath.

Mrs. Brimm offered a satisfied nod. "There now. A wedding at nine tomorrow. Doesn't it feel good to get the truth out?" She reached for her teacup and once more took a sip.

Lucas braved a sideways look at Flora, who appeared to have given up any effort of polite conversation. Rather, she was studying the trim on her sleeve with far too much interest to actually be seeing buttons and lace.

He rose. "Well, now that we have that handled, maybe I ought to leave you two ladies to—"

"Sit."

Millicent Brimm's demand had Lucas back in his chair before he realized he'd complied. "Yes, ma'am," he added before he could stop himself.

"Flora, dear," she said sharply, "are you certain of this marriage?"

She glanced over at Lucas and then back at her grandmother. "Yes, I'm certain."

"And the agreement?" her grandmother asked. "Is it a sound one with airtight terms and no room for unfortunate surprises?"

Flora avoided her grandmother's steady gaze as she nodded. From where Lucas sat, he could see the difference in how the old lady looked at her granddaughter and how she regarded the rest of the world. He would stake good money on the fact that no matter what Flora Brimm thought, the Brimm matriarch believed Flora could do no wrong.

"And you used a good attorney?"

When Flora told her the man's name, the old lady's iron-gray brows rose, though the name meant nothing to Lucas. "Well done. Using the family attorney would have been an awful risk. I'm very glad you picked one of the young men

I've chosen to assist with their political aspirations instead." She paused. "One wonders, however, if the gentleman in question was led to believe I am in agreement with this endeavor."

Her granddaughter's smile was faint and fleeting. "He might have been under that assumption."

Another nod. "Very well done indeed." Mrs. Brimm paused to allow her regal gaze to sweep over Lucas before returning her attention to Flora. "Fetch it."

"It?" Flora looked to Lucas. He shrugged.

"The papers our mutual friend drew up. I'll need a look at them."

"But they're legal gibberish, Grandmama. I can't see why you would—"

"Fetch them now, please. As to the fact you cannot imagine I would want to see them? Darling, didn't your grandfather ever tell you who used to write all his legal briefs for him?" She turned her attention to Lucas. "Until the late Judge Brimm was elected to political office, that is. Once he attained that sort of status, he had no need of lawyering anymore. I'm sure you understand."

"Well, sure. A man has better things to do than lawyering when he's elected to office." He was jabbering. Talking like a fool. Lucas closed his lips and did his best to stop himself from saying anything else that would make him sound any more like an idiot.

Why in the world did this woman cause him to feel like a boy headed for the woodshed every time she looked at him?

Miss Brimm returned, papers in hand, to offer him an I-told-you-so look. She handed the document over to her grandmother and returned to her seat.

"You understand you're not just joining forces with this woman, do you not, Pinkerton McMinn?"

"I believe I was the one who explained the terms to her," Lucas said as he marveled at the woman's ability to change the subject so swiftly.

"Did you now?" She studied him intently. "And you're willing to complete all the terms? All of them?"

"Grandmama, please. He isn't the candidate, so if you're trying to be funny, you're not."

"Funny?" Mrs. Brimm gave Lucas an inquiring look. "Were you amused by my question?"

He looked to Flora, whose cheeks were now flaming red. What in the world was wrong with her? They were still talking about the personal custody agreement he'd struck with her, weren't they? The one where Will Tucker got caught.

Or were they?

"Actually, I'm confused," he finally said.

Silence fell as Mrs. Brimm began to read. Lucas glanced over at Flora, who appeared nervous as she watched her grandmother. The clatter of hoofbeats outside drew Lucas's attention, and he rose to walk to the window.

The railroad transport had rolled into place in front of the hotel again, its occupants spilling out to wait for the driver to remove their luggage. He watched the process, a smooth transition from emptying out the transport to readying it for the next trip, with detached interest until he spied a man conversing with the driver. Lucas leaned a little further out the window to catch a better look at the fellow.

Will Tucker.

If it wasn't him, the man was his twin. And if Lucas hurried, he just might catch him before the transport left.

"Miss Brimm, ring the front desk and tell the clerk I want him to hold the depot transport until I can get down there and inspect the passenger list."

Thankfully, she rose to carry out the request without questioning him as to why.

Lucas rushed from the room. "Carry on without me, ladies," he called just before the door shut behind him.

He had no doubt they would.

❈ NINE ❈

Flora completed the call and then moved to the window to see what sent Lucas running off in such a hurry. Other than the Frisco transport's driver loading up to leave, there appeared to be nothing exciting happening.

With no indication that Mr. Tucker might be downstairs, perhaps the lawman had an adverse reaction to a recent meal. Or, more likely, he'd had it with Grandmama's elegant but obvious abuse. In either case, he was gone. Both a blessing and a curse. For much as she enjoyed watching her grandmother's ire being directed elsewhere, she knew much of it was not deserved.

Turning her back on the events unfolding downstairs, Flora leaned against the window frame and crossed her arms around her waist. Grandmama's attention was still focused on the agreement with no indication in her expression of her thoughts on the quality of the terms.

It was a good deal for both her and Mr. Tucker, and that's all Flora cared about. She was able to keep everything she wanted, and she gave away far less than she might have should her husband-to-be have requested it.

She was about to say just that when her

grandmother set the contract aside to once again reach for her teacup.

"Well?" Flora asked.

Making a show of sipping slowly, her grandmother finally put the cup aside. "If this marital agreement is acceptable to you and your candidate, who am I to say otherwise?"

A smile began. There was only one reason Millicent Brimm would not offer an opinion on something with this measure of importance. "You approve." A statement, not a question.

Grandmama was far too regal to show any emotion in excess, so her chuckle was a nice surprise. "I do, though I must wonder why your young man would be willing to sign this."

Flora moved away from the window to return to her chair. "All that matters is that he and I get on nicely and he is willing to sign."

"I suppose that's enough for some. Now this fellow McMinn, the Pinkerton agent." She settled back against the settee cushions and fixed Flora with a stare. "Suppose you explain your association with him in more detail. Are you really helping him with a case?"

"In a manner of speaking. Mr. McMinn is under the mistaken belief that my fiancé is the man he's searching for. I've agreed to help him only so I can disprove his theory."

"I see." Grandmama paused. "As to Mr. McMinn? I didn't figure that one for a man who could be this easily taken." She shook her head. "No, that's a poor choice of words. I believe I should have said bought."

"Yes," Flora said quietly. "I don't mind admitting I'm buying a husband. Is that awful?"

Grandmama waved away any thought of it with a sweep of her hand, the precious stones in the jewelry encircling her wrist and fingers catching the sun to cause glints of light to dance around the parlor. "Don't be ridiculous. Our people have been buying and selling spouses for generations." She paused to lean slightly forward. "Though we would never be so crass as to admit it, now would we?"

Flora shared her grandmother's smile. "I wonder what Father will think when I bring home a groom."

"He will think whatever we tell him, dear." Grandmama shrugged. "He's a man. Yes, he cares for your welfare and, when it suits him, for your happiness. Tell him both are assured in this marriage and he'll be fine."

Of course Grandmama was right. Father was far too knowledgeable of the affairs of business and ignorant of the affairs of women to bother challenging any statement she might make on the topic.

"And to be certain of it, I'll be sure to arrive back in Natchez before you and your groom to smooth the way. I'll have the maids begin

137

packing tonight so we can leave on the first train tomorrow." Grandmama paused. "If you're certain, that is."

"I am."

"And your father? Have you written him?"

"Yes, I posted a letter today." At least she hoped the urchin had actually completed his mission. Only time would tell, though now that Grandmama was in on the plan, at least partially, she would write again and post it downstairs.

"So this man you'll wed, he is the one watching you on the porch?"

"He is."

"Not an altogether unpleasant man to look at. A pity he's disposable." She lifted her bejeweled hand to her chin and appeared once again to be deep in thought. "I must say of the two, I vastly prefer your Pinkerton agent, however."

"*My* Pinkerton agent?" Flora shook her head. "He's nothing of the sort."

"What is he, then? And why did he think it prudent to decorate your wrist with a handcuff?"

"As to what he is, I could give you a long list of thoughts I have on the matter. Suffice it to say he is bullheaded, arrogant, and . . . well, I won't go on."

"And the handcuff?"

"Yes, that is an interesting story. Before he knew I would cooperate, he thought he might secure my help by placing me in his custody."

"That explains why it was put on." She gave Flora a look. "Now tell me why it wasn't immediately removed."

"We had a little disagreement and then he was called away." She offered Grandmama a view of her wrist. "The cuff is gone now."

She conveniently left off the remainder of the explanation where she admitted that while the cuff was gone, apparently their custody arrangement was not. Grandmama did not need to know this.

"And so is your Pinkerton. Again."

Flora smiled. "I don't mind if he stays gone for a while." She settled back in the chair to enjoy an unguarded moment with her grandmother. Golden threads of afternoon sun wove a youthful color into her elaborate coiffure and traced a pattern across her refined features. A beauty in her day, Millicent Brimm was still quite a handsome woman.

Blue eyes that once had matched her own and a profile that could belong to Flora decades from now attested to the family ties between them. But a bond stronger than appearance held her to her imperious grandmother.

Flora reached for the agreement Mr. Tucker would sign tomorrow. "You're wondering why I would go to such lengths?"

"No, dear. I was wondering why your grandfather went to such lengths."

The will. It always came back to Grandfather

Brimm's will. The stack of parchment pages decorated in handwriting almost unreadable in its masculine scribble. And yet it was readable. And legal.

"He never much liked how your father turned out, you know." Grandmama was looking beyond her, peering into a memory rather than anything actually present in the room. "But you. Oh, my, he did adore you." Now she was watching Flora carefully. "And Violet. She was his favorite."

The air seemed to go out of the room at her grandmother's pronouncement. "It's not your fault," Grandmama added. "None of it. Winny egged the both of you on."

"How did you know?"

She patted Flora's hand. "Because I know. And your grandfather? He was as stubborn as your father. And Violet? Darling, I wager she was the one who talked you into joining her on that climb atop the old barn."

There it was. The statement absolving guilt that Flora had hoped to hear from someone. Anyone other than Violet, who regularly proclaimed her own guilt in the fall that rendered her house-bound.

Only she and Violet knew the truth. Knew that though Violet was the better climber, it had been Flora's inattention and near fall that had propelled her elder sister to come to her aid. A choice that changed Violet's life forever. And her own. That

Winny sat on the ground and shouted encouragement was merely the final straw.

As much as she felt as though Grandfather Brimm's will had been the punishment, it was also his affirmation that she could make the situation right again. That she could lay her life down for the life of her sister. For what might have been had Violet's body not been irreparably broken.

All the more reason that she would not allow Brimm lands to leave this branch of the family tree. Her grandmother's image swam in a pool of unshed tears as Flora willed away the emotions threatening to tumble with them.

"Come and sit with me, child."

Flora complied, as much to seek absolution as to recall what it had been like as a little girl to have a grandmother who could make all the problems of the world go away with a single lilac-scented embrace.

"So many years ago," Grandmama murmured as she gathered Flora in her arms. "So very many years to be carrying the burden of it all. Your sister will leave her nest. I promise it."

"Promise it or require it?" Flora said with a half grin.

"The truth of the matter is I am more than ready to require it." She shook her head. "The Lord is taking His sweet time in moving that mountain."

The parlor door flew open and Lucas McMinn barged in, both to the room and the memories. "So sorry ladies. I thought I had a situation to handle, but it turned out to be a false alarm." He stalked toward them as the door slammed shut.

Flora accepted the use of her grandmother's handkerchief to dab at her eyes. Did this man not do anything quietly? Or with any sort of manners?

His sharp gaze landed on Flora. "What did I miss?"

Grandmama waved away his question with a sweep of her hand. "Nothing but the things women discuss when no men are around."

He looked perplexed, but only for a moment. "Fine. I'll just be going. Miss Brimm, I'll remind you to recall the terms of our agreement and the time I'll be meeting you in the morning."

"Certainly," Flora said. "And if anything should change, where can I find you?"

He glanced around, picked up a chair, and nodded toward the door. "Right outside," he said as he walked toward the exit.

"Young man," Grandmama called. "I refuse to allow you to sit out there all night. It's most improper."

He set the chair down to open the door and once again picked it up. "I'm sorry, Mrs. Brimm, but this is government business and nothing you can have any say in."

"I assure you I've had plenty of say in government business," she said as the door closed with the lawman on the other side. "He's quite insistent on getting his way, isn't he?" she asked Flora.

"He is at that."

Grandmama smiled. "I like that in a man. Now if you'll excuse me, I must prepare for the evening. Would you mind fetching one of the girls to help me dress? I'm afraid when I told the general's wife I was unexpectedly unavailable for tea, she insisted I come around for dinner."

"But we're to stay in tonight," Flora protested. "Unless you wish to have that man out in the hall following us and causing a scene. And what of the packing you were going to have them do?"

"No, dear. *You're* to stay in tonight. I don't recall Mr. McMinn offering an opinion as to where I might go. I am keeping my appointment as scheduled. The packing can be done when I return. Surely you wouldn't expect otherwise?"

Flora let out a long breath. "No, of course not."

"Don't pout, dear. It causes wrinkles." Grandmama shrugged. "You'll be fine here with your Pinkerton agent. Though I would suggest you order him up a meal when you get one for yourself. It would be the nice thing to do."

"Dinner with Mr. McMinn without a chaperone?" she asked as she affected a dramatic pose. "Whatever would the gossips say?"

"Tomorrow you'll be married and no one will care what the gossips say. Now the maid. Please fetch her." Grandmama stood and began moving toward her room. "Oh, and Flora?"

"Yes?"

"Having the man you're marrying tomorrow up to your hotel room tonight is a risk you don't need to take, so do not assume that my statement applies to him."

"You trust Mr. McMinn but not my fiancé?"

"The Pinkerton agent does not appear to be the type who would be willing to sign away his rights as a husband. I like that in a man as well." She paused to stare at a marble statue of Cupid, bow drawn, that stood among several other decorative items on the table. "A husband by contract is so much less complicated."

"Well, there's nothing to worry about," Flora whispered to her grandmother's closed bed-chamber door. "It's likely I couldn't find Mr. Tucker to invite him if I tried."

That admission should have worried her. Instead, the words she had prayed returned to offer a balm of peace wrapping her heart. If tomorrow's marriage was not to be—if God closed the door—there would be another solution.

For the life of her, however, she couldn't figure out what that might be.

She picked up the statue, surprised by the weight of what appeared to be such a delicate work of art. "Maybe you can tell me, Cupid," she whispered as she returned the piece to its place on the table. "If only you could shoot an arrow in the direction of the man God has for me."

She rang for the maid and settled into a quiet corner of the suite with *Pride and Prejudice* and the hope that her grandmother and all the activity surrounding her would soon be gone for the evening. Yet after the whirlwind that was Millicent Brimm departed, Flora found the quiet extremely disquieting.

She rose to pace the parlor, allowing the details of the afternoon to return in snatched thoughts and uncomfortable recollections. Seeking out her writing desk, Flora began and tossed aside a half dozen versions of the same letter.

Each began with: *Dear Violet, tomorrow I am to be married.*

None continued past the second line, where she struggled to explain why.

Instead, Flora decided to begin at the beginning. To tell her sister the how instead of the why.

Dear Violet, tomorrow I am to be married. The man's name is Will Tucker, and he made me laugh once when I desperately needed to.

"Much better," Flora said as she rested the pen against her cheek. "Now what?"

She closed her eyes and thought of that afternoon. Of Clothilde Brimm's funeral and the steamboat *Archness* and the Mississippi River with the damp New Orleans air that swirled over the brown water to stir it up like fresh-made gumbo. Air so thick a soupspoon would likely cut it, and so warm it almost pained Flora to breathe it in.

As the vessel began its upriver trek to Natchez, Flora remembered finding solace in her state-room, where headache powders and iced coffees had failed to ease an ache that rested partly between her temples but mostly in her heart. Sleep was fitful, owing as much to poor weather as to her other complaints.

Worse, she'd traveled with a new maid, who spent most of the voyage downriver with her head over the side plagued with seasickness. Thus, Flora was well and truly fending for herself.

Loneliness, the specter that plagued her girlhood and haunted her still, now chased her down the passageway into the grand salon. Owing to the late hour, only a few passengers still sat at tables or relaxed in the seating groups situated near either end of the ballroom-like space.

Though the calliope had played jaunty tunes all during the meal earlier, the room now hummed with the voices of those in conversation, punctu-ated by the rhythmic splash of the paddle wheel and the patter of rain against the windows. Outside the river ran past in a wide and muddy torrent of water and tree stumps—this much Flora knew from the many trips she'd taken on this route. Now, however, nothing but blackest night showed beyond the rain-spattered glass, a tribute to the hidden moon and the weather that mirrored her thoughts.

Flora selected an oversized stuffed chair of

brilliant scarlet in a less busy section of the salon and fitted herself into its velvet embrace. From her vantage point she could watch the goings-on, what little there were, without being easily seen. It was a viewpoint she preferred, for people watching had always been a favorite sport between her and big sister Violet on these excursions.

If things had been different, would they now be huddled together wondering about the young couple dancing, though the music had long stopped? Clandestine romance, Flora would assert, though likely Violet would have called them newlyweds. Or the three elderly men up long past their bedtime to hold some sort of seriously animated discussion that involved cigars and amber-colored beverages? Politicians or pensioners? Elderly travelers or clandestine spies in costume? Their stories had known no bounds.

Now it was her grief that felt boundless.

Flora blinked away the thought and cast about for another passenger, another story to surmise. Finding a fair-haired man at the opposite end of the salon, she allowed herself to wonder what might have captured his attention so intently out the window. She studied his lean, broad-shouldered frame and decided he was of the athletic sort. Perhaps one of those fellows who enjoyed a bracing walk after dinner or a day's hike in the woods.

No, she decided, for his well-tailored clothes told her he could just as easily be a man of leisure. Or perhaps an up-and-coming captain of some sort of industry.

He shifted his position to check his watch and then returned to his vigil. About now Violet would be making guesses as to his reason for waiting. What caused him to watch the river, though it was obvious he could not see it.

A lost love. Or a missed appointment. Perhaps a broken heart. Generally Violet went on like this until Flora changed the guessing to something less romantic. Something such as the color of his eyes or whether he would be leaving at Natchez or going on farther north to St. Louis.

Flora shrugged off the silliness and opened the book she'd brought along. Violet had shared their mother's love of Jane Austen even before she left the schoolroom. Flora, for her part, was still working through the books on her sister's recommended list. When *Emma* failed to entertain, she'd turned to *Pride and Prejudice*. And though Elizabeth Bennet's antics served to amuse, tonight Flora seemed to be reading the same few pages over and over without recalling any of what was there.

With books as in life, it never failed that while the elder sister daydreamed of sweet drama, the younger craved detail and fact. Perhaps like her beloved Jo March in *Little Women*, she would have taken up literary work or followed in the footsteps of the intrepid Mrs. Gladden in *The Female Detective* to sign on as an investigator had she not been burdened with the requirement to produce a Brimm heir.

If only the Lord would solve that problem for her. Tonight.

Flora closed her eyes, emboldened. *I don't need love, Lord. I've had that more than once and what happened? All four of them died. So choose any man for my husband and send him my way, but please hurry. A husband in name only is fine. Just let him live long enough to fulfill the terms of Grandfather's will.*

Oh, that sounded awful. As if she might only use the poor fellow until the heir made an appearance. *Let him live a long life,* she amended, *though it doesn't have to be with me.* She breathed a sigh as she decided she was giving God far too many instructions. It was a particular fault of hers, this ordering the Lord around as if she and not He knew what was best.

All right, Father. Just please send me the perfect husband. And it would help greatly if he might announce himself that way just to make things simpler.

"Amen," she whispered.

"A pretty lady like you should never be without one essential thing."

Flora jerked her attention from the page to find

a most lovely pair of storm-gray eyes staring down at her. Up close his shoulders were much broader, his smile impossibly wonderful. And the concern on his face almost made her wonder if this fictional Mr. Darcy that Violet was so enamored of might have taken on flesh and now stood before her.

The fair-haired man from the window gestured to the chair nearest hers. "May I?" he asked. "Or am I intruding on your solitude?"

"The only things intruding on my solitude at the moment are a nasty headache and the inability to recall what I am reading." Flora folded down the cover of the book and regarded the stranger with emboldened curiosity. "Now, what's this about essential things, Mr. . . ."

"Tucker," he said with a tilt of his head in her direction. "Will Tucker. And the essential thing, at least in my estimation, is a smile." He shook his head. "Alas, you have none. So I thought I would offer you one of mine."

Then he smiled. "I have been meditating on the very great pleasure which a pair of fine eyes in the face of a pretty woman can bestow," he added as he gestured to the book in her lap. "That would be a direct quote from your Mr. Darcy there, though I must say it also applies to you very well. A lovely shade of blue, those eyes of yours."

She gave him a sideways look, unable to tell whether he was serious or still making a joke so as to cause her to smile. When he quirked a brow as if waiting for her reaction, the man got the smile he so obviously sought.

"I am Flora," she said, keeping her last name private for the moment lest he recognize it. "You've read this?" Flora indicated the book as she pondered his motives.

He shrugged. "I've known women who were fond of it. Myself, I have other preferences. What about you?"

"The same, I'm afraid. And yet you quote the hero beautifully."

Her challenge caused no reaction other than to broaden his smile. "A blessing and a curse. Anything I read, I can recall. No quote, conversation, or date on a calendar escapes me." He gave another self-deprecating shrug. "My mother once told me the skill would make me the perfect husband someday."

Her heart thudded against her chest as the words she'd only just prayed were reflected back to her. "What did you say?"

"Just that I've been told I'd be the perfect husband."

The sound of thunder jolted her, and Flora's recollection of that first meeting with Will Tucker slid back into the place where she kept her memories. She glanced at the letter on the table before her and cast it aside for a fresh sheet of paper. Now she knew what she would write.

Dear Violet, tomorrow I am to be married. I know in my heart he is the perfect husband. As your Mr. Darcy would say, "I cannot fix on the hour, or the spot, or the look, or the words, which laid the foundation . . . I was in the middle before I knew that I had begun."

And now she was, Flora hoped, at the end. Tomorrow things would be different.

Better.

Resolved.

❧ TEN ❧

The rumble of thunder drew Flora's attention away from her task. Leaving the letter unfinished, she set down the pen and moved toward the open window. Halfway there, the electric lights failed, leaving her in complete darkness.

She could have looked for a candle or rang for someone to bring up a light, but something compelled her to keep moving toward the window. Lightning zigzagged across the night sky as the wind lifted the edge of the curtains, the air heavy with the promise of rain.

Flora held back the fabric and leaned against the window frame as once again lightning teased the distant mountaintops and lit up the hotel entrance below. Tomorrow she would be leaving

Eureka Springs behind. The thought of just where she might go had not occurred until now. Perhaps the best thing for everyone would be to return to Natchez, where she could hide behind the comforting walls of home until the surprise of her hasty marriage died down. She could claim many things in regard to Mr. Tucker, but love at first sight was not one of them.

Perhaps a brief wait before attempting to produce the heir the will required was in order. Flora let out a long breath and leaned against the windowsill. Should a woman anticipating her wedding day feel such relief at the prospect that the marriage would not include a pregnancy for some time?

And yet a baby was the reason for the wedding.

Reason folded back against reason to form a confusing circle of promises and excuses that tightened around Flora's heart. "It's all so complicated," she whispered.

"There's nothing complicated about a rainstorm, Miss Brimm."

Flora jumped and turned to face the direction from where the voice had come. Seeing Mr. McMinn was impossible until another flash of lightning gave a brief glimpse of the lawman leaning against the door frame, his hat slightly askew and his arms crossed over his chest.

"You gave me a fright!"

A chuckle. "I guess that means you can't change

your name to Fearless Flora after tomorrow's big event."

"Big event indeed. I'm sure you'll be glad to have all of this resolved."

"You think that's going to happen tomorrow?"

"I do, but from the sound of it, you don't. Why is that?"

"Experience. My gut's telling me things are rarely as simple as they appear." A thud and a few choice sounds let Flora know he was making an attempt to move toward her.

"Trouble?" she asked sweetly.

"With you, Miss Brimm, there seems to be nothing but trouble."

"Are you having a problem? I can come and help you."

"Thank you." A shuffling sound followed by the creak of wooden furniture told her the Pinkerton agent had found a suitable resting spot. "But no, I'm just fine over here."

She couldn't resist a little teasing. "Are you sure you don't want to join me at the window? The view is beautiful when the lightning is just right. You can see all the way to town and beyond."

"I'll take your word for it."

"So what brings you in here? Were you worried about me?"

"I thought the weather and the power outage might have scared you."

"Thank you for your concern, but storms are

something I rather like. It's odd, I know, but I find there's nothing more soothing than a stormy night."

"I don't understand that, but you're entitled to your opinion."

Silence fell between them until once again lightning flashed. She spied her companion sitting in a chair near her writing desk, his frame dwarfing the chair and his elbows resting on his knees. He looked anything but fine.

"You don't like rainstorms?"

"I'm not particularly fond of them," he said slowly, "though that's probably because I've spent way too many of them looking for shelter under a horse blanket or inside a cave somewhere. I can't say as I can complain about having to spend this one in the dark indoors."

"Well, I can." Flora moved away from the window. "I'm starved and I've just realized it. Do you think we can order up a meal?"

"I'm not sure that's such a good idea. Even if someone down in the kitchen could manage to cook it, how are we going to see to eat it?"

"So it's 'we' now?"

"I could eat something if it were offered to me, but I don't know if I'm willing to go to all that trouble."

"I am."

Flora felt her way to the settee and then waited for the next bolt of lightning to illuminate the parlor. When it happened, she ran half the distance to the writing desk before her shin hit something hard.

"Ouch!" she said as she knelt down to rub her leg.

"What happened?"

Mr. McMinn must have intended to jump into action and rescue her. Instead, he slammed into her. The collision sent both of them tumbling. The next flash of lightning found them both scrambling to stand. Unfortunately, his foot got caught on a table leg, and he went down again along with the contents of the table.

"Ouch!" he yelled as something thudded against what Flora assumed was his head. Or the floor. Either was just as hard.

Then all went silent.

"Mr. McMinn? Are you harmed?"

"No," he said with a tone that told her otherwise. "I'm just fine, but this little Cupid statue has seen better days."

"Where are you exactly?"

"I'm not sure. I don't think I got very far before I was tackled." A crunching sound and then a groan. "I think that is a table," he said. "Or was."

She reached out in the direction of his voice. "Here, take my hand, and let's see if you can stand."

When her fingers hit skin, Flora froze. "Sorry," she said softly.

"Not half as sorry as I'm going to be by the time these bruises show. Not that the little guy's arrow hit me where any proper folk would get a look." He punctuated the claim with a chuckle, giving Flora reason to believe he was just fine.

He managed to grab her hand, and a strong tug almost sent Flora tumbling back to the ground, but she stood firm while he hauled himself to his feet.

Lightning illuminated the room again, this time from a greater distance, and bathed the scene in pale silver. The table nearest Grandmama's favorite sitting spot had been upended, but the only casualty appeared to be the marble statue of Cupid Flora had recently lodged a complaint to.

Apparently Lucas McMinn had been pierced by Cupid's arrow. The irony struck her as humorous, and Flora couldn't quite manage to contain a giggle.

"I'm glad someone thinks this is funny," Mr. McMinn said. "You figure the bellpull works? We probably ought to get one or two of those maids in here to help set this place to rights again."

"In the dark? I don't see how anything can be done until the electricity is restored." She paused. "Now, unless you're desperately in need of medical attention after your unfortunate attack by Cupid, I'm going to make my excuses and go downstairs to find something to eat."

"It's pitch dark. And I'm fine, thank you very much."

"Suit yourself." She took a few halting steps toward the door and reached out to touch the writing desk. Yes, she knew where she was from here. Three or four lengthy strides and she would reach the parlor door. From there, she could only hope there was some way to find the stairs.

Behind her came a scratching sound and then the odor of something odd. A pale yellow light danced to life as Flora turned around to see Mr. McMinn holding a glowing matchstick.

"I'm afraid I don't have any idea where the candles are," she told him. "And if you're not careful, you'll burn yourself holding that."

"Unless I've calculated wrong, this match should have three or four minutes burn time. It won't get us downstairs to the kitchen, but it will shed some light on the matter."

He appeared to wait for her to react to his silly pun. When she humored him with a shake of her head, he gestured for her to come toward him.

"Hold this for me, would you?"

She did as he asked, keeping her attention mostly on the flame burning ever closer to her fingers. "If this gets too near to my skin, I'm going to blow it out. So whatever you're digging for in your pocket, I certainly hope you find it quickly."

"Here it is." Mr. McMinn produced a thin brass tube with a circle of glass on one end and a cap on the other. "When I tell you to, I want you to touch the match to the end of this."

"What is it?" she asked as she eyed the contraption with an equal measure of curiosity and skepticism.

"I haven't given it an official name, but I guess you could say it was a pocket lantern."

He removed the cap from the end and stuffed something inside. After fiddling with the brass tube a bit more, he held it near the yellow glow of the now-dwindling match light and nodded.

"All right, Miss Brimm. Just touch the lit end of the match to this spot right here."

Flora leaned forward to peer at the spot he had indicated. "You mean at the bottom of the tube where the cap was?"

"Yes," he said as he held the tube out at arm's length. "Remember, just barely touch it with the fire."

She gave him a doubtful look. "It's not going to blow up, is it?"

"I hope not," he said with a chuckle. "I'm the one holding it."

"All right." Flora edged forward and held her breath as she reached to touch the flame to the end of the brass tube. "Now what?"

Before he could respond, something inside the tube sparked and the match went out. A sizzling sound was quickly followed by a soft puffing noise. An instant later, something inside the tube began to glow—first a pale green, and then a soft blue, and finally a brilliant white. The tube appeared to have something burning inside.

On closer inspection, there was no fire at all. Rather, whatever Mr. McMinn had placed inside the tube was somehow lit, and though the interior continued to glow, the exterior remained cool to the touch.

"Actually, it's more like a torch," she said. "A hand torch, maybe? How does it work?"

He shrugged. "I don't figure it would make any sense to you if I did tell you. And if it did make sense, I'd have to wonder whether you would tell our secrets for the formula." He paused to direct his attention at Flora. "So I think I'll keep that to myself if it's all the same to you."

"Our?"

"I collaborate with an old friend on many of the things I design. Sometimes he comes up with the idea and other times I do." He met her stare. "But neither of us like to talk about it, understand?"

Momentarily distracted by the brilliance of his green eyes when viewed in the glow of the odd invention, Flora could only nod. The circle of light, small as it was, caused the parlor to fade into darkness. The thought of being alone with Mr. McMinn—something that felt so innocent, even slightly irritating, just moments ago—suddenly seemed like something much more.

A thought occurred.

"If you had a match and this invention, why did you wait around in the dark until now to use it?"

He shrugged. "It's a prototype, and my associate, Mr. Russell, wasn't sure if it worked. Given the weather and the fact this hotel has chosen electric lights over the more dependable gaslights made me think I might have use of it."

"You're serious." Flora shook her head. "So you just carry things like this . . . this experiment . . . around on the chance that you *might* get to test them? Does Mr. Russell do the same?"

"No comment, Miss Brimm. And as to this device, it's a prototype, not an experiment. There's a difference."

"I'm sure you think there is, but right now I would much rather continue this fascinating discussion over a plate of cold chicken or a sandwich. What do you say?" She nodded toward the lighted tube. "Can that thing get us to the kitchen before it blows up?"

"The elements in this tube are not volatile," Lucas said, "though the man holding it just might be." He shook his head. "A joke. Brought on by the arrow that jabbed me."

"Cupid's arrow." The infuriating woman grinned.

"Imagine that. What are the odds of Cupid finding you, of all people, to jab?"

"Apparently the odds are pretty high, because it happened."

The Natchez belle snickered but said nothing further. The silence that fell between them was neither comfortable nor lasting. Outside the lightning that had been so frequent flashed across the western sky in a weak line that stretched across the mountaintops.

Miss Brimm had apparently had enough. "Well, if you've recovered from your injuries, I think it's time for us to see if we can find the dining room."

She opened the door to the darkened hallway and stepped aside to allow him to pass her. "After you, Mr. McMinn," she said as she tucked a hand in his elbow and followed his lead.

The hall was dark, its doors all thankfully shut tight. At the far end, where the maids' quarters were situated, Lucas could see an orange glow beneath the door. Likely that part of the hotel wasn't privy to the modern electrical conveniences like those reserved for their employers.

And yet tonight these girls were probably unaware of the situation outside their doors.

The pocket lantern did a passable job getting them down the first flight of stairs, but as they moved closer to the lobby, he decided it was time to extinguish the glow. No need for the device to make its debut any sooner than planned, especially as the patent hadn't been completed on the project yet.

Carefully replacing the cap, Lucas fitted the gadget back into his pocket and patted his jacket to be sure everything was in its place. "All right," he said as he blinked several times to adjust his eyes to the absence of light. "Whatever you do, don't let go of me. Understand?"

"Yes," she whispered, her breath warm against his neck. "I wouldn't let go if you begged me right now, Mr. McMinn."

Lucas's pulse quickened as he inhaled the scent of lilacs. "Yes, well, I don't plan on begging for anything, Miss Brimm, except maybe a sandwich."

The thought of the meal he'd missed was almost enough to make him forget that the woman's soft fingers had slid from his elbow and were now clutching his hand. Almost but not quite, for she gave his hand a squeeze and once again leaned in.

"Ready when you are," she whispered.

Lucas could hear the muffled conversations of guests and, above the chatter, the sound of what could only be described as an impromptu concert by the same orchestra that had entertained at the costume ball.

"Is that a waltz?" Miss Brimm asked. "It sounds as though we're missing quite a party."

"Likely just guests with nothing to do until the

electricity is restored," he said as he tried to look around the corner. He had a mirror that might do the trick, but the low light combined with the need to look as if he were a normal hotel guest should he be spotted kept him from making the attempt. Instead, he decided to rely on instinct.

"I hope that means the dining room is still open."

"We're not going into the dining room."

"I thought we were coming down here to have a meal."

He shook his head. "We're coming down here to *get* a meal and take it back upstairs. I'm not taking any chances that we might be seen together in the dining room, and if you would consider it, you'd agree."

"But I—"

"Miss Brimm, for someone who has asked that I not interfere with her wedding tomorrow, you certainly don't seem to care that your fiancé might see you breaking bread with a Pinkerton agent and hightail it out of Eureka Springs before the preacher can pronounce the 'I dos.' "

He heard her sigh. "I can see your point."

"Well, hallelujah for small miracles," he muttered.

"There is no need to be sarcastic. Let's get this over with before I faint of starvation."

"Just one more thing," he said as he made a feeble attempt to sound as if he were the one in control of the situation. "You're not to forget that you are in the personal custody of a Pinkerton agent. That means we're going to do whatever it takes to not draw attention to ourselves. Also, it means you're to follow my instructions at all times and to stay within my sight."

A giggle.

"What?"

"Well," Miss Brimm said slowly. "I'm afraid I'm already in trouble."

He let out a long breath. "And why is that?"

Another giggle. "You can't see me, so how can I stay within your sight?"

"Oh, come on." He grasped the rail with one hand and squeezed Flora's with the other as he slowly made his way down the stairs to the landing midway between the first and second floors. "Almost there," he said as he paused. "Are you all right?"

"Fine," was a breath against his skin as she nudged his shoulder. "But I'm truly starved. Can we move a little faster?"

"We could, but I'd have to throw you over my shoulder." He laughed as her grip on his hand tightened.

"Don't you dare. I thought the idea was to not draw attention to ourselves."

"Oh, really? And I thought the idea was for you to follow my instructions at all times."

"Touché, Mr. McMinn. Do lead on."

❋ ELEVEN ❋

The kitchen was closed up tight with no one around to offer anything to eat, but that didn't keep Lucas from stepping inside, taking Miss Brimm in with him. As soon as the door closed behind them, he released his grip on her and took a step back.

"Should we be doing this?" she asked, though she had professed no qualms about following him inside. "I mean, you are supposed to be upholding the law."

"We've already done this. Now, how about we see what's for supper?"

"Dinner," she corrected with enough of a grin in her voice to indicate she was teasing.

"Out on the trail," Lucas said with an exaggerated drawl as he began searching for a candle and matches, "dinner's what we had in the middle of the day, ma'am. Supper, that's the evening meal. I would think a Southern lady like yourself would know that."

She actually laughed. "You'd be surprised at how hard it was for me to remember to properly designate the titles of meals once I went off to boarding school. I was in such trouble for it." She paused. "Speaking of trouble, what if we're caught taking food without paying? I doubt the manager would appreciate trespassers in the kitchen."

"This is official business, and no one said anything about not paying. I'll see the manager in the morning."

The statement appeared to be enough to satisfy Miss Brimm's brief venture into a guilty conscience. "And I'll be sure and add a little to the hotel bill to cover whatever we take."

"I found the matches. I'm guessing the candles must be . . ." Lucas reached deeper into the closet he was rummaging in and retrieved several candles. "All right, I think just one will do." He made quick work of lighting a candle and then blew out the match and tossed it aside. "Now let's see what's on the menu for tonight."

He moved toward the center of the room, where a bounty of bread loaves and other bakery items appeared to be awaiting the breakfast crowd. Miss Brimm remained at his side just within reach of the candle's circle of light.

"See anything edible?" she asked. "I'm so hungry right now I'm truly not picky."

"Tonight I don't think you could be picky and find something here. However, let's see what's over there."

Lucas aimed the candle's glow toward a stash of covered plates. Apparently, the dining room had done a good business that evening, for there wasn't much left over from the dinner menu to call it a meal.

However, he managed to find the remains of a mouthwatering platter of perfectly cooked prime rib in the warmer. To this he added a partial loaf of bread from the counter. All told, the ingredients were just enough for two decent-sized sandwiches.

She came up beside him to snatch a bite of prime rib. "Delicious," she said before taking another. "What are you making?"

"Enough of that. Give me room to work here. I'm making sandwiches. And I am taking you at your word that you're too hungry to complain."

"No complaints, I promise," she said as she held up her hand.

"Good, now why don't you go look over there and see what else you can find. Don't get too far into the shadows. There's no telling what's back there."

A brow rose. "As in?"

"As in I don't know. There could be poison to keep the rats out. Just stick to where I can see you and don't dig too deeply into any of the cabinets, all right?"

She did as he asked, wandering over to the larder where she stopped short. "Oh . . . my . . . goodness."

Her breathless exclamation drew his attention, but only for a moment before he went back to his task. She had probably just found some crackers or fresh vegetables to go with their meal.

"Oh, this is simply divine."

"What is it?" When she didn't immediately respond, he glanced up to see her holding what appeared to be an entire chocolate cake. "It does look good. Slice a couple of pieces and leave the rest."

"Surely you jest," she said with what he hoped was an exaggerated expression of horror. "What if I cut the pieces unevenly and one of us gets more than the other? Or, worse, what if they are too small and we wish we had more?" She gave him a sideways look. "Are you willing to take that risk?"

Lucas shook his head. "I see your point. Now put that down and go find a basket big enough to hold the food. If we're carrying the cake we will need something more than just our hands to get everything back upstairs. And while you're at it, you might want to figure out how to bring that whole cake with us. If you can't—"

"Oh, I can," she interrupted.

She had no trouble fetching a basket that would work for the sandwiches, plates, and napkins. The real problem came when she tried to figure out how to escape with just enough chocolate cake so that it wouldn't be missed. Or at least that was Lucas's assumption as he watched her travel from cabinet to cabinet shaking her head and mumbling.

Miss Brimm handed him the candle and began opening cabinet doors until she let out a cry. "I've got it! It's perfect. We can put the cake in here." Her eyes widened. "The whole thing."

He turned around to see her walking toward him holding out an oversized silver serving dish with a domed lid of the sort used for serving large cuts of meat or whole poultry. The thought of a person of her size looking inconspicuous while carrying a contraption that large made him grin.

Then there was the idea that a woman dressed in such finery might actually make anyone believe she had a good reason for carrying a platter as if she were kitchen help. That made him laugh out loud.

"What do you think?" she asked with obvious pride despite his humor. "It's a great idea, isn't it?"

All he could manage was a shake of his head and another chuckle.

"What's so funny?" she demanded. "The entire cake will fit inside here, plus a serving knife."

Lucas leaned against the door frame to admire the woman's ingenuity. He couldn't resist another question. "Why not put the knife in the basket?"

Miss Brimm shook her head. "Think, Mr. McMinn. While we might not attract much attention with a basket of food and a serving dish, don't you think someone might be suspicious if they spied this?" She held a knife up so it glittered in the candlelight.

"You have a point," he said carefully.

"A point. Oh, that's funny. Was that meant to be a pun?"

Her smile was radiant, and it almost made him grin once again in return. Almost but not quite. For the image of a woman in his custody holding a knife that could do substantial damage to his person reminded Lucas that he was a man on a mission. Part of that mission was to bring Will Tucker to justice. If this woman were to marry Tucker, and he still had his doubts, that meant she could still be considered just as guilty as her fiancé.

She pointed the oversized knife in his direction. "Look. Now I have a point. A sharp one."

All right, enough knife humor. "Here, let me have that," he said calmly.

Miss Brimm placed the handle of the knife in Lucas's hand without any further comment and went back to her work of searching the kitchen.

"What are you looking for now?" he asked as he set the knife on the counter beside him and then made sure he stood between it and her.

"I'm not sure, but I'm sure I'll know when I find it." A moment later, she once again cried out in a happy exclamation. "I've got it!"

"It?" he asked, though he suspected whatever she found would be something she alone could explain the reason for.

"A tablecloth. We certainly can't sit on the ground."

"The ground?" He paused to allow the sound of clanking metal from her search to cease. "Just where do you think we'll be eating, Miss Brimm?"

"Never mind that. I have a great idea, but I'd rather it be a surprise."

"In my line of work, surprises are not considered a good thing." He rested his hip against the side of the cabinet. "So why don't we just agree to disagree and say we'll take this meal back up to your hotel room, where I'll have my sandwich in the hall and you'll have yours safe and sound inside your parlor with the door closed?"

She paused only long enough to give him a look. "You do realize my grandmother could have returned by now, don't you? And she's going to wonder where we've been. It's likely she may have caused a fuss because she returned and neither her granddaughter nor the Pinkerton agent who was supposedly guarding her is in the room."

Lucas opened his mouth to respond, but she held up her hand to continue. "And furthermore, what do you think she'll believe happened when she sees the mess we left behind? The table was overturned and poor Cupid." A pause. "How is that arrow wound of yours? I certainly hope you're not getting designs on me."

"Designs on you?" he sputtered. "Be serious."

Her laughter danced across the space between them. "You know what they say. When Cupid pulls back his bow, the lucky recipient of his arrow falls in love with the first person he or she sees. And that, you lucky man, was me."

Had she not been so obviously taunting him, Lucas might have thought she was flirting. "Miss Brimm," he said slowly, "I believe neither in luck nor in any silly stories about Cupid. Nor should you."

"Oh, I don't. Not really. Though it is fun to think of that sort of thing." She paused while leaning down to look in a cabinet. "Mama always said the Lord chose the fellow I was going to marry, and that someday He would be the one to tell me who that man was."

"And you figure He has done that?"

"I do . . . at least I'm fairly certain of it. I made a particular request of the Lord and then almost instantly Will Tucker appeared. It's as if it were meant to be."

"Meant to be," he said under his breath. "Not likely."

"If we borrow a pair of forks, I think we will have all we need for our dinner," she called over her shoulder. "Oh, look. Here they are." She held up the utensils, the tablecloth draped over her arm. "Now to assemble the getaway basket."

Though he had his doubts, Lucas stood back and watched while she maneuvered the chocolate

173

cake onto the platter. "The knife, please?" she said as she held her hand out toward him.

He wedged the knife partly under the dessert and covered both with the silver dome. Much as he hated to admit it, she was right. The knife fit under the cake, and the dome settled nicely atop them both.

She gave him a triumphant look. "Perfect. Now, which one do you want to carry?"

"Considering the fact you would look ridiculous carrying a platter almost as big as you are, why don't I take this and you can bring the basket?"

She looped her arm through the basket's handle and shifted it into the crook of her elbow. Giving the contents a pat, she nodded in the opposite direction from the door where they had entered.

"Come on, let's get out of here before someone comes in and wonders why we're helping ourselves to sandwiches and cake," she said as she pressed past him.

"Where are you going?" He gestured to the kitchen door. "The exit's this way. I think if you stick close to me and we don't act like we're—"

"Really, Mr. McMinn. Just once will you trust me?" She had the audacity to set the basket down and unlock one of the floor-to-ceiling windows that marched along the southern side of the kitchen. "If you'll just follow me, I can show you a shortcut to the place I have in mind for our picnic."

Before he could protest, she picked up the basket, blew out the candle, and disappeared out the window.

"Again with the window?" he called. "I've never met a woman who had such a propensity for using exits other than the door. And I've been a Pinkerton for almost as long as I've . . ."

He stepped out into an alleyway that led between the hotel and an accompanying out-building, likely the place where wood was stored for the atrium fireplace. Though there was enough light from the atrium here to shed a decent glow onto the path, there was no sign of Flora Brimm.

The cold, hard truth was that he'd been had. By a redhead in skirts carrying borrowed sand-wiches, no less.

"Pssst."

Lucas looked around, shifting the heavy platter as he made a full circle. Nothing.

"Pssst."

This time he looked up and spied her perched on the fire escape, the basket at her side. "What in the world are you doing?"

"I'm getting us out of the kitchen without being noticed. Come on!" She nodded toward the upper reaches of the fire escape. "Set the cake on the steps and climb up over there."

This time it was Lucas who did as he was told, placing the covered platter on the step just above him and then climbing over the guardrail and chain at the bottom of the fire escape. By the time he straightened to reach for the cake, his companion was already nearing the second floor.

Thankfully the storm had passed, leaving only the twinkling lights of the night sky and the shimmer of rain on the ground. The wind had died down to almost nothing and, with the temperature still unseasonably warm and the moon broad and round over the mountaintops, the night ahead appeared to be a fine one.

He looked up to see that she had bypassed the second floor entrance into the hotel and was moving at a rapid pace toward the third level. At this point, she could race him to the roof and win before he'd catch her.

"What is it with you and heights, Miss Brimm?" he called as he paused on the third floor landing to adjust the burden of the heavy platter. While he was at it, Lucas said a prayer that the knife he'd wedged under the chocolate cake would not fall out and do serious harm to anyone who might have the poor fortune to be standing below.

Ignoring his question, she kept moving forward until she had reached the fourth floor. This being the floor her suite was on, Lucas figured she might actually stop this silliness and cease her climbing. When she actually did as he expected, he shook his head.

"It's about time you came to your senses," he

said as he came up next to her and shifted the weight of the platter to keep from losing his balance. "Let me see if I can unlock this door. I have a tool I use for occasions like this in my pocket, but I'll have to put the cake down first. It's a little difficult to see well out here, but I think I can—"

"No."

He looked down at her and shook his head. "No?"

"No. I'm just pausing here a moment to check something. Here," she said as she thrust the basket toward him. "Would you mind holding this for a moment?"

"Holding this how, exactly?" Lucas nodded toward the covered platter that required both hands to keep it horizontal.

"Good point." Her gaze swept the length of him and then slowly a smile dawned. "Of course. This will work just fine. Hold still."

Before he could comment, she balanced the basket atop the domed platter. Turning her back on him and his predicament, she stepped over the rail and onto the ledge.

"Oh, not again," he muttered as he tried to figure out a way to divest himself of his burdens and give chase. But no matter how hard he tried to remove the basket, he only succeeded in coming nearer to dropping the platter with each attempt.

"Miss Brimm, you come back here this instant!

You are in my custody and I demand that you do as I say. Do not make me come after you!"

He tried to kneel and deposit the platter and basket onto the step. The effort failed miserably, though he was able to catch the basket before it tumbled down three flights of stairs. When she disappeared around the corner, Lucas gave up altogether and started trying to figure out how to get back down the stairs without harming anyone. For if he saw Miss Brimm, he just might be tempted to throw a sandwich in her direction. A much better choice than any of the heavier or sharper objects in the arsenal he currently held.

He let out a long breath and tamped down on his ill humor. Throwing things was about as childish as he could get, and if anyone was going to be childish, it was Flora Brimm, not he.

No, if he ever caught up to the infuriating woman, he would see that the handcuffs went back on immediately. After that, he would make short work of hauling her into Eureka Springs and handing her over to the sheriff.

Then he would stake out the lobby where she would be meeting Will Tucker and catch him while he was waiting. "Yes, that would work," he muttered. "And I sure wouldn't be dependent on that woman."

❈ TWELVE ❈

"Mr. McMinn, where are you going?" Flora called to his retreating back.

He paused to slowly turn around and face her. While the moon's light was not at its brightest tonight, the illumination was sufficient to see that he was doing a doubtful job at best of keeping their feast from tumbling to the ground below.

"Where have you been?" he demanded with no small measure of irritation. "Did you not listen when I told you that you must remain within my sight at all times?"

"Yes, but—"

"And did you or did you not hear me tell you to come back here when you headed off over the side of the fire escape and down the window ledge?"

She gripped the rail of the fire escape and climbed back over. "I did, but—"

"And did I or did I not tell you that you were in my personal custody?"

"Yes, you did," she snapped, "but if you would just listen!" She briefly closed her eyes and sighed. "Look, I'm terribly sorry. Truly I am. But I needed to see if my idea was correct, and it was."

Moving toward her on the stairs, he paused just

close enough to allow her to reach the basket's handle. Mr. McMinn shifted the covered platter and leaned against the rail.

"Let me get this straight. You had an idea that required you to risk your safety and my ire, and you thought it a good idea to act on it?"

"Yes. And it concerns . . ." Flora felt a check in her spirit that told her it was best not to mention anything about Mr. Tucker right now. If she did, she'd have to tell him about her theory that the railroad detective had used the fire escape to climb from his room on the third floor to hers on the fourth.

"Go on," he urged.

"Never mind," she said slowly. "It's nothing of any importance to a Pinkerton man. Just a situation with an accessory."

His eyes narrowed, but thankfully he did not question her any further. Instead, he nodded toward the fourth-floor entrance. "Let's just go on inside and eat, all right? And no more side trips to the window ledge on the front of the building, theory or no theory."

Flora grinned. "Oh, no you don't. We agreed that returning to the suite was not a good idea for several reasons."

"I don't recall agreeing to that."

"At least reserve your judgment until you see that I have such a better idea in mind." Flora put on her most pleading expression. It worked, for by the time he looked away, he'd also begun to grin.

"All right, since I didn't have to throw sandwiches at you—"

"Throw sandwiches?" Flora shook her head. "What in the world are you talking about?"

"Don't ask. The other option was to turn you over to the sheriff. But because you came back of your own free will, I guess I can humor you and at least let you show me where you want to have this picnic." He shook his head. "But I warn you, Miss Brimm. I refuse to carry this platter much longer, and I absolutely will not walk on any window ledges. Understand?"

"Perfectly," she said sweetly. "Now follow me. We're almost there."

She continued up the fire escape until it ended at the fifth floor roof. Here the staircase gave way to the topmost point of the hotel, the rooftop deck and, at its center, the half-story climb to the belvedere. Much like a square gazebo, the belvedere was open on all four sides and yet large enough for its gabled roof to provide shade from the sun and protection from the rain.

Flora knew this because she'd happily endured both up here during her stay at the Crescent. Tonight, however, was the first time she'd seen the view by moonlight.

Leaving the basket on the bench that ran the length of the structure's interior, Flora moved to the edge to look up at God's glorious heavenly

181

handiwork. What the rain had washed clean now sparkled beneath the almost-full moon. Lights twinkled in the city below, mirroring the stars above.

And though the sound of revelers in the atrium drifted up to the roof, Flora felt as though she were miles away from anyone. Then a clang of metal against metal followed by a string of muttered complaints behind her reminded her that she was far from alone.

"Welcome to my favorite place at the Crescent, Mr. McMinn. Isn't it lovely?"

"Lovely, yes," he said softly.

By the time he stepped into her peripheral view, Flora had returned her attention to the scene unfolding before her. The remnant of the rainstorm was evident in the distant streak of lightning that played across the mountaintops. The slim flash of white was so far away and so pale that Flora was left to wonder whether she'd seen it at all.

"There is still some weather happening over beyond the valley. You might want to be careful about straying too close to the rail. You never know when you'll get a surprise jolt."

"Don't be silly. The bad weather is miles away from here."

"That may be, but I have learned the hard way to respect an electrical storm, even if it doesn't look as though it's anywhere near."

"The hard way?" She turned to face him. "What do you mean?"

"Out on the prairie things travel far. A man can hear sounds that started out a mile or more down the road."

He paused to adjust his hat, and Flora took the chance to study him. With his features washed in silver moonlight, he looked much younger. Much more like a man who might be more fun and less fuss.

As if he'd read her thoughts, Mr. McMinn smiled. Then, slowly, he swung his gaze to meet hers. "I ought not to tell you the rest. I'd hate to scare someone as fearless as you."

She nudged his shoulder with her own. "You started this story and you'll finish it. So tell me, what does that have to do with lightning?"

He dipped his head. "Just that it strikes at the most unexpected times. The good news is I survived with nothing but this scar to show for it." He pushed back his collar to show her a faded pink scar that snaked down beneath his shirt. "Now, how about we go see if I'm any good at sandwich making?"

Though she longed for more of his story, Flora sensed she would get nowhere by asking. So she nodded and tried not to think of the scar and how very much it must have hurt him. Instead she watched him work quickly to prepare the make-shift meal. He was quite good at it actually, as she discovered after settling the tablecloth across the bench and taking her first bite.

"I am impressed. You have surprising culinary skills."

He joined her, placing a napkin carefully across his lap before biting into his own sandwich. "I'm much better with a campfire and a pot of beans, but this isn't bad."

"I'm not sure I could see you hunched over a campfire and stirring beans." Her gaze swept the length of him, from the top of his bowler hat to the tips of his well-shod feet. "You look far too comfortable in formal attire."

"This?" Mr. McMinn set his sandwich aside to pull at his collar. "Fitting in is what I do, Miss Brimm." He chuckled. "Though it certainly didn't work with your grandmother. She pegged me as a phony right away."

Flora joined his laughter. "True, but my grandmother is definitely an exceptional woman. You're not the first to be put in your place by her, nor will you be the last. Sometimes when she says things . . ." She looked at him and smiled ruefully. "I cringe when I think of how she offered to send one of the maids to the kitchen for a boxed lunch."

Mr. McMinn gestured to the picnic spread out between them. "Looks like I got one anyway. Or at least a boxed dinner."

"Look who's calling the evening meal dinner."

Flora lifted a brow in mock surprise. "At this rate you'll truly be considered cultured in no time."

"I assure you, Miss Brimm, there's no danger in that. Ask my grandfather."

"Perhaps someday I shall." She continued to study him as he returned to finishing off his sandwich. How Grandmama knew this man wasn't of their ilk was beyond Flora. Everything about him, from his mannerisms to the way he blended seamlessly into a more socially fortunate crowd, seemed to speak of a privileged upbringing and cultured existence. Until he opened his mouth, that is.

The sum of all those parts made Flora wonder which one was the affectation and which was the real Lucas McMinn. There was one way to find out.

He caught her staring, but she did not look away. "I wonder something," she said as she watched his face. "Who are you really?"

Her question must have been unexpected, for Flora thought she saw a moment's surprise before his practiced neutral expression returned. "And I thought you were going to ask me to pass the cake." When she continued to watch him, Mr. McMinn looked away. "So, the prisoner is attempting to overthrow the guard by using the power of surprise." His attention returned to her. "It won't work. I'm Lucas B. McMinn, Pinkerton agent, and that's all you need to know."

"I've already learned something new about you." The lift of one dark brow told her she would get no further response on the subject. "All right, if you insist, I'll tell you what I've learned. Your middle name begins with a *B*."

"There you go," he said with a smile as he swiped at the crumbs on his jacket. "I'm just an open book, aren't I? And you, Miss Brimm, are quite the detective."

"Why, thank you," she responded cheerily. "I learned from the best, you know."

"Did you now?" He shifted positions to toss the napkin into the empty basket. "And who is this expert?"

"Mrs. Gladden." When his expression showed no recognition, Flora continued. "From *The Female Detective* novels?"

His guffaw of laughter echoed in the belvedere. "So you learned your powers of deduction from a fictional character in a detective novel? That's about right, I suppose."

"Not just any fictional character. Some say Mrs. Gladden was a real person and the novels were taken from her actual case files. I will admit that theory is not without its problems. Especially as the books were written a full fifty years before the London police force admitted women. Nevertheless, Mrs. Gladden offers an interesting insight into the crime-fighting world."

"Fair enough. As I said, you learned your

powers of deductive reasoning from a detective novel."

"Novels," she corrected as the wind kicked up to tease the back of her neck.

"I stand corrected," he said dryly. "Novels. But detective work is one thing. Where in the world did you learn to walk around on window ledges like a cat?"

The question stung, but only because it brought forward an image of her sister. Of Violet and her uncanny ability to balance on the thinnest thread of wire or the narrowest plank of wood. Indeed, her elder sister possessed an ability that, in a family of lesser social leanings, might have earned her a valued place in Mr. Ringling's circus.

"Have I asked a question you don't want to answer?" He paused, his expression unreadable. "Doesn't feel so good, does it?"

"No, it's not that at all," she said as she forced herself to believe the words she'd just spoken. "I suppose you could say this skill of mine is a family trait." Flora paused. "Handed down from my sister. Unfortunately, my talent developed a bit later than hers."

Else I would never have lost footing that day and Violet would still be . . . Flora shook her head. No good would come from allowing yet another recrimination to surface.

"Well, thank goodness you didn't say your grandmother, otherwise I'd be wondering when the woman was going to walk around the edge of the building to join us for cake."

"Oh, cake!" Flora forced enthusiasm even as she began the process of tucking the memories of Violet back into place. "Yes, it's time for cake, isn't it?"

"You've only eaten half your sandwich," he protested.

Flora waved away his comment. "Nonsense. It's always time for cake."

Mr. McMinn rose to retrieve the covered platter and set it on the tablecloth-covered bench between them. "All right, Miss Brimm. Cake is served."

He pulled off the dome to reveal a dessert that hadn't traveled as well as expected. While it had been a beautifully frosted masterpiece of chocolate confection down in the kitchen, it was now an interesting pile of cake layers held together by globs of dark icing.

"What happened here? It looks as though you went rolling down the hill with this while I wasn't looking."

"You're close. I almost went rolling down the stairs while trying to keep from dropping the platter and the basket of sandwiches you so kindly left me with while you went in pursuit of your grand idea." He paused. "Not that I believe you for a minute that you were on some lark about accessories. No woman goes climbing over a stair rail and crisscrosses the length of a hotel to . . ."

The lawman shook his head. "What am I thinking? That is something you would do without question."

"I came back almost immediately."

"You were gone long enough to allow me to believe you'd escaped my custody." His eyes narrowed. "And with your skills as a tightrope climber, you know you could have easily hopped around the entire fourth floor until you found an open window." A pause. "Sounds suspiciously like the night we met, doesn't it? And you were certainly on the lookout for Mr. Tucker then."

"You're being ridiculous," she said, though he truly was being anything but. "I may have stepped out of a window the night we met, but I returned through an open door." She gave him a triumphant look. "And in neither case was I trying to escape anyone's custody. It is simply not something I would do."

"And you know this because you've been in a lawman's custody before?" Mr. McMinn stretched out his long legs as he studied her. "I suppose I ought to have checked your name for priors while I was down at the sheriff's office swearing out that warrant."

"You know what?" Flora said sweetly. "I've come to believe this whole matter of an arrest warrant is a complete fabrication."

"Have you now?" He shrugged. "Suit yourself. But there are two warrants, Miss Brimm. One for you and one for the man you think you'll be marrying in the morning."

"Yet you didn't turn me in when you had the chance." She shrugged. "As the granddaughter of a judge, I'm not so sure how a jury of my peers would like that. Why, you're practically holding me hostage without a fair trial. Shame on you."

He rose abruptly and circled her wrist with his hand. "Come on," he said as he pulled her to her feet.

"Where are we going?" Flora demanded.

"Good news." His smile was dazzling, his expression dangerous. Flora found she couldn't look away.

"And what is that?" she managed.

"You're being set free." His grin appeared to be caused in part by sarcasm and the remainder amusement. "I can see you're surprised. Don't be. I'll happily release you from my captivity and into the hospitality of the Eureka Springs jail."

Again with the threat of jail.

"Or," he continued, "we can eat cake, and you can stop complaining."

"Funny you should say that," she said calmly. "I was just about to offer to cut a slice for each of us. I'll defer to you on that."

"Looks more like a spoon would work better, but I think we can manage. And given your enthusiasm for the idea of bringing the whole cake with us, I don't suppose I have to ask if you would like a generous serving."

Flora lifted one brow, a sufficient response to a question obviously asked in jest.

He sliced and scooped enough of the mangled cake to fill each of their plates and then set the knife aside. She did not miss the fact that he placed it well out of her reach.

"Still don't trust me?" she asked as she picked up the nearest fork. "I'm devastated."

"I'm sure you are."

The first bite was divine, the second even better. "Oh," Flora said as she savored the rich chocolate. "Even mashed to a pulp, this is good cake."

"Mashed to a pulp?" Mr. McMinn shook his head. "You're one picky woman. I carried that cake all the way up here because you said you had to have the whole—"

"Oh, please. I said it was delicious."

The cake *was* good. Not the melt-in-your-mouth variety that Cook made back in Natchez, but definitely a passable second choice.

"It smells like rain. Maybe we ought to go before the weather turns bad again."

"Don't be silly," Flora said. "I'm in no hurry to leave."

"Because there's still plenty of cake?" he teased.

"Because my grandmother will demand an explanation of where I've been and why the

191

suite was left in that condition." She met his gaze. "And I'm not ready to have that conversation with her."

"If she hasn't called the law to report us missing," he added.

"Oh, she won't call the authorities, at least not officially. She may send a few discreet inquiries to a few high-placed friends who will make discreet inquiries of their own. Anything to keep the situation quiet, you understand."

Mr. McMinn chuckled. "I see how this works. Poor folks like me call the law. Rich folks like you and your grandmother call their friends."

"Exactly." Flora frowned. "Well, sort of. You don't have to be friends with a person to . . ." She shook her head. There was no need in trying to explain how things worked in Natchez to someone who had no idea of the ridiculous social structure and politics that went along with being a Brimm. "You know, I'm curious about something. I don't believe you've come from background much different than mine. Am I right?"

The wind shifted directions to tease at the edges of the tablecloth. A moment later the sound of softly falling rain could be heard. "You'd be surprised. And it looks as though we're in for another round of weather after all."

"You sound like my father," Flora said. "He might have been born a Brimm and expected to take up the family legacy, but he is an indigo farmer at heart. When we're both at home, I don't think a day passes that he doesn't make some mention of the weather to me." She paused to trace the edge of her plate with the fork. "Grandmama says his behavior is most pedestrian. I always thought it was something fathers just did."

"Predict the weather?"

"Well, yes, though now that you've said it, it does sound a little silly." A shrug. "It would be even sillier to say I miss it."

"Not at all."

She took another bite of cake to keep from responding further. Finally, only the remnant of her oversized slice of chocolate heaven remained. Icing clung to the cake crumbles, requiring Flora to lick her fork in order to get all of its gooey goodness.

"You know, this sort of behavior would be unconscionable back in Natchez," she said as she noticed one last smattering of frosting on the back of her fork and swiped at it with her index finger.

"So I'm privy to Miss Brimm misbehaving?" He chuckled. "What would your grandmother say?"

Flora set the fork aside and rose to move toward the rail. If she sat there any longer, she'd indulge in another piece, something her corset would not allow.

"My grandmother does not need to know about

my indiscretion with the chocolate frosting," she cast over her shoulder, "and should you be so uncouth as to tell her, I will deny it."

"Is that so? You've given in to the urge to eat chocolate frosting off a fork in the presence of a person who is not a member of your immediate family. That is absolutely scandalous."

She leaned over the rail just enough to allow the light mist of rain wet her fingers. "It is scandalous, isn't it?"

As was her desire to press past Lucas McMinn to dance in the rain. They were, after all, completely alone with no one to witness her silly behavior. Behavior that was simply not done by a Brimm.

And after tomorrow, when would she get the chance again? Once Mr. Tucker cleared things up with the Pinkerton agent, she would be a married woman, and Mr. McMinn would be off to follow where the trail led next.

And neither of them would need to mention her damp waltz beneath the Milky Way. The longer she stood there, the less ridiculous the idea seemed. Even if he did tell on her, it would be her word against his that she'd committed any sort of silliness while dining on the roof.

Oh, why not?

❈ THIRTEEN ❈

Flora turned to see Lucas McMinn walking her way.

"Deep in thought?" he asked.

Rather than respond, she allowed herself another moment to watch the lawman's purposeful strides before turning to walk by him. He caught her elbow. "Going somewhere?"

"Watch and see," she said as she slid out of his grasp. "Or join me."

"Join you? Out there?" He took a few steps toward the edge of the belvedere and paused to cross his arms over his chest. "It's raining, Miss Brimm. Have you lost your mind?"

"No," she said as her feet fairly flew down the short flight of stairs to the empty rooftop terrace. "For just a moment, I think I've found it. I'll soon return to playing the dutiful daughter and granddaughter and put my mind back where it belongs, but for now I'm taking one thing away from the list of activities that Brimms simply do not do."

"I'm not even going to ask what you're talking about now," he said as he moved to the top of the stairs and watched her waltz around the rooftop. "But know this. If you decide to try and disappear again, I'm coming after you. And I won't care about smashed cakes or falling knives this time."

"Falling knives?" she said as she lifted her face skyward to allow the soft rain to kiss her skin.

"Never mind. And know also that if I see even a hint of lightning, you're coming back under this gazebo thing before—"

"It's a belvedere," she corrected as she opened her mouth and caught a few sprinkles on her tongue.

"Whatever you want to call it, you'll be standing under it again before you can blink twice."

" 'God hath not given us the spirit of fear.' "

"What's that?" he said.

"Just quoting my grandmother."

Lucas inclined his head toward her. " 'Speak not in the ears of a fool: for he will despise the wisdom of thy words.' " He shrugged. "Just quoting mine."

"Duly noted," she said. "Are you coming out here to join me?"

"Thank you, but no. I've had plenty of chances out on the trail to get soaked to the skin and spend time out in the rain when I didn't want to be in it. I can't imagine why a sane person with a place where she could take cover would want to—"

Lightning zigzagged across the eastern sky. "All right, that's it. Back in here now."

Flora opened her mouth to argue and then

196

thought better of it. Instead, she dutifully returned to the protection of the belvedere. While she'd barely felt the rain while twirling around in it, she now realized how much of it had soaked into her clothing. Shivers snaked down her spine as she shook off the drops of rain that had collected in her hair.

"Cold?" he asked.

"No, just a little damp." She nodded toward the remains of their dinner. "Might I trouble you for the tablecloth? I think it will make a passable towel."

Mr. McMinn put the dishes in the basket and then the basket and platter on the ledge. Once the cloth was free, he picked it up and placed it around her shoulders. She offered a smile of thanks before turning her attention to the moon, now obscured by a cloud that rolled slowly past.

He moved closer to stand beside her at the rail. She felt she should say something. Do something. After all, they barely knew each other. And yet she remained quite still. And quite comfortable in his presence.

"So," she finally said, "I'd like to ask that you add this to the list of things you won't tell my grandmother."

"Another secret to keep?" He looked down at her, amusement evident in his eyes, even though the moonlight was nearly nonexistent. "You're making me wonder what other secrets you've been hiding from your grandmother, Flora Brimm."

"If I told you, they would no longer be secrets. And what of you? Dare I ask what you've been keeping from me?"

"That wouldn't be a good idea."

"No?"

She turned to face him, though he kept his attention focused somewhere beyond the roof. Whether he was staring down into the darkened valley or watching the now cloudy horizon for another quick flash of lightning, Flora couldn't say.

What she could say was that the atmosphere had taken a turn for the worse inside the belvedere as well as outside. So she joined him in looking out over the valley, keeping her comments to herself, even when the splatter of rain on the roof became the ping of hail.

"Maybe we should make a run for it," she finally said. "The weather isn't improving out there."

"All the more reason to stay put, Miss Brimm." He nodded to the horizon. "If we tried to go down four flights of stairs in this, we'd be fools."

Flora nudged him with her shoulder. "In that case, we could be here a while."

"Looks that way."

"Have you a chessboard?" She turned back toward the bench, and Mr. McMinn followed a step behind.

"Cute. But, no. It's a shame there are no potted palms up here to look behind. You just might find one."

"Humor. That's a diversionary tactic. It means you have something to hide or you want the topic of conversation to change."

When he did not answer, Flora shook her head and allowed silence to fall between them. A short while later, the combination of the patter of rain and the delicious meal she'd eaten lulled her into exhaustion. As her eyelids tugged closed, she let out a long breath.

"Tired?" he asked.

"Maybe a little." She opened her eyes to meet his gaze, emboldened by the fact she would no longer see him again come morning. "You know, you have beautiful eyes for a lawman. They are a lovely shade of green. Has anyone ever told you that?"

"You're the second person to do so."

"Not the first?"

"That honor belonged to a certain Irish cook." He shrugged. "But for the record, you're much prettier and at least forty years younger."

She smiled. "I just thought you should know. Seeing as how you're intent on not standing out. Those eyes of yours . . . well, let's just say they are counterproductive to your intentions."

"Interesting. I don't believe that fact ever came up during my training. I can't imagine why."

Flora snuggled deeper into the tablecloth that now served as a fine substitute for a blanket. "I'm glad I mentioned them. That will give you something to remember me by when we part ways tomorrow."

"Oh, believe me," he said as he leaned back and let out a long breath, "you've given me plenty to remember you by already." He paused. "Not that I'm saying we'll part ways come morning, though for your sake I hope we do."

Flora bit back the response she longed to give. The one where she told him just exactly what sort of man Will Tucker was and for whom he was working. But to give away his identity as a railroad detective was not an option. Not only would it possibly jeopardize any ongoing investigations her fiancé might be embroiled in, but it also would not speak highly of her ability to remain trustworthy.

And a woman who could not keep secrets had no business being married to a man whose business depended on them.

"You're thinking awful hard about something, Miss Brimm. Dare I ask what that is?"

"I was just wishing I could tell you the whole truth about things. About Mr. Tucker," she amended. "I assure you that when all the facts are heard, you'll believe me when I tell you he isn't at all the man you think he is."

A muscle in Mr. McMinn's jaw tensed. "And I

assure you he isn't the man *you* think he is."

"This is personal, isn't it?"

He rose to move the basket and platter away from the ledge, as the rain was splattering both, though Flora suspected he was merely looking for something to do to buy some time before he had to respond.

Finally he returned his attention to her. "The law is the law, Miss Brimm."

She thought a moment before speaking her mind. "That watch," she said as she studied his handsome features. "You think it belongs to someone you know. That's why you believe it's stolen."

"A man who's been in my line of work as long as I have learns to trust his gut on some things." He paused to settle back on the bench beside her. "Now, for instance, I can look at the night sky and see how hard it's raining and tell you with pretty good certainty that I believe the sun will come up shining in the morning and the rain will all be gone." Another pause, this time to brush an errant raindrop from his cheek. "Or I could look at you and that fiancé of yours together and say that I believe neither of you have spent much time in the company of the other."

The statement surprised her, both at his use of it as an example and at its accuracy. His expression dared her to argue.

"What does that have to do with what we're talking about?"

"Plenty." He swiveled to face her as thunder rolled around the belvedere's interior. "I learned those things from experience. On the other hand, you said I *believe* the watch is stolen. That's wrong. I *know* it is stolen because I've seen the police report. That exact watch, described right down to the monogram on the back, was stolen in New Orleans nine weeks ago."

"You could be wrong—"

"I'm not." He fixed her with a look. "When did you say you met Mr. Tucker."

"I didn't," she responded as casually as she could. In truth, she'd only made the railroad detective's acquaintance some six weeks prior, a full three weeks too late to provide a sufficient alibi for his whereabouts and for the provenance of the watch.

"The look on your face is answer enough, Miss Brimm."

Flora clutched the tablecloth in her clenched fists and tamped down on her irritation. What was it about this man that seemed to cause her perpetual frustration?

She adopted her most imperious tone as she determined to address this ridiculous subject for the last time. "I suppose we will see in the morning, when my fiancé clears up this whole mess with what I am certain will be a simple explanation."

Mr. McMinn's snort of derision was, she

supposed, an answer of sorts. Flora's fingers clutched the tablecloth even tighter as she focused her gaze out into the night rather than allow herself to look at her companion.

"I thought a man sworn to uphold the law was bound by an unbiased search for the truth," she said evenly. "It seems to me you have more than your share of bias in this matter, sir."

Flora waited for his response but heard nothing but the patter of rain on the roof and the occasional splat of drops as they found the few places where shingles were missing. She decided to try again.

"Of course, I understand if you're unwilling to admit you've made a mistake. A man of your experience likely doesn't have much cause to retract his statements or, for that matter, to apologize to persons who have been falsely accused."

This time he not only refused to respond, but he also crossed his arms over his chest and stared out into space rather than admit he'd even heard her. Well, two could play this silly game.

"Wake me up when it stops raining, please. Or if you receive an epiphany and require me to listen while you admit fault." Flora offered her sweetest smile. "Make that faults. I've counted several."

Rather than wait to see if her jab had hit its target, she closed her eyes and pulled the tablecloth up to her chin. By stretching her legs out, Flora found some measure of comfort, and resting her head on the back of the bench provided just the position she needed to happily close her eyes.

"Remember," she said as she felt her limbs grow heavy. "Wake me up the minute it stops raining. I'd much prefer to prepare for my wedding downstairs in my own room."

Instead, she slept through the rain and the sunrise. She discovered this when the sun rose high enough over the trees to shine brightly on her face. Only when she slid the pocket watch out of the sleeping Pinkerton agent's pocket did she discover that she'd missed her meeting with Will Tucker by almost half an hour.

Miss Brimm looked as mad as a wet hen. Groggy from sleep and aching from his choice to sit guard duty rather than get comfortable and perhaps fall asleep—which had happened anyway —Lucas watched her pace the floor like a man waiting for his firstborn to arrive. Then he scrubbed his face with his hand and rose to stretch. "What has you all in a lather?"

Miss Brimm thrust a pocket watch in his direction. *His* pocket watch. "You were supposed to tell me when the storm was over!"

He made a show of looking around and then returned his attention to his companion. "Miss Brimm, the storm is over."

"I know it's over. And so is my wedding unless I can figure out a way to get out of this mess you've caused."

"I've caused?" He shook his head. "You're the one who wanted to have a picnic on the roof. *I* suggested we go back to—"

"All right, never mind," she said as she waved away his protest with a sweep of her hand. "I accept responsibility for talking you into coming up here, but you said you would wake me up when the rain stopped."

"I said nothing of the sort." Lucas shrugged. "As I remember it, I didn't answer you at all."

Miss Brimm's swift change of expression told him he was correct. Then, slowly, she pointed his watch at him, and Lucas took hold of it.

"Stealing another watch, Miss Brimm?" he asked as he stuffed the timepiece back into his vest pocket.

"Never mind," she said as she halted her pacing to reach up to feel the damage the combination of sleep and rain had done to her hair. "Oh, I'm a mess."

Though her just-awakened look with the tangle of curls cascading down her back, the tug of a sound sleep still evident in her eyes, and the wrinkled dress made her look more beautiful than ever, Lucas doubted she would agree. Nor would that imperious grandmother of hers.

"I should have been in the lobby a half hour

ago." She continued to fret with her hair. "Worse, I need to be at the church *right now*. That is, if he's even there. What if he thinks I'm not coming? Surely he knows I wouldn't miss—"

"Here," Lucas interrupted as he spied a pair of hairpins dangling from her once-elegant hairstyle. "Let me see if I can help." At her skeptical look, he added, "I had a younger sister, so I have some experience in the arrangement of a lady's hair."

Lucas stuck both hairpins in his pocket as well as the other three he found as he ran his fingers through her snarled curls. Slowly he coiled one thick strand and then reached into his pocket for the hairpin to anchor it in place.

"Ouch," she said under her breath.

"Sorry," he said as he repeated the process, this time applying a bit less pressure to the hairpin as he slid it into a spot equidistant from the other.

Four more hairpins later, he'd completed his work. Now what to do? She stood close, far too close for comfort, and yet the last thing he wanted was to move away.

"Mr. McMinn? Is something wrong?"

Yes. He'd sat up most of the night watching her sleep. He'd even allowed her to rest her head on his shoulder so as to be more comfortable. And worse, he dozed off himself and missed the chance to catch Tucker as planned.

"Mr. McMinn?"

"That ought to hold," he said as he let his hands

fall to his sides. "It won't fool anybody with decent eyesight into thinking a lady's maid did the work, but at least you won't look like you spent all night on the hotel roof after dancing in the rain."

Miss Brimm whirled around to meet him face-to-face. "I thought we had an understanding about that."

He lifted one brow and waited until she decided to elaborate. In the meantime, he allowed his gaze to slide across eyes as blue as the Arkansas sky. Across cheekbones dusted by thick dark lashes that shouldn't have belonged to a redhead. Finally his attention stalled on soft, pink lips.

They were moving. Speaking to him. Was it lack of sleep that wouldn't allow him to hear or did he just not care what she said? Could have been either.

Or both.

"Mr. McMinn?"

"What?" he said as her use of his name hauled him out of his thoughts.

"We agreed that anything we did up here would not be fodder for discussion at a later date."

He heard what she said. Knew what she meant. And yet from somewhere deep inside him, the most ridiculous thought surfaced.

Kiss her.

Lucas blinked twice. Then twice again. Still all he could think was: *Kiss. Her.*

"Well, let's go," she said.

He stared down into eyes that seemed even bluer than just a minute ago. "Go?"

"To the church," she said as she turned to stalk away. "If I'm to have any hope of getting married, I'll need to get there quickly." She stopped short and turned to look in his direction. "We'll have to leave a note with the kitchen manager letting him know we've left some of the hotel's things up here. I don't want to take up extra time returning them. Is that awful?"

"No." He adjusted his coat lapels and closed the distance between them. "After you, Miss Brimm. Let's see if we can salvage a wedding."

Not that he held out much hope that Will Tucker would be waiting at the church, not with deputies stationed both at the entrance to the Crescent Hotel and at several strategic spots downtown. Last time, his mistake had caused Tucker to escape. This time, that wouldn't happen.

Because if Tucker wasn't cuffed to a deputy or waiting at that church, Lucas intended to keep his fiancée in custody until she could tell him exactly where the criminal had gone. Somehow that prospect seemed a whole lot more interesting this morning than it had last night.

One thing was for certain. He would never get so close to her again that he'd find himself thinking he ought to kiss her.

The red curls he'd sought to repair bounced a

few steps ahead of him as they began their descent. As he watched one pin fall, releasing a curl cascading down the center of Flora Brimm's straight and proper back, Lucas had to remind himself of the promise he'd just made.

No kissing Flora Brimm. Ever.

❈ FOURTEEN ❈

Flora rushed across the lawn and up the steps toward the atrium lobby, only slowing her pace to a more sedate walk once she came close enough to be seen by other guests. Conscious of her wrinkled dress and patting at the mess Lucas McMinn had likely made of her hair, she nonetheless squared her shoulders and stepped inside.

The lobby was almost empty as she paused long enough to catch her breath. Other than a pair of elderly gentlemen playing checkers beside the fireplace and a matron reading a newspaper near the entrance, only the hotel staff appeared to be in attendance.

She reached for her handkerchief to dab at her forehead lest anyone appear and catch her glistening. Ignoring the man shadowing her, Flora did her best to search the expansive space without appearing to be looking for anyone.

"He's not here," Mr. McMinn said when she stopped a few feet away from the front desk.

"I can see that, though I'm not completely convinced he's not watching us from a place where he cannot be seen."

"Such as in the shadows over by the elevator?" He offered a rakish grin. "Yes, I saw you there yesterday. Or maybe he's found a spot behind a large plant somewhere. We both know that kind of hiding place works well."

The door opened and two men of middle age walked in. Their conversation kept them from taking any notice of Flora and the Pinkerton agent. Still, she kept her silence until they were safely out of the range of hearing.

"You're not the least bit humorous, Mr. McMinn."

"And you look as if you just came in from dancing in the rain, Miss Brimm."

Flora tried not to groan. "What an awful thing to say."

"No, actually I like this side of you. And, for the record, there was nothing awful about watching you dance in the rain." He made a show of covering his mouth as if he'd said something wrong. "Oh, I'm sorry. We weren't going to talk about what went on up on the roof, were we? One of the things Brimms do not do."

"You're the worst sort of cad, Mr. McMinn, but at this moment I do not wish to discuss it, you, or anything you've just mentioned." She gave him a look that matched her mood. "If you'll go and get that transport, I'll see what I can find out from the desk clerk regarding my fiancé."

He appeared to consider her statement a moment. "All right, but do you see those two men by the fireplace?" When she nodded, he continued. "If you attempt any sort of escape, they will alert me. Understand?"

While the pair in question appeared to be oblivious to anything other than the checkerboard between them, Flora wasn't completely sure whether her companion was telling the truth or not.

"You're joking, right?"

Green eyes met her blue ones, his expression unreadable. "Do I look like I'm joking? Trust me, there's no need for any sort of diversionary tactics, Miss Brimm. Not right now."

"Oh, go on. I'll just make an inquiry of the desk clerk." Her eyes narrowed. "And I won't leave the building."

He looked beyond her to the checker players and then nodded. "Fine. I won't be long."

"Good. Please hurry." She waited until the door closed behind him before making her way to the front desk. "Henry, could I have a word with you?"

"Of course, Miss Brimm." He grinned. "I figured you would be along soon. He said you would."

"Excuse me?"

"That fellow you were talking about yesterday." He nodded. "You know. The one you and that Pinkerton fellow were looking for."

"Mr. Tucker?"

"That's the one. He was just here."

She leaned closer to be certain she'd heard the ever-so-helpful desk clerk correctly. "What do you mean he was just here?"

"You just missed him, ma'am, not five minutes ago." He punctuated the statement with a wink. "He seemed awful insistent I look out for your arrival."

She ignored familiarity. "Where is he now? That is, where did he go?"

"He slipped out those doors." He gestured to the rear exit. "He said those two fellows at the checkerboard were deputies hired to keep him from an important appointment."

Flora's heart sank. Of course. Mr. McMinn had told the truth.

"But he told me you might try and follow him if you showed up, and I'm to see that you don't."

"Thank you," she said as she turned toward the back of the hotel. A covert glance at the two men told her they were now watching her intently.

"Miss Brimm?" When she ignored him to pick up her pace, the clerk caught up to fall into step beside her. "Miss Brimm, Mr. Tucker left something for you." He looked around and then back at Flora. "I probably ought to go on back to the desk before I give it to you. We wouldn't want to draw any attention, you know."

"Why? What is it?"

He opened his coat just enough to show Flora a slip of white paper tucked into his pocket.

"Is that a note of some sort?"

"Can't say." He shrugged. "I don't ask questions of another railroad man, Miss Brimm. That wouldn't be right. So how about you and me walk over there, and I give this to you all casual-like?"

Flora cast one last look at the exit doors and then nodded. "All right," she said as she followed him back to the front desk.

While he went around to return to his position, Flora waited. Out of the corner of her eye, she spied Mr. McMinn speaking to the same doorman who had handed her over to be handcuffed just yesterday. The checker players had now gone back to appearing engrossed in their game, though Flora doubted they truly were.

"Miss Brimm!" The hotel manager emerged from his office to reach across the counter and shake her hand. "To what do I owe the honor of your presence this morning?"

Flora forced a smile. "I . . . that is, I was just told I had a message at the desk."

"Yes, well, let me check the mailbox for your suite."

The clerk palmed the slip of paper from his

213

pocket, placed it on the counter, and then pushed it toward her. Flora put her hand over the envelope and tucked it into her sleeve.

"I'm sorry but I don't see anything—" The manager saw the clerk and stopped short. "Ah, you've returned, Henry. Did this lovely lady receive any messages?"

"Messages?" He appeared to be thinking. "No, sir. I don't think so. I'm sorry."

"Well, there you have it," the manager said as the clock behind him chimed the quarter hour. Nine fifteen. "There must have been some mistake. If you'll excuse me, I have a pressing appointment. Give my regards to your grandmother," he said as he donned his coat and hurried away.

"Thank you," she said to the clerk once the manager was gone.

Again he winked. "Anything for a fellow railroad man."

The flirtatious gesture made Flora want to call the manager back and report the man. Instead, she smiled conspiratorially. "You won't tell anyone about this, will you?"

"Me? Of course not." He pressed both palms over his heart. "Who am I to stop the course of true love?"

True love. If only that were the case.

"Again, I give you my most sincere thanks." Flora hurried off to find a spot where she could read the note unobserved. She found just the place by slipping behind the kitchen door.

Unlike last night, the kitchen was bustling with activity this morning. Flora pressed her back to the nearest wall to keep out of the way of the staff and reached into her sleeve to draw out the message.

Her fingers shook as she unfolded the page. To her surprise, it was blank. It contained nothing but a pink ribbon, which fell to the floor.

As she bent to retrieve it, the kitchen door opened and Lucas McMinn stepped inside.

"Interesting place to wait for transport, Miss Brimm."

"I kept my promise and did not leave the building."

"This is true. And yet I'm wondering why you're in the kitchen. Asking for the recipe for chocolate cake, perhaps?"

She straightened and kicked the paper behind her, the pink ribbon hidden in her fist. "Well, actually I had thought to use my time wisely by coming in here to inform the chef that he should send someone up to the roof for the things we left there."

"Oh?" His expression told Flora that he didn't believe a word of what she'd just said. "And what was the chef's response?"

"I . . . I haven't exactly located him yet."

"I see. And were you going to tell him yourself

or had you planned to leave him some form of written message?" He bent down to reach around her. When he straightened he held Will Tucker's folded paper in his hand. "Like this one, perhaps?"

"Oh, yes. Thank you." She yanked the page from Mr. McMinn's hand and then reached out to tug on the sleeve of the first black-coated waiter who hurried past. "You, sir," Flora said. "I wrote a note for the chef. Do give it to him, would you? It concerns some items he will find on the roof."

The waiter's eyes narrowed. "I'm sorry miss, but—"

"No, please." Flora hoped her expression conveyed the urgency of the situation. "Take it."

"All right," he said before tucking the paper into his pocket. "For the chef?"

"Yes. The chef and no one else. Thank you," she called to his retreating back. Finally she returned her attention to the Pinkerton agent. "All handled. Do you have the buggy arranged?"

"It's waiting outside." He studied her intently.

"Then let's go," she said as she swept past him. When she realized he had moved no farther than the kitchen door, she turned around to retrace her steps. "We've no time to waste, Mr. McMinn," she said in her best urgent tone.

One dark brow rose, as did the beginnings of a smile. Still he refused to move. "If that's the case, why did you decide to waste time by making this detour into the kitchen, Miss Brimm?"

"I don't know what you're talking about," she insisted. "As I said, I only sought to use my time wisely. Now, come on. I have a wedding to try and salvage. Do you want to be any more responsible than you already are for me missing it?"

"I refuse to debate that point, Miss Brimm. But because I'm certain something's going on here, I'll take you into town."

He closed the distance between them and then had the audacity to link arms with her. As they reemerged into the atrium lobby, Flora spied the clerk watching them. For a moment she wondered what he might think of the convoluted situation.

Then good sense prevailed. "Would you excuse me just a moment? I believe that clerk is trying to get my attention."

"The desk clerk?" Mr. McMinn met the man's stare. "Did you promise him something to get him to let you go yesterday? He may be worried you're leaving before you pay up."

"I did nothing of the sort!" She let out a long breath. "He's just a very nice man who was sympathetic to a woman in distress."

"A woman in distress?" His chuckle held no humor. "Hardly."

"All the same, I really should see what he wants."

"Suit yourself. But just so you know, it has not escaped my notice that you're hiding a pink ribbon in your right hand."

She opened her mouth to respond but then thought better of it. There was no use denying it.

"It had better be there when you get back here."

Flora feigned disbelief. "You're suggesting I would offer a total stranger a pink ribbon? Truly, Mr. McMinn, I fail to see how that makes any sense."

"Well done, Miss Brimm. But it could be a signal of some sort. Maybe a way of letting Mr. Tucker know the coast is clear." He paused to fix the clerk with a hard stare. "Or not clear."

She made a show of walking off in a huff, though her insides were quickly turning to jelly. If the pink ribbon were a signal, she'd yet to decipher a meaning. A glance in the direction of the checkerboard told her the men were now gone.

Interesting.

When she reached the desk, the clerk gave her a curious look. "Back so soon?" he asked, though his attention appeared to be focused elsewhere.

"If Mr. Tucker returns—"

"He assured me he would not."

"All right," she said as her patience threatened to flee. "But if he should, please let him know I have received his message, though I'm unsure as to its meaning."

Henry looked confused. "He said you would understand."

"Miss Brimm," the agent called.

Flora considered adding more to her message but decided against it. Considering the man's uncanny ability to listen in on conversations and generally anticipate far too much, she decided to leave the remainder of her thoughts unsaid.

"Thank you," she added as she stepped away from the desk to join Mr. McMinn.

"Did you get your message passed on to Tucker?" he asked as he escorted her out the door.

"Don't be ridiculous," she said as she allowed him to help her up into the buggy. When he had climbed in beside her, Flora fixed him with a look. "And do not even think of using your handcuffs again, Mr. McMinn. I've kept my side of the bargain, and I will hold you to yours. Do you understand?"

"Perfectly," he said as he set the buggy into motion.

They rode the short distance down the mountain to Eureka Springs in silence. Had she been traveling with anyone else, Flora might have remarked on the lovely shade of green the trees had turned, likely owing to last night's rain shower. Or she might have commented on the freshness of the midmorning air, also likely washed clean by the storm.

Instead, she plotted how she might best escape her jailor should she spy Will Tucker walking along the city street. Or, better yet, if she found him waiting at the parson's after all.

The buggy slowed at the edge of Spring Street, and Mr. McMinn glanced over in her direction. "The plan is to stop at the church just to see if Tucker has showed up. If he's not standing out front waiting, you and I will go in and see the preacher together, and I'll do the talking."

"All right," she said as she looked away. "Though I will remind you again that you're going to be proven wrong once you hear Mr. Tucker's story."

Rather than respond, he snapped the reins and sent the buggy jolting forward. His driving was deplorable, though her ire came more from the way he whipped the buggy around corners and swiftly and skillfully maneuvered around obstacles such as people and slow-moving wagons.

By the time they stopped at the church, Flora was ready to scream. And yet he had done as she asked and hurried.

Definitely hurried.

He secured the horse and stepped around to help her down from the buggy. "Need I remind you that you are still—"

"In your personal custody." She rolled her eyes. "Yes, you have reminded me of that at least a hundred times. Believe me, I'm acutely aware of that fact."

"Are you also aware of the fact that your fiancé is not waiting for you on the church steps?" He gestured to a sign that read OFFICE. "Let's go see the preacher and find out if your man never showed up or just gave up waiting."

"Well, there you are," the pastor said when they rang the bell at the office door. "I wondered whether one or both of you had gotten cold feet." He looked to Flora's companion. "You must be Mr. Tucker."

"No," Mr. McMinn said as he opened his jacket to reveal his badge. "I am Pinkerton agent Lucas McMinn. But I have a couple of questions about this Mr. Tucker."

The pastor ushered them inside and, after offering refreshments, admitted he hadn't actually met Will Tucker.

"That much I figured," Mr. McMinn said. "But how did he set the appointment and obtain the license?"

"I don't handle licenses. You would have to ask the fellow at the courthouse. And a man up at the Crescent Hotel set up the appointment." He paused. "I don't recall him saying any name other than Tucker." The preacher turned his attention to Flora. "I'm terribly sorry you're not going to have a wedding this morning."

"As am I," she said as she rose to walk to the office door.

She was sorry. But why?

Because I said no to your plan.

Flora looked around for the source of the words and found Mr. McMinn and the pastor in conversation, neither paying attention to her. She moved into the doorway. Just beyond where she stood was the chapel, a small wooden structure of simple but elegant construction. The cross at the altar beckoned.

"Just how did this man from the Crescent Hotel set the appointment?" Mr. McMinn asked.

"Excuse me," Flora interrupted, "but if you don't mind I need a moment." She gestured toward the chapel's interior before returning her attention to Mr. McMinn. "You have my word I'll go no farther than the altar."

He seemed surprised. Then his face softened. Slowly, he nodded.

As the men returned to their conversation, Flora wandered down the narrow aisle, past the rough-hewn benches that served as church pews, and up to the altar, where a shaft of sunlight pierced the darkness and spilled warm and golden across the uneven floorboards.

She moved through the sunshine to pause at the pulpit. A Bible sitting there was open to Psalm 23. Flora smiled. This chapter had been her first memory verses as a child, and she still recalled every word.

Only now she correctly stated the last line, while as a girl she'd insisted the proper version was Shirley Goodness and Mercy, two sisters who shadowed the Lord's people and offered holy help in times of trouble. Flora smiled at the recollection of how she'd debated Grandmama until the older woman had finally given up.

Funny how a simple mispronunciation could cause such a difference in meaning. How many times had she looked over her shoulder as a child to see if Shirley Goodness and her sister, Mercy, were following as the Lord had promised? And how many times had she felt disappointment that they weren't?

"Surely goodness and mercy shall follow me," she whispered. "Indeed, Father, I am in need of both. And please don't say no to my plan."

She moved toward the altar, leaving the Bible and its words of comfort behind. There was no rail, no kneeling bench covered in tapestry, no candlesticks of silver and gold shedding light on the place of holiness.

And yet the Lord was in this place. His presence was so close she could almost reach out and touch Him.

Finding the roughly constructed altar first with her hands and then with her heart, Flora fell to her knees and bowed her head. Words failed her, and yet she knew God heard.

How long she remained there, she couldn't say. When she finally tried to stand, her knees had long gone numb.

She rose with difficulty and made her way back down the aisle to the exit and the midmorning sunshine. Mr. McMinn was waiting.

Of course he was.

Now that Will Tucker was officially not marrying her today, there was little to keep the Pinkerton agent from hauling her off to jail and the mercy of the Eureka Springs sheriff. Again she thought of the psalm she'd just read.

Shirley Goodness and Mercy, where are you?

Without a word, he escorted her to the buggy and helped her up. "I suppose you're taking me to jail now," she said when he had joined her on the bench seat.

"Yes, Miss Brimm, that's where we're headed. Whether you remain there is yet to be determined."

❊ FIFTEEN ❊

Lucas almost felt sorry for Flora Brimm. Almost, but not quite.

While her prayer time in the chapel seemed real enough, the fact remained that she was intent on hitching her fate to that of a criminal. And he was just as intent on seeing Tucker pay for the crimes he'd committed.

That was the real reason for his visit to the jail. If the sheriff had sworn out a warrant for Tucker, he'd be more than happy to continue his arrangement with Miss Brimm until the man was caught.

If not, he'd have to decide whether turning her over for receipt of stolen property was sufficient.

If she and Tucker were in communication, the arrest of the woman could bring him out of hiding. Or it could cause him to drop any interest in her and run for the hills—and for his next victim.

Lucas let out a long breath as his mind untangled the threads of possibility. The idea that Will Tucker felt allegiance to any female enough to turn himself in was doubtful. That left only one way to catch him: Stick close to Flora Brimm and keep her out of jail.

A sideways glance told him she appeared less than enthusiastic with her current situation. Not that he could blame her. Whatever reason had caused her to want to buy what Tucker was selling, she certainly wasn't finding any relief for it now.

Maneuvering the buggy into a tight spot in front of the jail, Lucas set the brake and looked over at his companion. To her credit, the woman who had slept at his side last night bore the idea that she might be heading for a jail cell with surprising dignity.

Miss Brimm caught him staring at her. "Can we get this over with?" she demanded.

Lucas weighed his options. If he took her inside, he would likely be required to leave her there. If he went in without her, the odds were she would not be waiting when he returned.

There was only one solution. "Miss Brimm,

I'm going to have to handcuff you again."

"Honestly," she said as she leaned away from him. "What do you think I'm going to do? The sheriff's office is just a few steps away from where I'm sitting. How could I possibly escape?"

"I'm considering leaving you here while I go in and have a talk with the sheriff. If you go in with me, I'm going to have to continue my search for Tucker alone while you spend the night at the jailhouse." He allowed her to think about that a moment. "So, what will it be?"

Without comment, she held out a wrist. Lucas slapped on the cuff and attached the other end to the buggy. "Do not move until I return."

While the handcuff was obvious to anyone who might come close enough to look inside the buggy, from Lucas's vantage point at the door to the jailhouse nothing appeared to be out of the ordinary. Only the stricken look on Miss Brimm's face gave her away as anything but a woman passing time on a sunny May morning.

"Smile," he called to her. "Or someone's bound to wonder what's wrong and inquire."

Her response was swift. Though she added a broad grin to her expression, nothing in her demeanor told him anything had changed.

The woman looked as though she would rather shoot him than take her next breath. Lest she might have a weapon hidden in her skirts, he scooted inside.

"Hello there, Pinkerton man," the deputy called as the door closed behind Lucas. "The sheriff's out the back seeing to some business with the undertaker. He ought to be here in a minute or two, but I'll let him know you're here."

"I would appreciate that," Lucas said as he found a chair. A few minutes later the sound of heavy footsteps told him he was about to have company.

"Heard you'd come by to pay me a visit," the sheriff said. "What can I do for you, McMinn? My deputies didn't catch your fellow?"

"Unfortunately, no. Apparently he slipped out another way, but I do appreciate your sending them and posting the others." Lucas rose to shake the sheriff's hand. "I thought I'd come check on that warrant I swore out."

The sheriff fitted himself into the chair behind his desk. "Had a little problem with that."

Refusing to take the bait or let his disappointment show, Lucas kept his voice neutral. "Did you? Anything I can help clear up?"

"Maybe." He leaned back in the chair and put both boots on the desktop and regarded Lucas with a look that told him there was more than just a little jurisdictional squabble here. "I needed some information about the charges pending on Tucker, so I thought I would shortcut the process by sending for the details of your open investigation. You know, lawman to lawman."

Lucas had a sinking feeling. "You talked to someone at the agency?"

"I did," he said, his gaze never wavering. "There doesn't seem to be an open investigation against our boy Tucker." He paused. "At least that's what the fellow in Chicago told me. Maybe he was mistaken."

How to answer? While Lucas refused to lie, the truth wouldn't get him what he wanted. He decided to take a plot of ground that met the two in the middle.

"It's true, Sheriff. As far as the Chicago office knows, there isn't an official investigation. They have their hands full up there, what with the Haymarket appeals and all." Lucas paused. "In fact, I would wager a guess you were told I'm working on my own time."

The lawman barely blinked. "I was."

Not a surprise, given the man's expression of doubt over the whole investigation. Lucas decided to come clean and tell him the whole story, or at least the part of it that pertained to Tucker's arrest warrant.

"I have a telegram in my pocket from my contact at the agency. Unless you talked to a Pinkerton by the name of Kyle Russell, you're not going to get the full story. He's the one I report to and the man who has been keeping tabs on what I'm doing down here."

The sheriff's demeanor softened, though only

slightly. "Don't believe that's the man I spoke to. Go on."

Lucas let out a long breath as he sent up a quick prayer for favor. And for the ability to convince this man to help him without resorting to deception. There had been enough of that already.

"The truth is, Tucker isn't far from being caught. I was close and I'll get him yet. Resources being what they are right now at the agency, I felt it my duty to use time I had coming to me to bring him in."

"There's still the matter of no official investigation or arrest warrant."

"True. Russell's working on the first problem, and you can easily solve the second."

The sheriff sat up, put his boots on the floor, and rested his elbows on his desk. "I'm a straight shooter, Pink, and I would appreciate the same courtesy from you."

"You can count on it."

"All right." He paused as if sizing Lucas up. "What's this Tucker done?" When Lucas began the laundry list of charges against Will Tucker, the sheriff held up his hand. "No, I have all that in the papers you filed. I mean, what's he done to you personally?"

Lucas sat back and searched for something to say to cover his surprise. "What makes you think it's personal?"

"Son, a man doesn't go to the trouble you've

gone to if he doesn't have a personal stake in it. Now, don't get me wrong. I'm committed to putting men who deserve it behind bars. Trouble is, I don't usually take off from my regular job to go out and do it on my own time." He crossed his arms over his chest. "So I'll ask you again. What has Will Tucker done to you personally?"

Weighing the cost of giving up painful and private information against the cost of letting Tucker go free took only a moment. "All right," Lucas said slowly. "Tucker made some promises to someone dear to me. He stole something precious."

"Jewelry?"

Lucas looked him in the eye. "That too."

"I see."

A shuffle behind him told Lucas someone else had walked into the conversation. He swiveled to see the deputy who had missed work yesterday. "Looks like somebody's feeling better."

The deputy ducked his head. "Not feeling too good about letting you down, sir," he said. "I just wanted to come and tell you that. And to apologize. I was awful sick. Ate something that didn't agree with me. One of those box lunches from the kitchen. That old lady sent it to me, and I figured it would be good, but it wasn't."

He looked the man over and decided he was telling the truth. Hadn't Millicent Brimm wanted to do the same with him? Perhaps his stubborn pride had saved him from a similar fate.

Slowly Lucas nodded. "Yeah, all right. I guess I can overlook it."

"Deputy, would you mind leaving me and Mr. McMinn here alone for a minute? You can close that door on the way out."

"Sure, Sheriff," he said. "And thank you for understanding, Mr. McMinn. I do appreciate that, one lawman to another."

After the deputy had made his exit and the door was closed, the sheriff returned his attention to Lucas. "All right. I'm going to send your man Russell a telegram to see if we can clear up this issue of a case against Tucker. Once I have confirmation of something I can use, I'll see that the warrant goes into effect."

"Thank you, sir. He ought to give you whatever you need to get this arrest warrant active."

"That's all I ask. It would help if you could tie her directly to Tucker."

"I'm sure she's the link there, but you know that."

He nodded. "I also know her daddy's lawyers would have her out of jail and heading home before she could blink twice and turn around. And in the meantime, she'd be instructed not to say a word."

"Exactly. That's why I need to keep her with me a little longer."

"Keep her with you?" The sheriff gave him an

incredulous look. "Son, are you harboring a prisoner?"

"Technically, she's not a prisoner until I turn her over to you." He paused to choose his words carefully. "And being a Pinkerton, I can make a good case for keeping her in personal custody rather than allowing important evidence to go undiscovered due to legal proceedings that her family might file." He paused. "She's much more valuable out there than she is in here, sir. But you say the word, and I will bring her in and turn her over to you."

"Would you now?" He paused to look out the window. "Whether I keep her or let you take her with you, you're still going to be looking for him, aren't you?"

"I am."

"Thought you'd say that." He shrugged. "Go on and see that you don't get into any trouble. If you do, send 'em to me and I'll see what I can do to help."

Lucas stood and leaned over the desk to shake the sheriff's hand. "Thank you, sir. You won't regret this."

"I think there's enough doubt about all this that I'm going to back you on the warrant. I won't issue it until all the *i*'s are dotted and *t*'s are crossed with your superiors, but I have a lawman's nose, and I can tell you something smells in all this."

"It does. I'm grateful for any help you can offer."

"Question is, do you want me to cancel the warrant for Miss Brimm?" He once again seemed to be studying Lucas. "I don't think she would be able to run far if she's in your custody. And I sure don't think she'd be hard to find if we had to go hunting for her."

"You might want to hold off on that a while. If you don't mind, I would rather keep things as they are. A warrant gives me leverage nothing else will."

"I see your point, McMinn. If you change your mind, let me know and I'll take care of it."

"Expect to hear from me." Lucas once again reached over to shake the sheriff's hand. "As soon as Tucker is caught, I'll want Miss Brimm to go free. Unless she's somehow implicated."

"But you doubt it."

"I do. But long as I've been a Pinkerton, I've still not learned how to figure out a woman. So in my book anything's possible until all the facts are in."

"That's the truth. You might want to watch your back while you're on the hunt for this fellow. If he's gone to this kind of trouble, he's either good at what he does or he's not working alone."

Lucas shook his head grimly. "Tucker tends to find the next victim while he's still warming up the current one. It's possible he has another woman under his influence already. Or maybe he's just that good. I know he's left a string of broken hearts in his path. What I haven't seen yet is him putting anyone in danger, so other than the obvious, I don't think he'll harm anyone physically."

Lucas then said his goodbyes and headed for the door. Stepping out into the sunshine, he blinked to allow his eyes to adjust to the bright light.

This accomplished, he walked over to the buggy and climbed in beside a scowling Flora Brimm. "It's about time. I swear, Mr. McMinn, if I freckle from being out here in the sun so long, I will hold you personally responsible."

"If you freckle?" He laughed as he reached for the brake. "That's the worst you can complain about?"

"Oh, never mind. So you aren't locking me up in jail?"

"No, ma'am. I'm taking you home."

"To Natchez?" She held on tightly as he turned the buggy around and headed back up Spring Street. "Whatever for?"

"To catch a crook, Miss Brimm." He spared her only a quick glance before returning to the task of navigating the steep, narrow street. "Like it or not, you're my best bait."

"Best bait," she muttered. "That's not exactly a compliment. I suppose this means our personal custody arrangement is still in effect."

"It is." He paused to allow a family of four to cross the road before setting the buggy in motion again. "Beats being in jail, don't you think?"

"That's not saying much."

Mr. McMinn's chuckle set her teeth on edge, but the events of the morning and the exhaustion tugging at her kept Flora from engaging in any further conversation. By the time they reached the hotel, she was nearly falling asleep sitting up.

The doorman hurried over to help her down, studiously avoiding eye contact. "It's all right," she whispered to him. "I know you were just doing your job."

Relief washed over the man's face. "Thank you, Miss Brimm."

She gave him a smile and then headed toward the front entrance of the hotel. When Lucas caught up with her at the door, she walked past him to step inside without comment.

If she had to travel anywhere, going home was the best choice. Flora decided this as she crossed the atrium lobby. At least there she could find solace with Father . . . unless, of course, he got wind of the fact that she and Grandmama were returning. In that case, he would likely find cause to travel and soon.

A letter. Yes, she would write and tell him she had important business to discuss with him. Letter. Her heart sank as she thought of the previous letter she'd written. The one where she'd summarily announced that she would be married the next time he saw her.

She would have to deal with that, most certainly. But how?

"Miss Brimm," the clerk's voice derailed Flora's thoughts. "Miss Brimm, you have a message."

"Oh, thank you."

Lucas stayed at her side as Flora walked over to receive the note from the grinning clerk. Before she could read it, he snatched the paper from her hand and gave the clerk a look that sent him skittering for the back office.

"I don't trust that man," he muttered as he opened the note and looked down at Flora. "It's from your grandmother."

"Probably a scolding for not returning to the suite last night." Flora folded the page and returned it to the envelope unread. At Mr. McMinn's amused look, she explained. "I'll just hear it again once we're with her. No need to read what she'll likely say."

He escorted her upstairs, where Flora found the door to the suite wide open and three maids doing what appeared to be swift and thorough packing. She walked past them to knock on her grandmother's door.

"Mrs. Brimm has already gone," a maid said.

"Already gone?" Her heart sank. Of course. Grandmama had hurried home to Natchez to prepare Father for the news that was to come.

"You're sure of this?" Lucas asked.

"Yes. Based on what my grandmother knew, she would definitely pack up and return to Natchez once she believed I'd gone through with the marriage to Mr. Tucker."

Mr. McMinn shook his head. "Think carefully now. Are you sure she wouldn't have tried to stop you? Maybe gone to Tucker and had it out with him?" A pause. "Or maybe she returned to the suite last night while Tucker was here. Might they have had words? Could things have turned . . ."

Flora gasped. "Are you thinking my grandmother might have been harmed by my fiancé? That is ludicrous!"

"Is it?" He studied her with good reason, and yet it still felt uncomfortable.

"Yes, it is."

"The ribbon," Mr. McMinn said. "Is it the same one you found on the ledge outside Tucker's window?"

"I don't know, but I can check my Bible to see if the bookmark is still there."

"Yes, do that." He followed her as far as the door and then leaned against the frame as she walked over to the table and retrieved her Bible.

"I don't see a ribbon in here, so I have to assume this is the one that's missing."

"And that he got it when he was in the suite after we left."

Flora nodded.

"All right. I want you to look around and see if anything is missing."

"Honestly, I cannot imagine that my fiancé would steal anything," she said as she thumbed through the New Testament looking for her place in First Corinthians.

He chuckled. "If nothing is missing, I will apologize. But if there's anything even out of place, I want to know about it."

She nodded, though a sharp response was on the tip of her tongue. Will Tucker had no need to steal from her, just as he had no need to gift her with stolen property. Not only did he have a good job as a railroad detective, but he also would receive far more than the price of a few of her baubles once he completed the marriage contract and went through with the wedding.

To suggest anything else was ludicrous.

Finding the book she was looking for, Flora turned partly away from the door and flipped the pages until she reached the thirteenth chapter. Someone had underlined part of verse twelve: *For now we see through a glass, darkly; but then face to face . . .*

Beneath the verse, that same person had placed an arrow pointing to the margin where he had written: *Face-to-face in Natchez. I will find you there and marry you. Trust me.*

"Trust me," she whispered. "Yes, I believe I

must, Mr. Tucker. You're still the solution to everything."

"Find anything missing yet?"

"Nothing yet," Flora responded with the beginnings of a grin.

"All right," he said. "Be thorough but don't take all day. If your grandmother's trunks and her maids are going to Natchez, so are we. And don't even think of arguing the point or stalling for time."

"No, of course not." Flora slid the pink ribbon back into place and closed the Bible. She looked at him and her grin became a full-fledged smile.

"Are you making a joke?"

"No, of course not." She placed the Bible beneath her reticule.

One dark brow rose as he crossed both arms over his chest. "So you're not going to give me any trouble about leaving on short notice?"

Flora shrugged. "You said yourself I was in your personal custody. I'll take Natchez over the Eureka Springs jail any day."

"No attempts to contact Tucker to warn him you're leaving?"

"No," she said solemnly. "If Mr. Tucker wants to contact me, he will."

And he will.

"All right." Mr. McMinn's expression indicated he still had doubts. "I figure it's just better if you and I travel with the maids. It saves the issue of reputation and gives me someone to keep an eye on you when I can't."

"Of course," Flora said. "Though you have my word I will not try to escape."

"In transit or once we get to Natchez?" he asked as his gaze swept over her.

She shrugged as she affected her most innocent look. "Mr. McMinn, I know you're a lawman, but truly you should stop being so suspicious. I want Mr. Tucker found as much as you do."

The truth. What she didn't mention was that unlike him, she had no doubt Mr. Tucker would be found. And likely married to her very soon.

❄ SIXTEEN ❄

The three-fifty train from Eureka Springs allowed passengers to check into the Pullman sleeping car and travel without changing trains all the way to St. Louis. This had proven to be a lifesaver for Lucas. Without having to worry that Miss Brimm or one of her maids might try to escape during a stop, Lucas was free to get a precious few hours of sleep.

At least that was the theory.

"You understand," he said, "that there's nowhere to run on this train?"

She stood her ground, and for that he had

240

to give her credit. "George," she called to the Pullman porter, "when you get a chance, could you turn down my bunk? I'm so tired I could fall asleep right now and not wake up until we get to St. Louis."

"Yes, ma'am," the uniformed fellow said with a grin. "Just let me get a couple of folks settled on the other side of this car, and I'll be back to take good care of you."

Flora Brimm looked up at Lucas, her blue eyes wide and her expression as innocent as a woman that beautiful could manage. "Now, what was it you were saying about running?"

An image of those same eyes looking up at him while she danced in the rain jolted him, followed quickly by the reminder of how soft her hair felt in his hand. How close he came to kissing her.

"Nothing," he managed.

"All right. I'll see you in St. Louis."

Miss Brimm quietly slipped behind the curtains of her sleeper compartment, and he didn't hear from her again the remainder of the day. Sometime after the evening meal was served, he sent a maid in to check on her, but the woman returned with news that Miss Brimm was attempting to sleep. A similar result came a few hours later when another maid was sent in to check on why Miss Brimm did not wish to eat the meal that was offered.

When the train finally arrived at the depot in St. Louis, Lucas breathed a sigh of relief. Then, as he always did, he tucked away the small sense of victory of getting this far safely and began planning for the next step of the mission to capture the individual he was pursuing.

This part of the journey would be the most tricky as he had little control over the goings-on aboard the steamboat. He could hardly confine Miss Brimm to her quarters, though he intended to highly encourage she remain there.

Now, however, he had to get her and the maids and the luggage transported between the train station and the docks without incident. A daunting task, to say the least.

"Miss Brimm, we've arrived. You'll need to leave the train soon."

No response.

Lucas moved closer to her compartment. "Miss Brimm?"

"I heard you," she said without moving the curtain.

"And?"

"And I will leave the train . . . soon."

"I'll just go see to the luggage. Please don't dawdle, though. We have a schedule to keep, and though I know you're Flora Brimm of the Natchez Brimms, I doubt the captain of the steamboat will wait for your late arrival."

He stood near the curtain for another minute

and heard nothing but silence. Shaking his head, he made his way toward the exit.

He stepped off the train into the St. Louis depot with his usual amount of caution. Though he'd never been ambushed in a rail station, there was always a first time.

He glanced around for the Pullman porter and found he'd already collected all the luggage and piled it neatly together. "Thank you, George," he said as he gave the man a generous tip. "And thank you for helping me keep tabs on the ladies."

The porter grinned. "You did all the work, sir. All I did was watch to be sure none of 'em took a mind to leave the train before it came to a stop here in St. Louis."

"That's true, I suppose." Lucas spied the maids gathering near the pile of trunks and bags.

After waiting as patiently as he could, he finally motioned for one of the women to come forward. "Please check to see if Miss Brimm will be joining us in St. Louis."

"Yes, sir."

A few minutes later, she returned. "Miss Brimm will be along directly, sir."

"And when, exactly, is directly?" He pulled his watch out of his pocket to check the time. "We need to be down at the dock right now." Again he beckoned the porter. "Might I trouble you to get the bags and those ladies into a transport so we don't miss our boat? I'm afraid I'm going to have to go in and haul out Miss Brimm by force."

"Goodness, no!" he said, though his expression showed he knew Lucas was teasing. "Don't be claiming that. I'd have to turn you in if I saw you mistreating that wonderful lady."

"Wonderful lady, indeed." Shaking his head, Lucas stalked back to the Pullman palace sleeping car. "Miss Brimm," he called. "I demand you present yourself immediately. I refuse to miss the boat just because a woman in my custody cannot ready herself in time to—"

"All right," he heard her say from behind the curtain. "I'm coming."

The curtains parted and she emerged. Apparently, though she had slept a great deal, she hadn't slept well, for dark circles were under her eyes. As he reached for the bag she handed him, Lucas noticed her yawning.

"Unhappy with your accommodations?" he asked as he slung the bag over his shoulder.

"No, they were fine." Another yawn. "I just don't sleep comfortably in a strange bed. It felt as though there were lumps of coal under the mattress."

"Like the story of the princess and the pea?" He allowed his gaze to sweep over her. "You don't look any worse for wear."

In fact, she looked absolutely stunning. The dress she'd donned was just the right shade of blue to bring out the color in her eyes, and one of the maids had dressed her hair in some sort of fancy style that made her look like the princess he'd just teased her about.

"Thank you," she said. "I think."

"Ready?" he asked for lack of anything else to say. "Or are there other bags I need to carry?"

"No, that's all. I'm ready."

Lucas followed her out of the Pullman sleeper and escorted her to a rather fine carriage pulled by a matched pair of bay mares.

"Where are the maids and all our trunks?"

"Already en route," he said. "There was no need for them to wait while you completed your toilette this morning."

Miss Brimm rolled her eyes as the carriage pulled away from the depot. "I'm not as regal as all that, you know. It's just that I've had the habit of traveling a particular way."

"Is that so?"

"Grandmama had a sleeper berth designed just for me that's dark and has extra padding on the mattress so I don't feel the motion of the train as much." Another yawn. "I'll likely sleep my way down the Mississippi, however. No trouble on steamboats unless I have too much tea before bedtime."

He should have felt bad about his teasing, but instead Lucas counted the infirmity as a plus. If she remained in her cabin, there was little trouble she could find there.

Once they reached Natchez there would be trouble enough. Lucas had a hunch he would find more than just Will Tucker to worry about once they disembarked in Miss Brimm's hometown.

Exactly what, he hadn't yet decided. Still, he had the distinct feeling he was walking into a trap. Before he could think on it long, the carriage had pulled to a stop.

The docks teemed with life, a population overflowing with everyone from baggage handlers and dockworkers to well-dressed men and women in their finery. Women like Flora Brimm.

"All right," he said. "Stay close."

Lucas helped her from the carriage and kept a tight hold on her elbow as he maneuvered her around crates, persons of all colors and ages, and more than a few animals to reach the dock where the steamboat floated at anchor.

She paused to smile. "I don't believe I've traveled aboard this one before. It's lovely."

The cabin-level entrance to the *Americus* was reached through a staircase some two stories in height. On either side of the staircase was an ornate column supporting an arch above proclaiming the vessel's name.

Oblivious to the chaos on the dock behind her, Miss Brimm swept up the stairs with only her handbag and the Bible she'd been carrying since she left the Crescent Hotel. If he hadn't been ashamed of himself for being suspicious, Lucas might have thought she was smuggling evidence of some sort inside the Good Book.

The staircase spilled out onto an oversized carpeted salon that appeared to run the length of this portion of the steamboat and most of the width. Crystal chandeliers as big as wagon wheels dotted the ceiling and marched in two rows above tables already set for what appeared to be a grand supper.

Or dinner, as Mama and Miss Brimm would have termed it.

At the far end of the room was a raised platform containing a grand piano and several stringed instruments. Apparently, meals aboard the *Americus* came with entertainment.

A balcony ran the length of the upper floor and, he assumed, allowed those with inside cabins to look down on the goings-on in the main salon. He'd already noticed the outside cabins had a promenade balcony that ringed the vessel. Given the choice between the two, the lawman would opt for neither. However, he hoped the rooms they had been assigned would offer fresh air rather than the sounds of an orchestra tuning up for the next meal.

"It's beautiful," Miss Brimm said as she came to stand beside him. "If I didn't know better, I would think we were in a lovely hotel in Paris or London."

"Your name and destination, please?" a steward asked as he hurried toward them.

"McMinn. We're headed to Natchez."

The uniformed fellow looked around them and then returned his attention to Lucas. "Just the two of you, sir?"

"I suppose you could say that." Lucas shrugged. "Two of us plus three maids and twice as many trunks."

If the steward thought the statement unusual or rife with sarcasm, he gave no indication. Rather he made a note in the pad he carried and tucked the paper in his jacket pocket and gave a curt bow. "Do come this way, please, Mr. and Mrs. McMinn."

"Oh, I'm not Mrs. McMinn," Miss Brimm protested.

The steward looked down his nose at her, and then he returned his attention to Lucas. He gave the fellow a don't-you-dare-protest look.

"Yes, well, this way," he said as he led them up to the stateroom level. "Our best passengers are on this floor. You'll dine in our dining room and can relax in our well-appointed lounge. I'm sure you saw those on your way up the stairs." His attention went to Miss Brimm. "There is also a ladies' cabin for your use and enjoyment should you wish an environment free of those of the male persuasion."

"Thank you," she said as she pointedly stared

at Lucas. "I'm sure I shall like that very much."

The steward gestured to a pair of doors side by side. "These are your rooms."

Outer cabins, Lucas noted. At least he would have a place to find some fresh air if need be. And then a thought occurred. "They don't connect, do they?"

"They do not, sir, though if you wish I could find a pair of rooms that do—"

"No," Lucas and Miss Brimm said together.

He retrieved the pad from his pocket. "I'll just check to be sure your luggage has been properly stowed and your staff shown to their accommodations. Will you be in need of anything else before dinner?"

"No, thank you," Lucas said as he placed a coin in the man's palm.

When the steward had hurried away, Lucas escorted Flora Brimm to her stateroom. He opened the door to take a quick glance inside. Unlike the lavish attention to decoration down in the salon, this stateroom was serviceable, almost plain.

One narrow bed lined up against a wall while a chair and dresser with a pitcher and washbasin sat across from it. A passenger who awakened during the night need only to lean out of bed and reach for the pitcher, so tiny was the space.

Light poured in through the windows on the door that led to the balcony ringing the upper level of the steamboat. When night fell, an oil lamp that hung over the lone chair would have to suffice.

"Not exactly fit for a princess," he said with a grin. "Should I check under the mattress for a pea?"

"I know you think you're funny," Flora said as she swept past him to place her Bible and handbag on the dresser. "But I think your humor is masking something." She gave him a pointed look. "The question is what?"

Ignoring the question, he stepped out into the hall. "I'll give you a few minutes to get settled, and then I would like you to meet me out on the balcony."

"Why is that?"

"Until this vessel sails, Miss Brimm, I plan to keep you within sight."

"I've told you repeatedly that I want Mr. Tucker found. And knowing what I do about his innocence, why would I risk him looking guilty?"

"Fair enough, but if you're being followed, I'm going to know probably before you do."

"You think Mr. Tucker could be aboard?"

He shook his head. "It's doubtful, but I am not taking any chances."

"Well, you have me next door to you. How convenient."

"Our cabins are side-by-side so I can keep tabs on you. As I said, nothing's going to happen to you on this voyage without my knowledge."

She shrugged. "I'm so tired I could be asleep within the hour, so honestly I don't suppose it matters where you or I sleep."

Oh, but it did. Lovely as she was, Lucas knew the woman could easily invade his dreams if he allowed it. And knowing they shared a thin stateroom wall might make those dreams much more difficult to dismiss.

"I'll be back in five minutes. Don't think of leaving without me. Remember, there is still a warrant for your arrest back in Eureka Springs. Once you're out of my personal custody, you're a fugitive, Miss Brimm. Do you understand?"

"I make no promises," was her cryptic response.

"You're not serious, are you?"

She waved away his question and turned her back on him to reach for her Bible.

Deciding she was properly warned and decently occupied, Lucas stepped over to open the door to his stateroom. Finding a room that was a mirror image of the one he'd just left, Lucas stepped past the bed and dresser to stand at the door leading to the balcony.

He drew in a deep breath of the humid air and then let it out slowly in hopes he could release some of his concerns too. It didn't work. Nothing but catching Will Tucker would.

Lucas thought of Flora Brimm. Of the Bible she carried all the way from Eureka Springs. He'd give his eyeteeth for a Bible about now.

Something that could give him the guidance and assurance he needed that the way he was now traveling was the right one.

That he hadn't gone off on this investigation with revenge as the only motive.

But the well-worn copy of the New Testament he usually traveled with now lay buried six feet under in a coffin made for a true princess. And like it or not, Will Tucker was the reason for it all.

Lucas stepped back from the window with its view of St. Louis and the docks and settled onto the chair to rest his head against the wall. Though he knew the woman who could lead him to Tucker was just on the other side of the partition, he needed to take a few minutes to get right with the Lord first.

Sliding off the chair, he knelt in the middle of the tiny stateroom and laid out all his complaints against Will Tucker, Flora Brimm, and the Lord Himself. When he was finished, Lucas remained right there, keeping his silence until he decided God wasn't ready to talk to him just yet.

Slowly he climbed to his feet and walked toward the door. He could practically reach Flora Brimm's cabin while standing in his own, so it only took a moment to close his door and knock on hers.

When there was no immediate answer, Lucas tried again. "Miss Brimm, open the door, please," he said none too quietly.

Of course she ignored him. First the Lord and now this aggravating woman. Didn't anyone want to speak to him?

Lucas tried the knob, which yielded to his hand. He opened the door and stepped inside. While her Bible remained on the dresser, the woman and her handbag were nowhere to be found. He went out into the hall and turned his attention to the steward at the end of it.

"Have you seen Miss Brimm?"

The fellow's shrug was not the answer Lucas wanted. He gritted his teeth. He would search every inch of this vessel if he had to, and if he did not find Flora Brimm, she and not Will Tucker would become the focus of the investigation. For while Tucker had fooled someone Lucas loved, Miss Brimm would have managed to fool him.

And that wasn't a possibility he wanted to consider.

❧ SEVENTEEN ❧

Five minutes were long gone, and the Pinkerton agent had not yet come knocking at her door. This was fine, because Flora wasn't quite ready to see Lucas McMinn again. Not when being without him meant she did not have to endure his endless attempts to remind her that she was, indeed, in his custody.

Personal custody. And it certainly is beginning to feel a little too personal.

Just what she felt was a matter she tried not to consider. For no matter how endlessly the man irritated her, there was something in the way he looked at her. Something that emboldened her to do things a Brimm just would not do.

Like stealing chocolate cake for a picnic on the roof and licking the frosting off the fork. Like dancing in the rain.

"No," Flora whispered. "I'm not going to think about that."

He said he would give her time to get settled, and then she was to meet him on the balcony. Yes, that was the better plan, she decided.

She closed the stateroom door behind her and walked over to the rail to look down at the activity below. What appeared to be chaos, much like an ant bed stirred up by a stick, was in fact an organized process.

Men carried the remainder of the cargo onto the deck and then reappeared to fetch more. Others carried logs she assumed would fire the engines that turned the paddle wheel. Still others traversed the narrow planking across muddy docks to escort travelers aboard.

It was all so fascinating, not because she'd never traveled by steamboat, but because she'd never taken notice of it before. Always she'd been escorted, either by her grandmother or some other family member. The only other time she'd managed to travel alone, she'd escaped the maid's attention and found her way into the main salon where she'd met Will Tucker.

She wondered now if that fortuitous meeting might have happened had she not determined to give Violet's copy of *Pride and Prejudice* one more try.

"How silly," Flora muttered. "We were meant to meet, and that's that."

The declaration said, she moved down the deck to find a chair where she could await Mr. McMinn. She settled just around the corner from where their rooms were. Not far at all. She was sure it would take him no time at all to find her whenever he was ready.

Flora found the tension easing from her. While the breeze could hardly be called fresh due to the combination of the smells coming from the dock and the scent wafting up from the river below, there was nonetheless something pleasant about being outdoors.

Others must have felt the same way, for the promenade was filled with travelers taking the evening air whether seated in clusters or walking the length of the deck. Minutes passed as she relaxed in the warm sun. She smiled and nodded to a trio of ladies as they strolled past, and then she returned her attention to the docks below.

A familiar figure caught her attention. Was that Mr. McMinn down on the docks having what appeared to be a heated conversation with someone? Flora rose to return to the rail.

Narrowing her eyes, she leaned forward to get a better look. It *was* Mr. McMinn. What in the world was he doing down on the docks with the *Americus* ready to sail at any moment?

While there was little chance he could hear her from this distance and even less chance she would make the attempt of shouting to him with so many fellow travelers nearby, Flora knew she might capture his attention should she move into view and fix him with a stare. Just to be sure, she punctuated that stare by placing her hands on her hips, the universal gesture in the Brimm household for indicating displeasure.

At least it always had been for Mama and Grandmama.

The last of the crew began removing the planks in preparation for departure, while down below a chorus of male voices echoed up commands to fire up the boilers. Still the stubborn man refused to look in Flora's direction.

At this rate, he would miss the steamboat for sure.

The thought caught hold as the final plank was pulled onto the deck, leaving the *Americus* free to depart. With Lucas McMinn no longer sleeping on the other side of her stateroom wall, she was free.

Free from the ridiculous arrangement of personal custody. From the shadow of supposed guilt over some unnamed crime that he believed she or Mr. Tucker or the both of them had committed.

Free to marry Will Tucker right there on the docks in Natchez by the first riverboat captain who would agree to it, should she so desire.

And should Will actually meet her there, as he had promised.

Slowly, she stepped away from the rail to blend into the crowd on the cabin deck. Once again she found a free chair and settled in to enjoy the view of St. Louis in the last rays of the afternoon sun.

Indeed the fresh air and open space worked wonders, for as the giant stacks belched their smoke and the paddle wheel began to turn, Flora felt nothing but exhilaration at her fortunate and unplanned escape from Lucas McMinn.

The city soon disappeared in the distance as the steamboat picked up speed. When a steward arrived on deck to announce that dinner would be served in a half hour, she reluctantly returned to her cabin, where she found a trunk had been delivered and her evening clothes had been prepared in her absence.

The dress left hanging on the hook behind the door was a green silk gown with beading that she could don without assistance, though she soon despaired of her hair and wished for her maid's help. Even the Pinkerton agent had done a better job of taming her curls than she did with her poor attempt.

Finally Flora gave up and returned her brush and mirror along with the remaining hairpins to the trunk. If only hats were in style this season.

A check of her wrist for the time caused Flora to recall the loss of her watch. A watch that would be returned once Mr. McMinn discovered how wrong he was about Will Tucker, she reminded herself. She thought of earrings and decided Mama's pearls would be just right.

A search of the trunk failed to locate them, so Flora opted for a pair of tiny emeralds that dangled from her ears. A pair of bracelets and an emerald-encrusted locket on a gold chain brought the outfit together, though it hardly made up for her poorly dressed locks.

Considering the likelihood that Mr. McMinn had missed the sailing, Flora decided not to wait for a knock that would not come. Instead, she gathered up her evening bag and tucked one last curl into place before walking out of her state-room and down the corridor. Before she reached the entrance to the main dining room, she could hear the three-piece orchestra tuning their instruments over the hum of the diners' conversations.

"Good evening, Miss Brimm," the steward said as she arrived at the double columned arches leading into the area reserved for seating. "Please come this way, and I'll show you where you're to sit tonight."

She followed the uniformed man around a maze of well-appointed tables, noting that a majority of the ladies and gentlemen had already been seated. "Miss Brimm, may I introduce you to your fellow guests, the Lennarts?"

The three women she'd seen promenading on the deck earlier looked up to greet her with smiles as the steward pulled out her chair. Upon closer inspection, Flora decided the trio was comprised of a mother and two daughters, an arrangement that made her think of those times when she'd traveled with Mama and Violet.

Unlike the Brimm ladies, however, these three had not only agreed upon the same fabric and color for their gowns, but they also wore the same style. Tonight that color was a vivid shade of purple, the style decidedly frilly with ruffles and puffs and a heavy decoration of ebony lace around the sleeves and neckline. All three wore matching necklaces of jet and black pearls.

"Welcome, Miss Brimm," Mrs. Lennart said. "What a lovely gown you're wearing. The green in those beads goes quite nicely with your emeralds and that red hair of yours."

Auburn, she wanted to correct, for she'd never liked any references to herself as a redhead. "Thank you," she said instead. "And you three look lovely."

The daughters, who Flora figured to be near her own age, giggled like schoolgirls. "Thank you," their mother said. "Did I understand you're a Brimm? Might you be related to the New Orleans Brimms?"

Flora nodded. "I am. Winthrop Brimm is my cousin. Our fathers were brothers."

"Winthrop Brimm," Mrs. Lennart said thoughtfully as she looked first to her daughter on the right and then to the daughter on the left. "Well, of course. I know him well. My husband has business interests in New Orleans, and unless I am mistaking him for someone else, I do believe he has certain ventures in common with your cousin. Isn't it a small world?"

"It is," Flora said as she glanced at the two empty chairs at the table. "Is your husband traveling with you?"

"Oh, no. He's hunting in India this month. In fact, I thought your cousin was in the hunting party. Perhaps I misunderstood."

Flora laughed. "Oh, it's very possible. For all I know, Winny could be out buying silk in China. I haven't heard from my cousin in ages, I'm sorry to say."

The orchestra struck up a lively tune as the food was marched in under silver platters that looked very much like the one she and Mr. McMinn had used to borrow chocolate cake from the Crescent Hotel's kitchen.

"What about you, Miss Brimm?" the Lennart girl on the left asked. "Are you accompanied tonight?"

"Actually, I—"

"Flora Brimm!" the Lennart on the right exclaimed.

She turned her attention to the girl. "Yes, I am Flora Brimm."

"Oh, oh . . . oh, I thought so. I do know you." She shook her head. "No, that's not true. Actually, I know *of* you through Winthrop."

"I should have mentioned that your Winthrop had thought to call on my daughter," Mrs. Lennart interjected. "I hope you understand, but at the time, well . . ." She leaned closer. "My Eudora had, well, other prospects who were a bit more favored by her father, if you know what I mean."

"That is not true," the girl in question said. "I always preferred Winthrop and so did Father. You know that he was just being awful after he heard the news about—"

"Eudora, hush this instant!" Mrs. Lennart said sharply.

All three sets of Lennart eyes turned to focus on Flora. The older woman's face had begun to turn an interesting shade of scarlet. The other two, however, appeared to suffer no such embarrassment.

"The news about what?" Flora asked gently.

"About you," the other daughter said.

"Delphinia, do stop talking at once," Mrs. Lennart snapped. "Can't you see you're causing this sweet girl distress? Surely the rumors about those poor dead men are just that." She offered Flora a placating look. "I am terribly sorry."

Flora's heart sank. So her fame had spread beyond the Natchez folk down the Mississippi to New Orleans. The ridiculous thought that Winthrop could at this very moment be carrying on a conversation with someone in Bombay who had heard of Fatal Flora came to mind.

"I assure you the entire thing blew over ages ago," Eudora said.

"That's true," Mrs. Lennart added. "I know it because my Martin had no qualms about going all the way to India with the man." She reached over to place her palm over Flora's. "So don't you worry. I certainly don't believe anyone gave serious thought to the idea that Winthrop Brimm might have done harm to any of your fiancés so that he might be the one to inherit the Brimm fortune."

"I . . . I'm sorry. I don't think I heard you correctly." Flora shook her head as her mind caught up to what her ears had heard. "People believe Winthrop—"

"Might have a good reason for stopping your grooms from reaching the altar," Delphinia said boldly.

"Yes, well, I supposed that's one way to put it,"

Eudora added, frowning at her sister. "But I never believed he was a murderer, and I was quite insistent to Father and anyone else who mentioned it that I felt all of those six men—"

"There were only four!" Flora interjected.

"Ah. Well, in any case, I always did believe him innocent, and never once did that belief waver."

"So, Flora, dear," Mrs. Lennart said. "May I call you Flora? You're so like my own girls."

"Yes, of course," she said, her thoughts still rolling around this new information regarding Winthrop.

"Flora, dear," Mrs. Lennart continued as she nodded to the empty seat beside Flora, "I've not asked if you're traveling alone."

"She is not." Lucas McMinn settled onto the seat beside her looking far too smug and even more handsome. He had exchanged his traveling suit for more formal attire, the growth of stubble on his chin for a fresh shave.

Had he been anyone other than the Pinkerton agent who had irritated her with his insistence on things like personal custody and Will Tucker's guilt, she might have allowed herself to be swept off her feet with the mere look of him. A glance at the Lennart women told Flora they certainly had.

"Well, now," Mrs. Lennart said with far too much enthusiasm. "Just who is this handsome man, Miss Brimm?"

"Is he your next fiancé?" Eudora added as

she unashamedly studied the man in question.

"He is *not*." After a deep breath in and a slow release of that breath, Flora was ready to continue. "Ladies, may I introduce Mr. Lucas McMinn? Mr. McMinn, this is Mrs. Lennart and her daughters."

"Charmed. And which of you is Mrs. Lennart?"

Mrs. Lennart beat her girls in reaching across the table in a most unladylike way to allow him to kiss her hand. "Oh, my, but you are quite the gentleman, sir. May I present Eudora and Delphinia, my lovely and currently unattached girls of marriageable age and sufficient fortune?"

"A pleasure, ladies," Mr. McMinn said as he made a great show of kissing their hands, a gesture that had worked so very well with their mother. A chorus of giggles followed. Flora, however, found it difficult not to roll her eyes at the ridiculous display.

"Mr. McMinn, it appears you have won over my daughters. Perhaps you'll do us the honor of paying a visit should you ever find yourself in New Orleans."

"Had you not introduced yourself as their mother, madam, I might have been hard pressed to know which of you was the parent and which were the daughters. I can certainly see where they get their beauty."

He actually said that to Mrs. Lennart, and with a straight face. Flora struggled to keep her own expression neutral as she watched Mr. McMinn completely charm the ladies in less than three minutes flat.

Had the food not arrived at the table at just that moment, it's likely the three women would have continued to fawn over the Pinkerton agent. Instead, while the steward distracted the Lennarts with their dinner selections, Flora seized the moment to speak to Mr. McMinn privately.

"Where have you been?"

"I could ask the same question of you, Miss Brimm." His smile never wavered, though his tone bore an unmistakably hard edge. "I specifically required you to stay close by until called upon and what did you do? You left without waiting for me to—"

"I was exactly where you told me to be, Mr. McMinn." She leaned closer so as to keep from being overheard. "You said I was to meet you on the balcony in five minutes. When I arrived on the balcony you were not there. I did in fact see you down on the dock in a heated conversation with a stranger, but I did not ever find you in the very place you demanded I should be." Flora gave him a triumphant look. "So, I will ask again. Where have *you* been?"

"Ladies," Mr. McMinn said, "would you excuse us a moment?"

"But your food's only just arrived," Mrs. Lennart said. "Are you already leaving?"

"No," he said firmly. "I just need to speak to

Miss Brimm. She's a little hard of hearing and the music . . . well, it's not easy for her to hear me." He gestured to the orchestra. "I'm sure you understand."

"Of all the nerve!" Flora said quietly but fiercely as he attached himself to her elbow and practically lifted her from the table.

She followed him out of the dining room as much because of his grip on her arm as to keep from making a scene. When they reached the corridor, she stopped short.

"All right, Mr. McMinn. That is quite enough," she said as she shrugged out of his grasp. "What in the world were you thinking telling those women I was hard of hearing?"

A steward passed them, his food tray over-flowing. Though he appeared far too busy to listen in, his eyes were trained on them.

"Out here," Mr. McMinn said as he turned Flora toward the exit. He placed his palm on her back and led her through the doors and out onto the balcony.

The night was dark, but the moon cast just enough light on the Mississippi River to cause a ripple of golden water to dance along beside the steamboat. The splash of the paddle wheel and sound of the boiler and the men who fired it was muted up here, combining with the sounds of the orchestra in the dining room and the night sounds on shore to make a symphony worth enjoying.

Unfortunately, being in the presence of Lucas McMinn meant that Flora would likely neither enjoy this nor wish to repeat the experience. So she decided to get the conversation finished quickly and return to the dining room before the Lennart ladies came looking for them.

"Mr. McMinn, I'll ask you again. How dare you tell those women I am hard of hearing? And what in the world has gotten into you? Was there a purpose for bringing me out here or did you just want to reinforce the fact that I am in your personal custody?" She paused but only long enough to take a breath. "Something, I might add, that you were willing to forget about when you left the steamboat while I was waiting exactly where I agreed to be."

The moonlight slanted deep silver across his face, casting his green eyes in shadow. And yet the amusement that touched the tips of his mouth was unmistakable.

"What is so funny?" she asked, her hands on her hips.

"Are you finished?" he asked in that irritatingly calm demeanor he appeared to enjoy.

"You are a most frustrating man, Mr. McMinn. Do you or do you not know that?"

He crossed his arms over his chest. He was standing close, far too close, though the walkway would allow no less. "Yes or no?" he demanded.

"I don't know. I've forgotten the question. Or

questions. Or . . . oh!" The deck shuddered under her feet, and Flora stumbled.

He reached out to grab her just as the railing behind her snapped. Hauling her back from the edge, he pressed her tightly against his chest. Flora looked over at the gaping hole where she might have tumbled into the river or, worse, down to the deck below.

And then she began to shake.

Be it fear or the realization of how close she came to disaster. Or perhaps it was all of the frustration she felt at trying to be a good daughter, sister, granddaughter, and bride-to-be. Or maybe it was just the fact that all of these things had left her clinging to the man whose very presence in her life threatened all the things she held dear.

"Hey, now," he soothed. "Everything's fine. You're fine."

She looked up into those impossibly green eyes and felt his strong arms around her. And then her tears began to fall.

"Oh, no. Don't you dare," he said softly, all pretense of the man-in-charge attitude now gone. "Don't cry. Not here and not now."

"I . . ." Flora blinked but her tears still shimmered. "I'm not crying. Not on purpose."

He held her against his chest, and she nestled against his heartbeat. "Flora," he said after a few moments, his deep voice rumbling against her ear. "Flora, look at me."

She did, moving slowly to stare up at him as he reached into his pocket with his free hand and dabbed at her tears with his handkerchief. "It's clean, I promise," he said.

Flora crushed the white linen square in her fist and once again rested her head against his lapels. For a moment the rumble beneath her feet and the symphony of noises melded together to soothe her. And then, slowly, Lucas McMinn began to move.

To dance.

"What are you doing?" she asked as she fell into step with him.

"I'm dancing in the rain," he said with a wicked grin.

"It's not raining—"

"Funny, but my shirt is wet," he said as he spun her around and hauled her back against his chest. Then he kissed her.

❈ EIGHTEEN ❈

He kissed her.

Lucas held Flora Brimm close, as much to keep himself upright as to buy time before he had to look her in the eyes. What was he thinking? Personal custody did not include acting like a love struck fool.

At least he told himself that as he swallowed hard and dug up the courage to hold her at arm's length. He should say something. Anything. After all, he was the one in charge here.

But her lips were so soft, and her eyes were so blue. And the tears that still dampened his shirt had also soaked right through his ability to think straight.

She looked up at him with a slow sweep of her gaze, finally colliding with his stare. Lips he'd just kissed now turned up in what could almost be called a smile.

"We should go back in there," she said softly. "People will be wondering where we are."

"You're probably right." He took his hand-kerchief from her hand and dabbed at her cheeks and then stuffed it into his pocket. Spying a curl that had come unpinned, he grasped her shoulders and turned her around. "Let me repair this so no one thinks you've come undone because of me."

She glanced over her shoulder, a thick strand of fiery hair still curled in his palm. "And yet I have, it seems."

So had he, but he would never admit to it. "Miss Brimm," he said with his most authoritative voice, "you should turn around now so I'm not tempted to do that again."

With a nod she complied. When he'd repinned that curl and several more that her maid had poorly styled, he turned her back around to face him. "All right, let's go back in."

Another nod and she did as he asked. Without comment or complaint. That's when Lucas began to worry.

He followed her inside. Just before they reached the dining room, he reached to stop her progress. "Miss Brimm," he said when he had her attention. "About that kiss."

She looked up at him, eyes wide, and her expression one of complete innocence. "What kiss?"

Lucas paused only a moment. "Yes, right," he managed as he watched her weave her way through the maze of tables to return to her seat.

If he waited until his heart stopped racing and his thoughts cleared, Lucas was certain he would be standing there like a fool until well past the time the steamboat docked in Natchez. And of all the inventions he and Kyle had created over the years, there wasn't a single one he could call upon to fix what he'd just done.

So he shouldered his pride and straightened his backbone and marched back to the table as if he hadn't just kissed the most beautiful woman in the room. By the time he reached his seat next to Flora, he'd almost convinced himself he could actually pull it off.

"Well, there he is," Mrs. Lennart exclaimed. "Everything all right?"

"Just dandy," he said as he braved a sideways look at his companion. "Right, Miss Brimm?"

"Dandy," she said with what he knew was forced good humor. "Yes, absolutely."

As the Lennart women dug in to their meal, Lucas tried to do the same. And yet every time he spied Flora out of the corner of his eye, all he could think of was how good she felt in his arms, how helpless he felt as her tears dampened his shirt, and how soft her lips were when they pressed against his.

It was enough to drive a sane man crazy. And yet Lucas somehow managed to plaster on an interested look while the Lennart ladies talked on and on about who knew what. He'd just about managed to get his mind back to where it belonged, and then the dessert course arrived.

The steward presented the silver serving dish and placed it at the center of their table. Then, with a flourish, he removed the domed lid to reveal chocolate cake.

Flora started to giggle, a quiet little sound that unless Lucas had been paying attention, he might have missed. He slid her a sideways glance and caught her looking at him.

That's when he burst into laughter.

"Oh, my," Mrs. Lennart said. "I wish you would let the three of us in on the joke."

"Actually, it's not really all that funny, I suppose," Flora said. "Mr. McMinn and I were recently in Eureka Springs. And during our stay there, we had the most delicious chocolate cake, didn't we?"

Lucas stabbed his fork into the cake on his plate and nodded. He might have attempted words, but at that point they likely would have made no sense.

"You and Mr. McMinn were in Eureka Springs together?" Mrs. Lennart asked.

"At the same time," Flora said carefully, "but no, not together. I was there with my grandmother. Perhaps you know her? Millicent Brimm?"

"Of course I know her. Lovely woman, your grandmother."

"Yes, she is," Flora continued. "She suffers a bit from aches that the waters in Eureka Springs tend to soothe."

"So, Mr. McMinn, how do you and Miss Brimm know each other?" Eudora Lennart asked, her attention fully focused on Lucas.

He couldn't resist teasing her. "We met while searching for a chessboard. Isn't that right, Miss Brimm?"

"Don't pay any attention to him," she said. "My fiancé is a mutual acquaintance of ours."

"And now you're traveling together?" Mrs. Lennart asked.

"No," Flora said quickly.

"Actually, yes," Lucas amended. "I'm escorting Miss Brimm to Natchez in her grandmother's absence. Mrs. Brimm had to leave the city early, so I agreed to see to the safe arrival of Miss Brimm and some of the Brimm household staff."

"So this fiancé. Is he one of the dead ones or is this a new man?" This from the other Lennart daughter. Delphine? Or was it Delphinium? He hadn't paid close enough attention to recall.

Whatever her name, this woman's expression told Lucas she was clearly pleased she'd jabbed Flora. Not a good reflection on the woman and, because the other sister and the mother didn't seem to mind the bad behavior, it wasn't a good reflection on them either.

He thought of several possible retorts but decided to remain silent. None of the things he wanted to say to this Lennart daughter would endear him to her or the rest of her family. Lucas settled instead for taking a bite of cake.

"Ladies, this cake is delicious," he said in an attempt to steer the conversation away from the current topic.

"He is my current fiancé," Flora said. "I'm sorry, but would you pass the water pitcher, Mrs. Lennart?"

"Yes, dear," the older woman said. "And, Delphinia, do have some manners. Can't you see it still troubles Flora to speak of her lost loves?"

Three sets of eyes peered at his companion, leaving Lucas free to try and swallow the bite of chocolate cake that refused to go down. One by one, the Lennart females shifted their attention to him.

Apparently it was his turn to contribute to the conversation. And yet he had absolutely nothing worthwhile to say.

"Good cake," he finally managed, which once again set Flora to giggling.

When he could keep quiet no longer, Lucas joined her and soon they both dissolved into full-fledged laughter.

"I wonder if they ever found those plates," she said.

"Plates?" Eudora asked.

Lucas instantly sobered. "Didn't you leave a note with the chef?"

"No, why would you say that?" Flora asked as she reached for her water glass.

He rested his elbows on the table and fixed her with an intense look. "Because that's what you told me. What was that you gave the waiter?"

Again the Lennarts were staring. Again, Lucas felt the pressure to say something to divert their attention. He ignored both.

"Oh. Well, about that." Flora swung her gaze to meet his for the first time since they reached the table. "I did send a note to the chef. That's true. The thing is . . ." She took a drink of water and then another. Finally she returned the glass to the table. "The thing is, the paper was blank."

"Blank?" He shook his head. "Why would you

pass off a blank note to the chef? That makes absolutely no sense."

"No, it doesn't, does it? Now about those elbows," she said as she leaned toward him. "It's bad manners to eat with your elbows on the table. Best remove them."

"I'm not eating right now, Miss Brimm, and you are dodging the question."

"No, what I am doing is merely saving you the embarrassment that bad table manners can offer."

He was not to be deflected. "Miss Brimm, answer the question."

"All right. I cannot tell you why I left a blank note for the chef." She turned her attention to the other ladies at the table. "Have you ever done something like that? Something that you looked back on it after the fact and just wondered what in the world you were thinking?"

"Oh, yes," Eudora said before jumping into a lengthy discourse about the multiple times she or her sister had committed some faux pas or another while in the presence of people whose opinions of her were greatly valued.

Lucas listened in stunned silence as he realized how quickly his investigation into his prisoner's questionable statement was utterly and completely derailed by the women at the table. Finally, he'd had enough.

"Ladies," he said as he tapped his spoon against his glass. "May I offer a challenge?" With all eyes on him and three of the four ladies nodding—Flora abstaining—he continued. "Can we turn the conversation back to the topic at hand and keep it there for more than five minutes?"

Eudora offered a broad smile as she leaned forward to also offer a view of her décolletage. Lucas quickly averted his gaze.

"Anything for you, Mr. McMinn. Now, what was the topic at hand, exactly? I believe I've lost track."

"Oh, that's easy," her sister said. "We were talking about Miss Brimm's fiancés. Remember how angry Father was when he discovered Winthrop might be involved in their deaths?"

Lucas jolted to attention. "What's this?"

"You weren't here when we discussed the matter earlier," Delphinia said sweetly. "You see, Eudora and Winthrop Brimm, that's Flora's first cousin . . . well, they were an item."

"Not exactly an item," her mother chastised. "Winthrop had an interest in Eudora that went beyond a friendship." She turned her attention to Lucas. "It might have been more than it actually was, but with the rumors and then the circumstantial evidence, well, what could a father do but put an end to a romance that might reflect poorly on his daughter?" Her attention skittered to Flora. "I do apologize, my dear, but the truth of it is you're not to be ashamed of things that are not in your control. And whatever was said about your cousin, well, that's neither your fault nor your affair."

"Thank you, Mrs. Lennart. It's very kind of you to say that."

Lucas shook his head. "I'm confused." He turned his attention to Flora. "What are they talking about?"

"Winthrop Brimm is my cousin," she said as she lifted her gaze to meet his. "Our fathers were brothers. While my father chose to stay in Natchez, Winny's father settled in New Orleans. Apparently, these ladies are acquainted with Winny."

"Father is hunting with him in India right now," Eudora exclaimed.

"Isn't that nice?" he said to her before returning his attention to Flora. "But what is this about murder?"

"Oh, that's the best part of the tale," Delphinia said. "Apparently all four of Miss Brimm's fiancés have failed to arrive at the altar for the wedding alive. The reason is cause for much speculation."

"Delphinia," her sister said, "don't be so ghoulish. Every one of those four men met their demise due to natural causes. To suggest otherwise would just be wrong."

"Then why suggest it at all?" Lucas looked to the three women. "Is there any evidence to support this?"

"There was talk that Winthrop stood to inherit should Flora . . ." Mrs. Lennart shook her head. "No, I will not repeat gossip."

The statement almost made Lucas laugh out loud. "Miss Brimm," he said slowly, "you don't know of any reason why your cousin would want any of your fiancés dead, do you?"

"No," she said quickly. Too quickly.

"If Flora doesn't marry and have a child before her cousin turns thirty, Winthrop is the sole heir. His grandfather set up the will that way. Apparently there was some sort of disagreement between Mr. Brimm and his eldest son, Flora's father. He should have inherited." Eudora shrugged as her mother and sister gaped in her direction. "What? It's the truth. Winthrop told me, and he told Father too. That's why Father decided I should find a more suitable suitor. He felt that a woman as beautiful as Flora Brimm would easily find a man who could live long enough to marry her and sire a child." Her gaze went back to Flora, and she said, blushing slightly, "Though you truly have little time left."

The other sister nodded. "Indeed, it can take a while to . . . well, there is an order to things that would cause one to believe three months or possibly four would be the most you could wait to—"

"Enough of that, girls!" Mrs. Lennart exclaimed. "Not another word."

Lucas couldn't help watching Flora during the other woman's diatribe. He didn't have to ask if any of it was true. The look on her face was answer enough.

No wonder Fatal Flora wanted to hitch her wagon to the first star that looked to be sturdy enough to survive. She didn't want to marry Will Tucker. She needed to.

There is nothing awful about the truth being known, Flora told herself as if she might actually become convinced of it. What else had Winny said? Had he thought to charm Eudora Lennart with promises of a fortune he had yet to gain?

"Flora," Mrs. Lennart said, "I'm sorry this dreadful topic has been resurrected. I intend to banish it immediately from the table, and I know my daughters will heed my warning about saying another word on the matter." She looked first to Delphinia and then to Eudora. "Won't you?"

Both women nodded, though neither showed much enthusiasm with the idea.

"Thank you, truly, but you'd be surprised how little this topic bothers me. Honestly, the idea that Winny might have something to do with . . . well, the unfortunate events? That's just ludicrous. And besides, I'm the one dubbed Fatal Flora. I just assumed that everyone blamed me."

"Oh, dear, no," Mrs. Lennart said. "You're a

darling for even broaching the topic, but I assure you that among the better folk of our set you are nothing if not a tragic figure."

Great.

"What I mean to say," Mrs. Lennart hastened to add, "is that you are well bred and impeccably raised, and there's no fault to be found in you, my dear. This I have heard both from the gossips and those who are in a position to know you."

"Thank you," Flora said, though she found the comment uncomfortable. Why did anyone make it their business to know the details of another's life?

To divert her thoughts, she turned to face the Pinkerton agent. "So, you see, Mr. McMinn, there is no mystery here. Winny is not a murderer, and I am of good character."

"Duly noted," he said as he turned his lips into the beginnings of a smile.

Lips she had just kissed. Flora pushed away her plate and placed her napkin on the table, the need to escape propelling her to her feet. "If you'll excuse me, I really should . . ."

Mrs. Lennart shook her head. "Should what, Miss Brimm?"

"Actually," Lucas said as he rose. "What Miss Brimm has forgotten is that while she and I met looking for a chess game, we've not yet managed to play." He gestured to the lounge area just beyond the dining tables. "Unless I miss my guess,

I believe we're about to finally get our chance."

He then offered Flora his hand. She took it without argument or comment. From his expression, Flora could tell Lucas McMinn didn't know whether to be pleased or worried.

"Ladies, it has been distinctly interesting."

Though Flora recognized sarcasm in his tone, the three New Orleans ladies obviously did not. He fawned over each in equal measure and made sure to kiss Mrs. Lennart's hand just as he had when he greeted her.

"Anytime you're in New Orleans, we would love to host a party for you, Miss Brimm," Mrs. Lennart said.

"And do bring Mr. McMinn with you," Delphinia added.

Eudora leaned close. "Perhaps you could bring along your cousin as well? I do miss his attentions."

"Well, that would be up to Winny, but I will certainly tell him of your offer—"

"Oh, no, you mustn't!" Eudora exclaimed. "He would think it awfully forward of me, especially given our issue with Father's lack of approval."

"An issue that's obviously been remedied if the two of them are away hunting in India." A thought occurred to Flora, both entertaining and mischievous. "You know, Miss Lennart, perhaps you should write to your father and ask him to rethink his misgivings about my cousin. He could easily converse with Winny on the spot and solve any differences he might have."

"That's brilliant!" She clasped her hands together and turned to her mother. "Don't you think that's brilliant, Mama?"

"It is," Mrs. Lennart said. "We could perhaps plan a party for Father's return. Yes, that sounds lovely. We shall." A stricken look crossed her face. "But what of Winthrop? Might you also write him as well?"

"I will," Eudora said with enthusiasm as she rose. "I must write him immediately. I'll tell him of the party we're planning and how I met his cousin Flora and she's just lovely."

"Please don't tell him you met me," Flora said quickly. "That should probably be a surprise."

"Yes, absolutely." Eudora kissed her mother on the cheek. "Thank you, Flora. You've been wonderful. And Mr. McMinn, it has been a pleasure to meet you. Now, if you'll excuse me, I have some letters to write." She hurried off.

"Isn't she the lucky one," Delphinia muttered.

"Now, dear, you'll have your turn." Mrs. Lennart offered Flora a shrug and a weak smile. "We can't have everything, can we? Do give your grandmother my best."

"I will," Flora said as she made her goodbyes and then allowed Lucas to lead her away from the table.

"What are you smiling about?" he asked when

they had moved a respectable distance away.

"Just thinking of how Winny will react when that girl's father goes to speak to him about her."

"Come with me," he insisted as he placed her hand in the crook of his elbow. When he paused just on the other side of the dining room and nodded toward an empty table with a chess set on it, Flora looked up at him.

"You're serious?"

He shrugged. "Miss Brimm, we've been looking to play chess since the day we met. Are you seriously saying that now we have the chance, you're going to turn me down?"

"Oh, Mr. McMinn, you have no idea what sort of trouble you would be getting into if you play chess with me," she said as she let go of his arm, sat down, and moved a white pawn. "I was the Dillingham Ladies Preparatory chess champion for three years running."

"Is that a challenge?" he asked as he took a seat across from her and moved a black knight.

"I don't know." She looked out the window at the moon shining down on the river and then back at her companion. "It's a lovely night. Maybe I'd prefer going for a stroll on the cabin deck and enjoy the moonlight on the Mississippi." Flora returned her attention to Mr. McMinn as she slid a white knight forward. "You know, the deck where you were supposed to meet me before we sailed this afternoon."

His brow rose, as did a wicked grin. "The deck where you kissed me?"

"Where *I* kissed *you?*" She lowered her voice. "It was you who kissed me, Mr. McMinn, and don't you forget it."

"Oh, I promise, Miss Brimm," he said softly as he shifted his black rook into place and looked up at her. "I won't forget."

❦ NINETEEN ❦

"Check," Flora said triumphantly. "Your king is in danger, Mr. McMinn."

It wasn't really, not fatally. And though Lucas could see three different ways to capture her king and win the chess game, he was enjoying the woman's company far too much to end things so quickly.

And beyond that, they still had business to attend to.

He moved his king out of danger and then sat back to watch her consider her next move. He did the same, though not with any thought to the game.

Instead, he studied her while he had the opportunity. She was truly beautiful, though that was not what drew him to want to know more about her. This woman of wealth and privilege had something else about her—an inner beauty—which he couldn't quite define. And then there was the thought that he'd met her before. Perhaps in New Orleans or during his days at Harvard.

He knew that was completely impossible, and yet the longer he sat across the table from her, the more he felt the odd sensation.

She looked up and caught him staring. "What? Did I make a bad choice?"

He looked down and saw she'd captured his rook. "No, you made a good one, actually." He countered with his queen and then continued his study of Flora.

Instead of making another move on the chessboard, however, she paused to meet his gaze. "I wonder if you've decided about me yet."

Lucas hadn't expected her to say anything like that. His response took a moment to formulate. "What do you mean?" was the best he could manage.

"Whether I'm guilty of the things I've been accused of." She paused. "I'm just curious as to whether you actually think I could have committed the crime you've sworn out a warrant for. Or are you only using me to get to Will Tucker? I have my opinion, but I wonder about yours."

She tilted her head slightly and a curl slid free to cascade down her back. Lucas's fingers itched to touch it, but he forced his addled brain back to the topic at hand.

"I've already admitted using you to get to him. That's the substance of our deal and the reason you're still walking around instead of sitting in a jail cell."

"I suppose that's true. And I'm helping you because I'm certain of my fiancé and his character. But as to my guilt or innocence?"

"You really don't believe he could commit any crimes, do you?"

"No, not really, though I believe all of us have the ability to make choices to do the wrong thing. That's human nature. However, in this case I am absolutely certain that Will Tucker would not have done what you think. If I could tell you the complete reason why, which I cannot at this point, I believe you would think the same."

There she went again with the same defense of the man for this mysterious unknown reason that would be cleared up when Tucker was cross-examined. What struck him most was her insistence that the man Lucas knew as a hardened criminal couldn't possibly be involved in wrong-doing.

Did she truly not know his past? His gut told him she didn't, and yet if he believed she was being used by Tucker, there was a whole lot more about her he'd have to change his mind about. And right now thinking of Flora Brimm as anything but a potential criminal in his personal custody was dangerous.

His finger went to his lips as he recalled just what could happen when he allowed himself to see her that way. Just as quickly, he let his hand fall to his lap and sent his thoughts back to the topic at hand.

The fact remained, though. Flora Brimm was a dangerous woman whether she was guilty or innocent.

"You're skeptical," she said as she toyed with a pawn. Her gaze lifted to meet his. "My guess is that's a hazard of your occupation."

"It is."

She moved the pawn to take out his knight. "Then I won't take offense. I only ask that you remain fair and impartial, and that you give Mr. Tucker an opportunity to explain."

Lucas wanted to give her a lecture right then and there about the character of her Mr. Tucker. About what he'd been known to do once a woman admitted her complete trust in him. What he could do to her next.

But if he got started, he'd likely say something he would regret. Something that might jeopardize the investigation. So, in the interest of seeing Will Tucker pay for the crimes he'd committed, Lucas chose to take the high road and keep his stronger opinions to himself.

"Mr. McMinn, you seem reluctant to respond."

"I am, but I will admit I'm keeping an open mind." The truth, though he hated to admit even that much of the doubts that had begun to dog him. "Though the evidence is overwhelming. The property you handed over to me was stolen."

"From someone you care very much for."

Her face looked so innocent when she said those words. And yet the insight behind them terrified Lucas. If she could see that in him, what else could she see?

"I prefer to keep the subject on someone *you* care for." He paused. "Tell me about Will Tucker. What is it about him that made you accept his proposal?"

She shifted positions to move her pawn. "If I told you, you wouldn't believe me."

"Try me."

"I had indications he was the one. That's all I'm going to say. And it's your move."

"My move?"

Flora nodded toward the game.

"Oh, right," he said as he slid his king over. "How well did you know Tucker before he became your fiancé?"

He watched as several emotions crossed her face. Finally she met his eyes with what appeared to be embarrassment or regret. Lucas couldn't tell which.

"I didn't know him at all before that day." She shrugged. "I know it sounds completely insane, and maybe it is."

"I never did believe in love at first sight, but if

you want to claim it happened to you, go right ahead."

"I'm not claiming that at all." She paused to move her queen within reach of his king. "You heard what the Lennart ladies said about me. About my grandfather's will. Those women were complete strangers to me, and yet they knew intimate details about very personal issues that only my family should be privy to. You have no idea how often this happens."

"You do appear to be a popular gal, Miss Brimm."

"There was a time I might have enjoyed that. Even cultivated it." Another pause, and this time she looked away. "I just got tired of being Fatal Flora and of having the weight of the family inheritance swinging in the balance between me and Winny. It seemed the easiest way." She shook her head. "The best way," she corrected.

"Do you want the inheritance that bad?" he said. "Bad enough to marry a stranger?"

He allowed that Tucker might be a stranger to her, but only as an experiment to check her reaction. To his surprise, her expression did not change.

"I don't want it at all. But my father does and so does Grandmama. And then there's Violet's welfare to consider."

"Your sister? What does she have to do with all this?"

Flora looked away. "She needs a home and full-time care. I can provide that if I keep Brimmfield. I don't trust Winny to provide for her if I don't."

An invalid sister and relatives scheming to keep what some old coot wanted them to fight for? And here was Flora apparently stuck in the middle. For a moment, his heart hurt for her. "So these people are depending on you to somehow save the farm by marrying a total stranger?"

"Not exactly. Father has no idea beyond what I've written to him, and Grandmama . . . well, she was only recently informed." She sat back in her chair, all pretense of playing chess now gone. "The idea was to wait long enough to become better acquainted before Mr. Tucker and I actually married. To answer the question you will likely ask next, yes, we did intend on eloping in Eureka Springs, though I had hoped to introduce him to Grandmama and to spend a week or two with him before we wed."

"But it didn't happen like that."

"No. Unfortunately, Mr. Tucker was two weeks late, which meant that Grandmama's departure date was nearing. Nothing happened according to plan, though I did tell her the day before . . . well, before we might have wed had I not missed the appointment."

Lucas ignored the barb. "No wonder you were in such a panic the night we met. I don't believe I've ever seen a woman negotiate a fourth floor window ledge in a ball gown as skillfully as you did."

Her soft chuckle was a welcome sound. "I owe that skill to Violet. She was the brave one . . . until her accident."

"The accident that made you the only Brimm daughter who could marry and fulfill Grandpapa's terms?"

"Yes." It was a mere whisper.

Knowing people like the Brimms, who could write in their wills whatever outlandish terms they wanted to manipulate children and grandchildren like puppets from the grave, Lucas didn't ask for clarification. Apparently Grandfather Brimm had set Flora and this Winthrop character up as cousins sparring for the same trophy.

"So, Miss Brimm, if you're willing to marry a stranger to please your grandfather's lawyers, what is your cousin Winthrop willing to do?"

Her confident expression faded. "You don't actually believe that any of what the Lennarts gossiped about is possible, do you?"

"Almost anything is possible." He shrugged, just a nudge and nothing that would indicate any sort of extreme interest in the topic. And yet at the same time, he continued to watch her keenly.

"Possible, yes," she said as she maintained an even gaze. "Probable? No, I don't think it is probable that Winny had anything to do with my current unmarried state."

"As in he didn't kill any of your fiancés?"

"Exactly, though it sounds so harsh when you put it that way." Her expression softened, and Lucas thought it possible that her eyes might have been hiding a few unshed tears. "Contrary to what you likely believe about me, I wasn't always so intent on marrying for anything but love."

"Oh?"

She'd definitely captured Lucas McMinn's attention with that statement. Flora steeled herself for the remainder of the admission she planned to make.

"Believe it or not, I was in love."

"With all four of them?" His tone did not offer the sarcasm she expected, nor did he seem to dismiss her statement offhand.

"Well, not at the same time, Mr. McMinn."

"Lucas."

Flora shook her head. "I'm sorry?"

He leaned forward and rested his elbows on his knees. "Call me Lucas. I think we know each other well enough to allow us that."

"All right. Lucas." She tried out the name tentatively, giving it less emphasis than it felt when she spoke the word. "As I was saying, yes I did love Simon Honeycutt. I'd loved him since childhood. We had a pact." Flora felt a smile rising despite the jab of pain at speaking of Simon. "When we reached the age of twenty-five, which seemed awfully old to us back then, if neither of us had married we were to become engaged. And then by thirty, which was all but elderly by a nine-year-old's standards, we would marry and have one child."

"Thirty?"

She shrugged. "We planned to travel the world first. And five years seemed like plenty of time to see everything at least once. His mother thought the whole thing amusing. Mine thought Simon was my perfect match. So, we were humored. Encouraged, actually."

Her smile dipped slightly at the corners at how simple that all sounded. How very easy it might have been to do as Grandfather asked had things not taken such a terrible turn for the worst with Simon and the fever that took him so quickly.

"If only I had the wisdom of a nine-year-old again," she said softly.

A moment passed as Flora looked beyond the chandeliers and champagne in the dining room to see the beautiful simplicity of the moon floating above the tree line through the high windows.

"What happened to the other three?" His question, though gently asked, still jarred her.

"Being a Pinkerton agent, I thought you'd know."

"I know what the file says." He paused to shift positions. "I'd like to hear it in your words."

"Always investigating."

"A hazard of the job," he said without any sign of apology.

"All right." She let out a long breath. "My first fiancé, Graham, and I were far too young to be considering marriage, but my mother had just died and . . . well, I suppose people marry at seventeen and do just fine. I'm not sure we would have."

When he nodded, she continued. "Graham asked me to marry him while I was away at Dillingham Ladies Preparatory. We wrote the most romantic letters back and forth." She paused to smile. "He was quite the writer."

"What happened?"

"His father and mine had a dispute over the price of indigo crops. Though we'd already announced our intention to marry, Father forbade me to see him." She shrugged. "We decided to run away together."

Lucas smiled. "So you have a history of eloping."

"Well, I have a history of attempting to elope. This one didn't work out, obviously, though it wasn't because the groom didn't show. Unfortunately we only got as far as Memphis. Father hauled me home, though I was none too happy about it."

"And Graham?"

"He wrote me twice promising to come and get me." Flora paused. "And then he stopped writing.

A few weeks later he was found in an alley in a rather seedy part of Natchez. Apparently there had been a robbery, though his body must have been dumped there, for he certainly did not frequent that sort of area. At least not that I knew of." She shook her head. "I didn't want to know the details. I'm sure you can find them easily enough."

"And fiancé number three?" he asked. "How did he meet you and then his Maker?"

She slanted him a look. "I met Alan while visiting my aunt in New Orleans. He and Winny were friends. He died . . ."

"Go on."

She knew what he would think, but the truth was the truth. "He was shot while hunting."

"And who was this man hunting with?"

"Well, there were a few boys from Tulane. He was attending school there."

"Anyone else?" He shifted positions in the chair. "Was your cousin Winthrop hunting with them? Apparently he likes that sort of thing."

Even if she were to deflect the question, Mr. McMinn likely already knew the answer. "He was," she said with a look that dared him to make any further accusations. "And if it makes any difference, I wanted to believe Winny did it. I blamed him at first, quietly and privately, and I think other family members did as well. But we all closed ranks and saw to it that we provided a unified front until the scandal blew over."

"What made you decide it wasn't him who pulled the trigger?"

Flora sighed. "Because apparently Alan was killed by his own gun. The man who found him said he thought the weapon had either misfired or he dropped it."

"Neither are likely for an experienced hunter." He paused. "How long had this man been hunting, Flora?"

"Truly, Mr. McMinn . . . Lucas. Why are you doing this?"

"Because I want to see if protecting people you care about is a habit of yours or just a one-time event that applies only to Will Tucker."

She crossed her arms, closed her eyes, and sighed. On the other side of the room, the orchestra had switched to an upbeat waltz that had people jumping up to fill the dance floor. For a moment, she considered making an attempt to redirect Lucas's attention toward dancing. Or anything other than this macabre topic.

"Let me get this straight," he said. "You lost one fiancé to a mugging. Definitely not something you could have any part in."

"Correct."

"Then there's an unfortunate illness that took fiancé number two." When she nodded, he continued. "And fiancé number three had a hunting-related death that left some unanswered questions."

"Yes, though in both Graham's and Alan's deaths—"

"I know, you believe them to be accidents. Duly noted." He paused. "Now by my count, we have one more. What happened to fiancé number four?"

"Logan was stuck by lightning." She shook her head. "You certainly can't blame Winny for that."

"Nor would I unless the circumstances warrant." Lucas paused. "Where was he when this happened?"

"Actually, he was with Winny. They were riding horses at the time. Winny was unharmed and able to go for help. Unfortunately, there was nothing the doctors could do." She paused. "Having been struck yourself, you surely know how it is with such an injury."

He did. Fortunately, his injuries hadn't taken his life, though it had given him a healthy concern for thunderstorms. Unless Flora Brimm was nearby.

Lucas cleared his throat and returned his thoughts to the question at hand. "So by the time help arrived, courtesy of Cousin Winthrop, Logan was dead?"

She lifted her gaze to meet his. "It wasn't like that—"

"You don't know what it was like, Flora. You weren't there, were you?" She shook her head as he reached down to move his queen. "Checkmate.

Now let's talk about our plan for finding your next fiancé alive, shall we?" He rose and offered her his hand. "Walk with me."

She fell into step beside him, as much to placate the man who was making such awful assumptions about Winny as to prevent any further contact with the Lennart ladies, who were watching from their table.

Just when she expected him to turn right to exit the room, Lucas led her forward to the dance floor. "Oh, no," she said. "I can't. That is, we shouldn't, should we?"

"Flora," he said as he leaned in so close she could smell the scent of peppermint on his breath. "We already have. Twice. But never an entire song without an exit to interrupt it."

Her laughter sufficed as an answer as he whirled her into the crowd. For all his rough edges, this Pinkerton agent was an expert on the dance floor. His touch was light but firm, and they moved through the maze of dancers as if they were the only ones on the floor.

It was exhilarating to be led, to think about nothing but holding on tight while the music flowed around them. When the song ended, she paused to clap, though she truly hated that it was over.

"All right," she said as she made a move toward the exit. "Now we've danced an entire song. Time to exit."

The first chords of the next song chased her, as did Lucas McMinn. "Not quite yet," he said as he wrapped his arm around her waist and slid her back toward him. "I don't know about you, but this one's a particular favorite of mine."

She easily fell into step as the beautiful and elegant strains of "Beau Soir," literally translated as "Beautiful Evening," rose in a haunting melody. "Why, Lucas McMinn," she said in her best boarding school voice, "I had no idea you were a fan of Debussy."

He did not immediately reply, giving her cause to close her eyes and allow the music to once again sweep her away. This song, this tribute to the end of the day with its celebration of youth and happiness, had once been her favorite. Dancing in this man's arms to a three-piece orchestra on a rumbling steamboat's dance floor had once again elevated the tune to that status.

And then he began to sing. Softly at first, so soft that Flora was unsure she'd heard him, and then rising as the song rose. His French was impeccable, his tone a wonderful rich tenor that embraced the French lyrics as if he had lived them himself.

"*Magnifique*," Flora said. "*Je ne savais pas que vous parliez Français.*"

He appeared surprised, almost as if he hadn't realized he had been singing. "Thank you," he said with a measure of what appeared to be embarrassment. "I speak passable French. My mother was . . ."

"Was what?" she asked as she spied the three Lennarts eyeing them with more than a little curiosity.

"A lovely woman." He shook his head and began moving toward the edge of the dance floor. "Never mind. I think it's time to exit." At the staircase, he nudged her toward the door leading to the exterior balcony.

Her heart lurched at the thought of once again standing alone in the dark with Lucas McMinn. A rough-around-the-edges lawman who sang in flawless French and played a decent game of chess. Who knew what other secrets he was keeping from her?

❊ TWENTY ❊

Flora knew one thing for certain. The kiss she preferred to ignore absolutely could not happen again. And in the moonlight, with no one to chaperone them, it was probably not a good idea to keep company with a man who tempted her so.

She was engaged to be married. The fact she did not exactly know the revised wedding date meant nothing. Above all, she must keep her head clear and her heart unencumbered. For eventually she would learn to love Will Tucker. Or, failing that, at least learn to have a long and suitable life as his wife. Thinking of a kiss that set her heart thumping and her toes curling would never do.

And yet, as the recollection of how the moonlight had slanted across Lucas McMinn's handsome features rose, all she could think of was how very soft his lips had felt against hers. How very strong his arms had been as he snatched her back from what surely would have been certain death had she fallen through the broken railing.

To dislodge her errant and disobedient thoughts, Flora shook her head. She also firmly looked anywhere but directly at Lucas.

"Something wrong?" he asked as he held the door open for her.

"No." She saw other couples promenading down the walkway and relaxed. Up ahead, someone had mended the broken rail with some nails and a piece of board. Flora studiously averted her eyes until they had passed the scene of her near miss with trouble.

No, she amended as she gripped Lucas's arm for support as the steamboat shuddered. Trouble had come after the broken rail.

"All right," the object of her thoughts said when they reached an empty seating area at the far end of the balcony. "We are agreed that you and I are both working on the same side in this matter of Will Tucker, correct?"

She looked up at the Pinkerton agent, his dark hair tossed by the breeze and his bowler hat in his hand. If only things were different and Lucas McMinn was not a lawman with a grudge . . . She sighed. Things were not different.

"Flora," he said firmly, "are you in agreement that you and I are on the same side in this case?"

She released her grip on his arm and settled onto a chair. "If by that you mean we both want Mr. Tucker found so he can prove his innocence, then yes."

"Close enough." Lucas paused to allow another couple to stroll past and then took the seat nearest to Flora. "I need to be able to move freely in Natchez society. My contacts say he's there." He appeared to study her a moment. "I know you don't believe he's guilty of anything—"

"No, I don't."

"I want to give him the ability to come clean, Flora, but he has to speak to the authorities for that to happen."

"I understand, and I'm not concerned about any conversation he might have with the authorities. So how can I help in this?"

"When we arrive in Natchez, you will introduce me as your acquaintance and houseguest. In truth, I will be both, so I am not asking you to lie."

"You will be staying at Brimmfield?" Her eyes narrowed. "You do understand that's my grand-mother's home."

"I do, and I will. The other choice is for you and me to find a place where I can securely keep you in personal custody until my mission is complete and I have Tucker." He paused. "Any suggestions on where that might be?"

Flora felt her shoulders sag in defeat. "No, I can't imagine that the gossips would mind telling that tale over and over should you and I . . ." She shook her head. "Fine, you'll stay with us at Brimmfield. Is that all?"

"I need to move around in society. Be accepted. That's where you come in."

"What do you mean?"

He smiled. "I'm going to be introduced as your new beau. That ought to get the job done."

"Absolutely not."

His smile went south. "You have a better plan?"

"I do. You will be introduced as a family friend. Remember, I'm trying to live down a scandal, not create another. And if I'm right and Mr. Tucker is innocent, I plan to marry him as soon as possible." She paused. "It will just set the gossips talking if I marry him after claiming to entertain you as a beau."

"I suppose that makes sense."

"I warn you, however, that Grandmama may prove stubborn." The wind tossed a curl across her face, and Flora tucked it behind her ear. "And we both know that's a distinct possibility."

He rose and offered her his hand. "She's just

going to have to be won over somehow. The question is how?"

"You claim to have a way with her. Maybe you should charm her," she said as she stood and followed him.

"I don't recall that working so well last time." He opened the door and escorted Flora inside. "I don't suppose we could arrange for her to take an ocean voyage of some kind. Just for a month or two?"

She laughed. "She'd never go for it. Grandmama claims she's too old for trips that take more than a few days travel time. I'm surprised she decided to return to Eureka Springs this year. She'd been a little vague on whether she would."

"That would have been mighty inconvenient for you."

She shrugged as she paused in front of her stateroom door. "It turned out to be inconvenient anyway, didn't it?"

"I suppose so." He seemed reluctant to say good night, though Flora knew standing this close to him was far too dangerous to continue.

"I'll bid you a good evening, Lucas," she finally said. "Unless you want to tell me more about your family. Perhaps what life was like before working for the Pinkertons ruined you for polite society?"

His attention jerked to her face, where she hoped her features gave no indication of whether she was serious. Then he must have spied the beginnings of a smile.

"Well played, Flora. But no, I don't think I want to talk about things unrelated to this case. If you'll not have me as your beau, then I don't think my life is worth discussing."

The smile disappeared. "It's nothing personal," she hurried to say. "But I did meet Mr. Tucker first, and promises have been exchanged."

"I was teasing, Flora." He moved over to place his hand on the doorknob of his room. "Tomorrow morning at breakfast we'll talk more about what to expect in Natchez." He'd almost stepped all the way inside his stateroom when she called him back out into the hall.

"Yes?"

"Just one more thing. Please tell me we don't have to sit with the Lennarts."

Lucas laughed. "Table for two it is. I'll be sure to tell the steward."

Long after Flora had undressed and donned her nightgown, she thought about that laugh. About that table for two waiting for her in the morning. About Lucas's offer to play at being her beau. And about what sort of background he might have had. Was he cultured from birth or did he merely affect a background of ease with luxury when the case warranted?

None were unpleasant thoughts, but when she lingered on the memory of that kiss . . .

Flora reached up to place her palm against the wall that adjoined Lucas's room and wondered if he, too, was thinking about their moment together on the balcony during dinner.

Probably not, she decided as she allowed the slap of the paddle wheel against the water to lull her toward the promise of a sound sleep. Men like Lucas thought of much more important things than a kiss in the moonlight.

After backtracking his steps to find the steward and request a table for two for breakfast, Lucas fell asleep with Flora Brimm on his mind. He woke up at least twice, maybe three times, still thinking of the feel of her trembling in his arms after he'd kept her from falling. The thought of her smile as they danced across the floor. Of the kiss they shared.

Finally, somewhere before dawn he gave up on sleeping to wander out onto the balcony to watch the sunrise. As the purple of night faded to the pale orange of day, he went to stand at the door leading into her room. The window had been left open, the curtains teased only slightly by the light breeze.

Inside he could almost hear her deep draws of breath, the soft exhale, and the rustle of blankets. He could have gone back into his cabin and retrieved his hearing device to check for sure, but something about that felt wrong. Intrusive.

So he remained in place, wishing he'd either slept longer or made enough noise to cause Flora to join him. It would likely be another hour, possibly two, before she awakened, and yet here he stood like a fool waiting for her.

Returning to his cabin would only make the situation worse, so he walked down to the sitting area, retrieved a chair, and returned to get comfortable. With his feet propped on the rail, he leaned his head back and closed his eyes.

The next time he opened them, Flora stood over him. A few steps behind her was one of the Brimm maids.

"He snores something awful, Miss Flora," the maid said. "I pity the poor man's wife. She'll have him sleeping in the barn rather than listen to—"

"Hush, Lucy. I think he's awake now."

Lucas stumbled to his feet and did his best impression of a man who had been up and moving for hours. It failed miserably, however, when the maid gestured toward him and then hid her smile behind her hands.

"You want me to call the valet, sir?" she said. "'Cause someone needs to tame your hair, and I'm not so sure it's going to be something you can do without help."

Lucas reached up with both hands to slick down the mop of hair that was obviously showing the need for a comb. Generally his hat kept things under control, but when damp weather caught him unaware, things did not go well.

He met Flora's amused glance. "You do snore," she said as she gave a poor example of how to hide laughter. "But, honestly, I don't mind your hair in that sort of . . ." She shrugged. "Disarray, I suppose, is the word. It's refreshing to know that not everything about you is perfect."

With that she stepped back into her cabin, leaving her maid to gape and Lucas to wonder if he'd heard her correctly. Perfect? Well, now that was some statement.

"Come and help me with my hair, Lucy," Flora called.

"I'll help you all right," the maid said as she turned her back on Lucas, "but I tell you there's no help a woman of my skills can give to that man."

"Oh, come now," Flora said as the door shut behind the maid. "I think it's rather attractive. His hair reminds me a little of that adorable King Charles Spaniel my father once owned. Remember him? What was his name?"

"I can still hear you, Flora."

"I know," was her cheerful response. She came to the door just as he'd picked up his chair to return it. "But I am famished, so whatever you end up doing to get ready for breakfast, be it hat or valet, I do wish you'd hurry."

Precisely five minutes later, Lucas knocked on

her door. Lucy opened it and then scurried past without sparing him a glance. Flora stepped out a moment later. Today she wore a yellow dress sprigged with tiny red flowers that fit her just right, her hair secured in a cascade of curls that teased her neckline. Unlike Lucas, she looked well rested and ready to go.

"Excellent, Mr. McMinn. You are right on time. Isn't it a beautiful morning?"

"It is, Miss Brimm," he said as he escorted her to the dining room. "And other than the prospect of dining alone with me, is that the only reason you're so happy this morning?"

She gave him a look. "Once we arrive in Natchez, this whole silly mess will be cleared up. That's a good reason to be happy, don't you think?"

"You seem pretty sure of yourself." He nodded to the steward, who led them to a table for two as promised.

"I'm confident. But more than that, I'm almost home. And that means something, doesn't it?"

He smiled. "I wouldn't know."

She leaned back to allow the steward to place the napkin in her lap. "What do you mean?"

This wasn't the topic he'd hoped to discuss first thing in the morning. He picked up his menu and pretended to study it. That only worked until she reached over to snatch it from his hands.

"Hey," he said as he made a swipe for it and

missed. "How am I going to know what to order if I don't have a menu?"

"It's a diversion," she said as she neatly tucked his menu inside hers. "Pay attention and perhaps I can be persuaded to give it back."

"I'm listening."

"I have a brilliant idea, Lucas. If you want to meet Natchez society, the best way to do that is to throw a party in your honor. What do you think?"

The last thing a man working undercover to solve a crime needed was to be made the center of attention. What was she thinking?

"No."

Her smile fell. "No?"

Lucas retrieved both menus and placed Flora's in front of her and then went back to reading his. Once again, however, the irritating woman stole it.

"This can work. You just have to hear the whole plan."

Lucas leaned back in his chair to focus on her lovely face. "All right, Flora. Tell me your whole plan."

"Grandmama has no option but to be nice to you in front of her friends. After all, a woman of her breeding would never consider being thought of as a bad hostess. And apparently you do come from quality, even if it is not Natchez people."

She said that in an imitation of her grandmother that was dangerously close to the original. Lucas chuckled.

"And though you're the reason for the party, you don't have to worry about being the center of attention. I promise I'll be the one the gossips talk about the next day."

"How are you going to manage that?"

"That's the best part of the plan." She paused to look around. "Mr. Tucker and I will announce our plans to marry." She shrugged. "Or maybe we'll elope and then announce our wedding? It will all depend on how quickly the irritation of your little investigation is over."

"Flora," he said gently, "if the 'irritation of my investigation' is over, why would you possibly want to give a party for me?" He held up his hand to prevent further discussion. "The point is to draw Will Tucker out of hiding or, failing that, to introduce me to people who may have knowledge about Tucker and his whereabouts. Beyond that, I do not care for any sort of social event either for me, about me, or where I am invited."

He finished his speech and watched for a reaction. Slowly her enthusiasm turned to something else. Was it anger? Not likely.

"No, Lucas," she said patiently, "you're the one who doesn't understand. When I get home and tell my grandmother I am still not married, I do not know what her reaction will be. She may be quite happy to hear it, or she may be upset. But if you're there as a diversion . . ."

Flora looked at him as if he should pick up the thread of the conversation and continue.

"And?"

"And while she's fussing over you and the party we're giving, she will be far too busy to bother either of us. That leaves us free to clear Will Tucker's name so I can marry him."

"Or to see that justice is served and Tucker is thrown in jail."

The idea went against all he knew to be good lawman's techniques. And yet it was just crazy enough to work. Unless Tucker had connections far superior to his own, Lucas doubted the crook would know who he was. He certainly wouldn't know of any personal connections between them. Pride had seen to that.

"He's going to disappoint you," Lucas said. "He always does."

"You don't know that," was her response, though he couldn't help but notice that she put far less enthusiasm into that argument than she had anything she'd said previously.

Flora Brimm had her doubts. She had carefully hid them until now.

And so did he, but not about Will Tucker. He knew exactly what Tucker would do. All he needed to figure out was how, when, and where.

"Will you cooperate with the idea of being the guest of honor? Maybe we could throw another costume party. That would be fun."

"That would completely defeat the purpose of having a party, Flora. Think about it. If you require the guests to wear masks, how will you know which one is Tucker?"

"I would know."

"Well, I'm not committing to this harebrained scheme of yours just yet. I'll have to give it some thought."

She shrugged. "Suit yourself, but don't think too long. Both of us are in a hurry to find Mr. Tucker. I don't see how waiting around and trying to make a decision is going to further that goal."

"As long as you're in my custody, I make the plans. And right now I'm still deciding. All right?"

"All right," she muttered as she turned her attention to her menu.

"Now, about the arrangements at your home. Keeping to propriety means you will be on your honor not to leave the premises without me. Should that occur, you will be jailed for fleeing. Understand?"

"Truly, Lucas, why would I want to run away and risk that sort of humiliation in my hometown? Isn't losing four fiancés enough? I cannot imagine a good reason to leave without you, though I will hold out there could be one."

"Flora . . ." he said, his tone serving a double dose of warning.

"It's the best I'm willing to offer. Take it or leave

it. I'll not lie and give you an absolute promise when I have no idea of all the possible—"

"Fine," he said, holding up his hands to indicate he was done listening. "Have it your way. Just understand I'll not be pleased if you defy me."

"And I'll not be defying you if there is good reason to act in a particular way."

He could have argued the point further, but he knew no good would come of it. The woman was bent on irritating him beyond toleration, that much was plain to see.

"When the boat stops next, I'll ask the steward to send a telegram informing my grandmother of the change of plans regarding my wedding and that you are coming as a houseguest. That way you won't be a surprise."

A nod served as his response as the steward returned to attend to them. By the time the meal was over, Lucas had decided that Flora's plan wasn't half bad. He wouldn't tell her just yet, though. Not until he had a chance to speak with Kyle and get the update on any surveillance information that had come in.

For while they had been taking a train ride to St. Louis and then a lazy float downriver aboard the *Americus*, Pinkerton agent Kyle Russell had his men doing advance preparation that would lay the groundwork for the arrest Lucas knew was coming.

Of course, that was pending the news that the

Tucker investigation had become an official case. With warrants for Flora and, Lucas hoped, for Will Tucker on the books, there should be no reason why the agency would balk at putting a man on the case.

❈ TWENTY-ONE ❈

After the steamboat docked in Natchez, Lucas's first order of business was to seek out the telegraph office to make contact with Kyle. Listing his location as the Brimm home was risky, but Lucas decided it was worth it.

If Tucker had a connection at the telegraph office in Eureka Springs, which Lucas had surmised was a possibility, he might also have one in Natchez. However, there were enough telegraph offices in the city to seriously lessen the odds of walking into the wrong one.

Or the right one.

His mission complete, he went back aboard the *Americus* to fetch Flora and her entourage. The Brimm family, obviously familiar with how Flora traveled, had sent a carriage as well as a large wagon. In all, there was enough room on the wagon to fit the three maids and the luggage, leaving Flora and Lucas to ride alone together up the hill and away from the docks.

They sat in silence, the clatter of the wheels against the uneven pavement making for a bumpy trip. By the time the carriage passed through the ornate gates of Brimmfield, Lucas felt as if his insides were going to jolt out.

But once they were inside the Brimm property, the road was smooth and level. A perk of privilege, Lucas surmised as he settled back against the seat and awaited his first glimpse of Flora's home.

As with most houses that predated the war, Brimmfield was large, lavish, and set up on a rise with a view of the Mississippi River beyond the indigo fields. A quick tour of the interior, gained as he made his way up the stairs behind a uniformed valet, proved the home bore no signs of ill use during the war years.

The walls were covered in what appeared to be silk, and family portraits of men, women, children, and even the occasional loyal hound paraded down the distance between the two floors. A crystal chandelier hung halfway between the two levels, casting light on the Persian carpets and the curved ebony stair rail.

"You're probably wondering about the house," Flora said as she trailed just behind him. "Why we fared so well when others in Natchez did not."

"I was actually."

"That would be my grandmother's doing." They reached the second floor landing, and Flora fell into step beside him. "While she has great concern for the less fortunate, Millicent Meriwether Brimm does not abide interlopers in her husband's family home. Apparently, she told every group of Yankee soldiers the same thing when they arrived on her doorstep. She also paid a visit early to General Grant when he and his men were looking for a home to appropriate for their headquarters."

"Oh, Flora, are you telling that story again?" Mrs. Brimm stepped into the hallway, her eagle eyes trained on Lucas with what felt like disapproval but with her smile showing nothing but welcome. "I simply explained to the general that Brimmfield was not to be touched under any circumstances. I do not allow dirty boots to mar my carpets and uncouth men to cross my door-step in peacetime. Why in the world would I allow it during a war?"

"Whatever the reason," Flora said, "the soldiers bypassed Brimmfield and made their camp at Rosalie, the next plantation down the road."

"General Grant promised to pack away all the furniture and valuables, and he did. But poor Fanny Rumble. She was still finding carpets rolled up and stuck in the attic years after the aggressors went home." A pause. "You just never know when strangers are allowed to stay."

Something in that speech was directed at him. Lucas was quite aware that the old woman's gaze swept the length of him. He surreptitiously checked his boots to be sure he hadn't committed a travesty against the Brimm carpets.

"I wish I could say this is a surprise," she said to him, "but I've had advance warning of your arrival." She shifted her attention to Flora. "Warning but not explanation. Might I have a word when your guest is settled, dear? We've a dinner with the Chamberlains at eight, so do remember to have Lucy put one of your nicer dresses out."

"Not tonight, please, Grandmama. I've only just returned."

"Darling, you're being dramatic. You act as if you carried your luggage on your back. The Ellicotts will be there."

"I just don't want to go tonight." She paused. "I already made plans."

This was news to Lucas, though he half hoped Flora might be bluffing to get out of a social engagement she wasn't keen to attend. In either case, she wouldn't be leaving without checking with him. Much as he would hate to lose his best bait to the Natchez jail, he couldn't have her colluding with Tucker or, worse, running off to marry the crook and then seeing to his escape.

Grandmama appeared ready to respond but unwilling to speak in front of Lucas. For her part, Flora seemed not to care.

"A little warning that you're as yet unmarried would have been nice. Thankfully, your father has not yet returned."

"Should I have sent something so personal in something so public as a telegram?"

Both women looked at Lucas. Mrs. Brimm sighed. "Am I wrong in asking this of her, Mr. McMinn?"

"Honestly, ma'am, I'd rather not say."

She offered her granddaughter a triumphant smile. "Well played, Mr. McMinn." She returned her steely gaze to him. "Is it true that Augustus Girard is your grandfather?"

He paused only a moment. Obviously she knew the answer, so his response would change nothing. "He is."

"A fine man, and quite the dancer. Your grandmother was a lucky woman."

Well, now. Lucas let out a long breath. "I'll take your word for it, ma'am."

He spied the valet standing in front of an open door at the far end of the hall and gave thanks for the means to exit the conversation before it became too personal. "If you ladies will excuse me, I'll just go settle in."

Both women spoke of him though he wasn't even there. "Flora, dear, please tell me you didn't marry that one. Much as I loved a good waltz in his grandfather's arms, he is from New Orleans, for goodness' sake."

"Grandmama, truly you're insufferable. Tell me everything you know about him."

"I'll do nothing of the sort. That man's secrets

are his own to tell. Now, you and I have some plans to make."

Lucas knew a good time to make an exit when he saw one. He left them standing in the hall and moved as quickly as acceptable to duck inside his room. The bedchamber assigned to him bore a man's touch in the dark paneling and deep green curtains that all but blocked out the afternoon sun.

Waving away the valet, he waited until the door closed behind him and then walked over to the window to open the curtains. Fields of indigo danced in the distance, rolling down the hill to the brown ribbon of the Mississippi River.

Another home of similar size—Rosalie, he surmised—could barely be seen on the horizon. The road running between them apparently marked the place where the Brimm property ended. There he spied a small cottage that appeared almost out of place in the midst of the fields.

Wrapped in a simple clapboard siding painted a stark white, the little home appeared far too domestic to belong to hired help. And the purple wisteria climbing the porches front and back made the cottage look more like a hideaway for an aging relative than any sort of service building.

He reached into his pocket for his extra-vision spectacles. While he could see almost every leaf on the indigo plants, the closed white lace curtains of the cottage revealed nothing of what might be inside. Lucas set the glasses aside. Unless he wanted to read the names of the vessels plying the river from where he stood, there was no need to wear them.

A knock on the door announced the return of the valet, who carried a silver tray with a telegram on it. "Where would you like this, sir?"

Lucas gestured to the writing desk fitted beneath the eastern-facing windows and waited until the man had left to retrieve it. The telegram was from Kyle. *WT seen exiting steamboat. Staking out docks for possible sighting. Making progress on calling this investigation official. Hope to advise soon. KR*

If Will Tucker showed up anywhere near the Natchez docks, he would be taken into custody. Let the Brimm ladies enjoy their dinner plans. He had more important things to do tonight.

Lucas folded the telegram, slid it into his jacket pocket, and then went to open his travel case. He'd packed a few items especially handy for nighttime surveillance.

"This is the end of the line, Tucker."

❀ TWENTY-TWO ❀

His pockets now packed with all he needed for a night's outing, Lucas went in search of Flora. He found her on a bench in the garden, her paints and easel laid out nearby.

The May afternoon had grown warm, the breeze so wet with humidity that the very air felt thick. Lucas jerked at the fresh collar he'd just donned and wished, not for the first time, that this investigation didn't require him to dress as a gentleman.

It was his least favorite occupation. One he'd managed to avoid except for visits home and in times like these.

And yet for all his discomfort, one glance at her told him she was right at home in this garden. In the not yet blistering heat. She looked as fresh as a summer blossom in an afternoon gown trimmed in cornflower blue that he would bet matched her eyes. Her flame-colored curls had been tucked up under a little hat that was more ribbon and fluff than substance, and from where he stood he could see she was studying a paintbrush she weighed in her palm.

His boots crunched on the path, but she seemed oblivious. The temptation to stand and just observe bore hard, but there was a case to solve and a criminal who must be caught. Maybe the Lord would grant other times to spend with her—unless she was right and his search had led him to the wrong man. Then she would be married and he would be . . . gone.

That was all he could predict. Life as a Pinkerton man meant you were more gone than home, but it was a noble calling and he'd taken it on willingly.

Perhaps not the whole truth, but it was the truth he told himself.

"You were painting the first time I spoke to you," he said as he walked up to the beautiful woman, who was obviously deep in thought.

When she turned to face him, Lucas could see the remnant of tears on her cheeks. "At least I actually made an attempt at painting something, though I will admit my efforts are poor at best. Right now it's just a pretense so I can be left alone out here."

Lucas sat down beside her. "Didn't work."

A wobbly smile. "No, I suppose not."

He paused to choose his words carefully. "Your conversation with your grandmother did not go well."

A statement, not a question. Something Flora apparently felt no compunction to answer.

"Well, then," he said as he leaned forward to rest his palms on his knees. "I'll be going. I just wanted to remind you—"

"Not to leave Brimmfield," she supplied as she swung her gaze up to meet his. "Yes, I know. Personal custody and all that."

"Right." He paused a moment and then stood. "Well, my errand may take some time, so please don't hold dinner for me."

"Lucas, wait." She placed the paintbrush on the bench and rose. "This is about Will, isn't it?"

"I can't say." That was the most truthful response he could manage.

She reached out to grasp his sleeve. "Take me with you."

Lucas's breath caught as he realized the hint of lilacs he smelled did not come from the garden. That if he were to lean just a little closer, the scent of those lilacs would be every bit as intoxicating as the taste of alcohol once had been.

But he'd given up spirits at the same time he'd given up any right to have feelings for a subject in a Pinkerton investigation.

"No," he managed, as much to quell his racing thoughts as to indicate the Natchez belle would not be accompanying him on tonight's adventure. "I can't," he added as an additional response to both issues.

"Of course you can. I would be of great help to you. I know the city well."

"Not the part where I'm headed." He paused to allow his gaze to wash over her lovely features one more time. "At least I hope not."

Before he could change his mind, he placed his hand over hers. A diversion in the conversation was in order for both of them. "Be nice to your grandmother. I'm sure she loves you no matter what your differences might be."

The beginnings of a smile lifted her lips. "What makes you think I've had differences with my grandmother?"

He shrugged. "I don't know." Lucas lifted his hand to allow his knuckle to brush her cheek. "Maybe the tears you've been shedding out here while you tried to pretend you were painting."

"Is it possible those were tears of joy at my triumphant return to Natchez?" She shook her head. "I'm sorry. The deportment instructor at Dillingham was adamant that we learn sarcasm is never attractive."

Lucas inclined his head toward her. "Your instructor was wrong. You still look lovely despite the sarcasm. Perhaps you're not trying hard enough."

She smiled. "And yet I'm not feeling so lovely. I assume you received your stack of invitations after you settled in."

"I did."

Her soft chuckle held no humor. "Those are for parties being held in my honor." Her wavering gaze landed on him. "Grandmama mustered her friends to begin the round of parties celebrating me. Thank goodness she wasn't specific in what was to be celebrated, because it would be awfully uncomfortable to attend a wedding reception without a groom. That's an exceptionally poor time to not have a date, you know."

"Well, done," Lucas said as he defied logic to inch closer to her. "That was a good attempt at sarcasm. You're looking lovelier by the minute, however, so I'm still going to have to press my argument that your manners instructor was wrong."

"Deportment," she corrected. "But thank you."

"And for the record, I don't have a date either."

She lifted one brow. "Mr. McMinn, are you asking me to accompany you?"

He wasn't, but the idea was a sound one. "Why not? If your grandmother's friends don't know what they're celebrating, maybe we'll come up with something."

"Grandmama told me she hadn't breathed a word about the marriage. Or rather the marriage she thought I'd gone through with." A shrug. "I'm hoping by the time the day of the first party comes around, everything will be sorted out and Will and I can announce our nuptials."

"Yes, well, for your sake, I hope you're right."

Her smile vanished. "So we're back to that."

"If you mean my doubts about your fiancé, then yes, we're back to that."

A steamboat's horn sounded down at the river, its booming sound muffled by the distance it traveled over the indigo fields. And though the Mississippi was close enough to walk to in a quarter hour or less, the distance between Brimm-field and the place he was going was miles—and worlds—apart.

Lucas allowed the river and its late afternoon activities to hold his attention just long enough to brave himself for another look at Flora Brimm. When he returned his attention to her, he realized she was no longer standing nearby. Instead, she'd wandered back to the bench, where she'd once again taken up the paintbrush.

"All right," he said. "You know the rules."

She waved away his comment with a sweep of her hand. After another moment of studying the would-be artist, Lucas turned his back on her and began the walk toward the main gate. He'd barely rounded the bend to follow the path into a copse of cottonwoods when he heard her footsteps behind him.

"Flora, I told you that you cannot go with me," he said as he turned around to face her. "And nothing you say will change my mind."

Likely her deportment instructor would claim that the way she hurried toward him was most undignified, and yet he'd never seen her look more beautiful.

She threw herself into his arms, and as he wrapped her close in a reluctant embrace, Lucas once again smelled lilacs. "Don't hurt him," she said, her cheek pressed against his chest. "Promise me that."

Surprised, he held her out at arm's length. "What are you talking about?"

"He's not guilty until a judge says so. If you harm him in pursuit of your revenge, I will . . ."

A lone tear slid down her cheek, and with it any chance of his getting away from her without some measure of penance. Of all the things he'd become immune to over his years with the Pinkertons, why was it that a woman's tears took him down quicker than a bolt of lightning or the bullet from a man's revolver?

"Hey, now. I've had plenty of chances to harm your Mr. Tucker. So far I've exercised restraint. I want his guilt to come from a judge and jury. That's going to be my ultimate revenge."

Another tear slid down the same path, and so did Lucas's resolve to keep this woman at arm's length. Time to go. He couldn't miss his meeting with Kyle.

And yet he couldn't resist just one more attempt at getting the remainder of the truth out of her—if there was any truth to the reason she was such a staunch supporter of Will Tucker's innocence.

"Just tell me what you know, Flora. I want to know why you're so adamant that he's innocent."

Another tear and Lucas felt his knees getting weak. Behind her the sun had dipped nearly to the tree line, casting Flora's face in shadow and lighting her curls with touches of spun gold.

Despite all good sense, Lucas reached to touch a lovely curl. To wrap it around his finger.

The steamboat's horn once again blared down at the river, and the moment was broken. Lucas released her curl and took a step backward to offer his handkerchief.

"It's clean. Relatively," he said with a wink that drew a grin from her.

Around them the leaves of the cottonwoods shimmered as the breeze kicked up. Lucas looked up at the darkening sky through a canopy of green to spy the first star of the evening.

"I used to make a wish on the first star," she said wistfully as she swiped his handkerchief across her cheekbone. "I always wished the same thing."

"And what was that?"

"All I wanted was a happily ever after." She sighed softly. "I'm still wishing for that."

He shook his head.

"What?" Flora asked as she dabbed at her damp face.

Green eyes collided with hers, and Flora felt the impact all the way to her toes. "I was just thinking that it's hard to believe that someone with all these things the Lord has blessed her with would still want more."

He was right, of course. Mostly.

"I am blessed with a life of privilege and wealth that only a few ever know, Lucas, and I do realize that. I'm thankful, yes, very. But that's not what happily ever after means to me."

In an attempt to divert the conversation to a less dangerous topic, she grabbed his wrist and dropped his handkerchief into it. "It's clean. Mostly."

"Thank you. And yes, that was sarcasm again." He nodded toward the path leading back to the house. "You should go inside now. It's getting dark, and I couldn't help overhearing that you have plans with your grandmother."

An impertinent expression crossed her face. At least that was the impression she hoped to convey. The truth was, after her conversation with Grandmama, she wanted nothing to do with Natchez society until she could return to it with a husband on her arm.

Or a complete explanation.

And right now she had neither. But if he had a plan for the evening, then maybe she did too.

"I wouldn't dream of going out with Grandmama tonight. Not when I've promised you I would stay right here at Brimmfield unless you accompany me."

"Prearranged excursions are allowed as long as I approve them."

"So you wouldn't mind if I went into Natchez?"

He gave her a sideways look. "To the

Chamberlains with your grandmother at eight? The Ellicotts will be there."

"You listen far too closely to my grandmother."

"And I don't think you listen enough." A muscle clenched in his jaw.

She paused to size up her adversary. If he'd just let her accompany him, they would have a much greater chance of finding Will. An idea dawned. "You know, you're right. I really should listen more."

Of course, he had no idea what her grandmother had been advising her. He would have been surprised, to say the least.

"Is this more sarcasm?"

"No, this is my grandmother's wisdom. Know when to pursue and when to retreat. So now that you've bested me in this argument, might I suggest you use one of our buggies to go into town? It would prove much faster than walking." She paused just long enough to make him believe she was speaking off the cuff. "Or you could have one of our men drive you in and drop you wherever you'd like." A shrug, nonchalant and yet not too casual. "Then you would arrive unseen."

He crossed his arms over his chest. "You're awfully helpful all of a sudden."

"Again, Grandmama's wisdom."

"Know when to pursue and when to retreat? Or did she tell you something else?"

Flora smiled congenially. "Yes and yes. Now, if

you're intent on walking, good luck. If you'd prefer the use of one of the Brimm vehicles, I can arrange it."

"Or you can go get ready for your party and I'll arrange things myself."

He caught her by the elbow and set her in motion. She went willingly, though she would never hint at the fact she could have resisted and left him stranded. Or that she might have mentioned that he was going the wrong way.

After a few minutes, Lucas stopped to look around. "We're not going toward the barn, are we?"

Flora smiled. "Father prefers to call it the carriage house, but no, we're not."

"And it's almost dark."

She shrugged. "*Apparement*," she said in her best French just to see if he might respond in kind. Instead, he ignored her.

Oh, my, but he is handsome, especially when befuddled.

He let out a long breath as he reached into his jacket and retrieved an odd-looking brass sphere. A flick of his wrist and the top of the sphere slid back to reveal some sort of glass covering. "This way, Flora," he said as he turned and headed in the correct direction, leaving her to follow.

As the carriage house came into view, Flora caught up. "Nicely done. What sort of device is that?"

"A direction finder," he said as he slid the covering back on the orb and returned it to his pocket. "Rather than using magnetic north as a compass would, my device can discern size based on heat and other factors and allow the user to decide where . . ." He shook his head. "Never mind. It got us here, and that's what counts."

"Yes, it does. What other inventions do you have in your coat pocket?"

"Other than the personal torch and spectacles, which you've seen? I have climbing spikes, a hearing device, and a bullet for my revolver that contains a filament line for . . . Well, never mind."

"You're an interesting man, Lucas McMinn of the New Orleans Girards." She paused to make one last plea. "Only a smart man would think up things like that. So, since you're a man of high intelligence, I'll ask you again to take me with you this evening. I promise I will do exactly as you say and stay out of your way."

"You will?" he asked as he leaned closer. "Promise?"

"I promise," she said with a smile. "Definitely promise."

"Flora?" He lightly grazed her cheek with his knuckle. "No."

"Oh!" She swatted in his direction, but he easily deflected her blow. "You're insufferable. Completely and utterly insufferable!"

He had the audacity to laugh. "Yes, I am. Now go inside or I will think you're planning to follow me."

Then he had the nerve to stand right there and watch as she turned and stormed off. Of course, she played up her irritation to the hilt. What he did not know was that while she'd earned championship honors in chess at Dillingham Ladies Preparatory, she had also been named Thespian of the Year. An honor she would have won all over again had her classmates seen her performance as she played an obedient but defeated damsel.

❄ TWENTY-THREE ❄

Natchez Under-the-Hill was poor relation to its wealthier and safer cousin up on the bluff, a fact that caused Lucas to keep one hand on the reins and the other on his revolver until he'd safely parked the borrowed rig. If he was lucky, he wouldn't have to buy Mrs. Brimm another horse and buggy to replace this one.

Keeping to the shadows, Lucas easily found the place where Kyle was waiting. Situated next to the telegraph office, the bar was seedy, even for this part of town, and filled wall-to-wall with fresh-off-the-steamboat river rat types and the women who were paid to pretend an interest in them.

Though his best friend and cohort at the agency wore clothing no different than the other toughs who frequented this sort of place, Lucas would have recognized him anywhere. Such was the bond of friendship, and theirs had been forged over years and miles.

"You're making some folks at the agency awful skittish," Kyle told him when Lucas settled down beside him at a table with a clear view of the door.

Lucas chuckled as he glanced around, half expecting Flora to be hiding in some dark corner. "What's the verdict? Did the boss send you here to tell me I'm fired?"

"That was one of the options." He paused to glance up at three potential jailbirds as they walked in. "A promotion was the other," he said when the trio passed by them to find places at the bar.

"I'm guessing you're here to tell me either could happen at this point."

"You're right, but I also have a little good news. Thanks to the warrant sworn out in Eureka Springs, an official case has been opened."

Lucas swallowed the whoop of joy that likely would have gotten them shot or stabbed. "That *is* good news," he said instead.

"The boss wasn't keen on it, but apparently

someone above him in the Chicago office vetoed him. The news isn't all good, though. The other message I was sent to deliver is that you have three weeks to bring Tucker in and make the charges against him stick."

Three weeks wasn't nearly enough time should Tucker slip past him here in Natchez to escape again. And yet Lucas knew he would manage it somehow. He hadn't come this far to fail.

Still, Tucker had proven how elusive he could be. "And if I don't?"

"Case closed. And you're either on to something else or . . ."

"Fired?"

Kyle shook his head. "I prefer to think of it as reassigned. I hear the railroads are hiring men with detective work experience."

"Duly noted."

Lucas's friend leaned forward. "Any more news on Tucker?"

"I had a quick meeting with a telegraph man who swore he'd seen him. Said Tucker sent a message here to Natchez." He paused. "He claimed he couldn't remember the name of the recipient."

"They never do."

Lucas shifted positions to steal a glance at the door. When he returned his attention to Kyle, he said, "He did recall the message was that he'd be seeing the recipient soon."

"So there'll be a wedding after all?"

Everything about that idea sat poorly with Lucas. "Could be," he said, though he knew he would do everything in his power to keep that from happening. Despite Flora's penchant for irritating him beyond his tolerance, Lucas had developed a fondness for her. He would certainly not like to see her hurt by Tucker.

"Give me a rundown of any new facts," Kyle said. "I'll need a description if you have it, and any contacts you know of."

"The facts are the same. Flora still believes he is innocent, and—"

"Flora, is it?"

Lucas ignored the friendly jab as something he deserved. After all, the two of them had a long history of teasing each other that dated back to their school years. "She's in custody and nothing more," he asserted. "As I was saying, she claims she can find him. She also tells me there's a good reason why he's innocent, and if I will just hear his story I'll understand."

Lucas shook his head, and Kyle did the same. "Typical woman covering for her man?"

"No. There's nothing typical about this one."

"I'll take your word for it." Kyle glanced around and pulled an envelope from his coat and pressed it across the table to Lucas. "From the department. For expenses."

Lucas shook his head. "I can't take this. You keep it."

"But it's yours, Lucas. You're getting paid for this now."

"Actually, I will keep it, but I'm going to use it to hire you."

"Hire me?" Kyle's brows gathered. "What for?"

"I need to know what you can dig up on Winthrop Brimm. He lives in New Orleans, but he's a few years younger than us. It's likely you've never heard of him."

Kyle thought a minute. "No, I don't think I know him, but my brother might. What's the connection?"

"He's first cousin to Flora—"

"The pretty redhead you have in custody?"

"How did you know she's a redhead?"

Kyle grinned as he slid the envelope discreetly back into his pocket. "Don't look now, but there's a woman who doesn't belong in this bar trying real hard to look as though she does. And she's a redhead."

Lucas's temper flared. "What's she doing?"

His friend casually leaned slightly to the left, apparently to get a better look. "It appears she's in conversation with an older fellow. From the looks of him, I believe he's the head telegraph operator from next door."

"Interesting."

"Yes, she is," Kyle said before swinging his attention back to Lucas. "Give me a quick run-down on Winthrop Brimm before you have to leave to fetch your prisoner."

Lucas shook his head as irritation rose. It was bad enough that he had to deal with Flora tonight, but for his best friend to see how little control he had over a prisoner irked him even more. He gave Kyle the story in as brief a form as he could manage, given his Flora-induced current issue with concentration.

"Get what you can on old man Brimm's will. The grandfather, that is. Apparently, he's somehow managed to pit the two cousins against each other, and the stakes are high enough that Winthrop may have killed for them. They're certainly high enough that Flora—that is, Miss Brimm—is willing to marry Will Tucker to come out the winner in the matter."

He briefly filled Kyle in on the tale of Flora's four fiancés as best as he could recall and then eased a glance toward the door. Sure enough, she was dressed in an odd combination of working-man's cloak and workingwoman's dress. Keeping to some version of modesty, however, Flora had filled in her risqué décolletage with, of all things, what looked like a doily off of somebody's tabletop.

"Tell me the names of any Brimm relatives you can think of," his friend said, drawing Lucas's attention back in his direction.

"Grandmother is Millicent Meriwether Brimm, and trust me when I warn you to steer clear of her." He leaned forward. "Runs the family, that one, and does exactly what she pleases. She even claims to have sent General Grant packing when he came calling to borrow Brimmfield for his headquarters during the war. Though there was nothing she could do to circumvent her husband's will. I'm guessing that irks her something awful."

"Well, that sounds like a matter worth investigating." Kyle retrieved a pencil and paper from his jacket and jotted down a few notes. "Any contacts in New Orleans?"

Lucas told him about the Lennart ladies and their tale of the head of the household hunting with the subject in India. All the while he was itching to turn around and openly watch Flora to be sure she wasn't about to get her pretty little neck in trouble again.

Or rather in more trouble than she was going to find with him once he got her alone.

"This Lennart fellow. Did you catch the man's name?"

Lucas dragged his errant thoughts back to the conversation in the dining room of the *Americus*. What was wrong with him? He was usually so good at recalling the details. Unfortunately, what he most recalled was a kiss and a spin around the dance floor while he sang "Beau Soir" to the woman in his arms in his mother's native French.

"Lucas? Are you all right?"

He nodded. "Yeah, just thinking. I don't think it was mentioned."

341

"Not a problem. I can find that out." He wrote a few more lines and then looked up at Lucas. "Anything else?"

"Just keep your ear to the ground and let me know if any of your contacts get eyes on our fellow Tucker. I'd be much obliged for any help in that area."

"Glad to do it." His brows rose. "You might want to go save that girl from herself. Now she's arguing with the fellow."

Lucas glanced around to see that Flora was indeed attempting to use her powers of persuasion on the man. Thankfully, he was more interested in watching her than in listening to her. Or at least that's how it appeared from where Lucas sat.

Still she was drawing a lot of attention, something no one in Natchez Under-the-Hill did on purpose. Especially not after dark.

He bit back a few choice words he longed to say and shook hands with Kyle. "All right. I'm going to see if I can keep her alive a little longer. Are you heading out tonight?"

"Yeah. The steamboat leaves in an hour. I figured I'd check in and maybe wash the smell of this place off me before I get some sleep. Lucky for you I was headed to New Orleans anyway. You know how my mother gets when I miss her birthday."

"I wish I were going with you," Lucas said and found he meant it. "Once I get this case behind me, how about we get together and work on some of the plans you've been sending me? I've had occasion to use several of our devices, and they've worked out well."

"I've been meaning to tell you. I'm revising the calculations on the weight load on the wire we used in those special bullets. I'm concerned it's going to snap if you get anything close to two hundred pounds on it."

Lucas chuckled. "Then I'd best watch my weight."

"Speaking of watching things." He nodded toward the door. "She's gone. Good luck catching her."

"Believe me, buddy, luck has nothing to do with it. I could use your prayers."

"You always have those, friend. Always." Kyle rose to clap Lucas on the shoulder. "Keep in touch, and I'll do the same. And watch your back."

"I always do," Lucas called as he slipped through the crowd and followed Flora's path out onto the street.

It took only a few moments to find her. Red curls bobbed beneath a hat that was far too fancy to fit in anywhere but up on the bluff. Two toughs had fallen in behind her and appeared to be arguing silently about which one would get the privilege of getting to know her a little better.

Lucas snagged the bigger of the men by the neck and held his revolver to his temple. He said softly, "I'm going to count to three, and then you and your buddy, you're going to run." He gestured in the opposite direction. "That way. Understand?"

He released the man on three and both disappeared into the crowd. Now Flora had a lead on him, though Lucas could still see her up ahead. He'd learned early on in his career as a Pinkerton that he could either make fast tracks or he could make silent ones.

With Flora's lead gaining every moment he dawdled, Lucas decided for fast. Pressing past anyone who got in his way, he managed to catch her just about the time she turned the corner and left Spring Street behind.

Hauling her against him, Lucas clamped a hand over her mouth as he tucked her into the nearest alley. Though she tried to scream and clawed to be released, he held on tight.

"Enough," Lucas snapped. "The party's over, Flora. You will come quietly, or I will throw you over my shoulder and take you back to the rig that way." She stilled when she recognized his voice, and he risked removing his hand, though he still kept one arm around her. A moment later he turned her around and stared directly into her wide blue eyes. He continued in a low tone. "Right this minute I do not care which option you choose."

"Lucas?" She shook her head and the ridiculous hat flopped to one side. "How did you know it was me?"

"You're joking, right?" He reached to straighten her headgear. "My question is how did you know where I would be? I know you didn't follow me. I'm certain of it."

"Well, you're right. I did not. In fact, I had my own reason for being in Natchez tonight."

"Natchez is up there on the bluff. You're in Natchez Under-the-Hill, and no self-respecting lady would be here on purpose." His gaze scorched the length of her. "And they certainly wouldn't be dressed like this." A pause. "Wait, let me guess. The Chamberlains were holding a costume party, and you and Grandmama came dressed as . . ." Another slow glance before meeting her eyes once more. "Honey, I can't figure out what you're dressed as. I'm guessing the Ellicotts are down here with you and your grandmother. Was that old man you were keeping company with back in the bar Mr. Ellicott?"

"Sarcasm," she said as she straightened her spine and turned to walk away.

"Oh, no you don't. You're in my custody and an escaped prisoner at that."

"I'm right here, Lucas. How could I be considered escaped? And don't you even think of pulling out those handcuffs again," she called over her shoulder as she picked up her pace. "We're in Natchez now, and I promise you it won't go well if word got out that you were bullying me."

"Bullying? That does it."

He closed the distance between them to snatch her off her feet. Once again she screamed, but this time she directed her ire at his intention to haul her home. "I am not ready to leave yet, so put me down!"

"And why's that?" Lucas turned the corner and almost banged her feet into a stack of barrels outside some sort of seedy establishment. "Meeting with our friend Mr. Tucker? My guess is the old guy who runs the telegraph office is your contact." He turned another corner and then gave thanks that the horse and buggy were still parked where he left them. "You're not answering me, Flora."

"Lucas, if you don't put me down, you're going to regret it."

"I already do." Spying a group of less than stellar citizens eyeing the buggy, he picked up his pace. "Now, for once since we met, just do what I say. These men are not going to think you're nearly as adorable as I do."

She pressed her palm against his chest. "But you're going the wrong way. I need to—"

"Stop talking, Flora," he said as he saw one of the men breaking from the pack to move toward them.

"But I—"

"Stop. Talking. Now. I'm busy." He set her on her feet and wrapped one arm around her, his other palm resting on the revolver at his waist. "Evening, gents," he said, purposefully choosing the most imposing of the group to greet.

"Isn't she a pretty one?" one of the fellows called as Lucas strolled past. "Got some spunk in her, she does."

He moved Flora from his side and into his arms again in one swift motion and practically tossed her into the buggy. By the time he climbed in and grabbed the reins, the men were upon them.

To his surprise, Flora kicked the biggest in the eye and sent him howling to the ground. At their champion's quick demise, the rest of them skittered away like the wharf rats they were, leaving Lucas free to turn the buggy around and head back toward Spring Street and the bluff.

"What were you thinking?" He demanded and then he immediately shook his head. "No, you weren't thinking. You were playing spy. Do you have any idea how close you came to something terrible happening?"

"I am the one who bested that mob, Lucas McMinn, not you. Don't I get any credit for that?"

"Credit? For almost getting both of us killed? No."

She sat in stony silence, both hands gripping the buggy seat. Even in the moonlight he could see that the incident had affected her. He could also see the stubbornness he'd come to know of her in the slant of her mouth and the stiffness of her posture.

Speaking to this woman and actually having her listen had never worked well. And yet he would play the eternal optimist and try again.

"You know, Flora," he said as firmly as he could manage without shouting, "you and I had an agreement. You broke it. I have every right to keep on driving until I get to the jail."

"You won't," she said with far too much confidence.

"You're wrong. I cannot work an investigation and try to keep you safe at the same time." He paused to slide a look in her direction. "If throwing you in jail is the only way I have to keep you safe while I bring a guilty man to justice, you'd better believe I'll do it."

Her ridiculous hat flopped into her eyes, and she reached up to shove it back into position. "I don't believe you."

Lucas pulled back on the reins and brought the buggy to a stop. To his left the Mississippi River ran muddy and wide down below the bluff, vessels bobbing at anchor in the moonlight. Above, the sky was clear and bright. A million stars exploded with tiny points of light, the edges of the moon ringed by the mist that always preceded a rainstorm.

But on his right, Flora Brimm sat straight and

still in her ridiculous costume, her gaze trained on him as if she expected him to say something brilliant and conciliatory that would make everything between them right again. Something that would excuse her dangerous and irresponsible behavior.

All he could manage through clenched jaw was, "You don't *believe* me?"

"No," she said, though Lucas thought he detected slightly less starch in her spine than before.

He waited a moment. Counted to ten. He even searched the sky until he found the North Star. Any diversion to bring his temper below the boiling point and his words to something that he would not regret.

"That is your problem, Flora," he finally said as he swiveled to face her. "You never seem to believe me."

Oh, but she was beautiful in the moonlight. Even wearing an outfit that looked as if she'd stolen things at random from a clothesline and then dressed in the dark with her eyes closed.

"That's not true," she stated as she gave him a triumphant look and pulled the tweed cloak closer around her.

"Give me one instance since you and I joined up on this ridiculous endeavor that you've simply done as you were told without question or comment. Or, worse, without ignoring my orders altogether and doing whatever you please. Can you do that?"

Her smile was broad and immediate, the look of satisfaction that followed curious to Lucas. What could she possibly be thinking, this woman who vexed him so?

"Of course I can."

"Well, go on. Let's hear it."

Flora crossed her arms in front of her. "All right. Just yesterday when we boarded the *Americus*. You told me to meet you at the seating area on the deck." She paused and gave him a triumphant look. "And I did."

"Any other examples?" He cocked his head to one side to make a show of listening intently for the answer he knew she couldn't give.

She shook her head. "You're insufferable. Truly."

"Me? I am the one trying to keep you alive. Trying to catch a man before he breaks your heart and leaves you ruined like he did to Mary-Margaret, and *I'm* insufferable?"

Silence fell between them as, by degrees, Lucas realized how much he'd just revealed. How much he wanted to take back and pretend he hadn't said.

Flora leaned forward to press her index finger against his lapel and, despite the borrowed costume, Lucas caught the scent of lilacs. Sweet lilacs. Likely dabbed on her neck from one of those expensive perfume bottles he had seen in her suite back at the Crescent Hotel.

"So," she said slowly as she smiled sweetly up at him. "You think I'm adorable?"

"No!" He shook his head and tried to clear his thoughts. Still there were the lilacs. And her smile. "Yes. Oh, I don't know."

He'd already decided she was insufferable. Unscrupulous, as witnessed by the deception she'd played on him tonight. And decidedly dangerous, as witnessed by the way she had of making him feel like a fool just by leaning closer.

By smiling up at him with lips that begged to be kissed.

By allowing the index finger pressing into his lapel to slowly become the palm that rested against his furiously beating heart.

Night sounds enveloped them. The slap of an oar oddly echoing from down on the river, the call of a night bird, the chirp of night creatures. Everything seemed amplified in her presence.

The ire.

The interest.

And then she sighed. "Lucas," she whispered.

"What?" Though he intended to say the word sharply to indicate his displeasure with her, instead his question fell from his slack mouth in a single barely breathed syllable.

"I think you're adorable too."

❊ TWENTY-FOUR ❊

Lucas turned around and grabbed the reins, leaving Flora to hang on tight as he maneuvered the buggy over the ruts in the road. The only measure of satisfaction she took from the man's discomfort was the change of topic.

"Did I say something wrong?" she managed while trying to keep from sliding off of her seat.

"Nothing any worse than the things you've been saying tonight." He shook his head. "Adorable," he muttered. "One more mistake to add to the growing list."

Though she'd been too frightened to let on, Lucas was right. The entire evening had been a mistake. From the lack of cooperation she received while trying to talk sense into the stubborn telegraph office manager to the rudeness of the band of ruffians near the buggy, nothing had turned out as she had hoped.

Sliding a glance at him, Flora's heart softened yet again. He had told her too much with his slip of the name Mary-Margaret. Who was she? A relative? A friend? A sweetheart?

This last thought caused the oddest twinge of jealousy.

She wouldn't ask, of course. Not after seeing

the discomfort in his eyes when he realized he had said her name. So she sat next to him in silence, knowing she would eventually have to explain her reasons for being in that awful tavern and wondering how she would make sense of it all when the time came.

At least Father and Grandmama would never know of her transgressions. She planned to distance herself from Lucas McMinn as soon as she could manage it. For should either of them get wind of the fact she went down to Natchez Under-the-Hill in clothes she borrowed from the charity bin, she would never hear the end of it.

That is, if she arrived home in one piece. At the rate Lucas was driving the buggy, the likelihood was growing dimmer by the moment.

"You can let me out to walk the remainder at any point," she said sharply as he once again took a bend in the road far too quickly for her liking.

"You? Walk? Not likely."

"Why do you think I'm some sort of helpless woman? I assure you that I'm not."

His snort of derision only served to make her smile.

"I'd rather take my chances with coyotes and highwaymen than to be thrown from the buggy due to your excessive speed."

"I doubt you'll find either in this part of Mississippi, though you didn't mind associating with vermin tonight, now did you?"

"Nor did you, apparently, or you wouldn't have been in Natchez Under-the-Hill. I don't suppose you want to tell me why you were there."

A lock of dark hair fell into his eyes, and he pushed it away. "No, I do not."

"And I would further guess it didn't completely have to do with Mr. Tucker, did it?"

She was digging in a sensitive spot. She could tell that from the way the muscle in his jaw jerked at the question. A sensible woman would have left the topic alone.

But not when curiosity tugged at her and there were still a few miles to go before the gates of Brimmfield would appear.

She leaned over to see if he smelled of alcohol. When he did not, her heart sank. With it, her ire—or was it jealousy?—rose.

From what she could discern, there were only three things men went down to that part of town for. Two of them were business and drinking. Lucas had already eliminated the first with his admission that Pinkerton duties were only part of his reason, and Flora's sense of smell had eliminated the second.

"Do you frequent these places because of Mary-Margaret or in spite of her?"

No response.

Flora cast a covert glance at the lawman and found his expression grim, his knuckles white. She'd gone too far with her question. Amends were due for stomping all over what was obviously very private territory.

And yet an apology refused to form.

Then she caught him staring at her.

"Whatever you're thinking you want to say . . . do not." He bit out the words and then turned away from her again.

Surely he didn't mean it. He was just irritated because she hadn't apologized for her indiscreet remarks.

"You don't have to explain yourself to me," she said gently. "You're entitled to spend your free time however you wish without being accountable to—"

"Flora."

His voice held far too much warning for her to ignore, and yet not enough to completely take him seriously. Instead, she decided an apology was the only way to remedy the situation.

"All right. I'm truly sorry that I brought the subject up at all. It's just that when you mentioned Mary-Margaret, I assumed you might be looking for some conversation and maybe—"

"Not . . . another . . . word."

This time she felt his look before she turned to see it. She opened her mouth to agree, or apologize further, or something—anything to placate the unreasonable man.

"No."

So she clamped her mouth closed and turned to

shut him out of her vision even as she tried to keep his bad-tempered attitude out of her thoughts. For though she hadn't succeeded in her mission to find Mr. Tucker's telegraph operator friend, she had come extremely close. The man in the tavern had at least admitted he knew the Wilson fellow Will Tucker had addressed his coded telegram to.

Returning to Natchez Under-the-Hill during daylight hours would be difficult, but she would somehow manage it. And when she did, she would find Jack Wilson.

A thought occurred, and Flora caught her breath. What if Will Tucker was trying to reach her? What if he depended on her to be at a certain place at a certain time, and that dependence had been somehow conveyed through the message he'd left.

She sighed. There was nothing for it now. If she'd missed his attempts at contact, she could only pray that Will Tucker was still in Natchez and willing to wed.

Perhaps she could find a way to ask Lucas about this. Surely in all his Pinkerton training he encountered the need to get a secret message to someone or to make contact without being found out.

"So," she said slowly, "if you were looking for a woman, how would you—"

"You just cannot let it alone, can you, Flora?" he snapped.

She let out a long breath. The man was

absolutely impossible. He was, however, the only person who might be able to answer her question.

Thus, she decided to try one more time. "But, Lucas, I'm just trying to ask about—"

"Stop. Asking."

That did it. She'd had enough.

"Fine. I'll just handle the matter myself, but remember when you get mad at me that I tried to talk to you about it, only you refused to let me and then I did it and . . ." She paused to take a breath and found he'd not only stopped interrupting her, but he had also stopped the buggy.

"Go on," came out as menacing as two innocent words could.

Flora let out a long breath. "I'm just asking your advice." She paused. "If I've missed Will Tucker's attempts at finding me, how do I find him?"

"You don't find him, Flora," he said with what appeared to be difficulty. "I am the one who will find the man. You have nothing to do with it."

"I have *everything* to do with it. Without me, you can't catch him. If you could, you would have by now."

Even in the moonlight she could see the vein throbbing in his neck. "And *with* you I am so busy playing nanny to a spoiled child that I'm too distracted to do my job."

"Don't blame me for your distraction. I'm the one trying to help."

"Then stop helping," he demanded. "And just do what I tell you. Which includes, as I've told you, not going anywhere without my prior approval or—"

"Or you'll have me thrown in jail." Flora shook her head. "That's a tired old song you're playing, Mr. McMinn. I think I've heard it one too many times. I don't believe it anymore."

"You don't?" He nodded only once, his expression grim and yet thoughtful. "Well, all right."

The lawman slapped the reins and urged the buggy back into motion. At the bend in the road he turned right instead of left, something that Flora instantly questioned. Of course, the man refused to answer.

Oh, surely not. She tried to bluff her way to sounding brave. "Suit yourself, but when you find out you're lost, let me know and I'll help you get back to Brimmfield."

Again he remained silent. Flora sat back, her expression pensive. At least she'd managed to change the topic and redirect his ire if not the carriage.

Or she thought she had. Until the lights of Natchez came into view.

"Believe me now?" she asked. "Just turn around up here and I'll show you where you made the mistake."

"No, Flora. You're the one who has made the mistake."

Though he said nothing more, Flora was now certain where he was headed. Her pride, however, kept her mute. Even as he pulled the buggy to a halt in front of the city jail, she remained silent.

Lucas walked around to reach for her, but she saved him the trouble and exited the buggy herself. She also walked up to the sheriff's office of her own accord with Lucas following close behind.

A deputy she recognized but did not know personally rose when she stepped into the office. "Evening, Miss Brimm," he said. "How can we be of service?"

"I need to speak to Sheriff Lambert please," Flora said as she adjusted the doily protecting her modesty.

"No," Lucas said. "I'm the one in need of speaking to the sheriff."

The deputy shifted his attention from Flora to Lucas and then back to Flora. "The sheriff isn't here. I believe he's at the cotton exchange event tonight with your daddy, Miss Flora."

"Oh, of course," Flora said, though she doubted her father had returned to Natchez so soon.

"Are you the man in charge?" Lucas asked.

"I am." The deputy rose from behind the desk and walked around to shake hands with Lucas. "Are you Miss Brimm's new fella? Talk around here is that she'd already up and married, but the boss says no, that she's just got her cap set for someone and the wedding hasn't happened yet."

Flora gave Lucas an I-told-you-so look he ignored. "No, I'm a Pinkerton agent who has personal custody of Miss Brimm. And tonight she violated the terms of that custody. I'm prepared to write up a full report for the sheriff."

The deputy stood openmouthed for what felt like a full minute. "He's telling the truth," Flora supplied, "though he left out the part where I was just doing a little digging to help him solve his case."

Again the deputy shifted his stare from her to Lucas. "Let me get this straight. You want me to throw Flora Brimm in jail?"

Lucas drew in a long breath and let it out slowly. "Yes. If you'll just confirm, she has a warrant on her out of Arkansas signed by the Eureka Springs sheriff."

A trickle of perspiration slid down the man's forehead as he tugged at his collar. "For what?"

"Receipt of stolen property." Lucas paused. "That's a felony in Arkansas."

"It's a felony in Mississippi too, but I can't imagine this gal would willingly accept stolen property." He looked over at Flora. "Would you, Miss Brimm?"

"No," Flora said in her most angelic voice. "Of course not." She paused. "In fact, the item he claims I stole is in his possession. Technically, *he* took it from me."

"Confiscated." Lucas gestured to his pocket. "My name is Lucas McMinn, and I have a badge in my coat. Would you like to see it?"

"I would." The deputy watched closely as Lucas pulled out his badge and thrust it toward him. After a minute, he turned it over and then nodded. "Looks real enough. What can I do for you, Pink?"

"You can put this woman in jail," he said evenly. "As I said, she has violated the terms of our custody arrangement. Therefore, I am revoking her release and committing her to jail, where she will be safe."

"Is she in danger?"

"Only from herself," Lucas snapped as he replaced the badge in his pocket.

"And you have her property?" the deputy asked.

"The property has been confiscated as part of the investigation. It will be returned to her if and when it is determined to be hers." He shook his head. "The watch is in no danger of being lost."

"I don't recall getting a receipt for that," Flora said.

Lucas silenced her with a look and returned his attention to the deputy. "If you'll just show me where to sign, I will leave the prisoner in your capable hands."

"I don't believe so, sir." The deputy snuck a quick glance at Flora before addressing Lucas again. "I can't lock up Miss Brimm. Her grandpa, he was something around here. So's her daddy. And her grandmother . . . well, she'd have my hide for sure. Even ol' General Grant didn't mess with Mrs. Millie."

Flora suppressed a smile.

"Deputy, I'm sure you'll hear from the Brimm family, but the law is the law, and I'm turning custody of Miss Brimm over to you."

"No, sir. You are not."

A dull red began to climb up Lucas's neck, and for a moment he appeared unable to respond. Then he began in a deadly tone. "Are you saying that because you know this woman and her family, you are ignoring the warrant issued for her arrest in Eureka Springs and are refusing to accept the prisoner I have brought in tonight?"

"Yes, sir. That's exactly what I'm saying."

Lucas looked about ready to take the fellow to task. "And there's nothing I can do to get this woman put in jail, where she belongs?"

"Of course there is. You can take her back to Eureka Springs, where that warrant of yours is good."

"Sir, you are aware of the fact that Mississippi and Arkansas are both part of the United States of America, and as such recognize and cooperate with the laws of each state?"

"That's a pretty speech, Pink, but the fact remains that I'm not going to hold Miss Brimm on an out-of-state warrant when she and her family have been outstanding members of this city's citizenry since well before the war."

Lucas shook his head. "All right, I'm going to try this again. There is an active Pinkerton case in which this woman's warrant has been recognized as valid and material. I can get you whatever information you'd like on that case to have the sheriff swear out a warrant. How's that?"

"That would probably work, but first you'd have to get the Pinkertons to verify and then get the final answer on it from the sheriff once all the paperwork has been handled."

"I see. So what you're saying is I'm stuck with Flora Brimm—at least for now."

The deputy grinned at Flora. She, of course, returned his smile. "Yes, sir," he said as he looked again at Lucas. "She's all yours."

"Wonderful," he muttered as he gave Flora a look that would wither cotton. "Let's go."

She followed a step behind and allowed him to help her into the buggy. Without a word, he climbed up beside her and pointed the horse toward home.

They rode in silence, as much because Flora no longer cared to invoke Lucas's ire as to allow her a time of quiet reflection under the stars.

"Lucas," she finally said. "Are you talking to me yet?"

"No."

She giggled. "You just did."

Apparently the man had lost any sense of humor he might have once possessed. Flora giggled again anyway because it was truly funny. All of it was.

At the entrance to Brimmfield, she fully expected him to make her walk the rest of the way, but instead he drove right up to the front of the house almost at breakneck pace. When the carriage halted, an efficient houseboy had her feet on the ground before Lucas could climb out.

Just as well, for she intended to seek the solace of her room and a long visit with the Lord rather than spend any further time with the angry lawman. Worse, she couldn't possibly see Father or Grandmama wearing this horrid ensemble— that is, if Father truly had returned.

The front doors opened as they always did by the time Flora reached the first of the fourteen marble steps leading to the entrance, thanks to a pair of Brimm footmen who both bowed as she walked past. One of the maids hurried in her direction to retrieve her hat and coat.

"Might I draw you a bath, ma'am?" she asked, nothing in her expression giving away what must be surprise at her odd choice of outfit.

"Yes, please, and make it extra hot. And ask Lucy to give you some of those lovely lilac bath salts Father brought back from Paris, please," she said to the retreating maid's back. "I believe she put them in the trunk with my perfumes before we left Eureka Springs."

"Hold off on drawing that bath," Lucas called.

Flora spun around to see that he had not only followed her inside, but he seemed intent on continuing their conversation. "You there," he called to the maid. "Is this woman's father at home?"

"He's just back, sir," the maid answered. "You'll find him in the library."

Flora's heart lurched. And to think she had decided the evening couldn't possibly get any worse. If Lucas spoke to her father in this mood, the end really would come for her plans.

Of all the men in her life, only Lucas McMinn was less reasonable than Father. And even then, the race was close. And if Grandmama got wind of any conversation that might prove interesting, sparks really would fly.

She had to do something. Quick.

"Oh, no," she said to the maid. "This man may be a guest, but he is not going to see Father."

Then she turned to Lucas. That same lock of hair had fallen into his eyes but, from the look of him, he was too irritated to care.

This did not bode well.

"Lucas, you are *not* going to speak to my father. Not tonight. He is . . ." She tried to think of a reasonable argument. "He's indisposed. Yes, that's right. You can't see him now because he only just returned from Memphis. I haven't even seen him yet. Don't think of ruining our reunion."

Slowly he reached up to swipe the lock of hair into place. His gaze met hers but only briefly before he turned to look in the direction of the maid. "Where is the library?"

"Top of the stairs, first door on the right," she said, eyes downcast. "Shall I show you, sir?"

"No, thank you. I think I can find it." He returned his attention to Flora. "And you, Miss Brimm, are coming with me."

❋ TWENTY-FIVE ❋

Flora stared the Pinkerton agent down. "Absolutely not. I refuse to allow it."

"That's where you're wrong," he said as he advanced on her. "You do not get to decide."

She skittered out of his reach. "Lucas, have you lost your mind?"

"No, Flora. I've finally found it."

With that statement, he strode toward her. Flora squealed when he made a reach for her elbow, just missing it to make contact with the wall. The family photos shuddered, but Lucas seemed not to feel any pain.

"Come here, Flora. I'm in no mood to chase you, but I will if I have to."

"Really, I—"

He made another lunge for her, this time capturing her wrist. "All right," he said with deadly calm. "Let's go talk to your daddy. I couldn't turn you over to the deputy sheriff, but I can certainly turn you over to your father. Whatever it takes to keep you from ruining my investigation."

She took two steps forward with him and stalled. "I won't. What are you going to do, tell on me for not listening to you?"

"I thought I'd let you do that." Flora felt the impact of his stare. "I'm sure you'll come up with a better version anyway."

"Version of what?"

"The whole story, beginning to end." Green eyes narrowed. "Starting with the warrant for your arrest and your insistence on ignoring—"

"Not so loud," she said in a hushed voice. "Someone's going to hear you."

"That's the intention." He shook his head. "Now are you coming with me or do I need to pick you up and carry you? Either way there is going to be a conversation with your father tonight so I don't have to worry about what you will do to endanger yourself or my investigation tomorrow."

Panic stole her breath. "Honestly, Lucas, I am not a child," she finally managed. "And I do not appreciate your references to me as such."

"No, you're not a child. Things would be much

easier if you were. You're a full-grown woman, and I refuse to let anything happen to you."

"Mr. McMinn," she said as her gaze darted around for some means of escape. "You almost sound as though you care for me."

"I do, Miss Brimm. I don't know what I would do if something—" If his admission surprised Flora, it seemed to cause an even stronger reaction in him. "All right," he said with a tone that was brusque, even for him. "Last chance to walk upstairs with me without assistance."

When she hesitated, he reached for her.

Before she could react, the horizon tilted and the stairs came into view as he swept her into his arms. Though the staircase comprised the full height of the foyer, he ascended the steps almost as quickly as he'd driven the buggy.

"I believe you now. I do. Please just put me down."

"Too late," he said as he reached the top of the stairs and paused only long enough to turn toward Father's library.

"As least put me on my feet," she pleaded. "Let me walk in rather than being carried. I know you're angry, but think of how it will look to my father if you haul me into his office and unceremoniously drop me at his feet."

She could see the indecision on his face and celebrated a small victory. Out of the corner of her eye, she spied Father's valet watching from the door to the back stairs. When their gazes met, the man disappeared, likely headed down to the servant's kitchen to announce the latest Flora-induced scandal. He would tell her father what he saw at his earliest opportunity.

The horizon tilted again as Lucas set her on her feet. She wobbled a bit until he steadied her.

"Thank you," she said as she adjusted her hat. "There's just one more thing." She held her thumb and index finger up in an approximation of an inch. "Just a little tiny thing. Nothing, really."

He did not look impressed. Thus, she offered her best smile and continued. "Just let me change into something more presentable."

When he didn't respond, she tried again. "I know you're angry, Lucas, and I don't blame you. I realize on occasion I can be a little difficult—"

"A *little* difficult? You accused me of arranging illicit meetings with women in Natchez Under-the-Hill when I was merely meeting with a fellow Pinkerton, and all the while you were there in that ridiculous costume risking your life to speak to some man who would rather guess what you're hiding under your grandmother's doily."

"You're right," she said, wanting to choose words that placate rather than irritate. "About all of it. Please, can't we just start over?"

Lucas muttered something under his breath as he tightened his grip on her elbow. "Forget it, Flora. Let's go."

"No, wait!" She dug in her heels as he tried to pull her toward him. "I'm just thinking of you."

His laughter held no humor. "Really? All right. It seems at this moment I am just crazy enough to ask you how in the world you figure you're thinking of me? The only person you *ever* think of is yourself. So this ought to be good."

The accusation stung, though she knew she deserved it. Part of being Flora Brimm of the Natchez Brimms meant cultivating the persona of a pampered and cosseted pet. And had Father got his way, that is exactly what she would have become.

And yet the truth of the matter was that she rarely thought of what was best for her anymore. Not when she was so busy seeing to the needs of the others God had placed in her life.

"If Father sees me dressed like this while under your care, he will not be happy." She ignored his snort of derision. "And that unhappiness will likely reflect on you, not me. I'm his precious daughter, but you're the stranger who put me into a dangerous situation."

He began to protest and she waved away the comment with a swipe of her hand. "Go on," he muttered instead.

"If you will just let me change into something that will not steal Father's attention from the speech you wish to give to him about me, I think both of us will be better received."

She paused to watch his expression go from aggravated to thoughtful. Then abruptly he shook his head, all the while keeping a firm grip on her elbow.

"I know women, and they do not dress in a hurry, especially when a man is waiting on them. However, as much as I hate to admit it, some of what you've said makes sense. So," he said on an exhale of breath, "I'm going to do something I hope I do not live to regret."

Flora tamped down on her smile. "What's that?"

"I am going to give you ten minutes to find something to put on." He paused. "Lucy?"

To Flora's surprise, her maid crept around the corner to offer a downcast and decidedly shocked expression. "Yes, sir?"

"How quickly can you get Miss Brimm changed into something decent?"

Wide-eyed, the maid clasped her hands in front of her as she appeared to consider the question carefully. "Miss Brimm generally needs a half hour to complete her toilette once she's bathed and had her hair set up just right."

"Can you rid her of this ridiculous costume and dress her in something decent in no more than ten minutes?"

"Ten minutes, sir?" She shrugged. "Maybe a morning dress or . . . well, yes, I think I can do that."

Lucas turned his attention to Flora. "Do not make me regret this. Which room is yours?"

"My bedchamber?" She gestured toward the end of the hall. "That one nearest the windows. Behind the column."

"Lucy, you will remain with her at all times. Understand?"

"Truly, Mr. McMinn," Flora said, her hands on her hips. "This poor woman doesn't work for you. It's hardly appropriate for you to be giving her orders."

"Suit yourself, Flora. Let's go see Daddy."

He made a move as if he might once again sweep her into his arms, and Flora knew she'd pushed him as far as she could. The time had come for retreat and a few moments to revisit her plan.

"No, no. I'm going," she said as she hurried past Lucy. The maid followed and shut the door behind her.

"Ten minutes," she heard Lucas say. "And should you attempt to do anything foolish, I'll be waiting just outside."

Flora sank down on her bed and looked at Lucy. Her maid was trying not to smile as she shook her head.

"Miss Flora, that man, is he crazy or does he just love you very much?"

"Love me?" She laughed as she pulled the doily out of her cleavage and tossed it aside. "Don't be ridiculous."

372

"Oh, he loves you, all right. It's all over him." Lucy went to the armoire and pulled out a morning dress of mint green. "This one?"

"Yes, that's fine," Flora responded, though she knew she would not be greeting Lucas or Father in that dress—or in any other one tonight. Not with what she had planned.

She slipped out of her borrowed clothes and kicked them aside. "I'm curious, Lucy," she said as she bent to allow Lucy to slip the dress over her head. "Why do you think Mr. McMinn is in love with me?"

The maid grinned. "We all think that, miss. Mostly because of the way he looks at you when you're not watching. Can't you see it?" She laughed. "No, I suppose you can't, what with it happening when you're not noticing."

Flora straightened and turned around to her image in the mirror. "No, I don't suppose I can. But truly, he is insufferable. All he wants to do is complain."

"Yes, miss," the maid said demurely, though Flora knew she was only agreeing to be polite.

She walked to the window and Lucy followed with the remainder of her ensemble. From where she stood, Flora could see the little cottage and the single light that always burned in the window.

Most nights the light gave her comfort. Tonight, however, the image unsettled her. If Violet would just set her pride aside and . . .

No, that was a thought for another day.

"Oh!" Lucy exclaimed as she handed a folded piece of paper to Flora. "I almost forgot that I was sent up here to give you this. It came for you after Mr. McMinn carried you . . . that is, after you and Mr. McMinn arrived in the second floor hall."

Flora turned around to open the note as Lucy attended to the fasteners along the back of her dress. *Must follow the job to New Orleans. Marry me there? Jackson Square. Noon on Friday.*

She quickly folded the page and held it against her heart. Two days? Convincing Father of the need to visit New Orleans was a simple matter. She traveled between the two Brimm homes frequently.

Making the trip without Lucas McMinn was another matter entirely, especially since the man had already admitted he was from the city. Flora gave the matter some thought. And then the most brilliant of ideas occurred. *Yes, of course.*

"There, miss," Lucy said as she stood back to admire Flora. "You're all done, and according to your mantel clock you've a full minute to spare."

Flora tore her attention from the cottage and turned to face Lucy. "I do, don't I?" She nodded toward the door. "Tell Mr. McMinn I'll be out directly, please."

She gave Flora a doubtful look. "I . . . I believe I'm to stay with you, Miss Flora."

"Until Mr. McMinn pays your salary, Lucy, you'll not be taking orders from him. Do you understand?"

"Yes, ma'am," she said, her eyes downcast.

"I'm sorry I snapped at you. I'm just weary, and my patience is stretched beyond bearing by that man out there in the hall."

"The man who loves you," Lucy reminded her.

"Well, if he does, he certainly hasn't mentioned it."

"No?" Lucy asked. "Nothing at all?"

"Nothing." Except the kiss she hated to admit she still found herself thinking about. And the fact that tonight he declared he cared for her.

That was a surprise because most of the time he acted as though he was tired of dealing with her. Well, he would not have to deal with her anymore. Not if she could find her way out of this room and into the arms of Will Tucker on Friday at noon in Jackson Square.

The thought of Mr. Tucker's arms around her was quickly replaced by the recollection of the same embrace by Mr. McMinn. Why was it that the Pinkerton agent insisted on pestering her even when he was not in the room?

Again the light in the cottage caught her attention. "Of course," she whispered as the final piece of the plan's puzzle clicked into place.

❊ TWENTY-SIX ❊

Lucas removed his pocket watch to check the time. Exactly nine minutes. He leaned against the carved column adjacent to Flora's bedchamber door and closed his eyes. How had it all come to this?

Flora Brimm was a Pinkerton agent's worst nightmare, the type of woman who would niggle her way into his thoughts at the oddest moments, work her way into his heart, and all the while irritate him beyond description.

The fellow he'd seen spying on them from what he assumed was the back stairs once again poked his head out of the door. Looking around, he obviously did not see Lucas partially hidden behind the column, for the man skulked forward within reach of his hand.

Only when Lucas grabbed him did the man's eyes go wide. "Oh, sir, you startled me," he protested. "I only just wondered if you might need assistance before you turned in for the night."

"Is that so?" He gestured to the opposite end of the hall. "Then you took a wrong turn. My bed-chamber is that way."

"Yes, s-sir," he stammered. "I suppose I was misinformed on which room you would be using."

Lucy opened Flora's door and shut it quickly as she hurried past without acknowledging either of the men. Lucas released the valet and then watched both of them disappear down the back stairs.

"All right, Miss Brimm. Your time is up." Once again he removed the watch from his vest pocket to check the time. Eleven minutes. He paused and then knocked. "Flora, you've had an extra minute. Please do not try my patience any further."

When she did not answer, Lucas reached into his hat and connected his listening device. Pressing one end of the tube against the door, he held the other near his ear.

Nothing.

He tried the knob. Locked.

And then a thought occurred.

"No she didn't!" he muttered as he raced down the back stairs two at a time. Emerging into the servant's hall, he looked around for the first uniformed employee he could find.

"You!" he called to a footman. "Where is the nearest back door?"

"This way, sir." The man quickly led Lucas through the kitchen and past a cluster of maids folding laundry. A moment later, he emerged into the thick night air.

"Thanks," he called as he hurried around the corner of the building to find the approximate place where Flora might have climbed out of the window. And there she was above him, nimbly making her way around the back of the second floor of the three-story home.

A call to her would have alerted Flora to his presence. With tools to close the distance between them waiting in his pocket, Lucas decided to try another way to confront Flora Brimm.

Removing the bullet from his revolver, he inserted the special canister and made sure the weapon was once again ready for firing. Judging the distance to the ledge above him, he smiled as the shot hit its mark just around the corner from where Flora was heading.

Lucas returned the revolver to its holster and pulled the spikes from his pocket and attached them to his boots. Giving the filament line a yank, he curled it around his waist three times to anchor himself and raised his foot to begin the climb up the side of the structure.

Though the going was slow due to the poor visibility from the clouds covering the moon, Lucas managed to reach the ledge before Flora came around the corner.

"Oh!" she shouted as her forehead slammed into his shoulder.

He caught her before either lost their footing and then, to be sure she was safe, he released the clip and wrapped her against him with the wire. A turn of the notch and they were secure.

"What are you doing up here?" she demanded.

"I came to see a woman about a meeting with her father. If you will be still, I will get us both down safely."

Instead of not moving, Flora twisted around to see how they were connected. Lucas tumbled sideways and took her with him. Holding her tightly, he fought to connect his boots with the ledge.

"What are you doing?" she demanded as her nails dug into his back and her head rested against his chest.

"Trying to keep from landing on the ground before I'm ready."

Unfortunately, they were dangling just far enough away from the ledge to prevent him from using the spikes to gain control. All he could do was release the latch slowly and begin a descent to the ground.

A stiff breeze rocked them against the house, slamming Lucas's back against the ledge. He bit back the choice words he once would have said and focused on keeping control of the situation.

"Be still, or we're both going to end up in your grandmother's roses."

"I am being still, but I will ask you again. What are you doing? You were supposed to be waiting in the hall."

Lucas laughed at the absurdity of the situation. At the way she could take any kind of trouble she'd created and turn it into something she had no part of.

"I was waiting in the hall for you," he said as his fingers slid the notch on the wire down just enough to lower them a few inches. "You were supposed to come out as you said you would."

He felt her grip on his back loosen, and he swiftly tightened his arm, holding her close. "Hang on, Flora. I'll have us out of this mess in a minute."

"I could have kept us out of this mess, Lucas. If you hadn't stood in my way, I would have simply walked over to the cupola and climbed down the trellis. It's not a difficult . . . oh!" she exclaimed as the wire gave way a little too much and they plummeted several feet before he caught the notch and ceased their movement.

Flora held on very tightly now, and her talking had finally ceased. Lucas was sure he would be able to continue lowering them in a slow and measured manner.

Their swift descent had left them still several feet above the ground and well within view of anyone who might be seated in the dining room or formal parlor. Thankfully, tall shrubs kept them all but invisible from anyone who might be standing outside.

Lucas eased up on the notch and nothing happened. The wire seemed to have snagged.

Trying again, he found the workings had jammed. A glance up the length of the wire, at least from what he could see, showed him there was no reason from above that it would not be working.

Reason from above.

The idea caused him to shake his head. As did the unmistakable feeling of a fat raindrop as it plopped on the back of his neck and began a slow trickle down his spine. Along with all of this, he recalled Kyle's mention of the load limit on the wire. Though Flora was tiny, there could be no doubt their combined weight exceeded the two-hundred-pound mark.

All he could do was laugh.

"Mr. McMinn, I fail to see what could possibly be so funny. We are dangling a ways off the ground yet, and apparently your contraption has ceased to work. Is there something humorous in this situation I am missing?"

Another raindrop followed, this one slanting just enough to hit him beneath the rim of his hat. Meanwhile, Flora had her arms wrapped around him, her blue eyes trained on his face, and her beautiful, kissable mouth blessedly closed in a tight line.

"Face it, Miss Brimm," he said as he gave up on the wire and wrapped his free hand around her. "This is your fault."

"Mine?" Her eyes narrowed. "You are the one who was standing in my way, and you are certainly the one who created this ridiculous contraption that now has us both dangling and stuck." She closed her eyes briefly and sighed. Looking back up at him again, she said, "With all of those inventions of yours, can't you come up with something that will solve our problem? Perhaps you have a machine that will allow us to fly down to the ground in that pocket of yours next to the extra-vision spectacles and the human torch and who knows what else?"

"It is a personal torch, and there's no reason to use it. I can see you just fine." A pause. "And must I say, you look quite lovely in the moon-light. Much better now that you've given up on wearing doilies."

"Of all the nerve." She slanted a look up at him through thick lashes. Just as she appeared about to add more to her complaints, a raindrop splattered against her cheek. "Oh, no, Lucas. It's raining. Do something!"

"And what would you suggest I do, Flora?"

"I suggest you explain yourself, young man," said a gruff voice from the window below.

Lucas angled himself just far enough away from the wall to see who had spoken. From the age and appearance of the man in question, it did not take a Pinkerton agent to surmise that this fellow was Flora Brimm's father.

"Just the man I've been looking for," Lucas said. "Give me a minute, sir, and I'll bring your daughter down. And then you and I have some talking to do."

"Don't listen to him, Father. We're just having a little trouble up here. Could you call for a ladder or some shears to cut the wire?"

"I should call for the sheriff! And I still may."

"Yes, please do," Lucas said.

"No, don't." Flora implored. "Just get us down, and I promise I will explain everything."

Mr. Brimm gave her a doubtful look. "I will keep that thought under advisement, young lady. For now I'll ring for Harrison. Do not even think of going anywhere until one of us returns."

"Where would we go?"

"Yes, a good point indeed. But do understand, Flora Brimm, that I have ignored many of your antics over the years, including ones that might cause another parent to declare you completely beyond repair. Until now I assumed you would someday settle down into a more sedate manner of behavior. Unfortunately, I have once again been proven wrong."

Lucas could see his nemesis go from blustering to crushed with her father's words. Something in him, call it a lawman's instinct, told Lucas that Mr. Brimm was the one who was wrong.

"Father, truly I did not expect to—"

"Watch out, Flora," Lucas said as the wind kicked up again and tossed the two of them against the building. This time Flora's shoe went through the window just above her father's head.

From Lucas's vantage point, he could see Mr.

Brimm's color redden beneath his substantial facial hair. With a shake of his head, he moved away from the remnants of the glass and was gone.

Flora looked up at Lucas, her expression anguished. "We have now officially gone too far. My father is not an easy man to irritate, but I have never seen him that angry." She paused. "We've really done it."

Lucas looked down at the woman in his arms. "We?" He shook his head. "We? As with just about everything else that has gone wrong since the day I met you at the Crescent Hotel, Flora, this has been completely your doing."

"I wasn't the one who invented this thing."

"No, that was me," he said as he removed a tiny device hidden in his jacket lapel. Not only did the invention have a blade sharp enough to do substantial damage despite its size, it also contained a serviceable pair of wire cutters.

Lucas gazed into the cornflower blue eyes of the most maddening woman on the planet. A moment later he said, "Put your head against my shoulder. I'm going to cut us down, and I'll do my best to break your fall and keep us from landing in the broken glass."

"Lucas, don't—"

"Okay, here we go." A snap of the wire and her words became a squeal that chased them the remainder of the distance to the ground. Lucas's landing was softened by the garden soil, while he broke Flora's fall.

She shakily lifted her head to look at him, her nearness distracting him even as he grasped for the cutting device that had rolled just out of reach. "You are absolutely certifiable, Lucas. We could have been seriously injured."

"Are you hurt?" he asked as he quickly inventoried his own limbs and declared himself fit.

"No, I don't think so," she breathed. "But all the same, I could have been."

He leaned just a little more to the right and inched toward the device. "Hold on," he said as he moved their bundled selves toward it. Finally his fingers touched cold metal, and he palmed the little instrument.

"Did you get it?" she asked, a fiery curl falling over her face as she looked down into his eyes.

"Yes. Don't move or I might cut something I don't mean to." That stilled her until he could make short work of releasing the circle of wire that bound them. Jumping to his feet, he hauled Flora up and into his arms. "Why is it things are always so complicated when you're around?"

"Me? You're the one complicating things."

"We'll see about that." He leaned back a little to look at her. "I believe you and I were on our way to see your father before you attempted this ridiculous escape."

A rustle of noise beyond the shrubs diverted his attention. A man who appeared to be a gardener hurried in the wake of the man Flora had called Father. In Mr. Brimm's hand was an oversized pair of shears. Lucas let his arms fall from around Flora, though he stayed close beside her.

"Is this the husband you wrote me about, Flora?"

Her father was tall, though not as tall as Lucas, and his posture spoke of boarding school and years following in the footsteps of his ancestors. He knew the type. If not for Kyle Russell and the Pinkertons, he might have been the type.

Mr. Brimm brandished the pruning shears far too near to Lucas for his liking. "Sir, I will have an explanation of what you are doing dangling outside my home while inappropriately entwined with my daughter."

Where to start?

"Go ahead, Lucas. He'll find out eventually. You should probably tell him now."

The pruning shears caught the gaslight inside and took on a decidedly sinister golden glow. "Tell him what?"

"Indeed, daughter. Tell me what?"

Flora shook her head, and another of her curls sprung loose. "We were going to tell you eventually, Father. Lucas and I are working on a case and hoping to give chase to a criminal without alerting him to our presence."

"That is the most ridiculous statement I've heard in quite some time," Mr. Brimm stated. "Almost as ridiculous as the letter you sent informing me you were to be married. Thankfully, your grandmother tells me that hasn't happened yet."

"No, sir," she said softly, her eyes averted.

"Actually, sir," Lucas said, looking the man in the eye. "I am a Pinkerton agent. If you'll set those shears aside, I will reach into my pocket and show you my badge."

Mr. Brimm gave him a doubtful look. "And what would that prove? I fail to see how your employment as a Pinkerton could possibly explain why you were hanging outside my home with my daughter, sir. And in the rain, no less."

"It has everything to do with it, Father." She paused to give Lucas what he assumed was supposed to be a meaningful look. "We only just received a message from the man that Mr. McMinn is tracking. Because he managed to deliver the message to Brimmfield unseen, it is likely he could still be watching the house now."

"We did?" Lucas whispered, his lips against Flora's ear.

Flora nodded. "Please, let's just go inside and we will explain everything."

"You're in luck. I've never been fond of standing in the rain unless I must. My dear, inside with you. And you, sir," Mr. Brimm said to Lucas, "shall find another place in which to carry out your investigation."

Linking arms with Flora, Lucas stopped her progress. "Sir, I know she is your daughter, but she is helping me with an investigation. I wonder if I might speak to her privately for just a moment before we join you in the house."

"I'm afraid not." He yanked Flora's other arm and set her back in motion.

Lucas thought to register a protest and insist on his legal right to interrogate a prisoner, but if Mr. Brimm was at all as stubborn as Miss Brimm, it would do no good anyway. Resigned for now, Lucas followed the pair inside and across the entry to a room beneath the staircase.

From the looks of the dark, wood-paneled space, it was being used as some sort of study. One of the walls was covered in paintings of horses, while two others bore framed maps hung in orderly grids. The fourth wall was dominated by a large oil painting of a dark-haired couple seated before a roaring fire. In the woman's arms was an infant dressed in a long white gown and matching bonnet. Standing beside the man was a girl with long dark curls and big blue eyes. Balancing out the painting was a pair of wolfhounds resting at the man's feet.

"Sit, Mr. McMinn."

Lucas complied, but only out of deference to the man's position as Flora's father. Flora followed a step behind, taking a seat beside him without being told. When Mr. Brimm walked over to close the door behind them, Flora passed Lucas a note.

He opened the torn page discreetly. *Must follow the job to New Orleans. Marry me there?* was scrawled at the bottom of the page just above the place where the paper was torn. Intuition told him there was more to the message, but there would be time to look into that later.

Coming back to the front of the room, Mr. Brimm said, "I believe I would first like to see your badge, young man."

Lucas silently handed it over. After studying it a moment, Mr. Brimm handed it back.

"It appears to be in order. So what's this about dragging my daughter into a Pinkerton investigation?"

"With all due respect, sir, your daughter invited herself into it. I am tracking a criminal who may have chosen Miss Brimm as his next victim. Had Miss Brimm not been insistent on withholding key information, I would not have need of keeping her in personal custody."

Mr. Brimm's bushy brows shot skyward as he shifted his attention to Flora. "What's this, daughter? Mr. McMinn is not referring to the man you wrote me about, is he?"

"Yes, but it's all a misunderstanding, Father. The man Mr. McMinn is looking for is innocent, and I want to see that the facts are heard."

"Then give him the facts, Flora. All of them."

Her face reddened. "I . . . well, I cannot. It would mean betraying the confidence of someone who trusts me."

"That is ridiculous," he blustered. "Sir, I demand to know why you're using an innocent girl as part of your investigation. She obviously is not keen on giving a straight answer."

"I'm not *using* her, sir. She is in my custody at the moment because she is, at the least, a material witness in an ongoing investigation conducted by the Pinkerton Agency. Any more than that I cannot tell you at this moment because it is classified."

"That's the same reason I cannot tell you why Mr. Tucker is innocent," Flora interjected.

"Did we call a family meeting and forget to invite Grandmama?"

All eyes turned toward the Brimm matriarch, who stood at the door and allowed her gaze to sweep the room before landing on Lucas. "Mr. McMinn, it is always interesting when you and my granddaughter are in collusion. To what do we owe the honor tonight, and is it true you were found dangling up in the air with Flora?"

"He was just leaving, Grandmama," she said as she swiped at the curls that had fallen. "He's going to New Orleans in the morning." She paused only a second. "And I'm afraid I must accompany him."

"No, dear, that's quite impossible." Millicent

Brimm swept into the room and seated herself behind her son's desk. "You cannot possibly leave until the following day. Tomorrow we are hosting a reception for you."

"A reception for me?" She shook her head. "When was I going to be told?"

"Or I?" Flora's father asked.

Mrs. Brimm waved away the protests with a sweep of her bejeweled hand. "It's all quite impromptu, but it should be a lovely afternoon event."

"Afternoon?" Flora turned to Lucas. "We can still sail tomorrow evening."

"No, dear," Mrs. Brimm said. "Tomorrow evening you will be attending a ball held in your honor. It will be a bit of a push to have the house ready for two events, but I'm sure the staff will manage."

"Grandmama, why am I being honored at both a reception and a ball?"

The older woman shrugged. "I may have mentioned on the train from Eureka Springs that my granddaughter did not accompany me on the return trip because she was betrothed."

Flora groaned. "So your friends think I am engaged."

"I'm afraid so. Unfortunately, we will need to borrow a prospective groom for the occasion."

All eyes in the room now swung toward Lucas.

"Oh, no," he said a moment later, grasping their

meaning. "I can't. I . . ." He paused to think about the situation in a rational and calm manner. "Honestly, I cannot think of a worse idea."

"That's funny," Flora said, "because I think it solves everything."

"For you maybe, but . . ." He shook his head. "No. I'm sorry but no. I didn't create this problem, so I fail to see why I should solve it. Not when there's an investigation in progress."

She leaned over to whisper, "It keeps me out of trouble for two days and gets us where we can meet with Mr. Tucker. I don't see the problem, do you?"

"What's that Flora?" her father asked.

"I was just reminding Mr. McMinn of how well he danced aboard the *Americus*. He's quite good." The statement sent Flora and her grandmother off on a conversational tangent about dancing that finally had Mr. Brimm lifting his hands.

"Quiet!" he demanded. "Ladies, I wish to speak to Mr. McMinn alone. Flora, you will go with your grandmother and wait in the hall. As you will both likely stand at the door with your ears pressed against it, I will demand your ear trumpet, Mother, and I will declare that should you eavesdrop, Flora, my valet will alert me to it and you shall find yourself in more trouble than you are already. Now please go, both of you."

"Son, you're not actually asking for my trumpet?"

He held out his hand, waited until his mother complied, and then watched them walk out the door. When they were gone and the door was shut behind them, he turned his attention to Lucas.

"All right. What exactly did she do?"

"I don't know what you mean—"

Her father leaned against the desk and crossed both hands over his chest. "What is my daughter being charged with?"

Ah. "Receipt of stolen property." He paused. "But if it means anything, I don't believe she knew it was stolen."

"And yet you claim she is in your custody."

Lucas shifted positions to rest his elbows on his knees. "Yes, sir. Until I knew for sure she wasn't in cahoots with this Tucker fellow, I needed to keep the suspect—that is, Miss Brimm—close."

"And are you sure now?"

"I am, but I still need her."

"Are we still talking about the investigation?" he asked, one shaggy brow lifted.

"We are, sir."

"Fair enough. I will allow my daughter to see this investigation through on one condition."

Lucas bit back a retort regarding the older man's ability to stop a Pinkerton investigation or to hold back material witnesses. Instead, he inclined his ear toward Mr. Brimm as he swiped at a raindrop that dripped off his hat.

"And what is that, sir?"

"That should you find that my daughter is somehow involved, you will inform me before you make an arrest." He stood. "I love Flora, Mr. McMinn. She has taken on more responsibility for this family than anyone realizes, and yet she still seems to find herself in predicaments that are well beyond what anyone expects."

"Yes, sir. I've seen that."

He regarded Lucas for a moment. "I'm curious. How did the two of you really end up in such a predicament?"

Lucas told him, beginning with the part where he suspected she would climb out of the window, and ending with the explanation of how he got up to the second floor. "We didn't create the device with two persons in mind, and my colleague had just suggested a weight limit of two hundred pounds. My guess is that's where the trouble was."

A look of interest flashed over Mr. Brimm's features. "So you invented this contraption that helps you scale walls?"

"I did, sir. Creating new things is a hobby of mine."

"Have you invented anything else?"

Lucas told him of some of the things he and Kyle had perfected, as well as a few ideas he had been working on.

"You're an interesting man, Mr. McMinn, and well-matched for my daughter. I wonder if you've given any thought to an actual engagement with her."

He certainly hadn't expected that. "I don't think she would have me, sir. Your daughter has her opinions, and I doubt she holds a very high one of me right now."

Mr. Brimm chuckled. "Because you tell her no and refuse to allow her to go off and do things that are unsafe for her? I say bravo to the effort, even if I do not completely approve of the execution of the plan."

"Yes, sir. I suppose that's the problem right there."

"Then I say continue with what you're doing, and please, for my sake, do a passable job of pretending to be my future son-in-law. I would consider that a personal favor. And perhaps you will find you like the job."

"Yes, sir. I will." He rose to shake the older man's hand. "Though with all due respect, I doubt I'm up to the task for longer than a few days."

"We shall see, won't we? Oh, and son, the next time I find you dangling from the second floor with my daughter, all bets are off on what I will do with the pruning shears. Understand?"

"Clearly, sir."

❊ TWENTY-SEVEN ❊

"Come with me, Flora," Grandmama insisted. True to Father's prediction, they had listened outside the door until the men finished their conversation. Slipping into Mrs. Brimm's private parlor, Flora couldn't help but tease her grandmother.

"So," she said as she settled on her favorite spot, a floral divan with a tasseled ottoman for resting her feet. "I couldn't help but notice that you heard the conversation on the other side of the door better than I did."

"Don't be silly." Seated in a lemon-yellow chair nearest the window, her grandmother changed the subject. "I noticed you coaxed Violet out into the sunshine earlier today. Well done."

She had, though it had taken the promise that she would read *Pride and Prejudice* aloud to her to achieve the feat. "I wish I could have done more. Why does she insist on living down there at the cottage?"

"Have you asked her?"

"Repeatedly. She refuses to leave. I did offer up a quote you might recall." At her grandmother's lifted brow, Flora continued. " 'God hath not given us the spirit of fear; but of power, and of love, and of a sound mind.' "

"Well done, my dear." With a soft sigh, Grandmama appeared to turn her attention to the trim on a pillow at her side.

"I won't stop trying. She is just as much a member of this family as I am, and I hate it that she will not be attending the ball."

"Flora, dear, you must be patient."

How could she be, with Brimmfield slipping a little further from her grasp every day? "She is happy there, isn't she?"

"I believe she is," Grandmama said. "Violet has all the comforts of Brimmfield without the invasion of privacy that too often happens here in this house. For now, at least, the cottage suits her. I hope someday soon that will change. In fact, I plan to have her accompany me to take the waters next year. I think it would be quite beneficial. Now, may we speak of something else before your father barges in and interrupts us?"

Violet take the waters? *Yes, Lord, please.* "Of course."

"I've worked hard to keep our family name unsullied. Do not leave out any of the details when you tell me what your plans are with Mr. McMinn."

"Plans with Lucas?" Flora let out a long breath. For once, the demands of the Brimm matriarch did not frighten her.

"Ladies, are you in there?"

One gray brow rose as Flora's grandmother continued to watch her. "We are, son."

Father opened the door, his expression far from grim. "Thank you for your discretion in giving me time alone with Mr. McMinn." He crossed the room to hand Grandmama her ear trumpet.

"I trust you had a worthwhile conversation in our absence," she said as she fitted the device to her ear.

"Yes, very." Father turned his attention to Flora. "You will give your best cooperation to the Pinkerton agent, though you may continue to vex him should he broach propriety."

Flora grinned. "I shall, though I doubt that will be a concern."

Father and Grandmama exchanged a look. "Of course," he said before making his excuses and his escape.

"Do you love him?"

"No, of course not, Grandmama. Why on earth would I love Lucas McMinn?"

Another smile, this one much slower to grow into a broad grin. "Oh, dear, it's much worse than I expected. You're completely smitten and vexed all the same."

Ire rose, as did Flora. "Truly, Grandmama, I thought you were on my side."

"I am, dear. I just find it interesting that when I said *him,* you assumed I was speaking of Mr. McMinn." She gave Flora a pointed look. "You'd best get that sorted in your mind before you marry the wrong man."

The next evening in preparation for the ball in her honor, Flora had Lucy lace her corset tighter than usual. She did this only because she didn't want to give those who tended to gossip a reason to suspect she had any cause to marry quickly other than for love. *If only love really was the cause,* she silently lamented.

Duty would have to suffice.

She held tight to the bedpost and held her breath in while Lucy completed the work of perfecting her tiny waist. As the process of dressing continued, she allowed herself to think of the plan she and Lucas had agreed upon.

This afternoon's reception had gone very well, mostly because he had not been required to attend after all and her grandmother had not mentioned their conversation of the previous evening. Though Grandmama's friends grilled her without ceasing about every detail of her engagement, Flora was able to handle the questions and returned to her bedchamber exhausted but ready for the next event.

Lucy completed her dressing duties and stepped back to offer Flora the mirror. A nod and the maid was gone, leaving Flora alone. Again she went to the window, and this time when she saw the light in the cottage window across from her, she smiled. "It's Wednesday," she whispered. "Two more days and our problem is solved."

A knock diverted Flora's attention. She went to answer the door and found Lucas standing there. Gone was the Pinkerton agent with little regard for fashion or society. In his place stood a well-groomed and well-dressed gentleman with a smile that appeared to be only for her.

"Breathtaking," he said in a voice so soft that she wondered if she had actually been meant to hear.

He offered his arm, and together they walked down to the ballroom, where the band was playing a sedate violin concerto by Vivaldi. At Flora's arrival, the conductor gave the signal to cease the music. Someone must have sent word to Father and Grandmama that they were on their way down, because both of the elder Brimms awaited Flora and Lucas on the dais.

"Ladies and gentlemen, please welcome my daughter Flora and the man who has undertaken the daunting task of seeing to her well-being, Mr. Lucas McMinn."

Interesting how Father managed to speak the truth while giving the impression that Lucas and I are, indeed, engaged.

A round of applause filled the ballroom. "While I'll not ask Mr. McMinn to make a speech at this juncture, I will ask him if he would lead off the dancing tonight."

The next thing Flora realized, Lucas was leading her around the dance floor and the tune had switched to a waltz. Other dancers joined them, including Simon Honeycutt's parents. As the older pair danced closer to Flora and Lucas, she began to cringe.

"What is it?" Lucas asked.

"Mrs. Honeycutt. I don't know what to say to her. It's just awful whenever I see her."

A breath of laughter was in his voice. "Yes, I've seen the lengths you go to avoid her."

He moved her deftly around a slower-moving couple and picked up the thread of conversation once more. "What do you wish you could tell her?"

"How very sorry I am about Simon." She paused. "How deeply I cared for him. And how much I still miss his smile."

He slowed their pace to match the Honeycutts just as the waltz ended. "Then that's what you need to tell her."

For the first time since meeting Lucas, Flora decided to take his advice. Once they had parted, she reached out to Mrs. Honeycutt, and after a long hug, she told her dear friend's mother exactly how she felt. Though tears fell, Flora walked away from the conversation with a deep peace and gratitude that the Lord had somehow used Lucas McMinn's wise words to restore a once-lost relationship.

"That was very nice of you," Grandmama said

a moment later, discreetly handing Flora a scented handkerchief. "I'm sure Miriam heard what she'd hoped from you."

As Flora dabbed daintily at her eyes, she looked out over the crowd and saw Lucas deep in conversation with her father. "What she'd hoped?"

"Yes, dear. All she's ever wanted to hear from you is how very dear Simon was to you. She just needed to know he was loved."

Flora smiled. "I told her that."

"Good girl." Grandmama patted her arm. "Now I must go and mingle."

Seeing that the ballroom doors were open to the balcony overlooking the gardens, Flora slipped outside to breathe in the night air. Strains of a vaguely familiar song drifted toward her on the breeze and settled deep in her heart. As with the last time she stood beneath the stars, Flora found the night sky far too beautiful for words.

"Lovely," Lucas said as he came to stand beside her.

She rested her palms on the rail and let out a long breath. "Yes, the night is beautiful."

"No, Flora," he said gently. "I meant you."

"Thank you." She slid a glance in his direction with a smile. "You clean up quite nicely yourself."

A dip of his head served as his thanks. How long they stood side by side, Flora couldn't say. All the while her conscience niggled at her until finally she turned to face Lucas.

"I need to apologize to you."

"Oh?" He lifted a dark brow. "For what?"

She smiled. "Though I'm sure it would be far more satisfying if I offered up a laundry list of offences to which I would plead an apology, suffice it to say that I realize I've been a pain. Worse, I have put myself and your investigation in danger on more than one occasion."

"You have indeed." Lucas showed the beginnings of his own smile. "Am I to understand you are mending your ways?"

"Mending is such a harsh term. I think I prefer amending."

Lucas chuckled. "And what's the difference, other than one vowel?"

"I am amending the ways I already have. Not changing, but rather refining them." She shrugged as she struggled to keep a straight face. "You see the difference, of course."

"Is that something you learned at that fancy ladies school?"

She turned back to the rail. "I assure you that very little of what I learned at Dillingham Ladies Preparatory School has been of any use to me since I met you." She laughed. "I think my gentle education has been more of a hindrance, actually."

A round of applause indicated the music had ended. Flora looked at him again, and her breath caught as she noticed the angles of his face silhouetted in the moonlight. The cut of his coat and the turned up corners of his smile.

Though the entire image formed an unimaginably handsome whole, the true beauty of this man was in his tenacious search for justice. Whoever this Mary-Margaret person was, his quest was on her behalf. And right or wrong, the loyalty he felt to her was what led him to seek answers in the person of Will Tucker.

It was a revelation. Flora felt as if she were seeing Lucas McMinn for the first time.

Once again the strains of a violin drifted toward her. "Beau Soir," she whispered.

"By special request," Lucas said as he reached out toward her. "May I have this dance?"

Flora smiled. "I would be delighted."

Lucas swept her into his arms, her feet barely touching the ground as they danced. This time it was she who began to sing, and only after the first verse did he join her. They circled around the balcony with the stars for a canopy until the song ended.

"Thank you for the dance," he said though he made no move to step away.

"Your French is flawless."

"Merci."

She met his eyes and then moved out of his arms to twirl as the next song began. "It makes me wonder whether you learned the language at home or took instruction elsewhere."

He lifted a brow as he stood in place. Apparently, he was finished dancing even if she was not. "Flora," he said softly, "please leave the detective work to me."

Coming up to him and offering her most petulant face, the one that almost always worked on her father, Flora decided to try another attempt at prying information from the secretive lawman. "But I know nothing about you, Lucas. After all we've been through together, can't you tell me anything more than the meager details you've shared?"

Lucas leaned closer, his lips almost grazing her ear. "Flora?" he whispered.

"Yes?"

"The answer is no."

She feigned irritation. "That's not fair, Lucas. Just tell me one more thing about you."

"One thing?" He shrugged. "For some unknown reason, I like dancing with you." With this declaration, he drew her close and once again set her in motion to the sound of the orchestra. It was a waltz, though a slow one, and conversation soon became impossible because she was completely mesmerized by the feeling of being held in his arms.

But when the music ended, she found her voice. "Who are you, Lucas McMinn? Really?"

His chuckle was soft, his expression softer. Slowly he slid her a look. "All right, Flora. I suppose you've earned a little trust." He angled closer. "I went to Natchez Under-the-Hill last night to meet with my best friend Kyle. He's a Pinkerton agent too. We joined up together, and until he was assigned to the Denver division and I to the Chicago office, we hadn't been apart much since we were little boys growing up in New Orleans. And he's not only a fellow Pinkerton, but he's also my collaborator on many of the inventions you've seen me use. There. Now you know a little something about me."

Lucas gave her a satisfied look and once again was about to set her in motion. This time she dug in her heels and stalled his dancing.

"That's it?" She shook her head. "Your best friend, Kyle, is an inventor and a Pinkerton agent?"

He shrugged. "Yes, that's it. However, you may meet him in New Orleans. Maybe you can get more out of him than you can out of me, though I doubt it."

She moved away from him to lean against the rail. "You're not working on this case alone?"

"Not anymore," he said as he came to stand beside her. "Kyle has information that says your Mr. Tucker booked passage to New Orleans. When you showed me the note, I was only half surprised."

"Why half?"

"Because you only showed me half the note, Flora."

She jerked her attention up at him. How had he known this?

His green eyes narrowed. "Where are you meeting him?"

"Who is Mary-Margaret?"

He stepped back as if she'd pushed him. And maybe in a way she had.

"One question has nothing to do with the other," he said through a clenched jaw.

"Not true." Flora reached to close the distance between them and then placed her hand atop his. "I need to know if I can trust you, Lucas. You say I've earned a little trust. Show me by answering my question."

He let out a long breath. "She was someone I loved."

"I see."

Disappointment obviously colored her words, for Lucas shook his head. "Not in the way you think. She was family."

Family. Her heart sank even as a tiny part of her felt relief at knowing she was not standing in the shadow of some used-to-be love. "Was?"

"Yes, and as you may have guessed, she is the reason I began this quest to find Tucker." He paused. "She is not the reason I continue it, however."

"And what is that?"

"You, Flora. Even though you're obviously in this for what you will gain from your grandfather's will, you don't deserve what Tucker will do to you."

She squeezed his hand. "How sentimental."

"There's no room for sentiment in a Pinkerton's life," he said slowly as if his thoughts were elsewhere.

"Liar."

"What did you say?"

She grinned. "Oh, come now. You make your life sound so . . ." Flora searched for just the right word. "Dire. Yes, that's it. You sound so dire."

"Dire?" He shook his head. "I don't know about that. What I do know is when a Pinkerton is on the job, there should be no distraction to interfere. Sentiment can be dangerous. It can get me killed."

He thought of the information Kyle had forwarded to him this afternoon on Winthrop Brimm and his mounting debts. Any of the men to whom Brimm owed money might decide Flora posed too great a threat should she be allowed to marry.

"Lucas?"

He softened his expression. "And right now it could get you killed too."

"Oh, please. There is nothing dangerous in this investigation. At the worst you will capture a man who has been doing some bad things, though none of them worth killing someone over." Flora paused as an awful thought occurred. "Oh, no.

You don't think he killed her, do you? Your Mary-Margaret? She's dead, isn't she."

"She is."

"Is Mr. Tucker suspected of her murder?"

A muscle in his jaw clenched. "No," he said slowly, "he is not."

"There, you see?" She shrugged. "I'm very sorry for your loss, but once you talk to him and he shows you his credentials, everything will be just fine."

"What credentials?" he asked, suddenly alert.

Flora pressed her lips shut. She'd said too much. What was it about the moonlight and the nearness of Lucas McMinn that had her wanting to talk without thinking first?

"Flora," he said, his voice deep and very serious. "If you know something that is pertinent to this investigation and you don't tell me, be it the particulars of your upcoming appointment or the details of Tucker's credentials, you're going to be considered just as guilty as he is."

"In this country a person is considered innocent until proven guilty, Lucas McMinn, and you know that is the truth. As for those other things?" She paused to swipe at an errant curl loosened by the evening breeze. "You're just going to have to trust me."

"Trust you?"

She looked up into his beautiful green eyes and smiled. "I know I've said this before, but it bears repeating because you tend to forget. You and I are on the same side. We both want Mr. Tucker caught. And since I simply cannot marry a man with any sort of cloud of suspicion hanging over him—or us—I also want all the facts out so the matter can be handled with the utmost expediency."

"Then tell me what you know and be done with it—"

"I made a promise, Lucas. And even though I've come to care deeply for you, I have not yet found a reason to break that promise. You're just going to have to wait."

There was something new in his eyes as his hand closed over hers. "Flora Brimm, did you just admit that you care for me?"

She had. Heat climbed into her cheeks as she searched for a way to undo the damage she'd just done. For nothing good could come of admitting her growing feelings for this man.

Nothing at all.

"Well . . . of course, I do," she said as casually as she could manage. "You and I are on the same side of this endeavor. Why wouldn't I wish the best for you?"

"That's not what you said, Flora." His voice was low and gentle, his hand suddenly warm atop hers.

Strains of a violin solo drifted past. Grandmama's favorite. She would have Father out on the dance floor for her lone dance of the evening. And then she would plead her usual headache and retire, leaving the "young ones" to their merriment.

Life certainly went on as usual at Brimmfield, even when everything else in her life seemed doomed to tumble forth and change.

"Flora?" Lucas urged her attention to return to him by gently lifting her chin. "You said you care deeply for me. Did you mean it?"

She gazed into his eyes and found she couldn't look away. "You know, Lucas, I did learn one thing at school. A lady is never the first to speak of such things."

The corners of his lips turned up in a wry smile. "Is that so?"

"It is," she said as she leaned slightly forward. "My deportment teacher was adamant."

His arm went around her waist, his palm pressing against her spine, drawing her close. "Adamant? Sounds like any sort of violation of that rule might cause a real problem."

"Problem," she echoed as she lifted up onto her toes. "Yes, absolutely."

"Yes," he said softly, his lips nearly touching hers. "Absolutely."

And then he kissed her.

"Flora," he whispered, his breath warm against her cheek. "I don't know how you've done it, but you have me roped up and moonstruck."

"Is that a good thing?"

"A very good thing, though I don't think we ought to advertise that fact."

"No?" she said softly.

"No." He kissed her again.

And then came the applause.

Flora turned around to see that all of Natchez society, including her father, had come to stand by the open ballroom doors during their kiss. Apparently Grandmama had already pleaded her headache and left, or she likely would be up front offering her opinion.

"Bravo," someone called.

"Bravo, indeed," another shouted.

Lucas immediately did what he did best. He took charge.

"Thank you, ladies and gentlemen. Now, if you will excuse us, I believe my intended and I are going to enjoy a walk in the moonlight."

They descended the stairs that led down to the garden hand in hand and walked away to the fading sound of more applause and the rising notes of a brisk tune. At the edge of the garden, he paused and took her in his arms again. "About what happened back there . . ."

She looked up, hoping to see love, devotion, or at least the need to kiss her again. Instead, his handsome features gave no indication of his feelings, though his embrace told her otherwise.

"We should go back inside. I don't want your

father coming after me with the pruning shears."

"I think my father's going to allow us our walk. It's what would be expected of the father of the bride-to-be, and my father always does what is expected."

"I see." He reluctantly released her but then took her hand again in his warm clasp. "Then that means we have some time to discuss this investigation a little more. If you don't trust me now that I've admitted I'm falling for you faster than a buggy down an icy road, I don't know what will."

"True, though it might help if you kissed me again."

He lifted a dark brow. "Flora, you are incorrigible."

Flora's grip on his hand tightened. "Come with me, Lucas. I want you to meet someone."

"You're trying to divert my attention," he said. "Trust me with the rest of the information Tucker sent you."

"All right. Mr. Tucker has set a meeting place for Friday."

"What time and where?"

She shook her head and dropped his hand. "I've told you enough for now," she said as she moved down the gravel path that led through the garden.

"Oh, no you don't. You're not escaping that easily." He caught up to her and wrapped one arm around her waist to stop her progress.

"I'm not escaping. Remember, I'm amending my ways."

"Right. I'd almost forgotten. So where is it you think you're going?"

"We're both going." Flora nodded toward the end of the path, a destination hidden by the cottonwoods and gardens. "You'll just have to trust me."

He hauled her close, his palm pressing against her spine. "No tricks," he whispered.

"No tricks."

The moonlight filtered through the leaves of the cottonwood tree and splashed his features with silver. He dipped his head to kiss her again, and after his lips at last left hers and she looked up at him, she saw that the errant lock of hair she'd noticed yesterday had fallen onto his forehead again. When she reached to slip it back into place, he wrapped her hand in his.

"Flora," he said softly, "developing any sort of feelings for you is the worst thing I could do as a lawman. You do understand that."

"Yes," she whispered.

"All right. Lead on."

❄ TWENTY-EIGHT ❄

Against his better judgment, Lucas followed Flora down the path that wound through the garden and around the cottonwoods. Not that he had much left in the way of judgment. He'd abandoned that as well as any measure of good sense when he went looking for Flora and found her alone under the stars.

Somehow, admiring her had turned to conversing, and conversing had turned to kissing. And somewhere in between he'd admitted to feeling moonstruck and hog-tied. Lucas shook his head. How had she managed it, this blue-eyed belle? It made no sense.

Yet all he could think of was the feel of her in his arms, the touch of her hand in his, and the sweetness of her kiss. And lilacs. As long as he lived, the sweet scent of lilacs would forever be associated with Miss Flora Brimm of Natchez, Mississippi.

Flora Tucker, unless he managed to keep that from happening.

The sound of something akin to a loud explosion of gunfire caused Lucas to turn around. Yanking Flora against him, he scanned the perimeter. Shouts from the main house indicated the direction from which the shooter had fired.

Or, more likely, the direction the gun had been aimed.

He reached into his pocket and took out a weapon he'd designed for situations such as this and then pulled Flora beneath the low-hanging limbs of an ancient magnolia tree. He put the device in her hand.

"What is it? It looks like a comb." She turned her head to the house, her face stricken. "Lucas, what do you think just happened?"

"I'll let you know when I come back for you. Until I do, you stay right here." He put his hand under her chin and brought her eyes back to his. "And do not try my patience by ignoring my order. There could be a gunman loose, do you understand?" When she nodded, he continued. "The comb in your hand is a knife. If you press that little button at the end, a very sharp blade will come out. Keep your fingers free of that area at all times." He paused. He didn't want to leave her there alone. "Are you going to be all right?"

"Yes. And I promise to stay here. I don't want to be the cause of your distraction."

He gave her one last look and then kissed her quickly before heading toward the main house, his pulse beating staccato as he ran. As he passed the edge of the formal gardens and emerged into the clearing between the woods and the Brimm home, Lucas kept to the shadows.

A few partygoers were still racing down the back stairs to join those already gathered in clusters on the lawn. Spying Mr. Brimm comforting a matron who appeared near fainting, Lucas jogged toward him with his revolver at the ready.

"What happened?" he asked the older man.

"No idea. One minute we were dancing and the next there was an explosion that sounded as if it was right there in the ballroom with us. We all evacuated as quickly as we could."

"I thought the Yankees had come back for us," the older woman said as Mr. Brimm continued to fan her with his handkerchief.

"Sir, I need to ask you to keep everyone out here and away from the ballroom and any windows. Do not under any circumstances come inside until I release you to do so. Do you understand?"

"I do, Mr. McMinn. Thank you for taking care of this matter."

"I'll do my best." Lucas made his way as quickly as he could manage through the crowd and then took the steps two at a time to arrive on the balcony. A quick glance at the perimeter told him if the shooter was hidden, he could strike again at any moment, such was the depth of darkness there.

Pressing his back to the wall, he held his revolver at the ready. Inching toward the edge of the first window, he took a deep breath, offered up a quick prayer for safety, and then leaned over to glance inside the empty ballroom. He repeated the process each time he passed an open window until he arrived at the last one.

There he paused only a moment before bursting inside. A preliminary sweep of the perimeter told him the room was empty.

Then a sound behind him caused Lucas to whirl around, his gun drawn. Mr. Brimm's valet was standing in the doorway.

"I'm sorry for the trouble, sir." The valet raised his hands, one holding a cleaning cloth and the other a small brush.

"Did you see where the shooter went?" Lucas demanded as he lowered his weapon.

"Shooter?" The valet's eyes went wide as he dropped his hands back down by his side. "Oh, no! Was someone shooting too?"

Lucas gave the perimeter another sweeping glance before returning his attention to the valet. "Too?"

"Yes, well Mrs. Brimm's favorite Italian mirror is irreplaceable. It's thirteenth century, from the palazzo on Lake Como where she and Colonel Brimm spent their honeymoon. Thank goodness she had already retired for the night so she was spared seeing it broken." He paused. "But to think that on top of such a tragedy someone would resort to gunfire?"

The odd thought that Millicent Brimm might

indeed consider breaking her favorite Italian mirror occurred but he quickly discarded it. Another idea, much more plausible, came to mind.

"Show me the mirror."

"Of course, sir. What's left of it, that is."

Lucas followed the man, his weapon still at the ready. Through the open doors he could hear the hushed sounds of the people outside. Somewhere down below the property, likely aboard a river vessel, a bell clanged.

"That one." The valet gestured to the far end of the room, where the remains of a mirror glittered under the chandeliers' light, its ornate gold frame suspended the full length between the ebony floor and the gilt ceiling. Pieces of the mirror covered a fussy-looking table similar to the one in his mother's formal parlor and stuck out in odd angles from the remains of the candles that had been burning there.

He moved closer, shards of glass crunching beneath his feet. The valet carefully picked his way around the debris.

Lucas nodded to the cleaning cloth and brush in the valet's hands. "Did you see this happen?"

"I did, sir." The valet ran his hands over the edge of the gold-leaf on the frame. "During the course of the ball, the candelabra on the table was accidentally pushed directly up against the mirror. I saw that from a distance away, and I suspected that the flame from the candles, which are quite large and specially made for Mrs. Brimm here on the property, might generate enough heat to cause trouble with the glass, which is somewhat fragile. It is hundreds of years old."

"Indeed. Go on."

"I immediately walked over to remedy the situation, but I wasn't able to move the candelabra in time."

Lucas nodded thoughtfully. A mirror this large—at least fifteen feet in length—would have broken with great force and greater noise. The loud explosion would certainly have sounded like gunfire.

But he needed to be sure. "Except for the loss of Mrs. Brimm's favorite mirror, there have been no casualties or injuries here tonight?"

"No, sir."

After one last sweeping glance around the room, Lucas nodded again. "All right. Carry on. I'll inform Mr. Brimm that his merrymaking can continue."

He left the valet sweeping up the mess. Flora's father met him on the lawn. From the look of the number of people still milling about, curiosity had won out over concern to keep them waiting for any sort of news.

"Did you catch the man who did this?" Mr. Brimm demanded.

"There was no gunman, sir. Just a candelabra set too close to a mirror."

Mr. Brimm shook his head, his expression shifting from relief to concern. "Oh, no! Not Mother's favorite Italian mirror. She brought it back from her honeymoon at Lake Como. It's quite old and very precious to her."

"The good news is the frame is still intact."

Mr. Brimm gave a weary nod and then ascended to the third step of the balcony stairs to address his guests. His voice chased Lucas down the path and into the cottonwoods.

"Flora?" he called when he reached the tree where he'd left her.

No response.

How Will Tucker had found her, Flora could only imagine. That he'd risked detection to slip up beside her while she hid behind the tree was proof he'd gone to great lengths to achieve a meeting. What he hadn't expected was to find her armed with a comb—that was also a knife.

Knowing Lucas could return any minute, Flora had marched her prisoner some distance from the magnolia tree to back him up against the little white cottage at the edge of the property.

"I want some answers from you. Understand?"

He nodded but said nothing. A good sign she had him properly frightened for his well-being.

"All right. First and foremost, I want you to tell me who your employer is, Will Tucker, and I want the truth."

In an instant any fear or respect was gone. In its place was the charming, rakish grin of the man she'd met on the steamboat weeks ago.

"Sweet Flora," he said as he leaned against the cottage and affected a casual pose. "I've told you more than once that I am a detective in the employ of the Frisco Railroad. What brings you cause to ask again?" He nodded toward the knife. "And to accost me in such an unfriendly way? If I were a less understanding man, I would take serious offence."

"Then I suppose we're both fortunate you're an understanding man." She nodded to his coat. "However, if you have a badge in there, now would be the time to produce it."

"My badge?" He shrugged. "I can't do that, Flora."

"Because you're not a detective?" she said as her heart lurched.

"Because when I am working undercover, it would be foolish to carry a badge. You do understand, don't you?" He leaned forward as if to touch her sleeve, and Flora moved to counter him by swiping the knife in his direction. His eyes widened. "You're really upset with me, aren't you?"

She allowed her gaze to scorch the length of him. "You have caused me no end of trouble, Mr. Tucker. You have no idea what I have dealt with since you left Eureka Springs. My grandmother has questions, and my father—"

"I'm a topic of conversation? Well now, I like the sound of that," Mr. Tucker interrupted. "So the old lady approves?"

"My grandmother trusts my judgment. Should she ever hear you call her 'the old lady,' however, she would not only disapprove, but she would likely have your head on a platter."

His attention went to her hand and then back up to Flora's face. "Appears to run in the family."

"This is not the time for jokes, Mr. Tucker. I am very close to calling off our arrangement."

Flora paused to allow herself to believe she'd just spoken her thoughts aloud. For though she was mightily irked at the man's casual attitude to their impending nuptials, she was even more bothered by the feelings she had for Lucas McMinn.

Could she truly marry another when her heart refused to allow room for anyone other than the irritating Pinkerton agent?

"All right," he said, his tone placating. "I deserve that."

If he expected her to respond, to make some sort of allowance for his behavior, he could wait all night. It simply would not happen.

"See, Flora, it's like this." Mr. Tucker leaned toward her, and she once again pointed the comb at him.

"You're still in trouble, sir, so do not presume to come any closer until I allow it. Do you understand?"

"Perfectly. As I said, I know I deserve this." He paused to give her a look that should have melted her heart. "I wanted to be with you. You cannot imagine how difficult it was to attend to my duties when I had nothing but you on my mind."

"What duties, Mr. Tucker? You've not yet proven anything regarding duty. How am I to know that you're telling the truth?"

"You just have to trust me. Yes, that's right, Flora. Trust me. That's what wives do. They trust their husbands. And you have to admit I've kept in touch. You have no idea what danger I've courted just by showing up here tonight." He paused. "But I wanted to see you. Needed to, actually."

A bell clanged out on the river, and he glanced over in that direction. Flora, however, kept her attention focused on her intended.

"That's my signal. Will I see you in New Orleans on Friday?"

"I think the real question here is will I see you?" she said as she retracted the blade and tucked the comb into her pocket.

"Of course you will. I'm as good as my word, and I give you my word."

"And the license?" she demanded. "I suppose you have that already?"

He had the audacity to wink. "Of course not. But one of my men is seeing to it. A trusted associate."

"Mr. Wilson?"

He flinched at the name. "Don't you worry,

Flora. Now, dare I approach to give my bride-to-be a kiss on the cheek, or should I take my leave and be glad I am in one piece?"

Flora crossed her hands over her chest and gave him a severe look. "I think for now you'd best choose the latter. We can discuss the former once the state of Louisiana declares our marriage legal and final."

Was it her imagination or did his confidence slip slightly? If so, the moment was fleeting, and Mr. Tucker gave her a wink and a smile. "Have it your way." Another bell and he shrugged. "The last warning. I must say goodbye. Until Friday, sweet Flora."

He turned to go, and only as he was disappearing into the thicket did a question occur to her. "Mr. Tucker," she called to his retreating back.

"Yes?" he responded over his shoulder.

She was careful to move close enough to see his handsome face. "Does the name Mary-Margaret McMinn mean anything to you?"

Even in the moonlight, she could see the change in his expression. She had guessed the last name, but his face told her she'd guessed correctly.

His mask of calm swiftly returned. "Why?"

"I'm asking the questions, Mr. Tucker."

His shoulders sagged. "All right. My associate Jack Wilson and I are investigating her death." He paused. "We believe it wasn't an accident, given that her brother is the only witness. Now, unless you have more questions, I'll see you Friday."

"No," she said softly. "Nothing else."

As Flora watched him slip away into the thicket, she tried to sort the facts from whatever fiction one of the two men in her life had created. Was Lucas McMinn searching for Will Tucker, or was the opposite true? And why did she feel completely safe in the Pinkerton's arms and ever wary in the presence of the railroad detective? It was all too confusing.

"Flora?"

Lucas.

She sighed. Of course. "I'm over here," she called as she watched him slip from the shadows onto the path.

True to form, he was scowling. "Once again, Flora, you did not do as I asked." He moved closer. "What happened?"

Her fingers trembled as she kept them away from the wrong edge of the comb. Anything to divert her attention from her racing thoughts. "What happened at the house? Was that gunfire we heard?"

"Candles were too close to a mirror and the heat shattered it." He paused. "Now, please answer me. Why did you once again ignore my instructions to remain in place until I—"

"He was here," she interrupted.

"Who was here? Tucker?" He looked around

and then back at Flora. "Which way did he go?"

"That way. Toward the river." As he turned to bolt in that direction, Flora grabbed his wrist. "Wait! I need to know something first. Was Mary-Margaret your sister?"

❦ TWENTY-NINE ❦

Lucas ignored the question to race off in the direction Mr. Tucker had disappeared. For the first time, he left no instructions for Flora. Why bother? The infuriating woman did what she wanted anyway. And there was no telling what lies Tucker had passed on to her.

As he ran, he kept his eyes trained on the perimeter with the knowledge that Tucker could be anywhere. Even as he followed the criminal's trail, his mind returned to Flora.

He traced several paths to the river and used his personal torch to search the water's edge. Even with the help of the light, Lucas could only see a limited distance across the Mississippi, allowing for a man in a boat to have fled, given the opportunity. Donning his extra-vision glasses and fitting in the hearing device from his hat, Lucas still didn't see or hear anyone.

His frustration rose.

Putting away the hearing device, he kept the

glasses in place and went back to the most likely place where Tucker could have made his escape. Another close inspection of the bank showed at least two possible places where someone could have recently launched a skiff, giving further weight to his theory.

With Tucker once again eluding capture, Lucas went back to find that Flora had actually waited for him right where he'd left her, though she was not alone. The person attending her wore the Brimm family uniform, indicating she was a servant.

"Tell her I will be in to visit momentarily," he heard Flora whisper to the older woman. She nodded in response and slipped back inside the cottage.

"What else did he tell you?" Lucas demanded once the door had closed.

"He said you were the only witness and might be implicated in her death. Or responsible. Or something. Oh, I don't know. But he was investigating."

Struggling to remain calm, Lucas measured his words carefully. "Who did he claim he works for?"

She handed him back the comb and shook her head. Lucas couldn't help but notice how close she remained to him. And, of course, there was the scent of lilacs. Always the scent of lilacs.

"The railroad."

"Which one?"

"The Frisco." Flora lifted her gaze, her lower lip quivering. "He asked me to keep that confidential, but I don't know what to think, Lucas. Truly I don't." She put her hand in the crook of his arm and leaned against him, her head on his shoulder.

So Tucker was masquerading as a railroad detective. That alone would bring another host of charges to the already growing list on his warrant.

"What did he want?" He made a decent attempt at sounding gruff, but the feel of Flora next to him undid any irritation caused by her misbehavior. "Tell me exactly what he said."

She took a deep breath and let it out slowly. "That's all, really. Except that he wanted to be sure I would still meet him in New Orleans."

Lucas slid the comb back into his pocket and put his arm around her, hugging her to him. Slowly he lifted his gaze to meet hers. "Details, Flora? Trust me."

She blinked. Twice. "Yes, I think I do. Friday at noon. Jackson Square. That's all I know."

Studying her a moment, he knew she was telling the truth. "Thank you," he said as he wrapped his other arm around her. "For trusting me," he added.

She pressed her palms against his chest to lean back just enough that her eyes once again met his. "Trust me," she whispered. "And tell me about Mary-Margaret."

He froze.

She kept silent. A rare thing for a woman so bent

on stating her opinion. Lucas would have given anything for her to start talking so he did not have to.

Tell me what to say, Lord, was the best prayer he could manage as he looked up at the stars and then back at Flora. "She was my sister, and I failed to protect her," he said when his voice would allow.

"But you're a Pinkerton," she said, oblivious to the stab of fresh pain the statement caused.

"Yes. I couldn't save Mary-Margaret, but I won't fail to protect you, Flora." He paused to wait out the lump in his throat. "You're just going to have to trust me."

She rested her head against his chest. "More trusting?"

A chuckle rumbled in his chest. " 'Fraid so."

Again she leaned up to seek his gaze. "Come with me and meet my sister."

Her fingers reached for his as she slipped out of his embrace and led him around the corner of the white cottage. After a quick knock she stepped inside with Lucas a pace behind. The servant he'd seen Flora speaking to before now rose to greet them.

The contrast between the humble exterior of the cottage and its elegant interior was striking. Furnishings that would have appeared right at home up at the main house filled the tiny space with a comfortable yet formal arrangement.

Gaslights hung overhead and cast a soft light on the room, while the thick tangle of roses climbing the eastern side of the building was the likely culprit for the heady scent in the air. Above it all, however, was a deep feeling of peace that permeated the structure.

He caught a few words and watched as Flora spoke, but his attention remained on the parlor where he now stood. Lucas couldn't help but notice some baskets in the almost child-size room, filled almost to overflowing with what appeared to be letters and postcards.

"Did she have a good afternoon?"

"Yes, ma'am," the maid said. "She's sleeping now, but I can wake her up."

"No, don't do that. We can come back another time—"

"Flora, don't go," came the soft voice of a woman in the other room. "Send Daisy in to help me, please."

As the maid disappeared into the other room, Lucas glanced over to the open door and what was obviously a bedchamber beyond. The same pale white of the walls continued into that room. Over the fireplace he saw a painting of two laughing girls. A dark-haired girl of not more than seven or eight stood beneath the gnarled limbs of a giant magnolia tree. Nearby a slightly younger female child sliced through the air in a swing, leading with her bare feet and trailing with long locks of glorious red hair.

"The Brimm sisters," Flora said as she came over to him. "Grandmama thought it scandalous that we were painted with bare feet, but Mama insisted."

"And your mother won. She must have been a formidable woman." Lucas knew from the dossier on the family that the late Mrs. Brimm had succumbed to yellow fever several years ago.

"Apparently it is a trait among Brimm women."

"What happened?" he said softly. "And why is she out here?"

"She's here because it's where she's happiest." Flora shrugged. "I know that sounds completely crazy, but she rests comfortably here."

"It doesn't sound crazy at all."

"Her nurse thinks it's the quiet and coziness of the little cottage." Flora paused. "I think it may be because Grandmama built this for use as the family chapel before Father fitted it out for Violet and her nurse. In either case, the presence of the Lord seems quite real here, and I think Violet senses it. Unfortunately, it keeps her from rejoining the family up at the big house, something I feel is completely wrong."

"I heard that."

Lucas turned toward the voice and saw a beautiful woman staring openly at him. Though her eyes were a match for Flora's, her smile was purely her own. A blanket swaddled her, and her arms were thin, her fingers lying still in her lap as the maid pushed her chair into the parlor.

He greeted her with a smile of his own. "You must be Violet."

She dipped her head. "Might you be Mr. Tucker or Mr. McMinn?"

"Lucas McMinn."

"The Pinkerton." She nodded toward Flora. "My sister speaks highly of you."

"Does she?" He met Flora's gaze. "That is a surprise."

Flora playfully nudged him before looking away.

He gestured to the baskets. "What's the story with the letters and postcards."

Flora said softly, "Those are from me."

"You?" He glanced around the room again. "All of them?"

"She writes every day when she's away," Violet supplied. "It gives Daisy something to read other than the books I've heard far too many times."

Flora worried her sleeve before lifting her gaze to meet Lucas's. "And it lets me feel as though I'm doing something to help pass the hours she spends here when I'm not at home." She turned to face Violet. "For some reason, she refuses to move back into the house with us. Or rejoin the world. It's quite maddening."

"I like it here."

"I know you do," Flora said gently as she moved

to kneel beside her sister's chair. "But the truth is, I'm concerned."

"I'm fine, Flora."

"It's not you I'm concerned about. Grandmama isn't getting any younger, and Father's mostly away when she's here." She paused to shake her head at her sister's attempt to speak. "Please just consider it. Grandmama needs you, Vi. More than you need your privacy. Contrary to what she believes, Millicent Brimm is not going to live forever. She wants you to take the waters with her."

Violet seemed to consider the statement. "I don't know. There are so many—"

"People? Yes, there are. And some of them may see you in this chair." Flora rose and crossed her arms. "So what? Then they will see how very brave you are." She shook her head. "You saved my life. Do not let my stupid mistake take yours."

Violet looked beyond Flora to meet Lucas's gaze. "Is she this bossy with you?"

"Regularly."

"Then she must love you too."

"Violet Brimm, that's enough out of you," Flora said. "Just promise me you will consider what I've asked of you."

"I promise to consider it."

They made their exit a short while later and left Violet in the capable hands of the maid. Emotion gripped him, and Lucas had to swallow the lump in his throat as a thought occurred. "What will happen to her if your cousin inherits Brimmfield?"

She looked up sharply. "He won't," she snapped before moderating her expression and her tone. "I will not allow it."

"Because he will not permit Violet to stay at Brimmfield?"

"Because he will not permit either of us to stay. Once Grandmama is gone, Brimmfield will be put up for sale if Winny inherits it. He has already made it abundantly clear that he considers Natchez far inferior to New Orleans. Keeping a home here is not his intention."

He let out a long breath as the spoiled and pampered princess changed before his eyes to become a caring sister willing to put the welfare of another ahead of any idea of her own happiness. He also thought of the debts Kyle had uncovered. Nothing other than ridding himself of Brimmfield would likely make sense to Winthrop Brimm.

"But if you marry Tucker and produce a child, you will inherit Brimmfield and secure your sister's welfare." Her refusal to meet his questioning look was all the answer he needed. "You can't do this, Flora. Surely the Lord has another way planned."

"If He does, He is remaining awfully silent on the matter."

They strolled the remainder of the distance back to the house in silence, the moonlight following them down the path and then up the front steps. A few stragglers remained in the ballroom, their merrymaking apparently no longer affected by the earlier excitement. As Lucas walked a step behind Flora up the stairs to part ways at the second floor landing, the orchestra played them to their rooms.

He paused at his door to glance down to the opposite end of the hall and caught her doing the same. Lucas quickly closed the distance between them.

"If Father were to catch you anywhere near my bedchamber door, he *would* take the pruning shears to you," she said, though she made no move to escape his presence.

"I would expect nothing less." He reached to touch a fiery curl and wrapped it around his finger. "However, I am willing to risk his wrath to thank you for introducing me to Violet."

She remained silent, though her eyes never left his.

"I want you to know," he said softly, "that while I do not believe you are going about this the right way, if Will Tucker somehow proves his innocence, I will wish the two of you the best."

"Will you?" she said, her gaze sharp. "Or is that just what you had to say to make me feel better about marrying for something other than love?"

Lucas released her curl to touch her lips with his finger. Then he slowly removed his finger to press his lips gently against hers.

"Good night, Flora Brimm," he whispered against her ear. "And the answer to both of those questions is yes."

He walked down the long hall, feeling her watching him every step of the way. And long after he was lying down and trying to sleep, his eyes remained open and his thoughts remained centered on Flora. If he'd been this wrong about her and her motives, what else had he misjudged about her?

When he climbed into the carriage to find she'd beat him there the following afternoon, Lucas was still wondering about the beautiful Miss Brimm. As they left the gates of Brimmfield behind, Flora leaned back against the seat and closed her eyes.

"Tired?" he asked.

"Yes," was her soft response. "I didn't get much sleep."

Tempted to concur, Lucas instead merely nodded. "Maybe you'll stay in your stateroom and rest." He waited for her to open her eyes and look in his direction.

Then he winked.

"You are incorrigible."

"No, Flora, I am practical."

The corner of her lips turned up in the beginnings of a smile. "Remember, I've amended my ways."

His snort of disbelief caused her maid to turn and peer back at them. "Is something wrong, Miss Brimm?" the elderly busybody asked.

Of course Flora's father would send his daughter with the one member of the household staff who appeared immune to Lucas's charms. It was exactly what he would do if he had a daughter.

Thank goodness he never planned to fall into that sort of trouble.

Once aboard the *Leviathan*, his prisoner and her guard in petticoats disappeared into Flora's stateroom. When the dinner hour arrived, Lucas stood in front of the door trying to decide whether to knock until Flora finally opened it.

"I grew tired of waiting," she said as she swept past him dressed in a deep blue that matched the night sky, leaving Lucas to trail behind her.

Owing to the fact this steamboat was much smaller than the grand *Americus*, Lucas found himself alone with Flora at a table for two. He glanced around, half expecting to see her maid watching from behind a curtain or staring back from some dark corner.

"What are you looking for?" Flora demanded as she pushed around the same bite of food she had been toying with for the past five minutes.

Lucas nodded toward her almost-full plate. "I could ask you the same thing."

Giving up any pretense of continuing with her dinner, Flora set the fork aside and sighed. "I discovered that my mother's favorite earrings are missing. I've looked for them everywhere, and they're gone."

"I see," he said as evenly as he could manage. "Any idea what happened to them?"

"Don't toy with me, Lucas." She tossed her napkin on the table. "I don't want you to be right. I hope you know that."

"If it's any consolation, I'm not taking any pleasure in this."

"It is, I suppose. I just thought that maybe . . ." Another sigh. "Oh, I've been completely single minded and obtuse, haven't I?"

"Single minded and obtuse?" He suppressed a grin. "You're going to have to help me with that."

"All I could see was how to best fix the problem of Grandfather Brimm's will. And because of that, I've been blind to anything else, including the possibility I might be wrong about Mr. Tucker."

Well now. He bit back the *I told you so* he wanted to say. "I would have to agree," was his response instead.

Their gazes met and Lucas felt the collision down to his toes.

"I want my mother's earrings back. If it means I must beg some sort of arrangement with Cousin Winny to keep Violet safe rather than marry Will Tucker, I don't care."

The vehemence with which she spoke surprised him. The expression on her face gave him cause to worry.

"Flora, I understand, but you need to leave the detective work to me. Do *you* understand? I'll need a detailed description of them for my report."

"Of course," she said as she gave him her sweetest smile and rose. "If you'll excuse me, I think I'm ready to go back to my stateroom."

Lucas followed suit, even though it meant leaving half a plate of delicious food on the table. He followed her bouncing curls until she wove her way out of the dining room. Then he caught up to fall in step beside her.

"You're not thinking of trying to get those earrings back on your own, are you?"

She continued walking in silence until she reached her room. Lucas placed his hand over the knob and himself between her and the door.

"Flora." While he hoped his voice conveyed the appropriate amount of warning, her expression told him it did not. "Flora Brimm, do not even think of doing anything without my knowledge. Are we clear on this?"

She looked up into his eyes, and Lucas swore he saw a twinkle there. "Of course, Lucas. Perfectly clear. And remember," she said as she placed her hand over his. "I've amended my ways."

"Why am I more concerned now than ever?"

he asked as he bent down to draw her into an embrace. "For once, please listen to me."

"Oh, stop talking and kiss me, Lucas, before I'm forcibly hauled back into my stateroom by the nanny Father sent to protect what remains of Fatal Flora's reputation."

So he did.

❧ THIRTY ❧

The following morning, Lucas awoke to a knock on the door. How he'd managed to oversleep and miss the vessel's landing, he could only attribute to once again losing far too much sleep thinking about Flora Brimm. Thankfully, his years as a Pinkerton had taught him how to step out of his bedroll and into his clothes in record time.

Still adjusting his collar, he met Flora and her maid on the dock. A carriage had already been delivered for their use, and someone in livery—presumably from Winthrop Brimm's household staff—was loading their bags.

"Good morning, ladies," he said as if he hadn't sprinted until just before he reached sight of them.

Lucas noticed Kyle Russell leaning against a shed a short distance away. When their eyes met, Kyle nodded.

Flora touched his sleeve, drawing his attention

away from his fellow Pinkerton. "When you weren't at breakfast, I thought you'd decided to leave me to my own devices."

"And I still might. If you'll excuse me just a moment, I need to speak to someone."

"But what if we're ready to go and you're not back?" she called.

"Then it would be in your best interest to wait," he said over his shoulder as he closed the distance to greet his best friend.

After the pleasantries were exchanged, he got down to business. "What have you got for me on Brimm?"

"As far as I can tell, the guy's clean. He's strapped for cash, but he's been throwing around some sort of big inheritance he's due to come into."

"Brimmfield?"

"It's possible. The old man's will is sealed, so I would have to have access to family to get a look at the terms." Kyle glanced past Lucas. "Or I could just ask your friend Flora."

"Right." Lucas turned to see the woman in question walking their way and suppressed a groan. "Anything else before she joins us?"

"Just that the word you had on his India hunting trip wasn't exactly correct. He backed out at the last minute. My source couldn't say why, only that he'd practically dropped the news as the men were getting on the boat."

"Money troubles." A statement, not a question.

"Could be, but if that's true, he's likely not the only one. I did some checking, and the only one of those men who concerns me is Martin Lennart. His wife and daughters are expensive, and I'm not so sure his companies are completely able to handle that kind of financial drain."

"Could Lennart be leaning on Cousin Winny to pay a debt? That would explain his reluctance to spend a month with the man and his hunting rifle."

"It's possible." He paused. "McMinn, that is one fine-looking woman. And if I weren't such a good judge of character, I would think she only thought of you as the Pinkerton out to jail her fiancé."

Lucas turned to face him. "What does that mean?"

"Just that it doesn't take a fool to see that Flora Brimm's crazy about you, pal. If I were you, I'd watch myself around her."

"Doesn't do any good. She's already crawled up under my skin. The sooner this case is over, the sooner I will forget about her and have a good night's sleep."

"I doubt that," Kyle said as he once again fixed his attention to a spot behind Lucas. "Well, hello there, Miss Brimm," he said with the smile he reserved for only the prettiest of pretty women. "Kyle Russell, inventor, Pinkerton agent, and unfortunate acquaintance of your Mr. McMinn since well before his mama allowed him out without his nursemaid."

Kyle thrust his hand out toward Flora. Instant jealousy flamed when Flora not only smiled but also allowed his old friend to kiss her hand.

"Yes, of course," she said as the smile broadened. "Mr. McMinn has spoken of you, Mr. Russell. Though I must say he did not tell me how very handsome you are."

It was all Lucas could do not to gape at the woman. Was she actually flirting? And with his best friend?

"Likewise, ma'am. I wonder if I might walk you to your carriage. This late May sunshine can wreak havoc on a lovely lady's skin if she's out in it too long. At least, that's what my New Orleans mama always said."

That was what *his* New Orleans mother always said, not Kyle's. What in the world was his soon-to-be-former best friend up to?

"Thank you. It's so kind of you to consider my welfare." The latter she said to Kyle while looking directly at Lucas. "A true gentleman is a rare thing."

"So is a man who tells the truth," Lucas echoed as he fell into step beside them. Looking past her to fix his attention on Kyle, he gave the man a look that would have withered cotton. Of course, Kyle ignored it.

Reaching the carriage, Flora allowed Kyle to help her up. "Might you join us? We're headed into town."

"Thank you, Miss Brimm. Actually, that would be most kind of you." He shot Lucas a glance that appeared to ask for him to play along.

Lucas gave an almost imperceptible nod, though he also offered up a hard look that told Kyle exactly what he thought of the too-familiar banter between him and Flora Brimm. Before he could climb in to take the spot next to Flora, Lucas elbowed his way in front of him.

"Don't even think about it," he whispered as he made himself comfortable beside Flora. Only then did he realize that, from the seat opposite her, Kyle not only held Flora's attention, but he also sat in the one spot where it was impossible for her to look away.

They rode into New Orleans with Flora and Kyle making small talk while Lucas sat quietly and glowered.

"Isn't that something?" Kyle said, laying his charm on thick as he leaned across the space between them in the carriage. "Here I was just saying hello to an old friend, and now you and I are practically—"

"And we're here," Lucas announced. "Sorry we can't stay and chat longer, but I'm sure you have things to do that are much more important than that."

445

"No," Kyle said thoughtfully. "I don't believe I do."

"Well, isn't that lovely?" Flora beat both of them to the punch by allowing one of the liveried Brimm housemen to help her from the carriage.

As the servants unloaded the carriage, Lucas took Kyle aside. "If you could stop the flirting for one minute, I'd like to finish our conversation."

To Lucas's supreme irritation, his friend laughed. "Flirting?" He shook his head. "That was nothing of the sort. Has that woman got you so head-over-heels that you've forgotten everything you learned in training?"

Lucas inclined his head, all the while watching Flora as she was deep in conversation with her maid. "So you were getting cozy with her to see what you could find out about her cousin?"

"No. To see what I could find out about the two of you."

"And?"

He slapped Lucas on the shoulder. "And you probably ought to just marry her. Pending final analysis, there's likely no basis to the rumors of her fiancés' early demises, so I'm reasonably certain you're safe. There is the issue of Flora Brimm being party to a Pinkerton investigation, but, of course, I'm sure that with you being a professional and all, that won't be a problem."

"Mr. Russell," Flora called, interrupting any

possible response. "Won't you join Lucas and me for tea? I would so love to continue our conversation."

"What she's saying," Lucas added, loud enough for Flora to hear, "is that she wants to pry any possible details of my childhood and the Tucker investigation out of you." He shrugged. "Of course, I'm sure that with you being a professional and all, that won't be a problem."

Kyle slipped past Lucas to take Flora's hand and once again press it to his lips. "I regret I must decline your generous offer after all, Miss Brimm, though I will be most glad to see you again tonight at the Governor's Ball. I do hope you'll save room on your dance card for a Pinkerton agent."

She met Lucas's eyes. "Yes," she said, smiling, "I've saved plenty of room on my dance card for a Pinkerton agent." Abruptly, her attention returned to Kyle. "However, as you and I are barely acquainted, I fear the Pinkerton lawman who has claimed my dances is Mr. McMinn. I'm sure you understand."

He nodded and released her hand. "I do indeed." Kyle stepped away toward Lucas. "Well," he said quietly with a grin that made Lucas want to punch him. "I'd say I've found out exactly what I needed to here."

"And that is?" Lucas growled.

"I don't know how you've let it happen, old

friend, but you've fallen hard for that pretty gal. The bad news is, if I had to guess, I'd say she feels the same way."

Lucas watched Flora and her maid walk up the stairs to the front door of the Third Street house. "Just be sure her cousin isn't in on things, will you?"

"A few introductions from you tonight, and I ought to have what I need." He paused. "The question is, do we involve Miss Brimm or keep her unaware of what we're working on?"

"She knows enough," Lucas said. "I think we'll find better access to the people you need to speak with if she's the one making the introductions."

A nod. "I'll come up with a list and have it sent over before so the two of you can review it." Kyle paused. "Now, unless you really do want me to join you for tea, I'd better make myself scarce."

"Scarce is a good idea right now, because if you stick around much longer, I'd have to ask you what in the world you're thinking to tell me I should marry a woman who is in my custody."

Kyle nodded toward the house. "Looks like it might be the other way around."

Lucas turned to see Flora watching him from the door. "I'll look for that list to be delivered in a few hours. Anything else we need to talk about before I rejoin my fiancée?"

His friend smiled at that, but then his expression became serious. "Afraid so. I know I'm giving you a hard time about this beautiful Southern belle, but can I just be straight with you for a minute?" At Lucas's nod, Kyle continued. "In all the time I've known you, I've never seen you as involved in a case as you are in this one. Perhaps because Tucker was involved with your sister, or maybe because of your feelings for Flora Brimm. Whatever it is, I just need to warn you that if you're not careful, you're going to lose your edge." He paused. "And we both know what happens then."

He did. He'd seen it happen . . . just not to him.

"Once Tucker's in jail, I'll have more time to think about Flora." Lucas let out a long breath. "And yes, you've guessed right about my feelings for her. And possibly hers for me. But we both know we'll get over it. She has her family to see to, and I have the law to uphold."

As he said it, Lucas knew those were thin excuses. And yet he couldn't imagine asking for Flora's hand in marriage. Not that she would ever accept. She was a lady used to fine things, and he was a Pinkerton agent used to sleeping in a different town every few weeks and putting his job above everything else.

Which is why he would never ask.

A few hours later, Flora stood at the window and watched Lucas disappear around the corner, his gait indicating that whatever mission he was conducting now was important. Well, so was hers: to send a telegram to the man who managed the telegraph office in Natchez Under-the-Hill requesting he invite his friend Mr. Tucker to tonight's party. The details would have to be brief but sufficient to draw the man to the correct location at the appointed time.

She'd almost made her escape through the front door when Winny arrived at the house. "Leaving so soon, Flora?" he said, though his tone told her he cared little for the answer.

"I just thought I'd take care of a small matter." She stepped aside to allow him entry. "I won't be long."

With a shrug of his shoulders, Winthrop headed upstairs without comment. His snub might have bothered her had she not been in a hurry.

Inquiring of the best place to send a telegram had taken some doing, but before long Flora returned to Third Street, her mission accomplished. Now to wait and see whether that awful telegraph operator in Natchez Under-the-Hill would pass along the invitation she'd sent to his pal Will Tucker. If anyone knew how to find him, it was that man. Or, at least, he should if Mr. Tucker's assertions were true and the two men were working together on an investigation.

Slipping back inside the Brimm house, Flora felt a thrill of excitement at a job accomplished without detection. Was this what it felt like to be a Pinkerton?

"Back so soon?" Winny looked up from his afternoon glass of bourbon. "I don't see shopping bags, so I'm left to believe you slipped out to meet someone. Not slipping around behind your fiancé are you?"

Of all the insolent questions! "I suppose it would make you happy if our wedding was called off," she said snappishly.

His expression did not change, though he did sit up a bit straighter in his father's favorite armchair. "What are you insinuating, Flora?"

She gathered her arms around her waist and fixed her cousin with an even stare. "Only that you would have much to gain should I be unable to produce a Brimm heir."

Winny took a slow sip of the brown liquid before setting the glass aside. "Flora Brimm, do you really think I'd be so vulgar as to impede your happiness?"

"Vulgar?" She shook her head. "Not you. Unless you had a good reason."

He leaned forward, elbows resting on his knees. Finally, he sighed. "We both know I have plenty of reasons." A shrug, and he once again reached for the liquor. "Tell me the truth. Are you marrying for love or so that I don't sell Brimmfield out from under your addlepated relatives and your crippled sister?" At Flora's

451

gasp, he continued. "Is she still afraid to leave that cottage? It would be a pity if something happened and she was forced to rejoin the world, wouldn't it?"

Rage blinded her as Flora launched herself toward Winny. She lifted her hand with the intent to slap him.

"Go ahead. I deserve it."

What had she become? Lowering her arm, Flora began to shake, either from anger or in the knowledge that in that moment she'd wished harm—serious harm—on Winthrop Brimm. And that made her no better than he.

"The simple thing would be to blame Grand-father Brimm," her cousin said, "but the truth of it is that we're both at fault."

She found it impossible to respond.

"I've collected debts almost as quickly as you've collected former fiancés. Ironically, mine were acquired in the name of love, though I doubt you would believe me." He lifted his glass. "To the Brimm frauds. Anything for money, eh?"

The Brimm frauds. If only she could argue the point.

"Apparently, I've struck a nerve." After another swig of bourbon, he pointed the empty glass at her. "The trouble is you don't want Brimmfield any more than I do. It's just a means to an end."

"It's my home," she finally managed.

"It's your sister's home. If you win this contest,

she'll never be forced to return to the world." The tumbler fell from his hand and shattered. "At least with Brimmfield gone, she might actually have to begin living again."

He paused to give her a look. She returned it with a vengeance.

"You know it's true, Flora. You're not responsible for her fall, and don't forget I was there too. I saw it all. But you will be responsible if you continue to allow her to hide away from the world."

"You don't care about Violet. You laughed and said we couldn't do it."

A shrug. "I was wrong. But I do care."

"How much money will it take to buy Brimmfield back from you?"

His smile ratcheted up a notch. "Ah, now look who's conceding defeat."

"How much?" she demanded even as she heard the door open behind her. "Name a sum and I'll raise it."

"How, Flora?" Winny said. "By marrying the Irish whelp? Do you have any idea who McMinn is? His mother's good enough stock, old New Orleans money, but his father—"

"What's going on here?" Lucas demanded.

"Tell her who you are, McMinn." Winny rose. "Then see if she still wants to marry you."

Rather than give Lucas the explanation his expression required or Winny the clarification that Lucas was her fiancé in name only, Flora straightened her spine and walked away. Somehow through shimmering tears she found her room, locked her door, and buried her face in her pillows. When she rose a while later to prepare for the evening ahead, she had replaced the tears with a calm resolve.

Winthrop Brimm would not touch Brimmfield, nor would her sister's carefully contained world be shattered. Of this Flora would make sure. And as to who Lucas McMinn was—at the moment it didn't matter. He was her fiancé, at least in name, and together they would put an end to whatever larceny Will Tucker intended with the next poor woman who fell for his charms.

For tonight, this would be enough. Tomorrow she would demand to be allowed to return to Brimmfield. She would just have to figure another plan while there was still time.

Not how she'd hoped Fatal Flora would return to Natchez.

Shrugging off the thought, she donned a Worth gown of deepest sapphire trimmed in black lace that nipped her waist and accented her eyes. Tiny drop earrings with perfectly set pearls dangling among sparkles of diamonds, aquamarines, and sapphires completed the ensemble and caused Flora to smile. The earrings, borrowed from Grandmama, were an exact copy of the pair that Will Tucker appeared to have stolen.

She told herself it didn't matter what Lucas McMinn thought of her ensemble. And yet when she spied the reflection of herself in the mirror, she hoped to offer a striking ensemble that would set Lucas McMinn's heart racing. From the expression on the lawman's face as she made her way down the stairs, it appeared she had succeeded.

She tore her attention from Lucas to meet Winny's stare. Nothing in his expression gave away his thoughts, though neither man appeared happy to be in the company of the other.

Flora ignored her cousin to address Lucas. "Shall we?"

He took her arm, and then, as Winny disappeared out the door, leaned close. "Are you all right?"

She looked up into his beautiful green eyes. "Yes. Though I might be in need of hiring a Pinkerton agent very soon."

"Oh?" He regarded Winny's retreating back with a suspicious look. "Has he made threats?"

Her cousin had already taken his place in the carriage. Flora, however, was in no mood to join him just yet. "He's far too certain of victory to resort to something so vulgar."

"Vulgar?" Lucas muttered under his breath. "I'll see that doesn't happen, Flora. You have my word."

"How? By marrying me and providing the Brimm heir?" Before he could respond, she hurried to continue. "Please forgive me for saying that. I shouldn't have. I just don't know what to do. I made him an offer of money for his inheritance. Pray Grandmama is willing to go along with the idea."

"Is that legal?" he asked as he moved her toward the door. "According to the will, I mean?"

"Anything's legal if you word the documents properly." She lifted one brow. "I'm starting to sound like my grandmother, aren't I?"

Lucas grinned. "I'm afraid so, though that's not necessarily a negative, depending on who is on the receiving end." He paused. "You may not have as much trouble getting your cousin to agree as you may think."

She allowed him to assist her with her wrap and then swiveled to face him. "Oh?"

Lucas seemed to be considering his words. "It's possible one of the men he's indebted to might be having financial trouble himself. He's made some threats over what might happen should Winthrop not repay him. Serious threats."

Flora gasped. "Oh, no. Is Winny in danger?"

"He could be." Again he seemed to be thinking before he spoke. "It's possible those threats might extend beyond him. To you."

"Me?" She shook her head. "Why me?"

This time he met her eyes with an intent look. "If you inherit, he won't. That would make repayment of any loans, overdue or otherwise, difficult."

"So you think this man might want to see that I don't . . ." Her heart sank. "Oh, Lucas, do you think he might be responsible for any of the deaths of . . ."

She couldn't continue. Thankfully, she didn't have to, for he took her hand and squeezed it. "We're going to check on that. As soon as I get you inside, I'll have a quick meeting with Kyle to catch him up on all of this. Do you think you can behave yourself long enough to let me do that?"

Flora managed a grin despite the circumstances. "Do you doubt me?"

"I think the question is, do you doubt me?" Lucas said, his expression softened, perhaps by the question or maybe it was merely a trick of the deepening shadows.

"Trust you? Yes, I believe I do, though if I only knew more about you, Mr. McMinn. Just a little more information to lessen the mystery of who you are would do the trick, I believe."

"Like why your cousin calls me the Irish whelp?"

"Hurry along, will you?" Winny called.

Though Lucas had offered the opportunity to delve into his past, his expression told her of the cost involved. Kissing him quickly on his cheek, she turned to make her way down the front steps to the carriage, leaving Lucas to follow.

Had Flora not been preoccupied with her plans for the evening, she might have cared that Winny glowered at her the entire way to Prytania Street. Of course, Lucas returned the expression in kind, making it obvious to her cousin that should he intend an argument, he would find one with a Pinkerton agent.

For a few hours she would set aside the concerns of Brimmfield and the worry of whether Winny would cooperate in favor of a different mission. Tonight she intended on giving Will Tucker a piece of her mind and, she hoped, on setting the man off on a different path.

Perhaps one that did not involve offering hope and fraud in a measure equal to his substantial charms.

When the carriage took its place in the line of arriving vehicles, Flora focused her thoughts and memorized the brief speech she intended to offer Mr. Tucker. She even considered whether she should tell Lucas of her intentions, but she discarded that idea when her gaze met his.

With him watching, she would never be able to recall a word. She might miss Mr. Tucker altogether.

So instead, Flora linked arms with him and turned toward the entrance. "Let's get this over with," she said softly.

He stalled. "We'll be in presently," he said to

Winny, who ignored them both to disappear inside.

"Really, Lucas. We are expected."

His silence irked her, as did the sound of the orchestra as it spilled out into the waning sunlight of the Louisiana evening.

"We have a plan, Flora," he finally said, "and that plan involves the two of us—"

"Masquerading as an engaged couple." She paused but only for a second, her gaze flitting to the as-yet-empty second floor balcony, where she'd arranged her assignation with Tucker. "Yes, I know. Let's get on with it."

"You're claiming to be my fiancée. Aren't you the least bit curious about what those people in there know about me?"

Oh, but the man was far too handsome for his own good. Had her responsibilities not been elsewhere, she might have allowed that to distract her. To let him lead her into the ballroom on his arm feeling as if she'd snared the best catch in the room, even if it was all make-believe.

No, she wanted to say. *I don't care because it is all a ruse.*

And yet she did care. Deeply. Though her feelings for him were as doomed as the fiancés who came before him.

And yet her curiosity bested any other response.

"All right, Lucas. Tell me who you are."

❧ THIRTY-ONE ❧

Lucas reached for her, his hands easily spanning her waist as he lifted her to the ground. She might have protested had she the wherewithal to work up decent irritation in such close proximity. The last time he'd held her like this, a kiss resulted.

A wonderful, confusing, memorable kiss.

Despite her best efforts, Flora leaned slightly toward him. He moved, almost imperceptibly in her direction. Their gazes met. His lips parted slightly.

And then he turned away. "You're wasting time," he tossed over his shoulder. "We can walk from here."

Oh! Flora caught up and fell into step beside him, a step he likely slowed to match hers. Two blocks down, he paused in front of a distinctive Gothic-style home, the only one of that style on Prytania Street. She knew it well from the times she'd gone visiting with her aunt.

On occasion Flora and the daughter of the house had gone to the kitchen where they were treated to whatever sumptuous Irish fare was bubbling on the stove. Decadent indeed, though a grander sort of young lady would have preferred the teacakes and delicacies served in the formal parlor.

What was that girl's name? Time had stolen any recollection, unfortunately, though now that Flora thought on it, she remembered her eyes. They were such a unique shade of green. The Irish ladies with their lilting voices . . . yes, that she also remembered. The ladies called them lassies and said . . . and said that the girl, Marion? Marie? No, it was long gone. But the kitchen ladies loved to tease her and the elder brother, who often skulked on the perimeter but rarely approached, that they carried a bit of Ireland in their green eyes. Regarding Flora, they said she must truly carry the sky for the shade of blue she'd inherited. A much-reduced legacy in Flora's young opinion.

"That kitchen had the most wonderful smells."

He turned and their gazes met. "Stews bubbling on the stove and—"

"And always something sweet under glass waiting to be dealt out to extremely bored young visitors curious about life outside their rather sheltered world."

"Or a young gentleman of the house who had a foot in both worlds." Lucas blinked, his expression soft. "The girl with the sky in her eyes. That was you?"

She searched his face even as she once again begged her memories to tumble forward. "The very serious elder brother with Ireland in his eyes?"

"Not so serious," he said as he covered her hand with his. "Shy, mostly. But I was often accused of being the one who watched while everyone else went about their business." Lucas shrugged. "A talent that has served me well as a Pinkerton, so I guess it was meant to be."

Flora shook her head. "But how? That is, why do you say you were in both worlds when you speak perfect French and have a last name that is obviously . . . Irish?" She paused to grip the fence rail as things began to make sense. "One of your parents was a . . . that is you were born out of a relationship between . . . oh, I'm making a mess of this."

Lucas's soft chuckle almost made up for the heat rising in her cheeks. "Yes, Flora, I'm half-French and half-Irish. The Irish whelp."

"Oh, Lucas, I didn't mean to imply—"

"I know. Now hush and let me finish." He pressed a finger softly to her lips to emphasize the point. "As you've guessed, my grandparents were less than thrilled when my mother chose the cousin of our Irish cook over the well-born gents who had been coming to call."

He paused as if remembering. "Father was a prizefighter. A good one, from what I understand, and a mountain of a man. He was killed by a bunch of thugs who took exception to the fact he wouldn't throw a fight. My mother was expecting Mary-Margaret when she got the news. Some say that once my sister was born, nothing else held her here. She didn't last a week."

"Oh, Lucas, I'm so sorry. First your father and then your mother. That must have been terrible." *And now your sister* remained unsaid. The effect of that loss was something she had seen for herself.

"A Pinkerton man put those criminals behind bars for life." He paused to allow a deep breath. "I wasn't but seven or eight, but I knew I would be one of those Pinkertons someday. As soon as I could I made that happen, though Grandfather Gus was almost as displeased as when he was introduced to my father." Another pause. "His exact words."

"Whatever for?" Flora demanded. "Being a Pinkerton is an honorable profession."

"Not when you've been sent off to Harvard and groomed to take over the family cotton business."

"I supposed not," Flora admitted.

"Definitely not, though I wager Grandfather is more perplexed that I work at all. He settled my mother's inheritance on me years ago in the hopes I might give up the Pinkertons."

So Lucas McMinn wasn't the man Grandmama had assumed at all. Nor, however, was he what she had assumed either.

"Thus far, the Pinkertons have suited me well. I've found no need for my mother's money, though I hope to put it to good use someday."

"I see." Flora shifted positions to link her arm in his and lean against him as she allowed her gaze to dance across the fanciful facade of the home. Shutters of deep mossy green stood out against the pale exterior, each of the three windows pointed at the center. As a child, she had always thought those windows looked like church windows. Even now, though they were shadowed in darkness, they still did.

"What happened to your sister?" she asked gently.

Lucas stiffened beside her, though his hand moved to cover hers on his arm. "She met a man who stole her heart. Grandfather insisted on a church wedding, likely because his own daughter had refused one. He was stubborn like that." Lucas paused. "Still is. Anyway, when Tucker didn't show . . ."

"She was humiliated," Flora supplied.

"Worse. She ran out of the church and directly into the path of a streetcar."

"Oh, Lucas. I'm so sorry. What a tragic accident."

He leaned away, and instantly she felt his absence. "Was it?" He shrugged. "I saw it with my own eyes when I watched her run out of the church, and yet knowing the temperament of the women in my family . . ." He let out a long breath. "Grandfather Gus and I are all that's left."

Something inside her shifted. Flora moved to

wrap her arms around him. "Lucas," she whispered against his neck, "is your grandfather still alive? I would like very much to meet him."

A smile dawned. "You would like him, I believe. And I know he would like you."

"Then let's go inside." Flora reached to open the gate, but he halted her progress.

"Not tonight," he said firmly. "We have an appointment elsewhere. And besides, we'd likely find him already in bed."

The darkness of the windows and the stillness that surrounded the home backed up his claim. "Tomorrow morning then?"

He seemed to consider the question a moment before offering a curt nod. "We may have things to do before your meeting with Tucker at noon, but I'll consider it," he said as he turned her around and pointed her in the direction they'd just come. "Now, if your curiosity is satisfied, we should get back to the real reason we came to New Orleans."

"Temporarily satisfied," she amended as she took Lucas's arm and allowed him to escort her back to the party.

"Flora," he said as they stepped into the circle of a streetlight's glow, "aren't those the earrings you claimed Tucker stole?"

So he'd noticed. "It just so happens that Grandmama has a matching pair. Don't you think they look lovely with this dress? Now come on, let's go in."

Lucas stalled. "Flora . . ."

"All right. I sent an invitation to Mr. Tucker. And don't give me that look. I don't know where he is, but I paid a visit to a place where I might find someone who does." She slid Lucas a sideways look. "All I did was send a simple telegram to that man who ran the office in Natchez Under-the-Hill. Nothing more."

He groaned. "I told you to let me do the investigative work, Flora. You have a meeting with him tomorrow at noon. Can't we just stick to that plan?"

She shook her head and released her grip on his arm. "Please do remedy that expression of yours, Lucas. If we're to be playing a happy couple on the verge of marriage, don't you think we should look like it? Now, show me those eyes touched with the hills of Ireland, please."

With that she swept through the doors and into the thick of the crowd, leaving Lucas to either follow or watch as she worked her way through the greetings. She spied Kyle Russell engaged in conversation with two other men over in the corner. Only Mr. Russell looked up when she walked in, and he quickly went back to his conversation as Lucas joined them. After a perfunctory round of greetings, she excused herself to slip out to the upstairs balcony.

The shadows had rendered the secluded spot almost completely in darkness. Only a sliver of the moon cast any sort of light, and that was poor and silvery. Flora leaned over the edge to peer down at the street. A moment later, she felt a tug on her sleeve.

She turned to see that her invited guest had joined her. His hair had been cropped short, and on his face was the beginning of a beard. Her gaze sought out Lucas through the window. He was now deep in conversation with Kyle alone, his back to her.

Will Tucker's attention went to her ears, and for just a moment Flora thought she saw his good humor disappear. "Interesting that you would have an engagement party tonight with one man and a wedding planned for tomorrow with another. Care to explain, Flora?"

"Not really, Mr. Tucker." She made at playing coy. "However, if you insist, I will admit I much prefer a man who can produce a badge to one who only claims to own one."

"Flora, I told you . . ." He shook his head and went silent as his eyes seemed to be scanning the horizon.

As the orchestra finished their tune, the night sounds of New Orleans replaced the combination of voice and chamber music in the ballroom. The air was thick with the portent of rain, quite heavy and still. Even the wisteria vine that wound around the porch rails appeared to be drooping from the weight of it.

Slowly he returned his attention to her. Again she caught him looking at her ears.

"Do you like them?" she asked sweetly.

"Very nice." He met her eyes, this time with a measure of what she almost believed might be insolence.

Flora took a deep breath and let it out slowly. From where she stood, she could see the crowd through the closed French doors. Unfortunately, Mr. Tucker had chosen an unlit corner of the balcony, so it was quite unlikely anyone could see them.

She thought of Lucas and his sister. Of Irish eyes and then of Violet and Brimmfield. When had simple solutions become so complicated?

Her attention returned to the man beside her. A wrong word could cause more trouble than she wanted, of this she was certain. And yet he had lied to her. He had stolen the one possession she valued most. And worse, he had given her a hope that she might have gained a safe future for Violet through her marriage to him.

For that alone he deserved to go to jail.

Now, if Lucas would only hurry and miss her. Hurry and find her. Find them.

He moved a step closer and leaned against the balcony rail, his elbow touching hers. A sideways glance told her his attention was on the crowd inside.

"Why am I here, Flora? Are we to be married tomorrow or not?"

"My mother's earrings," she said with the same steel holding up her spine. "I want them back, Will Tucker." A pause. "Or whatever your name is. And no, I don't think marriage will suit us now. Not with what I've come to know about you."

To her surprise, he showed no sign of emotion. Rather, he swung around to place her between him and the rail. Now the eyes that she'd felt were so kind seemed harder, his touch that had been soft she now began to fear.

"My name is Will Tucker. I am a detective for the Frisco Railroad. I've told you all of that. As for the rest, I have no idea what you're talking about."

"Yes, you do," she said softly. "I know what happened to Mary-Margaret McMinn."

His eyes narrowed. He looked away, revealing a vein throbbing at his temple that she could see even in the pale moonlight.

And then in an instant his expression returned to neutral. "Detective Wilson and I are still investigating her death," he said lightly.

"Detective Wilson? Are you claiming that man at the telegraph office is—"

"A lawman? Yes. And if you've heard that woman's death was an accident, you're mistaken. Her brother was the only witness besides the driver, and those men aren't paid enough to tell the truth if a lie is more profitable. Anyway, once we finish our investigation, we can certainly take up another regarding your jewelry. Now what was it again? A watch?"

"No, Mr. Tucker. A stolen watch is what you gave me. Stolen earrings are what you're intent on passing forward to the next victim. Only there will be no next victim."

"Flora, truly I don't—"

"Enough!" With anger blinding her to caution, Flora reached out to jab him with her index finger. "I'm tired of hearing lies from you, Mr. Tucker. Someday the truth will catch up to you, but here is what I know for certain. You gave me Mary-Margaret's watch. Please tell whomever you're planning on giving my mother's earrings to that she will be prosecuted for receipt of stolen property. And, by the way, they are an exact copy of the ones I'm wearing, so obtaining a match for evidence will be quite simple. But you already noticed that, didn't you?"

"Flora," he said as he remained stock-still. "You're making some dangerous accusations."

"No, Mr. Tucker, I am merely stating facts." She rested both hands on the rail and prepared to hold on tight should the man attempt to push her. *Protect me, Lord,* was the prayer she breathed as she stared up into the face of the man she had almost married.

"You don't want to cooperate with Lucas McMinn."

"Well, that's where you're right. I rarely want

to cooperate with him. In fact, he would be extremely upset if he knew I was out here with you. However, I want my mother's earrings back. Just give them to me and we can both walk away."

"I don't make a habit of walking around with women's jewelry, Flora."

"Then find them and return them. Concoct a story. Drop them on my doorstep. Send them in the mail. I don't care what you do, but return them."

Mr. Tucker's chuckle held no humor. And then he was gone, vaulting over the railing to land on his feet in the courtyard below. Flora's shaking knees refused to move, her quivering lips unable to call out for someone to give chase.

And then she recalled just who she was. She was Flora Brimm of the Natchez Brimms. And she was the second best climber in all of Natchez.

Testing the rail, she looked around to be certain no one was watching. Lucas and Mr. Russell were still deep in conversation, giving Flora reason to believe she'd never have time to alert them and still catch Tucker.

Her decision made, she lifted her skirts to ease over the rail and then moved carefully to the narrow strip of windowsill. From her vantage point she could see that Mr. Tucker had run into a snag in making his escape. The courtyard where he'd landed had a locked gate. At present, he was attempting a climb that looked most unlikely.

Looking beyond the gates, she spied several carriages with drivers waiting. Unfortunately, the darkness that made the balcony an excellent meeting place also hid her from view. To call out would be to risk the criminal escaping another way.

Only she could stop him. What she would do when she caught up to him was the least of her concerns. All she knew was that he must be caught before he took advantage of someone else. Perhaps a citizen's arrest would be in order.

Or she could just club him over the head and wait for help. She sighed. Not likely, given the fact she couldn't even work herself up sufficiently to slap her cousin. And he was threatening her home and family.

The creep down in the courtyard had merely stolen baubles. Her mother's baubles, to be sure, but inanimate objects all the same.

For God hath not given us the spirit of fear; but of power, and of love, and of a sound mind.

Her courage bolstered, she edged over to grasp the worn wooden shutter, all the while praying the black iron straps securing it would hold. Inch by inch, she crossed the space between the windows until she reached the next one. Again, she prayed the shutter would hold until she could make her way past.

Unfortunately, it did not.

Air swirled around her as she tumbled backward, the worn green shutter besting her in its swift descent. Something zinged past her and then returned to cinch her waist, stealing the air from her lungs. A second later, the ground coming ever nearer, breath failed her and all went black.

❦ THIRTY~TWO ❦

Lucas hauled Flora against him and then cut loose the filament line that had caught her. As light as she was, her dead weight had made it challenging to raise her back up to the balcony. As he was pulling on the line and bringing the woman he loved to the shelter of his arms, Lucas couldn't help thinking that if he and Kyle never created another invention, he was perfectly happy with the knowledge this one gadget had saved Flora's life.

Unfortunately, the filament line had squeezed tight around her middle. Had she not been wearing a corset of hardy material, Flora might have had broken ribs—or worse.

Instead, she would be sore but otherwise very much unharmed.

"What the . . ." Kyle came up behind him, carefully closing the door. "I thought I saw you out here, but I . . . What happened to Miss Brimm?"

A movement down in the courtyard caught Lucas's attention. "She's fine," he whispered. "She almost fell climbing down the wall, but our filament line saved her. The breath has been knocked out of her, but she ought to come to in a minute." He made another sweeping glance of the courtyard. Yes, there it was again. "Stay with her while I check something out."

Kyle nodded and gathered Flora into his arms. Lucas yanked on the rail. Sturdy enough. Another look back to meet Kyle's gaze. "Yeah, I know. You love her, so I'd better keep her safe." He patted the revolver strapped to his side. "Go on. If she wakes up, I'll keep her out here until you return. Either way, we'll get her to safety together."

A nod and then he climbed out and followed what surely had been Flora's path across the front of the building. Carefully sidestepping the place where the wooden shutter hung precariously, he saw a drainpipe and lunged for it.

Capturing the metal with both fists, Lucas glanced back to be certain Kyle still maintained his vigil with Flora. At a nod from his old friend, Lucas put his mind to the task at hand.

With the orchestra playing an up-tempo song, the sound of his boots hitting the brick courtyard was, he hoped, sufficiently muffled. He could still see Tucker's fair hair as he gave up on trying the gate and moved across the courtyard toward the servants' quarters.

Lucas had grown up traversing most of the back gardens and alleys in this part of New Orleans, so it was a simple matter to duck under the rainspout and around the corner to follow the side yard until it met the back wall of the old summer kitchen.

A crunch of footsteps on gravel told him Tucker was nearby. Lucas palmed his weapon and moved forward, his own steps quiet as a cat from all the years of playing hiding games in places just like this one.

He reached the edge of the building and paused to take a deep breath. When the steps came near, he said a quick prayer and then rushed from his hiding place to tackle Will Tucker. The crook never saw him coming, though he did put up a good fight.

Two swings with his free hand, and Lucas had Tucker on the ground. He stood over the downed criminal with his weapon poised. Everything in him begged the man to break and run. Any excuse to shoot him.

Instead Tucker swiped at the blood on his cheek. "I guess I deserved that," he said slowly. "You gonna shoot me?"

"Nothing would please me more. Unfortunately, if I did that would make me no better than you. Get up and let's go."

Tucker did as he was told. When he was upright, Lucas snapped on handcuffs and led him out to the front gate. Summoning the Brimms' driver, he sent the fellow off in search of a police officer. He glanced behind him and looked up at the balcony to see that Flora was still in Kyle's arms. The fact that she was not yet standing troubled him, though he forced his attention back on Tucker. A thorough pat down revealed a Navy pistol that Lucas quickly pocketed.

"Got anything else you need to admit to?"

"Nope."

Lucas ran his hand over Tucker's jacket and felt a suspicious lump. "What's this?" he asked as he reached into the jacket and found a small box hidden in a pocket. He hoped it contained Flora's mother's earrings.

Pulling out his key, he unlocked one of the handcuffs. "You letting me go, Lucas? There's a good sport."

A moment later Lucas clamped the other handcuff to the gate and then gave it a tug to be sure it held. "The only place you're going is to jail, *sport*."

Flora awoke to the sound of her name, the soft whisper of a voice distinctly familiar. The whisper became more insistent—a demand, really—that required her to do something.

What? There was jostling about and something else. Someone called out. *Belles pralines*. A street vendor. Yes, she recognized the chant. And an orchestra.

Again she heard her name. This time Flora opened her eyes to see Lucas McMinn's face just above her own.

"You're awake. I'm going to sit you up. Easy now. You've taken a blow to the back of your head, so you might feel a little woozy."

The world tilted, and she watched Lucas once again appear. For a moment, his image swam before her, and then he came into focus.

"I'm sorry, Flora, but we're not staying to enjoy our party. But the good news is I'm taking you home to Brimmfield."

"The party." She closed her eyes and sighed. "Will Tucker was at the party," she said, and her eyes flew open. "He was there and then I chased him and . . ."

Lucas tightened his hold on her. "And then you fell."

"Yes, I did." She rubbed a hand over the ache beneath her ribs.

"Well, the short version is I caught him. And you. Remember that filament wire that had us both dangling off your home?"

She looked up into his eyes. Ireland green. The phrase made her smile. "Until you cut it just before my father threatened using pruning shears?"

"That's the one. Kyle and I had been playing with this device but it hadn't been tested. We added a nice little airfoil to a thin rope. It causes an unbalanced airflow that creates an elliptical path. In this case, the path wrapped around you. I held tight and so did the line."

"I have no idea what you just said."

Lucas sighed. "Basically a man can throw it out and it comes right back, similar to a boomerang. Anyway, it works."

"Oh, good." She moved and then winced. "I think we should stand, don't you?"

"If you think you're ready." His attention went to her side. "Likely you'll be sore there, but nothing's broken. Apparently, they make women's formal attire much stronger than men's. You hit the side of the house pretty hard."

"Apparently." She sucked in a breath as Lucas helped her to her feet. For once the stupid corset had actually proven to be beneficial. She looked up at him. "So Mr. Tucker has been arrested?"

"Kyle's seeing to the paperwork right now. But with a warrant out of Eureka Springs and an active Pinkerton investigation ongoing against him, I'd say he won't be seeing daylight for quite some time."

"What about the man in Natchez? The telegraph operator."

"I'll follow up on him once I get you situated at Brimmfield." A shadow of concern crossed his features. "Speaking of which, I need to take you home to Brimmfield. Tonight."

"Tonight?" She shook her head. "Why? You caught Mr. Tucker, so what's the hurry?"

"I'd rather explain elsewhere, but suffice it to say I have more information on the debtor I mentioned earlier." He gave her a sweeping glance. "Can you walk or do you need more time?"

"Yes, but—"

"Trust me, Flora. I'll tell you everything as soon as I can."

"Promise?"

At his cross look, Flora tested her ability to take one step and then another. Though her head swam and her knees shook, her feet seemed to perform upon command.

"All right, then." He held her at arm's length and then brushed his knuckle across her cheek, his expression softening. "We're walking out of here looking like a happy couple, understand?" When she nodded, he continued. "First, you will make your excuses to Cousin Winthrop. I don't care what you tell him, just don't tell him you're leaving New Orleans."

"But it will be the height of rudeness if I just abandon him in the middle of the night—"

"Flora," he said patiently, "you two didn't look as though you were worried about rudeness earlier, but if you insist, you can write him and explain."

"You're right. Let's go."

Before the doors opened, Flora had her smile pasted back in place. With Lucas guiding her, his palm warm against her back, she managed to navigate the substantial length of the room to find Winny deep in conversation with Eudora Lennart.

"Dora, you remember my cousin, don't you?" he asked the young woman.

"Yes, of course. We were on the *Americus* together. We had such a grand time, didn't we, Flora?"

Conversation with the Lennart ladies was not what she recalled when she thought of that voyage. Still, she managed a polite smile.

"Yes, we did." Flora turned her attention to Winny and saw no hint of the cold man she'd encountered at his home. Either that was an act, or this woman's attention had overridden any remaining ill will. "Lucas and I are going."

"Are you ill?"

"I'm afraid she's a bit overcome by all the excitement," Lucas said. "Her anticipation of our marriage causes this on occasion."

Flora jabbed the cad discreetly. Still, when Winny looked her way, she did her best to look as if she agreed.

"Use my carriage. I'll not have need of it for quite some time. That is, unless Dora is tired of me and wishes for me to accompany you."

"Don't be silly." Eudora looked around him to smile at Flora. "Take your time."

A short while later, Flora and Lucas arrived back at the house on Third Street, where she hurriedly threw a few belongings into a bag, and then she and a maid crept back out to join him in the carriage. He silently nodded toward the carriage driver and footman, still refusing to elaborate on the reason for their hasty departure.

Kyle found them before the carriage had completely come to a halt at the docks. "I've got some news. I think our man's on the *Bertolino*."

The two men exchanged glances.

"He just made it on. The gangplank was up and the boat had already begun to pull away. If I hadn't seen him make the jump myself, I wouldn't have believed he could do it."

"You're sure it was him?"

"I believe it was, but no, I didn't see him close up." He shrugged. "He gave the name of Winthrop Brimm to the fellow who sold him the ticket."

"I see."

"What are you two talking about?" Flora demanded.

He thrust some tickets in their direction. "We need to get moving. The *Venerable* sails in ten minutes. If we're on time, we'll get there right behind him. If we're lucky, we'll beat him there." Lucas turned to Flora. "Once we're settled onboard, I promise I will fill you in, all right?"

"All right," she said slowly.

Lucas sent the driver on his way and escorted Flora and the maid through the maze of containers and persons lining the New Orleans docks. As they stepped onto the deck, the *Venerable*'s bell began to announce its imminent departure.

"Were you able to alert the authorities in Natchez? A New Orleans warrant ought to get their attention," Lucas asked Kyle as they climbed the stairs.

"I was very clear that we were in pursuit of a suspect with a warrant, and that the suspect would arrive via the steamboat *Bertolino* midday tomorrow. To be safe, I let them know we were traveling with Miss Brimm."

"Good. Then if they find him when he steps off the boat, all we need to do is show up and file the paperwork."

"Ideally, yes," was Kyle's response as they reached the long hall leading to the staterooms. "And if he doesn't get off the boat, we track him to Memphis, because that's the next stop for that vessel."

The maid went off to find her quarters among rooms for the staff, and the other three walked in silence until the door to Flora's stateroom came into view. "This is where I bid you two good night," Kyle said. "I'll be right across the hall, so fetch me if you need me. Otherwise, I'll relieve you in a few hours."

Lucas nodded and opened the door for Flora. Glancing around the tiny stateroom, he gestured toward the chair in the corner. "Need that?"

"No, go ahead," she told him, and she then

watched as he carried the chair out into the hall and rested it against the door frame.

She looked around to be sure they were alone. "All right. Who is he, Lucas? Do I know this man you are chasing?"

He paused to watch her a moment. "It's Martin Lennart."

Flora gasped. "But . . ."

"Yes, *that* Lennart."

"But why?"

"Your death ensures that Winthrop inherits. And Winthrop's inheritance ensures that Lennart will have the money he needs to avoid losing everything." Lucas paused to look around and then returned his attention to her. "Or it would have. Unfortunately for him, he chose a Pinkerton informant to join him in the plan to kill you. Don't worry, Flora. We'll catch him. He'll not have the opportunity to harm you."

"Those poor girls." She ran her hand along the edge of the door. "Is my family in danger?"

"From what Kyle has uncovered, the only one in danger was you." He paused and once again seemed to be considering his words. "Obviously, he's now aware that we're on to him if he's taking such lengths to leave town under cover of darkness and using an assumed name. If he's headed to Natchez, we'll catch him before anyone is harmed. If he's going on to Memphis or elsewhere, which is my guess, then we'll still catch him." He put his hands on her shoulders. "Don't worry, Flora. I'll keep you safe."

"Thank you," she said as she reached up to give him a quick kiss on the cheek. "I'm sorry for all the trouble I've given you. Truly. I wish I'd told you all about Mr. Tucker from the beginning."

He held her against him for a moment and then released her. His smile lit his face. "It's what I do. Besides, I prefer my apologies in writing so you can't change your mind later." He paused. "When you amend your ways. Now get some rest."

"You are incorrigible," she said as she watched him settle into the chair. Then she closed the door.

This time there was no thought of cheerful banter or good-natured misbehavior. Flora remained in her stateroom all night, even when the ache beneath her ribs and the headache pounding at her temples roused her from her sleep. Finally the sun rose, and so did she.

Dressing hurriedly, Flora reached for the Bible she'd tucked into her bag. Instead of the words she read there, a quote from *Pride and Prejudice* rose high in her mind.

I was in the middle before I knew that I had begun.

And that, Flora knew, was the real problem in all of this. Before she'd listened to God—before she'd waited on His plan—she had gone ahead with her own. She had truly been in the middle of this plan that had seemed so well thought out and plausible before she realized the trouble had begun.

Before she'd known how far off the Lord's chosen path she'd gone to secure Brimmfield and a safe life for her sister.

A knock at the door jarred her thoughts. "Yes?" she called.

"It's Lucas. I brought you something to eat."

She opened the door and took the tray but knew she wouldn't eat a bite on it. "Did you have anything?" she asked when he returned to his chair.

"I'm fine."

"Then so am I."

"Oh, for goodness' sake, Flora. Eat. I'll have something when Kyle relieves my watch in a half hour." Tiredness etched the corners of his eyes. "I promise."

When she opened her door to check on him some time later, Kyle had taken Lucas's place. "Are you finished with that?" he asked, indicating her untouched tray.

She nodded and handed it to him. "Thank you," she said as she lingered in the doorway, "for taking care of us."

He shrugged. "It's what I do."

An echo of Lucas's words. She smiled. "No, I mean for worrying about Lucas enough to test my feelings for him." She paused to watch his expression. "I know that's what you were doing in the carriage."

He chuckled. "Lucas didn't. That almost got me punched."

"I hope you found what you were looking for."

"I believe I did." Kyle paused only a moment before he added, "He loves you, you know. I'd advise you not to abuse that."

"You have my word, Mr. Russell," she said as she let his statement settle against her heart.

"Under the circumstances, I figure you ought to call me Kyle."

The door across the hall flew open and Lucas came stumbling out, his shirt half buttoned and the tails hanging out over his trousers, with no shoes on his feet. "Is something wrong? I thought I heard Flora," he demanded, his hair sticking out at odd angles.

"Nothing's wrong. I was just returning my breakfast tray."

"Get some rest, buddy," Kyle added. "We've got another few hours before we dock in Natchez, and we both need to be ready for whatever happens."

In a bold move, Flora walked across the hall to smooth back Lucas's hair and kiss him soundly. Without a word, she turned back toward her stateroom.

"I'm supposed to get some rest after that?" she heard Lucas ask Kyle as she closed the door.

An eternity later, the *Venerable* landed at Natchez. From her stateroom window, Flora could see the collection of law enforcement officers awaiting the vessel. Or, rather, awaiting the steamboat carrying Martin Lennart. Apparently, their boat had bested the other in travel time, for none of the men with badges appeared to be holding anyone prisoner.

Flora took one last look in the mirror and frowned at the smudges beneath her eyes. There was no remedy for it except sleep, and she would be able to do that tonight back at Brimmfield . . . but only if the man who meant her harm was in custody.

The moment Lucas knocked, she opened the door and stepped into the hall. Whether he'd slept or just completed his grooming, her Pinkerton agent looked every bit the calm and collected lawman.

"I'm escorting you to your carriage, and Kyle is already doing a little reconnaissance. From what I can tell, the *Bertolino* arrived just ahead of us and is already discharging its passengers. My guess is our man won't walk onto the docks of his own steam with all the law in full view, so Kyle's going to see if he can get on board the other boat and have a look."

"What if he doesn't find him?"

"We'll worry about that if it happens," he said as he linked arms with her. "But I doubt seriously that will happen. There's no place for him to go and no place to hide."

"If you say so," Flora said as she allowed him to escort her down the stairs and onto the lower deck.

"I say so," Lucas said, squeezing her arm. "Once we get out in the open, you're going to have to stick very close to me. Ready?"

She nodded as she offered what she hoped was a calm expression. Once she reached dry land, Flora released the breath she hadn't realized she was holding. All around her were convenient places to hide. "Calm down," she whispered to herself, "and trust God."

"Miss Brimm?"

She looked up to see the deputy who had refused to accept her at the jail some nights ago now standing in her path. "Good afternoon, Deputy."

A flush climbed into his cheeks as he stepped between her and the exit. "I'm sorry, Miss Brimm, but you have to go with me."

"Go with you? Where?"

"To jail," he said, refusing to make eye contact. "You have an active warrant for your arrest on the charge of receipt of stolen property. According to Pinkerton Russell of the Denver bureau, we're to hold you over for trial or until the Eureka Springs folks come to fetch you."

"Don't be ridiculous," Lucas said. "You're

supposed to be arresting Martin Lennart, not Miss Brimm."

"They both have warrants, so we're to bring both of them in." The deputy squared his shoulders and looked as if he were preparing to do battle with Lucas. "I understand your irritation, sir, but the law's the law. I ought to have listened to you the first time you brought her to the jail, but I didn't. I'm sworn to uphold the laws of this state, and one of 'em is seeing that those with active warrants are brought in."

"Active?" He groaned. "I thought that had been taken care of. She's in my custody."

"Not anymore." The deputy reached for Flora's wrist to clamp a handcuff on it, but she jerked her wrist away.

"I demand to speak to my attorney. He will see that everything is cleared up."

"I'm sorry, Miss Brimm," he said as he reached for her again.

This time something inside her snapped. She would not see the inside of a jail cell. Not with the man she loved in harm's way.

She ran.

Eluding the slightly overweight deputy proved surprisingly easy as Flora ducked behind some stacked barrels and quickly made her way into the crowded waterfront. With lawmen everywhere, she knew she could not step into the open, so she paused to catch her breath and contemplate a plan.

A moment later a large hand wrapped around her arm.

"Let me go!"

"You'll have to take this up with the sheriff, ma'am. I'm just following orders." With that, the deputy led Flora away.

"Lucas!" she called as she stumbled forward and leaned heavily on the deputy's arm. "Do something!"

But he was nowhere to be found.

❄ THIRTY-THREE ❄

Lucas took three steps in the direction the deputy and Flora had gone and then stopped short. As much as he hated allowing this, at least she would be safe in jail until he could come for her. The fact that she might not forgive him was a risk he would have to take.

Kyle jogged up to interrupt his thoughts. "Where's Miss Brimm?"

"Thanks to you, she's in jail," he snapped. "What did you say to the sheriff?"

"Only that we were pursuing a suspect with active warrants and requested arrest upon sight." He paused. "Wait, are you telling me she still had a warrant? I thought you took care of that." Kyle hit his forehead with his palm. "I should have been more specific and told them it was Lennart we wanted, not her."

"You can explain that to Flora when she's released. Right now we have a man to capture."

They briefly discussed strategy and then parted, Kyle going aboard each of the vessels with one party of deputies and Lucas combing the waterfront with another. A third group went on to Brimmfield to search and then stand guard. Lucas personally alerted the authorities in Memphis.

By daybreak Lennart still had not been found. The likelihood he had remained in Natchez, however, dimmed with each moment that passed. It was time to go and fetch Flora from her prison cell.

"Keep at it," Lucas told Kyle as he turned away from the docks and headed toward the jail.

"Don't you want me to come with you to spring Miss Brimm? I figure you might need backup once she's set loose."

"Very funny," he said, though Lucas knew it wasn't far from the truth. Flora would be furious. And though Kyle's wording of the message hadn't helped matters, the reason she'd been arrested rested on Lucas.

He was the one who had sworn out the warrant.

"Get some sleep," he told his friend. "Lennart will show eventually, likely somewhere upriver, and when he does I'll need you rested so you can go get him."

By the time Lucas reached the jail, the sun was beginning to rise in earnest. After taking a side trip around the corner to rent a horse and buggy for the trip to Brimmfield, he returned to find an unfamiliar fellow asking questions of the deputy. It only took a moment for Lucas to realize the man was asking about Flora. Thankfully, the deputy didn't appear interested in answering.

"Who are you?" Lucas said as he stepped between the two. "And what business is it of yours to be asking around about my fiancée, especially here?"

The man's pale brows rose. "So you're the mystery fiancé. We had a tip that there was to be a wedding at Brimmfield, but due to an unfortunate mistake in addressing invitations, mine did not arrive."

"I see." He leaned closer to the man and put on the expression he generally saved for the more hardened criminals he dealt with. "I will repeat the question. Who are you?"

"Carlton," he said as he stuck out his hand in an attempt to shake. "Asa Carlton of the local paper."

Lucas ignored the gesture to narrow his eyes. "Reporter," he said with all the derision appropriate to this man and his ilk.

Carlton withdrew his hand and reached into his pocket to produce a pencil and pad of paper. "My sources say Fatal Flora was arrested upon her return from New Orleans yesterday afternoon.

Any chance you two were returning from your honeymoon? And what's your name by the way? Oh, what where those charges against Miss Brimm?" He shook his head. "If she's married to you, then she wouldn't be Miss Brimm anymore, would she? But if she's married, she also wouldn't be Fatal Flora anymore, would she?"

The barrage of questions died a quiet death when the reporter finally raised his eyes to meet Lucas's glare. At that point, he fumbled the pencil and then scrambled to retrieve it.

"Well, Mr. Carlton," he finally said. "Your sources were only partially correct. There is a major investigation underway regarding a suspect in a substantial threat to certain parties in this city. What your sources likely saw was Miss Brimm being taken to a place of safety so as to be removed from the imminent danger." He nodded toward the deputy. "Can you think of a safer place than right under the nose of the Natchez law?"

The reporter laughed. "I suppose you're correct. However, I'm told she was carried away in handcuffs and was quite uncooperative."

"Have you not considered that is *exactly* what law enforcement wished the suspect to see?"

Carlton was practically giddy with excitement at this idea. "Then do allow me to interview Miss Brimm. Or, rather, Mrs. . . . . what was your name, sir?"

"I didn't say."

He peered up at Lucas. "Yes, well, you'll have to say if you want to be named in the write-up."

"There will be no write-up. Security reasons. I'm sure you understand."

"No, actually I don't."

Lucas swiveled to turn his attention to the deputy. "Deputy, would you tell this man what happens to someone who interferes in an active investigation?"

The young man grinned. "That would be a charge of aiding and abetting a criminal, for one. Then there's the—"

"No need to continue," Carlton said quickly. "Just give me my scoop about the wedding, and I'll leave you to your investigation without a single mention of any part of it." He gave Lucas a pleading look. "I need my job, sir. If you're marrying Flora Brimm, just give me some sort of scoop about the when and where of it. Something, please?"

Lucas thought only for a moment. "All right. If you agree to say nothing about any of this, I will do what I can to see that you alone will have an exclusive interview with my bride and me. And, more importantly, you and your paper will never, ever refer to my fiancée as Fatal Flora again, or you will risk my wrath and legal action. Will that do?"

He nodded far too quickly. "It will indeed."

"And if you breathe a word of any of this,

Carlton," the deputy said, "you'll be back here and on the wrong side of a cell door before you can blink twice. Do you understand?"

The reporter scribbled something on the paper and handed it to Lucas. "Here's how to reach me. Now I will bid you a good day." With that, he was gone.

"Seems like there's always a reporter or a lawyer sniffing around here." The deputy gestured to his desk. "Speaking of lawyers, Miss Brimm's man was here yesterday and is in fact down at the judge's house right now getting a signature on the release papers. The judge is going to call when he—"

The telephone rang just then, and the deputy nodded toward it. "Likely him now." He picked the receiver up and listened a moment. "Yes, sir. Might I save him the trouble by releasing her to Mr. McMinn? He's standing right here." The deputy looked at Lucas. "You willing to take Miss Brimm home?"

"I am."

The deputy relayed the information to the judge and hung up. "All settled. I'll just go get the prisoner." He glanced back over his shoulder. "You sure you want her? Her lawyer said he'd come fetch her home. Might be safer."

"No," Lucas said on an exhale of breath. "I started this. I might as well finish it."

To his surprise, Flora stepped out to greet him

looking only slightly worse for wear. Someone had styled her hair, and she'd changed her clothes to wear a frilly dress that matched her eyes. Eyes that, upon close inspection, spared him little sympathy as he began his hastily prepared speech.

"Flora, I had no idea Kyle worded the telegram that way. Then I decided you'd be safer here than anywhere else, so I—"

"Lucas, can we just leave now before that awful reporter finds me?"

"I handled him."

She gave him a doubtful look. "How? Did you have him thrown in jail too?"

"No. I promised him the exclusive story of our wedding."

Flora groaned. "You're not funny."

"I wasn't trying to be." He escorted her out into the morning sunshine. By habit, he searched the windows of the buildings around them for the suspect, and then he scanned the horizon. Once he was sure all was well, Lucas released his grip on Flora's arm. "Your carriage, Miss Brimm," he said with a nod toward the buggy.

His hands spanned her tiny waist as he lifted her up onto the seat. Had he allowed himself, Lucas might have taken a long look into those impossibly blue eyes. Even now he couldn't believe the pretty girl with the sky-colored eyes was his Flora.

His Flora.

Lucas let out a long breath. No, he couldn't think of her as anything of the sort.

A few kisses and a declaration of some feelings of attraction did not a relationship make. Not exactly a statement worthy of Shakespeare, but it certainly fit the bill.

Now, if she loved him . . . well, that would be something altogether different.

But she was too busy solving the problems of the world—or at least the problems of her world—to consider marriage to a man who would well and truly love her.

Marriage. Where had that come from? Other than the obvious fact everyone outside of the people who truly knew them believed he was about to make Flora Brimm his wife.

He looked down and saw his knuckles had turned white from gripping the reins so hard.

"You look awful, Lucas. Didn't you get any sleep?"

"No," he said as he gave the reins a gentle slap and set the buggy in motion. "We were hoping we'd get Lennart. No one wanted to go home."

Her expression softened. "I appreciate that."

"Part of the service, ma'am," he responded with an exaggerated drawl that he hoped would continue her light mood. "How did you spend the night in a jail cell and end up looking so pretty?"

"According to Grandmama, a lady never goes out in public unprepared. So she made sure I was prepared." Flora paused. "Or rather the half dozen members of the Brimm staff who were sent over for the purpose made sure of it."

They fell into an uncomfortable silence, though that was preferable to any distractions a conversation might bring.

Flora leaned back against the buggy seat and closed her eyes.

"Tired?" he asked as he returned his attention to the road. With Lennart still on the run, he could be anywhere. One good shot and . . . no, he would not let that happen.

"Yes, actually. I'm completely tired of men."

"Of men?" He lifted a brow as his gaze continued to scan the perimeter. "All men or just a few in particular?"

"I suppose I could blame a few in particular. Such as my grandfather for putting me in this mess, or my cousin Winny for being such a poor handler of his money. Then there are Lennart and Tucker, two men I don't ever want to see again. Add in the reporter, the entire jail staff, and . . ." She let out a long breath before swiping at an errant strand of hair that had come loose from her elegant updo. "Or maybe I could rest the responsibility on you."

"Me?" He spared her a quick but direct look. "Why me? I'm the one trying to keep you safe."

"No, you're the one doing your job, which just happens at the moment to be keeping me safe."

Oh, that did it. "That is enough, Flora Brimm."

He gave the area a thorough scan and then veered off in a sharp right onto a dirt road that bisected a stand of cottonwoods. When he was fairly certain of the safety of their location, he pulled the carriage to a quick stop and then swiveled in the seat.

"Why are you looking at me like that?"

"I'm trying to decide whether to kiss you or take you back to jail and swear out another warrant."

"You wouldn't dare." She looked ready to bolt. "Would you?"

"What is it about you, Flora? You're the most irritating, agitating, beautiful . . ." He reached to haul her against him. "Do you really believe you're just a job to me? After all we've admitted in regard to our feelings?"

She looked deeply into his eyes, and something she saw there made her heart melt. "Oh, Lucas. Let me show you what I believe." Before he could respond she wrapped her arms around his neck and pressed her lips to his.

A shot rang out. Cursing himself for a fool, Lucas pushed her onto the floor of the carriage and covered her with his body.

"Do not move!"

"Lennart," she whispered.

"Probably." He leaned up on one elbow, his weapon at the ready. Another shot rang out, this one ricocheting off the back of the carriage and causing the horses to spook.

The carriage lurched forward as the terrified animals ran for cover. Somehow Lucas managed to capture the reins and halt their progress. When the next shot zinged past, he lifted his gun and fired twice.

Someone in the copse of trees cried out. Flora cowered on the carriage floor, all too aware of their near miss with death. Even more aware that her selfish tirade had landed them in this mess.

Silence reigned. Overhead a hawk circled and then called out.

"Give it up, Lennart," Lucas shouted. "You're already good as caught."

Nothing.

"Is he dead?" Flora whispered.

"Might be. Or he could just be reloading."

"But you hit him. I heard it."

A nod, and Lucas returned his attention to the direction where he'd last shot. "I'll believe he's dead when—"

Lucas fell backward, blood staining his shirt. Another bullet zinged by, this one ricocheting off a tree somewhere nearby.

Flora reached to grab the reins. "Lucas!" she cried, but he didn't answer. *For God hath not given us the spirit of fear; but of power, and of love, and of a sound mind.*

"Thank You, Lord." Brimmfield was too far

away yet, so Flora turned the carriage around and urged the horses back toward town as fast as they could go. "Lucas, don't you dare die before I get you to the doctor. Do you hear me?"

But the color was already fading from his face, and those long black lashes refused to move from the spot where they dusted his pale cheekbones. She reached over to place her hand atop his, but only for a moment.

Save him, Lord, please. I was in the middle before I knew that I had begun.

She slapped the reins and the carriage lurched forward.

Once they were back in the midst of the traffic that made up Natchez's main street, her prayers became more fervent, more immediate.

Let him live. I love him, Lord. Please let him live.

Finally, the doctor's office was just up ahead. "Thank You," she said as she drew the carriage to a halt. She jumped from the wagon and practically dragged the protesting doctor out of an examination and into the street to tend to Lucas.

Returning to the buggy, she pressed past the few bystanders who had already begun to gather. "Let the doctor through," she demanded as she kept a tight grip on the man's coat.

Lucas's shirt was soaked now, blood staining his chest bright crimson. If he breathed, she couldn't see it. And then he gasped.

"You're alive," she said as she pressed her

palms to his face. "I've brought help." His eyes fluttered open but his attention did not immediately fix on her.

"You there," the doctor said to a pair of men standing close by. "Help me get this man inside."

They complied, making short work of moving Lucas from the carriage to the operating table.

"Flora?" she thought she heard him say as the doctor used a pair of scissors to cut away his shirt.

"Yes, darling," she answered as she swiped at tears now freely falling. "It's me."

"Excuse me, Miss Flora," the doctor said. "Or, forgive me. Are you his wife?"

"No, but I am his fiancée."

"Close enough. What I'm about to do is going to hurt something fierce, so I'd advise that you hold his hand."

What the man did Flora couldn't say, for she turned her head. Lucas's screams, however, told her that the doctor hadn't lied in his warning.

"The next three hours will be critical," he said when he was finished. "And should he survive those, the next few weeks it will be essential that he remain as inactive as possible."

She pulled the watch from his vest pocket and wiped the bloody splotches off with his handkerchief. The time was straight up ten o'clock. Three hours would be one in the afternoon. Easy for God but an impossibly long time to wait.

Save him, Lord, this man of mine.

❊ THIRTY-FOUR ❊

"I hope you're listening to me, Lucas McMinn," Flora said as lightly as she could. And then came the crash of emotion, the strength of which sent her crumbling. "I absolutely cannot lose another man I love. Do you understand me?"

Green eyes fluttered open to capture her gaze and hold it. "You love me?" he breathed. "I was . . ." He paused to gasp for breath. "Was going to tell you . . . first. When I stopped the wagon. Only . . ."

"And you shall," she said as she once again swiped away her tears. She traced the scar where lightning had touched him then returned her attention to his eyes. "Properly and while standing upright. I must warn you I intend to hold you to it."

"You can count on . . ." He gasped and his eyes fluttered shut. "On that," he said with what Flora feared was his last breath.

"Do something," she demanded of the doctor.

Before the man could answer, Lucas began breathing normally, though his eyes remained shut tight. They stayed closed through the haze of activities that followed. Somehow Father appeared at her side to take her home, though she refused to leave until the three hours had passed. When the clock struck one and Lucas's breath was still shallow but even, Flora finally relaxed. *Thank You, Lord.*

Once at Brimmfield, Father had a bed installed in the parlor so as to avoid the question of whether Flora's reputation would somehow be compromised by her insistence at remaining at Lucas's side in his bedchamber.

She pulled Father's favorite chair closer so that she could lean back against the cushions and allow herself a quick few minutes of rest. When her eyes opened again, some hours later, the lamps had been lit and Lucas was watching her.

Flora almost fell out of her chair as she went to him. "Oh, Lucas," she said. "I thought I'd lost you and then the doctor said you must live through the first three hours and you did, and then he said . . . well, I'm just very glad you're alive."

"Apparently so," he managed as he struggled to sit up.

"Be careful. You've been shot—"

Lucas gave up and then reached up to wrap a strand of her hair around his finger. "While you were sleeping the doctor came. It looks as if I'm going to live."

"Well, of course you are." She grinned. "I had no doubt."

"Lennart. Is he dead or alive?"

Her smile faded. "Lennart was found. Dead.

Apparently he was already mortally wounded when he managed to fire off that last shot."

He drew in a deep breath and let it out slowly. Then he nodded. "I'd hoped he might live to stand trial. His wife and daughters will be . . ." His eyes closed and then slowly fluttered open again. "I didn't want it to end like this."

"I know." A pause. "You saved my life, Lucas. Thank you."

"Just part of the service, ma'am." He reached for the table beside him and then touched his chest. "My father's watch," he said. "It's missing."

She pulled it out of her pocket and placed it in his hand. "It's right here."

He began to cough, and pain contorted his expression. Flora soothed him as best she could until he breathed easy again. "In my jacket pocket," he said, once again looking around. "A box. From Tucker. Did it contain your missing earrings?"

She recalled the empty box the valet had brought her upon laundering Lucas's stained clothing. "No, it was empty." At his distressed look, she hurried to continue, "Rest now, Lucas. There will be plenty of time to talk later."

"Not yet," he said. "There's still one more thing." He paused to draw her near. "Flora Brimm," he said softly, "I know I'm not exactly upright yet, and I couldn't tell you what that doctor's put in the vile medication your butler keeps insisting I drink, but I can't wait any longer. I love you."

She smiled. "I love you too."

Lucas beckoned her to come even closer and then managed a soft kiss. "I want to marry you someday." He gestured to the bandages. "I had a different outfit in mind, so you might have to wait a while."

"I'll wait for you, Lucas."

"Promise?"

"Yes, I promise." Tears shimmered in her eyes as a prayer of thanks went heavenward. Even if the medication kept him from remembering, at least he had spoken from his heart. "Now promise me you'll get some proper rest. It's almost midnight."

"I will if you will."

Flora softly kissed his cheek and then stepped out of the parlor. In the pale lamplight of the hall, she found Violet waiting for her in her wheelchair. Daisy stood in the shadows near the door, her face beaming.

"How is he?" her sister asked, as if her presence there was not out of the ordinary.

"He is improving."

"Good." Violet smiled.

"What are you doing here?" Flora asked, and then she wished immediately she could take back the words. "Never mind." She knelt at her sister's side. "I'm so glad you are."

"This is my home, and it's time I returned to it." Violet reached to wipe away Flora's tears. "We have much to talk about, don't we?"

"Yes."

"All right, then. I have it on good authority that chocolate cake is in the kitchen."

"Chocolate cake?" Flora began to giggle. "Oh, Violet, we do have much to talk about!"

"Son, do you understand what I'm telling you?"

Lucas blinked hard, as much to adjust his eyes as to give him a minute to compose himself. The doctor stared back at him, his face kind and his eyes wearing the concerned look a man gets when he's delivered bad news.

And the fact that Lucas would likely never use his right arm again definitely qualified as news of the worst kind. What would a man who made his living with a sidearm do when he stopped being able to shoot? And how would he diagram his inventions when he couldn't even sign his name?

"Yeah, Doc, I got it. I'm washed up as a Pink and not much use to anyone who needs an able-bodied man. I wouldn't make much of a husband right now either."

The doctor adjusted his spectacles. "Now look here. I've seen worse than this and fellows managed just fine. The bullet zagged around a bit, so we can't know what other damage has been done just yet. That'll take some time and—"

"All due respect, Doc," Lucas said as he settled back against the pillows and prayed for the pain medication to take hold, "but what you've seen and where I'm lying right now are two different matters altogether."

The doctor reached for his bag. "I suppose you're right."

"Can you promise I'll make a full recovery? That I'll be the man I was before Lennart shot me?"

The older man rose and set his hat atop his head. "There's nothing else I can do here, but the Lord . . . He's only just started to work. Let Him do His job, won't you?"

"So what you're saying is that even if Miss Brimm would take me as a husband, it's likely she'd get a cripple in the bargain." He let out a long breath and paid for it with a searing pain in his chest. "Thanks, Doc."

"Son, I'm sorry. But you're alive. Give it some time."

Gritting his teeth, Lucas turned away to bite back a response he knew he would regret. Only when the door closed on the doctor and his bad news did he allow himself to form the complaint he wished to lodge against God. The trouble with that, however, was the fact that he knew the doctor was right. Things could have been worse.

●●●

The next morning Flora slipped in to see Lucas after the doctor left, hoping to be the first to break the news of her sister's victory over the fear that had kept her hidden away. Instead, she stalled at the expression on his face that greeted her.

Tilting his head toward his right arm, now bandaged and immobile, he let out a long breath. "I've no use of this arm."

A by-product of the shooting, the doctor had told her on his way out. While there was no limit to what the human body might do to repair itself, the likelihood that he might regain use of that arm was slim at best.

"Good morning, Lucas," she said brightly. "I have such great news—"

"Did you hear me, Flora? My arm. It's . . ."

"I heard," she whispered.

"This makes me useless as a Pinkerton agent." His Irish eyes met hers. "What good is an agent who cannot shoot his weapon or even sign his name?"

"You'll manage. Or learn. Or, who knows? Things may improve, and there's always your inventions to keep you busy. Surely you'll find something—"

"No, Flora. There's nothing."

"Nothing?" She shook her head. "But I thought . . ."

"Leave me." He paused to pull in a shuddering breath. Be it physical or emotional, pain obviously wracked him. "Just please go."

"But I brought a book, and I thought that perhaps we might—"

He looked away. "Not today."

She did as he asked and left, too proud to show her tears and too hurt to remain and fight. When her next several attempts at conversation were met with the same reluctance to speak, she finally gave up. Whatever battle Lucas McMinn was now fighting, he chose to fight it alone.

Like it or not, they were no longer a team.

Worse, the niggling fear that his feelings for her were only a passing medicated moment kept Flora worried. Four days after the shooting, he announced he would no longer keep to the makeshift sickroom and began to take his meals in the dining room with Flora, Father, and Grandmama.

Conversation at mealtimes was lively, mostly owing to the fact that Grandmama loved to reminisce about the old days before and during the war. And though Flora and Father had heard the stories a multitude of times, Lucas proved to be an interested audience. Refusing help, he fumbled his way through learning to feed himself with his left hand as he studiously maintained only the most distant demeanors toward Flora.

Through it all, nothing further was said about

the feelings they expressed on the day of the shooting. Nor did he hold much interest in keeping company with her at all. She began to believe she'd dreamed the whole thing. Or that his profession of love had indeed been the medication speaking.

About this time Father insisted Lucas take over the first floor library. A much more fitting space for a man, he'd declared as he left on yet another of his trips to buy seed or make purchases for the farm. Cleverly, he had also requested Lucas look over his business records in his absence.

Indeed, Father had never taken to the business side of things. Yet even then, he'd never shrugged from his duties. Though Flora suspected ulterior motives in Father's request, Lucas obviously did not. The man who swore he could never return to the Pinkertons now took to his new responsibilities with great gusto.

Such was his fervor with the project Father had left him that Lucas took to having his meals in the library. Any attempt for company was rebuffed.

In short, Flora had become a stranger. Or, rather, the man in Father's library had become one. She certainly did not expect this when he asked her to wait.

A week after the shooting, she wandered into the library to find him poring over something that looked suspiciously like blueprints. Though he had lost some weight, the maids had seen to tailoring his shirts so they still fit him quite well. From the width of his shoulders to the arm he'd taken to wearing bound in a sling, he was still quite a handsome and formidable man.

As always, her heart thumped at the sight of him. "Lucas?" she said softly.

He did not look up when she stepped inside, nor did he appear interested in conversation. When she cleared her throat, he finally spared her a glance.

"I wondered if I might get you anything." She craned her neck to see what he was working on. This certainly had nothing to do with Father's books. Rather, it appeared to be some sort of ladies' hat, its plume of feathers quite fashionable, though the maze of wires and things beneath the brim appeared baffling.

"Thank you, no," he said as he moved the papers out of her view. "Will there be anything else?"

She sank into the chair across from him. "Yes, actually. I was wondering . . . that is, you appear to be healing quite nicely. I wondered if you might want to . . ." She looked away. "Take a walk in the garden," she finally managed.

Silence.

When she returned her attention to him, he had already gone back to his drawings. She could see the concentration on his face as he attempted to draw a straight line with his left hand, mostly failing miserably.

"Lucas, did you hear me?"

"Yes, Flora, I did." He looked up sharply. "I'm busy. Do you mind?"

"Do I *mind?*" Her temper spiked. "Yes, Lucas, I mind greatly!" She rose to grab the papers and toss them behind her. "Oh, this is just wonderful. I regain my sister only to lose the man I . . ." She shook her head. "No, my deportment teacher was right. A lady is never the first to say . . ." Flora stopped herself, anger blinding her. "You don't remember a thing you told me when you first awakened in the parlor, do you?"

His expression went blank. Either he had no recall of the promise or he wished to forget it.

"Right." Flora let out a deep breath in hopes a small measure of her anger and despair might escape with it. The attempt failed miserably. "I promised to wait, but not forever."

Again she searched his face. Nothing.

"I see." She shrugged, hoping it would hide the deep wound forming. "Well, then. If you have no further need of me, I'll not take up any more of your time. Should you realize you miss my company, that's just too bad. I won't be back until I get an engraved invitation to visit."

A nod.

"Did you hear me?" she asked as she rose.

No response.

Humiliation forced her from the room, though pride propelled her with her spine straight and her eyes focused on the door. Only when she had given that door a good slam did she allow her feelings to take hold. Racing up the stairs, heedless of anyone's thoughts of impropriety, she found her room before her tears blinded her.

Everything in Lucas demanded he follow Flora up the stairs and set her straight. Never had he loved a woman so much as he loved her. It killed him to pretend he had no feelings left for her.

Every time he left a meal where he'd hurt her by ignoring her or bypassed an opportunity to spend time with her, Lucas told himself it was for her own good. She needed a man who could be a husband to her.

A man who was a whole man, able bodied and worth something.

A man who didn't awaken during the night in a cold sweat, reliving the moment a coward hiding in the bushes fired bullets that took him down.

Nine days after the shooting, Kyle Russell came to visit. The butler announced him, and Flora went down to offer her greetings. For all her anguish over the change in his friend, she held no ill will against Kyle.

With him in the foyer was an elderly man whose gait was surprisingly spry. "Do come in," Flora said as she greeted the pair. "Lucas is in Father's office, though I suppose it should be called his office as Father has happily ceded the space to him." She kept her tone intentionally light, her expression happy. Should Kyle learn of the change in their relationship, it would come from Lucas, not her.

"That's good to know," Kyle said.

She gestured toward the closed door. "Yes, well, I have no idea what he does all day, but it appears he's creating all sorts of designs."

"As requested," Kyle said. "You see we've had news on some of our patents and, well, where are my manners?"

She looked to the man at Kyle's side. "Is this your father?"

"No, he is—"

"Augustus Girard," Grandmama supplied as she descended the staircase.

"My dear Miss Meriwether." The old man's face beamed. "I never did get used to calling you Mrs. Brimm."

Grandmama's smile was brief but genuine. "You're awfully cheeky for a man who dared to break my heart." She allowed a chaste embrace, and then she said something in French before she stepped away. The old gentleman's response was brief, soft. His expression tender.

"Flora, dear, do stop gaping and say hello to my friend Monsieur Girard. He and I had occasion to make each other's acquaintance on many occasions before the war. Has it been so long?"

"Time is irrelevant where you're concerned," he

said to Grandmama before turning to Flora. "My dear," he said softly. "Do forgive an old man his surprise. When I first saw you I thought . . ." He glanced over at Grandmama. "Well, suffice it to say you do cause the years to fall away."

"Thank you," she said as she accepted his handshake.

"Shall we go in, then?" Grandmama said, indicating the closed door of the library.

"After you, Millie," Monsieur Girard said.

Millie? No one called Grandmama by that name—at least not to her face. Even Grandfather Brimm wouldn't dare.

And yet off she went, blithely followed by the stranger and Mr. Russell into Lucas McMinn's inner sanctum. Flora fell in line until Grandmama turned to stop her.

"No, dear," she said before closing the door in her face.

She'd almost reached the stairs when the door flew open again. There stood Lucas, rage causing his entire frame to quiver. "Are *you* responsible for this?"

"This?" Flora shook her head. "What on earth do you mean?"

"Lucas," she heard the old man say. "The girl did not contact me."

His expression softened, but only slightly. Another moment and he turned his back to close the doors again.

"Men," Violet said from the door to the parlor. "They are a confusing group. Come on, let's go for a walk." She looked down at her wheelchair. "Or rather, a roll."

"Only if you promise not to make me read *Pride and Prejudice*."

She stepped back to allow Violet to pass through the corridor ahead of her and then roll out onto the sidewalk on the specially designed ramp Lucas had hastily designed for her—the lone good deed the despicable man had accomplished since his injury.

"And before you start lecturing on the benefits of this great novel, Violet," Flora continued as she pressed away thoughts of Lucas McMinn, "you know I've tried to read it."

"Just as I've tried to read your lady detective books. Honestly, Flora, I do not see the attraction to law enforcement stories."

From her vantage point on the sidewalk, she spied Lucas deep in conversation with the elderly man through the library windows. He spared her a brief glance before turning his back on her. A moment later, Grandmama rose to close the curtains.

"You know, Violet," Flora said as she followed her sister down the path toward the cottonwoods and the river beyond, "I'm beginning to agree with you."

"Good, because today I brought *Little Women* to read. Can we both agree on that one?"

"Oh, yes. Lead on. I have all afternoon."

Violet caught the attention of the ever-present Daisy, who hadn't quite gotten used to her charge's newfound independence. "Might you have a late lunch brought out? Say in an hour? And tea later." When the older woman had left them, Violet returned her attention to Flora. "All right, tell me about Mr. McMinn."

"There's nothing to tell. He seems to be recovering nicely."

Violet fixed her with a look. "But you are not."

"What do you mean?"

"I mean that since our recuperating Pinkerton agent awakened after saving your life, both of you are quite changed." She shrugged. "He is closeted with Father's books and the odd drawings he attempts with his left hand." A pause. "Actually, I saw him practicing his signature yesterday. He's getting quite good."

Flora nodded as her sister babbled on about Lucas McMinn's many virtues. Finally the talking ceased.

"But you. Well, let's just say I know a woman who is grieving when I see one. Do you think you've lost him?"

Flora sighed. "I don't know if I ever had him."

The truth. So much for the happily ever after she'd wished for.

"May I change the subject?" At Flora's nod, Violet continued. "Your near miss at marriage with this Mr. Tucker . . . was it because of me?"

Flora looked away. "It was because of Brimm-field." A partial truth.

"And because I refused to leave it." Violet wheeled around to intrude on Flora's view. "Nothing holds you here, sweet sister of mine. Not even me. You've written of adventures. Perhaps it's time you go and have some."

"But Brimmfield—"

"Will prosper long after its inhabitants are gone." She reached to touch Flora's sleeve. "Including you and me."

"But the will." Her eyes searched Violet's face. "I must keep Brimmfield in the family."

"It's just a big expensive plot of land." She paused to glance around. "None of us will leave here destitute. Grandfather was not that cruel."

"I suppose."

"And Cousin Winny's not such a bad man, is he?"

Flora shook her head. Silently she looked back at the house and thought of the afternoon that changed them all.

"Stop. You're woolgathering. We're no longer children susceptible to whims and dares."

"No," she said softly, though Flora couldn't tell whether it was a statement or a question.

"Then go and have adventures. I dare you," she said with a twinkle in her eye.

Flora couldn't help but laugh. "All right, but

shall we read about the March sisters and their adventures today? I have plenty of time to see the world tomorrow. Or next week." *Or once my broken heart has healed.*

"Of course."

And so they read, each taking turns and pausing only for lunch and tea. Finally, when the sun dipped below the cottonwoods, Daisy came and insisted on taking her charge indoors lest she chill in the evening air.

Exhausted from their extended visit to the gardens, Violet retired to her room upon their return to the house. Flora wandered into the foyer, surprised to find the door to the library open.

She wandered inside, shocked to find that the person seated behind the desk was Winthrop Brimm. "Come to take over so soon?" Regretting her stinging blow, Flora shook her head. "Forgive me. That was uncalled for."

Winny rose to take a few tentative steps in her direction. "No, what was uncalled for was Grandfather's need to put us both in such an untenable position."

Flora nodded, unable to disagree. "Well, I cede the victory to you, Winny. I've been convinced just this afternoon that there are adventures outside of Brimmfield to be had, and I intend to find them."

"Good for you." His face went pensive. "Flora, I owe you an apology."

"No, honestly, you do not."

"Let me do this. I've made poor decisions in my life. Many of them. Some have only harmed me, but others have harmed people for whom I care deeply." He paused to touch the edge of the desk. "Violet shall hear this of me as well, but I beg your forgiveness for the childish taunts that caused her to fall." His unsteady gaze swung to meet hers. "Though I do not deserve it, might I have that forgiveness?"

She smiled. "Of course," she said and meant it.

Relief washed over his features. "This is not in my nature, though I'm becoming quite adept at it. There's another thing. The shooting." Again he paused, this time to worry his sleeve. "More ill-advised choices. I wish to plead love, but that sounds foolish." He shrugged. "I wanted to impress someone I cared for deeply, but, well, the funds I needed were tied up in business ventures elsewhere. When her father offered a generous cash settlement for a portion of his business, how could I decline? To become a partner in the family firm and have the means to court the daughter as well?"

"Dora Lennart," she said softly. "I understand, Winny. There's no need to go on—"

"But there is. I had no idea her father's businesses were in jeopardy. I was blinded by love and did not do my due diligence. Only when I began to ask questions did things get . . . ugly."

"Yes, I would imagine so."

"I never realized Martin Lennart would go to such extremes to see that I inherited all of this." He shook his head. "That a person could be so focused on money as to risk losing everything, including his life, was a sobering realization. I will not be that sort of man. Should you want to remain at Brimmfield, Flora, it is your home and shall remain so. I give you my word."

"But your debts." She pressed her fingers to her mouth. "I'm sorry, but Mr. McMinn told me."

He shrugged. "I'll manage. Dora and I are committed to coming through this together, and I am concentrating on that. Her mother and sister will need a man to guide them through this period of bereavement. I believe I am that man."

"I'm very glad."

He moved toward her, arms outstretched. "As am I," he said as he embraced her. "But now I must bid you goodbye."

"I see." She stepped back. "You're leaving so soon?"

"I just came at Grandmama's request. Now back to the city and Dora."

Flora bid Winny goodbye and then drifted upstairs to freshen up for dinner. When she arrived in the dining room expecting to find the chairs filled with the guests she'd greeted this morning, Flora found only Grandmama waiting.

"Violet's dining in her room tonight," her

grandmother said. "Apparently the afternoon tired her. I suspect, however, that her nurse is merely scheming to have some time with our girl to allow herself to believe the transformation. She is transformed, isn't she? It's just glorious."

"It is. So, where are the men?" she asked as she took a seat on her grandmother's right.

"All gone, I'm afraid," she said as she rang for the footmen.

"Gone?" she echoed. "Even Lucas?"

"Yes, your Mr. McMinn left as well." She gave Flora a pointed look. "It was time."

"Yes, I suppose it was," she said though her heart was not in the statement. "I thought he might have said goodbye, considering . . ."

"Considering?" Grandmama shrugged. "You know how men are. Always in a hurry to handle their business. It seems to be a singular focus of some of them."

Flora nodded mutely as the table quickly filled with the first course of a dinner she had no desire to eat. Hadn't she made the same accusation of Lucas just before the shooting?

Perhaps if they hadn't argued—and then kissed —Lucas McMinn would never have suffered the bullet wound that took not only the use of his arm but also his love for her. If the latter was ever there.

"You're woolgathering."

Flora mustered a smile. "You sound like Violet."

"Good." Grandmama reached over to touch her sleeve. "I've spoken with her. I think an adventure is exactly what you need. Just tell me where you'd like to go and I'll arrange it."

Where would she like to go? Somewhere with dizzying heights and no Pinkertons. Sacré-Coeur in Paris came to mind, though she doubted she could convince Violet to travel that far so soon. Perhaps next year. No, somewhere closer.

As the thought occurred, so did the beginnings of a true grin. "Actually, Grandmama, I do have a place in mind."

"Is that so?"

"Yes. May we go back to the Crescent Hotel? You, me, and Violet. Just the three of us."

"The Crescent?" She lifted an iron-colored brow. "Yes, well, that sounds lovely, dear but . . ." Something stopped her, and suddenly her expression changed. "Of course we can. I'll arrange it immediately."

"Grandmama, I saw Winny earlier. He said he came at your request."

"Yes," she said, her expression unreadable. "It was time for that too."

"Time for what?"

"Enough questions, child. Let's go back to planning our visit for the Crescent and leave the topic of your cousin for another day, shall we?"

❦ THIRTY-FIVE ❦

Because arrangements on the scale Grandmama required took time, three full weeks passed before the Brimm women arrived on the familiar steps of the Crescent Hotel. They were given the same suite as before, this time fitted out with a third bed for Violet. To her chagrin, Daisy was bundled off to the maids' quarters, where she could only dote on her charge from a distance unless summoned.

"The elevator was such a wonderful convenience," Violet said when they entered the suite. "Perhaps someday we'll have one at Brimmfield, Grandmama."

Mrs. Brimm merely inclined her head and did not offer comment. However, she did exclaim when she saw a wrapped package on her bed. "Oh, my. It is here."

"What is here?" Flora followed her grandmother into the bedchamber to watch her pulling a lovely feathered hat out to admire.

"Goodness, I don't think I've seen you so excited over a purchase before," she said as her grandmother adjusted the hat in the mirror.

"Oh, how very wonderful," she repeated. "I just cannot believe he would send such a wonderful gift."

"He?" Flora looked askance. "Do you mean that fellow Monsieur Girard? Grandmama, do you have a suitor?"

"Don't be ridiculous. I could have all the suitors I desire. I just don't want any right now." She gestured to the card attached to the wrappings. "See for yourself."

Flora picked up the tag and read it. *To the Belle of Brimmfield for sheltering a wounded Pinkerton. Lucas B. McMinn.* She couldn't help but notice it had been written by hand and hoped that it was Lucas's hand that had done the work. This must have been the hat he was working on.

Grandmama had it on her head and was fiddling with something. "Flora, what a marvelous invention. He's cleverly hidden a device inside so I can hear without using my trumpet."

Before she could respond, she heard Violet call to her.

"Oh, Flora, do come and see!"

She hurried to the chamber she shared with her sister to see that she, too, had received a package. Wrapped in similar paper, this box was much bigger than a hatbox. "Has he sent you a garden rake or perhaps a pair of stilts?"

Flora regretted that comment as soon as the words left her mouth. As yet she could not tell how much of Violet's bravery in public was truly felt and how much was pure bravado.

"Even better," her sister said, not offended at all as she pulled out what appeared to be an oddly shaped piece of lumber from the box. She set it aside as she removed a second one exactly like it. The third item inside was very obviously a lady's walking stick. "Come and see, Grandmama."

The nerve. Lucas knew Violet would never walk. Why did he send something so cruel? And why hadn't he sent her anything? Flora stepped over toward her bed and discreetly checked to see if her gift had possibly fallen over the side.

She saw nothing beyond the ever-growing stack of invitations that overflowed on her bedside table. While the topmost envelope was new, the calligraphy marked it as yet another event Grandmama would force her to attend. She swept it aside and continued her search.

Flora eased down onto the bed to reach under the pillows. Perhaps it had slid out of sight.

Nothing.

Just to be certain she threw back the blankets and swept her hand between the sheets.

"Flora, what are you doing?" Violet demanded.

Of course she couldn't admit to her reason, so Flora leaned back against the pillows and feigned exhaustion.

Immediately Violet set about reading the note, apparently a detailed set of instructions that Grandmama snatched away upon her arrival in the room. "How wonderful."

"Wonderful," Flora echoed as she noticed the tag and picked it up.

No longer a shrinking Violet. May you bloom wherever you choose to be planted and dance if you wish. Lucas B. McMinn

"What in the world possessed him to write something like—"

Flora's breath caught. Violet. She was . . . standing. Leaning heavily on the walking stick, to be sure, but all the same standing.

The tag fell from her fingers as she tried to make sense of what she very plainly saw. "But how?"

Violet lifted her skirt to show the wooden contraptions buckled to her legs.

"Oh, honey." Flora rose to approach her sister with care. "It's a miracle."

The sound of sniffling caused Flora to turn around. There she spied her very dignified grandmother, feathered hat still in place, with tears falling. Not once could she ever recall her grandmother weeping. Ever.

"Darling," Grandmama said. "I'm speechless. Just . . ." She moved closer to Violet but seemed afraid to touch her. "Just speechless," she said as Violet leaned into her arms. Flora joined them and, for a moment, all was well and right in the world.

And then Violet began to wobble.

"Easy there," Flora said as she helped her

sister sit on the bed. "It's been years since you stood. You're going to have to build your strength."

"But you're in the right place for it," Grandmama declared. "I'll just phone my physician here, and we'll get you settled into a program that will do the trick."

"A program?" Violet looked doubtful.

"Of course. Taking the waters, perhaps some sort of exercise to strengthen your muscles." She paused. "If you'll agree to it, that is."

Violet seemed to think a moment. "Yes. I believe I would like to give it a try."

"Excellent." Grandmama went off humming, and a moment later she was urging the hotel operator to ring the doctor.

"What have I done?" Violet asked as she ran her hand across her skirt, likely feeling the wooden contraptions.

"You've taken your first step. Well, almost."

Violet began to giggle, and Flora joined her. "Help me stand again," she said as she looked down at her legs, now resting straight out in front of her.

"Now what?" Flora asked when the feat was accomplished.

"Read the instructions," she said as she gestured with her walking stick.

Flora reached for the folded paper and began to read. As her eyes scanned the page, she found herself thinking more of the fact that the words had been written by Lucas rather than actually comprehending what the paper said. She finally shook off the thought of the absent Pinkerton agent and decided to read the thing aloud.

That did the trick. Soon she had Violet standing comfortably for brief periods without leaning on the walking stick. Between taking the waters, attending to a strict schedule of exercises as prescribed by Dr. Jones, and practicing, after a few days Violet took her first tiny baby steps without assistance.

And then just this morning, she had managed to cross the length of the parlor with only the walking stick for help.

The feat had taken just short of two weeks.

Oh, but what a glorious two weeks it had been. Most of the time Flora managed to stop thinking about the man who'd virtually disappeared from her life, only to make such a difference in her sister's. The conundrum confounded her, and yet given the choice, she far preferred to see Violet so happy.

And yet it had been five weeks since the afternoon Lucas McMinn disappeared without so much as a goodbye. The same Lucas McMinn who had declared his love, albeit under medication.

But wasn't that a truth serum of sorts? Flora made a note to ask Dr. Jones when next Violet saw him. And perhaps she would also ask for a remedy for her broken heart.

Not that she expected it to ever heal.

"Look, Flora," Grandmama said then stepped back to reveal Violet and the new gown the dressmaker had just delivered. "Isn't she lovely?"

Her sister beamed. "I can't remember the last time I wore a party dress."

"Lovely," Flora said, "and I hope you will soon have a chance to wear it."

"Haven't you heard?" Grandmama said. "She shall. And very soon."

Mrs. Brimm turned to Flora. "It's an Evening in the Ozarks masquerade ball here at the Crescent. Didn't you see the invitation?" She hadn't. Likely it lay in the pile of unread mail that had been stacking up on her writing desk since her arrival.

Invitations were cast aside in favor of her daily search for any sort of correspondence from Lucas. Grandmama dictated her calendar and Violet's anyway. Why bother reading the mail?

Violet looked away. "I've not yet decided . . . But yes, there is a ball. And perhaps . . ."

"You shall attend," Grandmama said. "You just must." She waved away any possible protest. "Lest you think you might cause a spectacle, don't give it a thought. The doctor has given his permission, and I have a brilliant idea for how we can get you in and out of the event without causing any notice."

"Truly, Grandmama, I just don't know . . ."

She patted Violet's shoulder. "Shall we plan on your attendance and then, if you so choose, decline later? The ball is a week away. Imagine what you can do between now and then. You are, after all, a Brimm, dear. And we Brimms are capable of doing exactly what we put our minds to."

Violet looked to her. "What do you think, Flora?"

"I think it's a grand idea. Now, shall we get back to practicing?"

Though Violet was the one who claimed concern over attending the masquerade ball, it was Flora whose nerves got the better of her as she stepped off the elevator. Grandmama and her sister followed, with Violet looking only slightly less worried than she.

"All right, dears," Grandmama said. "We are Brimms. Follow me."

To Flora's surprise, her grandmother bypassed the grand entrance to take a few steps down the side hall. There she had a wheelchair waiting for Violet.

"Trust me," she said as she pressed past, leaving Flora to push Violet in her wake. After a few turns, Grandmama stopped in what was obviously a servant's passageway. There a silver-haired gentleman was waiting: Violet's doctor and a young man he introduced as his assistant.

He offered Violet his arm, and she took it. "All right," he said as Flora pushed the chair out of the way. "Remember how we've practiced. Sixteen steps forward and then three to the right." When Violet nodded, he addressed the assistant. "I'll have you on my opposite side. And Flora, will you bring up the rear and see that your sister remains steady on her feet? Of course, Mrs. Brimm, you enter first and capture all the attention."

Flora grinned. The cad.

"Whenever you're ready," he said to Violet.

She grinned and fixed her mask in place. "Now, I believe."

The door opened and, to Flora's surprise, the room was bathed in darkness except for the tiny bulbs that twinkled on the ballroom ceiling and the candelabras that shone light on each of the tables.

The effect was lovely, turning the ballroom into a nighttime paradise—an evening in the Ozarks. It also served to hide the fact that Violet Brimm was being propelled across the short distance to their table with her feet a few inches off the ground. With Grandmama leading the way and taking the spotlight, depositing Violet comfortably at the table was simply and efficiently done with none of the guests any the wiser.

And with the table set into the corner in an alcove mostly hidden by tall potted palms, the

effect was to highlight those seated there without allowing more than one or two persons to
come near.

"Oh, Flora," Violet said. "This is lovely."

And it was. Truly.

She leaned back in her chair and watched as the
doctor captured Grandmama's hand and led her
onto the dance floor. As the music began in
earnest, the electric lights flashed on, illuminating
the room.

"May I join you?" the intern asked, though the
effort of speaking appeared to cost him reddened
cheeks.

"Yes, of course," Violet said. "Do, please."

A moment later the pair were in deep conversation about who knew what, leaving Flora to gaze
out the windows and try not to think of the last
time she danced beneath these chandeliers. Of her
climb out on that ledge and the exit she and Lucas
McMinn made by dancing across the ballroom.

He was a wonderful dancer.

Flora sighed as Grandmama waltzed past, this
time on the arm of yet another gray-haired gentleman. A moment later the pair disappeared into
the crowd, leaving her to wonder.

"Flora, do stop your woolgathering."

She looked over at Violet, who nodded toward
the intern.

"May I fetch you something to drink?" he asked
solicitously.

At her nod, the fellow made haste toward the refreshments.

"Well, now," Flora said as she leaned toward Violet. "Aren't you the belle of the ball?"

"Don't be silly. He's just a dear fellow who happens to work for Dr. Jones."

"Oh?" she said, though she knew what she saw on Violet's face. It was the same expression she'd once looked at Lucas with. Despite all predictions to the contrary, Violet Brimm was falling in love. And from the look on the intern's face as he earnestly balanced two glasses of punch, that love was reciprocated.

"How long have you known him, Violet?"

Her shrug was anything but casual. "Since the first time Grandmama took me to see Dr. Jones. Rudolph is a dear man, and he's been most helpful in my recovery."

"Rudolph?" She stifled a smile. "I see."

"Am I late?" Cousin Winny slid onto the chair beside her with Dora Lennart in tow.

"Winny? What are you doing here?" She glanced past him to his companion. "Hello, Miss Lennart."

"Are we late?" he repeated.

"Late for what?"

Winny shrugged. "Grandmama said she wanted us gathered precisely at eight." He removed his watch and checked the time. "And it's ten after." He looked at Dora. "We're late."

"I'm terribly sorry, darling," she said. "I—" Any further conversation ceased as Grandmama arrived at the table.

"Excellent, you're all here. Dora, dear, wouldn't you like to mingle?"

"Mingle, Mrs. Brimm? Why would I want to do that?"

Grandmama fixed her with a look. "Because it would be the appropriate thing to do at this moment." She paused and then, when it appeared Miss Lennart still did not understand, she leaned toward her. "Leave, dear. Winny will fetch you when we're finished."

At Winny's wave, she slipped away from the table to move toward the refreshments.

Grandmama nodded to the doctor, who gestured to his intern. Together the pair moved into position. Now the table was completely blocked off from the rest of the room.

"I made the decision to meet here in this public place to avoid any unpleasant scenes." Her gaze swept the three cousins seated before her. "So should any of you wish to cause trouble or complain, you will need to do so elsewhere, please."

"Grandmama," Flora said, "is something wrong?"

"No, dear," she said, her smile radiant. "Something is very right, though I will require you all to remove those ridiculous masks. I simply cannot hold this conversation while you are thusly costumed." She paused while they complied and

536

then continued. "Though we are all far too well-bred to bring it up, each of us has been affected by my late husband's will. You," she said to Winny, "have spent what you don't have in hopes of getting Brimmfield. You," she indicated Violet, "have used Brimmfield as a place to hide." Grandmama met Flora's gaze. "And you have allowed it to be an excuse not to live the life you were intended to live."

Because neither Winny nor Violet had voiced a response, Flora didn't dare be the first. And yet words of complaint were on the tip of her tongue, ready to be unleashed. How dare Grandmama think that she knew what sort of life she was supposed to be living?

"Winthrop, your debts have been paid and the Lennart family has been the recipient of a generous insurance policy they believe Martin Lennart purchased. You will not disabuse them of this belief. Do you understand?" He nodded but did not speak.

"Violet, an allowance has been settled on you that will allow you and your beloved nurse or whomever you choose to travel in safety and comfort. Or, if you choose, to settle somewhere and live a comfortable life."

Her sister reached over to grasp Flora's hand, smiling. Flora returned the smile.

"And Flora." Grandmama sighed. "Dear Flora. Oh, this was a difficult decision."

Flora's heart sank. "I still have time to inherit Brimmfield—"

"No, dear. I've sold it."

"Sold . . . Brimmfield?" Flora shook her head. "But how? The will—"

"Had a loophole. It took some doing, but after reading that brilliant piece of work he did for you in the form of the marriage contract, I had our mutual legal friend look it over again. Indeed, the judge intended for one of you two to inherit upon my unfortunate demise. However, there was no mention of me being unable to sell the property as long as I own it." Her smile brightened. "And be assured, I do own it."

"Actually," a familiar voice said, "I own it. As of yesterday afternoon, that is."

The doctor and his assistant moved aside to allow Lucas McMinn into their midst.

"You own Brimmfield?" Flora could barely breathe as she tried to get the question out.

"He has generously leased the property back to your father for a small sum," Grandmama said. "And I understand plans are underway for Mr. McMinn to build a home for himself on the easternmost side of the property."

"About that," he said as he extended his right hand to Flora. "I thought we might discuss the matter in private."

"I don't think so." She crossed her arms and tried not to let the overwhelming hurt that had been inside for more than a month spill out in a most unseemly way. "You left me without so much as a goodbye, Mr. McMinn, and now you want to waltz back into my life, buy my home out from under me, and then ask me to *discuss* it?" She rose, disgusted. "The time for discussion was before you walked out. Or at any point along the way where you realized how stupidly you behaved."

She stormed past him, trying to ignore the fact that she'd never seen the man look better. From the well-cut suit to the black mask covering all but those Irish eyes, the nearness of him made her knees weak.

"Stop, Flora. I can explain—"

Giving his request no heed, she walked toward the door. Unfortunately, she found it bolted shut. A look around the room showed her the easiest form of exit.

Without sparing Lucas a glance, she headed straight for the potted plants.

"Flora Brimm," he said loud enough for half the room to hear him, "come back here!"

She squeezed behind the palms, went to the window and unlocked it, and then raised the sash. Unlike her last venture out this window, the air was warm and the breeze was barely noticeable. She stepped onto the ledge and breathed in deeply.

She had no home. The man she once loved had stolen it away.

The sound of approaching boots told her he had followed her.

"I want your wish to come true, Flora. Your happily ever after."

She froze and then turned to face him as he joined her on the ledge. "Did I wish that?"

He smiled and lifted her chin to cause her to look into his eyes. "You may not remember, but I do."

"Go back inside, Lucas."

"Please just listen. I tried to contact you—"

"Then why didn't I get so much as a letter?" She held up her hand before he could respond. "Please leave me alone. I don't want to hear your excuses."

He let go of her chin and bent toward her. Quickly, she turned again and made her way past the windows to the far end of the hotel, where the veranda proved less treacherous.

For Lucas, not for her.

Glancing around, she knew she must choose between going back into the ballroom or . . . she looked up as lightning crossed the sky. Yes, the fire escape. He would never follow her up there. Not with his aversion to storms.

But he did, all the way to the belvedere where they had enjoyed a memorable evening what seemed like an eternity ago.

"You left me," she said when he moved with catlike grace toward her.

"I had to. If I'd waited to say goodbye, I never would have left." His eyes searched her face. "A man has to heal alone, to learn to be a man again. I couldn't keep letting you take care of me." Again he stretched out his right hand to her. "I still can't shoot the way I once could, but that's no matter. I've left the Pinkertons. I want to make a home with you at Brimmfield."

Now she was really mad. Of all the nerve! "If you wanted to make a home with me, why didn't you care to ask how I felt about the matter?"

Tears threatened, but she refused to allow them to fall. He might have broken her heart, but he certainly was not going to see her cry.

With a glance in his direction, she could see he didn't appear willing to respond. Or perhaps he didn't know what to say.

In either case, his silence stretched her nerves beyond the point of control.

"Lucas McMinn," she said through gritted teeth, "I am absolutely furious with you. Can't you see that? I declared my love for a man who then slipped out of my home and life without so much as a decent farewell, and now he's back and what am I supposed to think? Did you expect that buying Brimmfield would make everything all right? That coming to save me from my terrible fate would make me forget the fact that you walked out?" She fixed him with a look that told him exactly how she felt. "Well, it did not!"

Lucas winced as if she'd slapped him. He threw his mask aside as the moonlight washed his handsome features in soft silver shadows. "I did care. I do. I cared so much, but . . . well, I couldn't offer you half a man. I admit I didn't go about it the way I should have . . ."

"You're right about that!"

"I know," he said softly. "That's why I sent the invitations. But then, when you didn't answer . . ." He scrubbed his face with his hands and shook his head. "Flora, can't we talk about this inside?"

Her eyes narrowed. "What invitations?"

"Surely you cannot claim you didn't receive the invitations I sent. There had to be at least a half dozen of them. Probably more. Starting with the day I sent the gifts to your grandmother and sister—"

"I don't know what you're talking about."

He reached for her hand but she easily stepped away. "You said if I wanted to see you again, I would have to send you an engraved invitation." Their gazes met. "Well, I did."

She thought of the stack of invitations in her bedchamber, items she had cast aside while looking for a letter she hoped Lucas might send. Had she really told him that?

"I could send someone to fetch them," he offered. "I'm sure they were delivered. However, I'm not sure you read them."

Flora attempted to blink away her tears again. She failed miserably. "No," she admitted. "I didn't read any of the invitations I received. I had no idea . . . I mean, there was nothing to indicate . . ."

"That they were from me?" He grinned. "That was the idea. I was trying to be clever. Trying to tell you how much I wanted your forgiveness. And how very much I missed you." He reached for her hand again, and this time she allowed him to lift her fingers to his lips. "Will you forgive me? I've been the worst kind of fool, but you have my word I'll never make that mistake again."

The anger she'd held inside shifted, and with it went the hurt and disappointment. In its place was the warmth of her Pinkerton's smile and the knowledge that he had wanted her after all.

Or had he? The question sliced through her. Where was the proof?

Of course. It was in her suite.

Flora pulled her hand from his, picked up her skirts, and hurried from the belvedere toward the fire escape. Before she could forgive him, she had to know if he spoke the truth. She had already believed false promises. Now was not the time to fall for more.

"Flora, wait! Where are you going?"

"I've already had one man lie to me," she called as she turned to fix him with a look she hoped would cause him to stop his pursuit. "I have to know I'm not falling for another."

●●●

Lucas gave Flora a moment's head start before following after her. His arm ached but his heart hurt worse. Not the spot where Lennart had come within an inch of nicking it, but deep inside in that place he'd finally opened up to allow Flora Brimm in.

It didn't take a Pinkerton—or, rather, a former Pinkerton—to figure out where his bride-to-be was headed. Lucas knew which rooms the Brimm women were staying in; he'd found that out almost as soon as they had arrived at the Crescent. He could thank Flora's father for that.

That and a whole lot more. The man didn't have to welcome him as a prospective son-in-law and yet he had. Giving Brimmfield back to the head of the Brimm family had been an easy decision; the price of one dollar for a lifetime lease, even easier.

He arrived at the door to their suite and lifted his good arm to knock, but thankfully Flora had saved him the trouble by leaving the door ajar. He paused only long enough to get his bearings, and then he followed the soft sound of paper tearing.

"Lucas," she said when she saw him in her bedchamber doorway. "You did. You sent . . ." She gestured at the invitations now spreading across her bed like oversized confetti. With each envelope she tore open, another decorated the silken coverlet.

Leaning against the frame, he paused to watch her reading the words he had written. The engraved invitation to visit him in New Orleans. To allow him to return to visit her at Brimmfield. To meet in a neutral location such as, ironically, here at the Crescent or aboard some as-yet-to-be-named steamboat. To forgive him.

Each had been penned with his mind clear and lucid, his heart breaking.

Finally she spied the one he had sent in anticipation of today. Its pale blue color set it apart from the others.

It was the invitation to the wedding he hoped to pull off in the near future. For that he could thank Millicent Meriwether Brimm, for she and Violet had undertaken a project of the greatest secrecy and importance. And God for convincing Lucas he still had a chance with Flora.

If he could only convince her to return with him to Brimmfield, she would find that a wedding had been planned in her absence, complete with guests and an orchestra that would play their song upon their exit from the white cottage that was hastily being returned to its former purpose as a chapel.

Their reception would be a much grander affair in the Brimmfield ballroom, the place now set off with a trio of mirrors he'd had sent in from a buyer in Italy. Mrs. Brimm had been speechless when she realized they were an identical copy to the one that had been lost to the candle incident.

Millicent Brimm with nothing to say? That had been payment enough, but to know he had also gained the older woman's love and respect was priceless. Now to see if he could sway her granddaughter to give him the same.

Flora met his gaze, her eyes swimming with tears. "You sent all of these."

He crossed the room to tilt up her chin. "I love you, Flora. That's not medication talking or the silly infatuation of a man who got himself love struck. I want to build a life with you if you'll have me. And I've already had the papers drawn up to return Brimmfield to you. It's yours to do with what you want."

"Oh, Lucas. It's not Brimmfield I want. It's you. Us. It's . . ."

"Happily ever after?" He reached for his handkerchief to dab at her tears, and then he pressed his index finger gently to her lips. "I want to do this right and proper."

She glanced around, merriment in her lovely eyes. "Where are your gadgets, Lucas? Don't you have some invention to do this right and proper?"

"There will always be gadgets, sweetheart. That's part of living with an inventor. But I'm getting ahead of myself." He let out a long breath and moved to get down on one knee. From his pocket he pulled out a small black velvet box. "This is the only gadget I have to offer you. That and myself. Will you marry me, Flora Brimm?" he asked as he opened the box to show her a lovely aquamarine and diamond ring. "For the girl with the blue sky eyes."

"Lucas," she breathed. "This is better than the extra-vision spectacles, the portable climbing spikes, and all those other crazy inventions put together."

"That wasn't an answer," he whispered as he pressed his lips to her temple and inhaled the sweet scent of lilacs. "Tell me you'll marry me. It's all arranged. Your grandmother and Violet have seen to it, though I'm sure they've left some of the details for you to decide."

Her giggle sent his heart soaring. "Why do I suspect you're telling the truth?"

His knee complained, and his arm throbbed, but he was determined to keep his pose until the frustrating woman said yes. "Why do I suspect you're stalling? What's it going to be, Flora. Will you let me make your wish come true?"

"The girl who loves the boy with the Irish eyes," she breathed against his chest as she allowed Lucas to slip the ring on her finger, "says yes."

Later there would be time for telegrams and wedding announcements. For plans to return the Brimm entourage to Brimmfield for the wedding. For discussing the home he was building for her on the Brimmfield property that would have an inventor's laboratory for him and a nursery he hoped they would someday fill with children who were born out of love and not duty to some relative's will.

And, of course, he would alert that Natchez reporter so as not to break the promise he'd offered regarding the scoop of the Brimm-McMinn nuptials. He even had the headline already planned: FLORA'S WISH COMES TRUE.

But for now all Lucas could think of was holding Flora in his arms. Of the happily ever after he would make certain this wonderful woman would have.

The Natchez Weekly Democrat
August 11, 1887
        FLORA'S WISH COMES TRUE

Miss Flora Brimm of the Natchez Brimms was united in marriage with Mr. Lucas B. McMinn, inventor and former detective with the Pinkerton Agency. After a honeymoon trip to Paris, the couple will make their home at Brimmfield Plantation in Natchez.

And buried on the last page:

CRIMINAL ESCAPES FROM CHAIN GANG

Inmate William Tucker escaped police custody while being transported to the Angola Penitentiary to serve a five-year term for larceny and theft of property. The search for Tucker is ongoing.

❧ ACKNOWLEDGMENTS ❧

Thank you for allowing me to take you on a trip through one of my favorite parts of the world: the Southern United States. From New Orleans to Natchez, from Memphis to Mobile and beyond, there is just something about returning to the land of magnolias and the Mississippi River that slows this Southern girl's frantic pace to a more dignified stroll.

I credit this mind-set to the long line of Southern belles from which I descend. From my great-grandmother Viola McMinn to my grandmothers Dorris Simpson and Katie Aycock, I learned early on what it meant to be a lady of the Southern persuasion. The tradition continues in my mother, Bonnie Sue Miller, who faithfully took me to the Gates Library to feed my voracious need for the written word and who would never wear white after Labor Day. From the grit of these women comes the character of Millicent Meriwether Brimm. From the strength, intelligence, unaffected beauty, and good common sense of my own Southern Belle in Training, Hannah Y'Barbo, comes the essence of Millicent's granddaughter Flora Brimm. Thank you, ladies, for the inspiration on and off the page.

This book is also dedicated to my brother, Farris Miller, who endured life with three sisters and yet always managed to be the Southern gentleman Daddy taught him to be, despite all the grief we gave him. Lucas McMinn gets that from you.

In the writing of this novel, I took special care to visit most of the locations where the story was set, including the Crescent Hotel in Eureka Springs. While the greatest attention was taken in remaining accurate to the history of this lovely and grand establishment, I did take certain poetic license in several scenes. Foremost is the location of the ballroom, which in various reports was either on the topmost floor or on the bottom floor. Diagrams of the hotel show it to be on the ground floor, but currently there is a space on the fourth floor where it might have been. Owing to changes to the original blueprints as well as renovations over the years, I have chosen to place the ballroom in this tale on the fourth floor. This was a conscious choice that better showcased Flora Brimm's peculiar talent for nimbly traversing narrow walkways set at great heights. Any error or risk of mistake in this matter is mine alone.

Also, while there are now several lovely suites at the Crescent Hotel, an 1886 blueprint does not show this type of room. However, I imagined that Flora's imperious grandmother would settle for nothing less than a grand set of rooms on an upper floor with all the comforts and trimmings. Thus, this is what I gave her. What can an author do but listen when her character demands these things?

Though the popular myth of a writer's life might lead readers to believe that a book is written in solitary hours with only the author in attendance, nothing could be further from the truth. It truly does take a team to produce a novel, and I am blessed to work with some of the best individuals in the industry. A huge thanks to Kim Moore and the gang at Harvest House for making me feel so very welcome, and to Wendy Lawton, agent and friend, for her guidance down this publishing path.

Finally . . . and always . . . to my husband, Robert Turner, my Ephesians 3:20 man, for playing copy editor, chauffeur, eye candy, trip planner, bodyguard, roadie, photographer extraordinaire, and purveyor of Reese's cups in equal measure. Like Flora, I wished for happily ever after. In you, God allowed my wish to come true.

❈ DISCUSSION QUESTIONS ❈

1. Flora's wish is to live happily ever after. At the beginning of the book, she sets a plan in motion she believes will make this wish come true, but she forgets to consult God on the matter. What is the result? Have you ever stepped out toward a goal without first taking stock of the path the Lord wants you to walk to get there? If so, what happened? If not, why not? What was that result?

2. Lucas McMinn wants revenge so badly he's willing to go outside the bounds of his job as a Pinkerton agent to find Will Tucker and bring him to justice. Lucas excuses this choice even as his conscience is eventually troubled by it. What did you do the last time you got one of those jabs that cause you to wonder if you're doing the right thing?

3. Will Tucker offered Flora what she thought she needed—a way to keep what she had and take care of those she loved. But Will's offer of marriage was not what it seemed. Have you been confronted with what you thought was the answer to a prayer only to find it

wasn't God's best choice for you? How did this become apparent? What did you do?

4. Though Flora lost her mother, she has a grandmother who dearly loves her and takes on the role. Millicent Meriwether Brimm is a formidable woman who gives praise and correction in equal measure but always tempers both with deep love. Is there a person in your life, past or present, who serves in this role? What would you say to him or her if you were to write a note detailing what that meant to you?

5. Flora keeps a pink ribbon in her Bible to mark her favorite chapter in First Corinthians. What is your favorite verse, and do you have something special in your Bible to mark that place? What does that mean to you? What about the verse?

6. Grandfather Brimm wrote a special requirement into his will to control the people in his life long after he was gone. Are you guilty of trying to manipulate those you love to do as you wish? If you're not guilty of this, is there someone in your life who is? Have you turned this over to God to seek a remedy for it?

7. Flora's sister, Violet, is unable to live the life her family had hoped. Flora determines she will not miss out on a minute of what's going on and goes to extraordinary lengths to make that happen. Have you gone out of your way to do something special for someone who cannot offer thanks in return? If not, is there someone God has put in your life for this purpose? Think about what you can do and then do it.

8. Lucas McMinn became a Pinkerton agent because of something God allowed into his life that, at the time, was the worst thing he could imagine happening. But the Lord redeemed that awful thing and caused Lucas to use what came out of that for good. Do you have a similar story? Are you in that place now where you need to believe God will take you from this valley and cause what you've learned to place you on the mountaintops?

9. Lucas has a fondness for inventions. During the course of the story he uses a hat with a listening device, a pair of extra-vision glasses, a device shot from a gun that allows him to climb up the side of a building, and a precursor to a modern flashlight, among other things. If you had the power to invent

one amazing thing, what would it be and what would you use it for?

10. Throughout the course of the book, Flora has a difficult time listening to Lucas and following his instructions. In almost every case, something happens to cause her to wish she had paid heed to his warnings or done as he asked. Does this resemble you in any way? Who do you wish you had listened to and why? What happened?

11. Flora mentions her preference for detective novels over her sister's preferred Jane Austen books. What is your preference in leisure-time reading material and why? Is there a book or author someone in your world absolutely adores that you need to give a second try?

12. Lucas had a healthy respect—bordering on fear—of lightning. Do you have something like that in your life? If so, what is it and why do you feel that way? Is it something you can give to God and have Him heal?

13. The book stops with Flora and Lucas living happily ever after. However, I have left other story lines unanswered. What do you think happened with Winthrop and Eudora? Were they able to get past Mr. Lennart's criminal behavior to find love? And what about Will

Tucker? Do you think he's used this escape as a means to straighten out his life? What do you hope has happened?

14. Both Lucas and Flora have suffered the loss of loved ones. These losses have made them the people they are. What has happened in your life to make you who you are? How has that changed you?

15. Lucas and Flora do not start out on good terms, and yet by the end of the book they have found an unexpected love with each other. Do you have a love story like Lucas and Flora? If so, what caused you to fall in love? What about your love story with Christ? What caused you to give your heart to Jesus? If you haven't, what do you need to know to make that decision? I would love to chat with you and answer any questions regarding the best choice I ever made. Please contact me through my website at www.kathleenybarbo.com or go there and read the page titled The Greatest Story. I promise you won't regret it.

❊ ABOUT THE AUTHOR ❊

Bestselling author **Kathleen Y'Barbo** is a RITA and Carol Award nominee of more than forty novels with more than one million copies of her books in print in the United States and abroad. A certified family law paralegal and former literary publicist, she was recently nominated for a Career Achievement Award by *Romantic Times* maga-zine. A tenth-generation Texan, Kathleen Y'Barbo has four grown children, seven bonus children, and her very own hero in combat boots.

Find out more about Kathleen at
www.kathleenybarbo.com.

Center Point Large Print
600 Brooks Road / PO Box 1
Thorndike, ME 04986-0001 USA

(207) 568-3717

US & Canada:
1 800 929-9108
www.centerpointlargeprint.com